W9-CYB-080

The CATCH

1. Primrose Lake
2. Ed Bellichek's cabin
3. Brock Bellichek's cabin
4. Lake LaBarge
5. Duke Lake
6. Mike Jansen's cabin
7. Burwash
8. Mt. Logan
9. Kluane Lake
10. Kluane Park
11. St. Elias Mountain
12. Schwatka Lake
13. Pilot Mountain
14. Mt. Skukum
15. Kaskawulsh Glacier
16. Mackenzie River
17. Air route to Yellowknife and Tetcho Lake

The CATCH

Jonathan Hobbs

Cover design, Bassett & brush Design
Test design, Gopa Illustration & Design

01 02 03 04 05   1 2 3 4 5

ISBN: 1-58619-022-9
Library of Congress Card Catalogue Number: 00-111001

First Printing January 2001

Published by Elton-Wolf Publishing
www.elton-wolf.com
206.748.0345
Seattle, Washington

TO SNOUS

An extraordinary mother,
a patient wife,
a passionate lover,
and my dearest friend.

ACKNOWLEDGMENTS

I HAD ASSUMED writing a work of fiction could be accomplished entirely by using my own imagination. That was a staggeringly inaccurate and foolhardy assumption. Without the expert opinions and constant support of the following individuals, this story would still be an incongruous mess rattling around inside my head.

I would like to thank Dr. Duren Johnson. His expertise in pathology was essential; Captain Robert Pyde whose extensive knowledge of flying in the Arctic and the Canadian wilderness was a reliable and indispensable source of information; Perry Mazzone for his keen understanding of Canadian law; Patrick Scott and Dr. John Catalano for their tireless assistance in making my manuscript intelligible; Robert Thixton for being remarkably patient in a business not known for its patience; Joe Sparling of Air North, who took a chance on a tenderfoot pilot known as 'Hollywood'; Jack Edison Hobbs for taking a little boy flying and whispering into his ear "airspeed and altitude"; and to Elizabeth Birnie for her literary guidance and persistent belief in my abilities.

My thanks to James Torina, Phil Gerisilo, and Ms. Cuba Craig who forced the final summit; Ms. Beth Farrell and the entire staff at Elton-Wolf Publishing for their dedication and professionalism; Captain Dave Koseruba and Mr. Brad Oliver for their encouragement, support, and unparalleled friendship; and to the wind beneath my wings, Marshall, Cameron, and Connor. I salute their lawn care skills, which provided an extra day of writing each week, and their mature understanding every time Daddy smiled and closed his office door.

CONTENTS

FOREWORD

TWENTY YEARS EARLIER, the wide grooved snow tires of the rusted black Chevy truck sprayed slush onto the traffic circle before the worn brakes squeaked slightly, bringing the vehicle to a halt outside the school. Purposely hidden in the cab's shadow, the driver rolled his window down and blew tobacco smoke into the Arctic breeze. The rope on the silvery pole in the center of the traffic circle clanged against the aluminum mast, proudly waving the Canadian and Northwest Territorial flags. The driver knew the routine when the bell sounded, ending another day of high school in the small Northern community of Yellowknife. Bundled-up teenagers with frosty breath scattered in every direction and a few of the parents mingled with the teachers. This school was particularly sloppy. The catch would be today. He was familiar with his target. He had had dreams of the girl in the past. She wore the same blue hair bow every day. The others would like her, too.

The bell sounded and he quickly started the truck with a roar. He pulled away from the traffic circle and out of sight next to the Dumpster behind the gymnasium. Seconds later, the main doors of the school opened up and a wave of adolescent humanity spilled into the courtyard. Tossing the cigarette in the direction of the trash container, he hopped out and brushed along the shadowy side of the gym, strolling confidently toward the laughing children. As he approached the corner of the building, several screaming and giggling teenage girls startled him by running around the corner. Right behind the girls came the pursuing teenage boys. They deftly dodged the stranger without looking up. Unbelievably, the pretty one with the blue bow was strolling toward him at his shadowy vantage point. He tried to get her attention by waving and quietly whistling. She did not hear him, or chose to ignore him. It didn't matter. As she wandered next to the building, he reached out, gently gripping her tiny forearm and whispered into her ear. The speech was well rehearsed and flowed smoothly from his lips. The man quickly looked up. None of the teachers or parents noticed the man with the girl next to the gym. Why would they? Child abduction was a big city crime. Parents in the Arctic worry their children might become frostbitten, not kidnapped. He swiftly led her back into the shadows and in the direction of the truck. He smiled to himself at the ease of the catch.

The girl jumped into the man's warm truck with a wide smile. She had lived in the North her entire life and was trusting of everyone. She pushed the hood of her wool parka all the way back, allowing her chestnut brown hair to fall across her small shoulders. The sub-zero temperature made her cheeks glow and her nose run. Her blue eyes sparkled at the man behind the wheel. She smiled at him, exposing her new braces. As a teenager, she was attractive. Later in life, she would have been a beautiful woman.

This wasn't the first time her mother was late picking her up. Her mother often sent friends or relatives to pick her up after school. The man in the truck knew it. He had watched it happen several times. Her dad sometimes even sent one of the other men on duty when his wife was going to be late.

The driver smelled funny. Like gasoline. His shirt was not neatly tucked in. She knew her dad would not approve of his appearance. He had said so before. Sometimes, special assistants had to dress in normal clothes to go unnoticed.

Between smiling at the man and looking at her schoolbooks, she peered out the window. She watched the icy buds of Dwarf Fireweed and other wildflowers race by, dripping melting snow from the spring sun and preparing for their rebirth during the long warm days of summer.

Occasionally, the man looked over at the girl reading her schoolbooks. He was excited, though it did not show. The only other catch had been a homeless drunk native, someone likely never to be missed. This was a white girl. He knew it would be the last catch for a long time. Yellowknife would look long and hard for this prize.

He could picture their faces as he drove up to the small mine on Tetcho Lake. The others would be pleased. At first, he would act disappointed, as if he had failed. Then he would pull her up from the floorboards like a fresh steelhead. He felt his pants beginning to stir. He was becoming too excited. He had more than an hour drive before reaching the small lake north of Yellowknife.

It wasn't long before the girl realized the man was not driving to the center of Yellowknife's small business community. She asked him several times why they were going to her father's office this way but the man only smiled and said nothing. She trusted him.

Soon the young girl became upset and demanded an explanation. The man said nothing. She stared through the condensation on the window, sobbing at her foggy reflection, mumbling something about her father and his job. At one point, a Royal Canadian Mounted Police (RCMP) cruiser approached them on the bumpy highway. He grabbed the girl by the hair and thrust her head into his crotch. She screamed a muffled cry as the police car passed and the RCMP officer smiled and waved at the man in the truck. The man had heard enough whimpering from the catch. When the road was clear in both directions, he drove with his knees while duct-taping the girl's mouth and hands for the remainder of the trip.

The others were pleased.

They raped her continuously in the little shack sitting under the expansive Arctic sky. The night was so clear, every star's sparkle touched the crystal fingers of every neighboring star. The sobbing cries of a tortured young woman was a strange musical accompaniment to the aurora borealis dancing brightly and peacefully across the pristine Northern horizon. It was confusing to all of nature's wild creatures who listened in their burrows and warm dens. The cries of a tortured living being are alien to them. They kill for survival, quickly and without ceremony. Not these creatures. Drunk and exhausted, they passed out clutching the rope knotted to the small girl's waist. She dreamed of her room, her favorite stuffed animal, and a place called Heaven.

For all practical purposes, the life of the young woman ended shortly after she arrived at Tetcho Lake. Her body survived for three days. Her spirit died much sooner.

She was an only child. Her parents would never recover nor forget. Their tenuous belief in divine justice was all that kept them from instantly spiraling into a life of despondency and anguish. If there was to be justice, it would come. One way or another, it would come.

PREFACE

The Canadian exploration company, NorCan, had spent another unsuccessful summer exploring and drilling the upper ridges of the Tetcho Valley. The geologist had found traces of copper the preceding two summers, reinforcing the belief that a vein of rich minerals lay below the valley floor.

The drill site was 3,000 feet above sea level on a ridge overlooking Tetcho Lake. Although often obscured in a cloud of dusty drill mud, it offered an expansive view of the lake and the thousands of acres of Northern pine, birch, alder, and spruce surrounding the valley. NorCan engineers had plowed a smooth dirt road into the territorial tundra to access the lake.

The operations vehicles were parked at the bottom of the mountain by the creek leading out to the main road. More than a mile from the parking lot and deeply set into the bushes by several hundred feet, a rotting shack lay half collapsed in the dark recesses of the brush. An old miner's shack, it was almost impossible to recognize unless one studied the landscape closely.

It was late afternoon in September, near the end of the exploration season. The sky turned dark early and winter's freeze began to push most vestiges of life into hibernation or south of the 49th parallel. NorCan had all but given up on the supposedly "mineral rich" Tetcho Valley. The company realized it was within days of shutting down the Tetcho Lake operation for the season and possibly forever.

The heavyset mechanic had worked all day repairing the hydraulic arm on the D-9 bulldozer. He was cold and tired. He lit the glow plugs, pushed the starter, and cursed the mighty diesel until it roared to life. Feeling smug, he manipulated the arm in every direction. Three thousand pounds per square inch and the seals didn't leak a drop. Before shutting down the big Cat, he tested the repair with a load on the blade. The bulldozer rumbled toward a muddy ridge at the end of the clearing. The mechanic gently dropped the blade to the ground as the mud and bushes loomed larger. He sliced into the earth, rolling tons of dirt off the top of the monstrous steel blade. The exhaust stack bellowed black smoke with every application of the accelerator. He was about to take one more pass at the ridge when he noticed a parka-clad figure off to his right, waving and pointing toward the rolled earth. In front of the big D-9 blade, fixed and working so well, was a pile of freshly turned half-frozen dirt. Even with the onset of darkness, the mechanic could see two black skeletal eyes sunk into what appeared to be a tiny human skull.

DAY 1

TRAVIS BANKS unwound the electrical cord attached to the chrome grill of his Chevy truck, plugged the block heater into its outlet, kicked off his snow-encrusted boots, and entered Arctic Air's gray steel and white wood hangar. A blast of freezing air slipped in behind him, whipping across the floor and rearranging the papers on the receptionist's desk.

"Well, thank you, Travis," Peggy Rand said with a wry smile.

"No problem." Banks winked at the portly Miss Rand. She might not be the most beautiful of God's creations but she was the kindest soul he had ever met. A plump, plain woman with light red hair and fair skin, she had a half dozen freckles on each cheek that belied her forty-five years.

"You're looking particularly ravishing this morning, Peggy."

"Yeah, sure." She blushed in spite of herself, a faint pink that spread from her neck to the roots of her hair.

Banks leaned his lanky form over her desk, looked her square in the eyes, pulled a cloth rose from behind his back and placed it into her hand.

"When you look into the eye of a rose, unencumbered appreciation flows like water from Niagara Falls."

"And you," she said, "are full of shit." She regarded Banks coolly, repressing a desire to laugh. "Let me guess. You want me to do your job and file your flight plan to Primrose Lake?"

"You *are* amazing, Peggy. Thank you." He pointed to the office door over his left shoulder. "Is the She-Wolf in her den?"

"I heard that!" The voice shot from around the corner of the only truly private office in the hangar. "I need to see you before you head to Primrose."

Travis smiled at Peggy pleadingly and turned up his palms in mock appeal. He handed the receptionist a blank flight plan form to file with the Ministry of Transport Flight Service Station. Banks blew her a kiss and headed toward his boss's office.

Like the hangar itself, everything in her office was a testament to the longevity of khaki paint and steel, part of the detritus left behind by U.S. Army engineers forty years earlier when they'd carved out the Alaska Highway through Whitehorse and the Yukon Territory. No aesthetics, but sufficient for a company doing no more than half a million dollars' worth of business a year.

Kayla Jackson was punching numbers into her overworked computer when he tapped and entered in one smooth movement. The intoxicating aroma of lilac immediately infiltrated the pilot's senses. The wonderful perfume always accompanied Ms. Jackson.

Kayla waved her hand without looking up, indicating she'd be finished in a minute.

Everything was perfect about her, Banks thought, as he flopped into a chair opposite the tank-sized desk: the sandy blonde hair piled on a delicately sculptured head to the gold wire-rimmed glasses perched on a perfectly curved button nose. Just his luck that his boss happened to be the living fulfillment of a recurring fantasy he'd had as a teenager—the intellectually appealing librarian whose image kept him locked in his bedroom scouring the underwear section of the JC Penney catalog.

Kayla pushed her chair back from the computer and reached for a file on the side of the desk.

"I've got a DC-3 charter to Yellowknife tomorrow. You interested?" She stared at him.

"Of course." He unsuccessfully tried to shelve his fantasy for a later date.

The other pilots at the small airport had often organized lake parties in the summer in the off chance she might show up in a bikini, but Kayla never obliged. She wore denim jeans and simple blouses in the summer and was never without her parka in the winter. She paid no attention to the advances. Her life up to this point was her company. She was quick to point out to new pilots smitten with her looks that the unemployment office was downtown in the Federal Building, right next door to the Equal Employment Opportunity Commission. She worked the pilots hard but was fair. She cut them slack in the slow winter months after they had worked long hard hours in the hectic summer months flying tourists, hunters, fishermen, and mining exploration personnel.

"Well?" Kayla Jackson questioned the bush pilot.

Banks sat up. Would he like a trip to Yellowknife? It was a silly question and she knew it. Long charters in the DC-3 were prime trips in the winter. The bigger the ship, the farther the trip, the more money you made—the ground rules of commercial aviation.

"What about the old man? He's senior to me."

Kayla motioned to Banks to close the door. He obliged by turning sideways and shoving the door closed with his foot.

"I'm not running an airline, Travis. Seniority doesn't mean a damn thing around here." There was a sharp edge to her lowered voice. "Flemming's an ass. He's upset customers I've spent a great deal of energy securing. I've decided to make a change. He's on his way out. Unfortunately, I can't afford to let him go until I get the fleet off skis. He's got 2,000 hours on ice. Our insurance company loves him."

"Well, I couldn't agree more."

"What? That he's indispensable?" Kayla was surprised.

"No. That he's an asshole."

Frank Flemming was Arctic Air's chief pilot, a pickled old fart who'd been flying in the North before Banks was out of diapers. Naming Flemming chief pilot was designed to satisfy the Ministry of Transport and the insurance company. Kayla kept her grip on every shot called but Flemming reveled in his imaginary authority. He was proud of his gray hair, potbelly, cauliflower nose, and shot liver, and he saw them as living testimony to his qualifications. He believed those attributes made you a good Arctic DC-3 pilot; that's what separated the men from the boys. What actually got Flemming's goat was the fact that

Travis had made it to the airlines and chose to return to bush flying.

"When his time's up, Kayla," Banks smiled but spoke softly to his boss, "can I give him the news?"

"No, Travis. In fact you'll say nothing until I get this fleet back on wheels and floats for the summer, O.K.? Hopefully within six months, you'll have enough ski time to pass muster with the insurance company."

Banks nodded. It was best to let it go. Hell, he just might get drunk and tell the old bastard anyway. It would be the highlight of his aviation career. "About this charter. People?"

"Yep."

"No freight?"

"Nope."

"What's the catch?" Banks respected Kayla's ability to manage her staff. She had a fix on each one of them.

"There's no catch," she said lightly. "But I do have a little favor to ask of you."

"Never would have guessed." Banks turned his head slightly and eyed her cautiously.

"Are you still seeing that . . . uh . . . nurse? . . . What's her name? Mary something . . . ?"

"Michelle. And she's a doctor, not a nurse."

"Right."

Banks grinned. Even Kayla, with her drop-dead looks and hard-to-come-by Airline Transport Pilot's License, was typical of many successful women—insecure about other successful women. She'd defied all the macho bush pilot rhetoric by becoming the first of her gender to own a small airline north of the 49th parallel, yet apparently still hadn't made it into the personal security zone. She knew Michelle's name and profession as well as he did.

"Sometimes we still get together." Travis felt his way. "But . . . it would be a stretch to say we're an item. Why?"

Kayla moved a couple of papers on her desk with a neatly manicured fingertip. Her pink tongue flicked across her lip. She looked up, took a deep breath, and fired.

"I have to attend the Rendezvous Dinner put on by the Whitehorse Chamber of Commerce this Saturday night. I'd prefer not to go alone. It doesn't really matter, mind you," she paused uncomfortably.

"Look, it's a suit and tie affair. God only knows if you even own a suit and a tie but if you do," she looked back down to her desk- top, "would you be interested?"

Banks knew the invitation had nearly killed her.

"Well, stone the crows, Ms. Jackson, are you asking me out on a date?" He was careful not to be too playful.

"Keep your voice down!" Kayla pointed at the door angrily. "You know perfectly well what this is. You'd simply be an… I don't know… an escort!"

"Wow. How can I turn down such a gracious invitation? You've made me feel warm and fuzzy all over." He tried to keep the tone light and hoped she couldn't hear his heart beginning to thump against his ribs.

"After eight years, I should be able to trust you," Kayla added. "That's more than I can say for the vast majority of your sexuallyclosed-minded-testosterone-driven peer group. I'm assuming afterward you'll be discretionary in discussing our dinner. It will be strictly platonic."

She lifted her eyebrows in the hope of some sort of assurance from Banks. Not a word, not even a murmur indicating understanding.

"In other words," she blundered on, "I trust you won't concoct some outlandish sexual exploit at the expense of my character."

She stared back at the pile of work on her desk and, without glancing up, said, "Think about it and let me know."

Banks said nothing but he didn't move either. He figured that if he sat there long enough, like it or not she'd finally have to give him the smile the librarian of his dreams had never given.

Seconds passed. Finally Kayla looked up, her gold-rimmed glasses balancing on the edge of her nose, her mouth pursed, her bun intact. The librarian incarnate.

"Don't you have a trip to Primrose?"

No smile.

Ed Bellichek's breath shot into the air with the rasp and rhythm of a carpenter's file. His stained sleeping bag, piled onto a canvas cot buttressed by a foam mattress, was pulled up to his nose. It was thirty below zero outside the shack and not much warmer inside. The smell of smoldering alder was ebbing. The night fire in the tin barrel stove rarely made it until daylight.

The trapper's sleep had been restless, full of strange dreams. Half-awake, he morosely eyed the wooden beams stretching across the ceiling, the walls lined with canned food, the Coleman lamp on the beaten-up trunk, the long johns strung in front of the stove, the pot of water for coffee. Time to get out of bed, whatever time it was. He had no watch, didn't need one. Winter in the Yukon had its own timetable. The sun rose at ten, skimmed the horizon, and was gone by three in the afternoon.

He rolled his eyes toward the window by the door and saw that the sun was creeping up Mount Skukum above the hazy ice fog over Primrose Lake. The silence was absolute. It would be a brilliantly bright February day and bitterly cold. A good day to work his trapline. He struggled to get going. Trapped wolverines loved to chew their feet off before noon.

Bellichek unzipped his sleeping bag, lifted his legs onto the cold floor, and was fully dressed and into his wolf-trimmed parka in less than a minute. He never washed when he worked the trapline. Said the clean smell frightened away the wildlife. Never washed in town either, for that matter.

After a few phlegmy huffs and puffs into the stove, Bellichek stuck in a log and transformed the embers into flames. Soon the strong aroma of coffee filled his nostrils. He tore off a piece of caribou jerky with tobacco-stained teeth, chewed it with all the grace of a hungry wolf, slurped down a bourbon-laced coffee, and rolled his first cigarette of the day.

With the cigarette stuck between his wet lips and the smoke burning his eyes, Bellichek shook the sleeping bag until his mukluks fell out onto the floor. He liked to start the day with warm feet. He slipped on his foot coverings, belched, farted, spat black tobacco juice onto the sticky stained floor, and quickly checked his rifle before opening the door. Not every hungry bear hibernated all winter. The grizzly ate early, sometimes at Bellichek's restaurant where drying beaver pelts were the breakfast special.

The stark, freezing air burned his lungs and assaulted his senses. He reached up and unhooked a dozen size three and four leghold traps from the side of the shack. His trapline was currently sixty traps long—each trap with teeth as serrated as a tiger shark. It had been a good winter for marten, lynx, and wolverine, and he wanted to add a few more traps, as well as replace any that had broken. A cold trapline wasn't the place to fix anything. He tossed the jagged devices on the small sled hooked to his snowmobile and noted his drum of gas was getting low. Supplies would be arriving by air from Whitehorse soon, provided the good weather held.

Taking the empty water bucket, Bellichek crunched through the dry snow down to the edge of the lake. Occasionally, a wolf met its demise walking too close to his cabin. It was easy to spot wildlife against the flat white backdrop of the Primrose Lake shoreline. Looking over the mile-wide frozen lake, Bellichek saw nothing. The other shoreline, part of the Saint Elias mountain range stretching endlessly into the bright blue northern sky, butted up against the mountains at almost ninety degrees.

Bellichek poked around the icy shoreline like some mangy water rat come to shore. Reaching a certain spot at the water's edge, he poked a hole in the ice with the butt of his rifle. The hole had to be popped open a couple of times a day. Left untouched for more than a few hours, only an ax and a lot of sweat would open it again.

Bellichek filled the water bucket and hauled it back to the cabin. He stoked the fire with Northern alder and spruce and, by the time he was back outside, the dry fir had begun crackling.

He would work the trapline on the south side of the lake in the morning to take advantage of the early sun, and finish up on the north shore close to the warmth of Jack and the cabin. Jack Daniel's was his best friend, always faithful, always waiting to put a smile on his face when he returned with a sled covered in dead animals.

Twenty years earlier, he would have had to feed and care for a dozen sled dogs all winter. He missed their company but not their all-night barking every time a squirrel pissed in the woods. The thought reminded him of his next task.

In over three decades of trapping and mining in the Arctic, he had never found a pleasant and comfortable way to crap in the woods. It was a cursed chore—the fumbling with mitts and jackets, the clumsy undressing, the sheer misery of cold so cutting it burned. But building a proper outhouse at Primrose Lake would require a Herculean effort in the bitter cold. He'd rather shit outside for another thirty years before making such an effort.

The trail leading to the dumpsite wasn't hard to follow, even when he had to go at night with Jack Daniel's running interference. He pulled down his pants and settled on the large branch he used as a seat. The loaded rifle lay across his lap. Hungry enough, wild animals would eat anything, including human excrement. A disgusting thought, even for the lowly Bellichek. He finished quickly, slid off the bough and quickly went to work buttoning up the trap- door on his long johns.

As he bent over with both hands behind his back, he noticed an unusual track in the snow ten feet away. It ran by the tree line where he burned the used toilet paper in the spring. It wasn't any animal track he recognized. He closed the breech on his rifle and inched forward toward the trees, his pants around his ankles.

Another inch forward and the sound that exploded was like a jail door slamming shut. Bellichek had one second in which to try to raise his rifle but he was already crashing onto his knees into the snow, his whole body filled with a pain so intense it seemed to have no place of origin. He could see his cheeks rounded next to his nostrils but could not hear the sound of his own screaming.

The rest of Primrose Valley heard. High atop Mount Skukum, the Dall sheep were momentarily startled. Their heads jolted upward and their jaws stopped their ruminative chewing as they froze into statues. After a few seconds, the biggest ram acted. He sensed that the screaming posed no threat to his species yet he discreetly turned toward a higher elevation. The other sheep slowly followed, moving in a scattered file that occasionally stopped along the way to forage and feed on clumps of frozen grass.

Down in the valley, writhing on his back as he went into shock, Bellichek watched the bright Yukon sun spin above his head. His legs seemed bound by something other than the pants at his ankles and, rolling over, he tried to pull himself up. On all fours, he stared in horror down his chest, passed his genitals, and between his bloodied legs.

A size-one bear trap was clamped around his ankles, its carnivorous teeth entrenched in his bones like the mouth of a hungry shark.

Twice he reached down bellowing with rage and fear, feebly clawing at the jaws of the trap whose embrace was draining away his life. He knew it was futile to struggle. It took more than 100 foot pounds to spring a bear trap. For a little longer, he thrashed around, then his movements became slower, and he lay quietly and watched his breath roll into the sub-zero morning air. Steam wafted from his body. The ice, crimson under his imprisoned legs, spread about him like a pink and purple blanket.

In the darkest recesses of the trapper's mind, something like laughter arose. Were the animals he had trapped and tortured over the years laughing? Could they see him now as they had once been? Bellichek's mind felt cold and dark. Even the sparkling sun had suddenly disappeared, blocked by a large shadow approaching from the east. He could hear the crunching in the snow. An animal? The shadow grew larger but the sounds it made were becoming more distant. He felt warmer. Peaceful. By the grace of God, Ed Bellichek drifted into unconsciousness.

Banks checked his watch. The conversation with his boss about a date had taken his mind off his trip to Primrose Lake. Ed Bellichek did not like waiting for his groceries and supplies, especially when Travis was carrying a case of Jack Daniel's.

The pilot quickly walked through the dark, dilapidated hangar toward the ramp and his aircraft. He waved good morning to Arctic Air's three full-time mechanics and slid back the heavy metal side door, exposing the snow-covered ramp.

A fuel truck was pumping in the last of 100 octane low lead into the red and blue de Havilland Beaver, which stood in a cleared area banked by high snow. The Herman Nelson gas heater alongside the twenty-year-old aircraft—registered with the Canadian government as "Charlie Golf Kilo India Delta" or "C-GKID"—shot hot, undulating exhaust into the air.

Dale McMaster had almost finished loading it with cargo. Clumps of ice had formed on his sandy brown mustache and a hand-rolled Players cigarette hung, as usual, from his lips. His bloodshot eyes gave away his activities from the night before. Another few minutes of forced hot air and the frozen Pratt and Whitney radial engine would be unlocked and ready to start.

"If I had a pilot's license, I wouldn't need you," he greeted Banks, shouting over the roar of the gas heater.

"If I enjoyed loading airplanes, I wouldn't need you," Banks responded. He opened the left door to the tail dragger and threw his David Clarke headset onto the front seat.

"Is that a little brown spot I see on the end of your nose?" McMaster smirked while he tightened down the last strap around the drum of gas behind the two front seats. "You were in the boss's office a *long* time."

"She only wanted a date." Banks made it sound like a lie. "Did you put my Redhawk back in the survival kit?"

"Even cleaned and oiled it. You've got your weapon, I've got mine."

McMaster patted the Nikon 35mm camera that had become a fixture at his side. Years earlier, he'd gotten into wildlife photography as a hobby. But after he'd turned the only clothes closet in his apartment into a fully functioning darkroom, it had become his consuming passion, his only passion apart from drinking.

"Right," said Banks. He was picky about his survival kit and didn't care who knew it. He knew from experience that most people who died in Northern plane wrecks died from exposure while waiting for help. Comparatively few died from the impact itself. So he'd created his own kit rather than copy Ministry of Transport specifications. The custom-made affair was only two feet square and weighed less than forty pounds but, if it wasn't on board, he didn't go. Each item in it could mean the difference between life and death: the sleeping bag, space blankets, dry long johns, one man tent, dehydrated food, medical kit, flammable gels, flashlight, military eating utensils, collapsible fishing rod, handheld ax, disassembled Winchester .30-.30 rifle with ammunition, large Buck knife, several signaling devices, a PSE hunting bow, and a Ruger .44 Redhawk.

The Redhawk was his handheld cannon. If he ever found himself injured and stuck in the frozen recesses of the Yukon Territory, it would be his last line of defense.

"Ready?" Banks pulled the old gas heater across the icy ramp clear of the aircraft.

McMaster pointed toward the sky and climbed into the right seat.

After a quick preflight and run-up checklist, the airplane lifted off the southbound runway of the Whitehorse Airport and turned west toward the Saint Elias mountain range.

Banks opened his flight plan by making radio contact with the Whitehorse Flight Service Station, aware even as he did so that a flight notification would have made more sense. He'd have given the same information whether he'd filed a flight plan or a flight notification—aircraft type, registration, owner, pilot's name and license, true airspeed, route of flight, and departure and arrival times. A flight notification afforded him some leeway over a flight plan. Notifications were filed for flights that might last days or weeks in remote areas where there was no ability to contact the air traffic authorities. If an aircraft didn't show up as scheduled, nobody panicked. Only after twenty-four hours of no-show would the Canadian Armed Forces Search and Rescue Team launch a search. But if an unclosed flight plan had been filed, a search would be started within an hour of an aircraft's failure to arrive.

Banks put it out of his mind. No matter what, there'd be no problem. The flight would only take an hour and the Beaver's on-board HF radio could reach the company from Primrose Lake. If Arctic Air wanted, it had the authority to change or cancel any flight plan or flight notification.

The sun glared through the windscreen as the Beaver smoothly rose.

The winter morning was bright and crystal clear with a visibility that seemed endless. The steamy, billowing exhaust from the Schwatka Lake Power Station spread a milky blanket of ice fog over the waking Northern community. The town slowly slid out of view from beneath the aircraft's left ski.

Once clear of civilization, Banks descended to an altitude no higher than required to miss the white tops of the lodgepole pines, mountain ash, and birch trees passing underneath. Wildlife scattered in all directions and the earth slipped by at 100 miles per hour. Soon the two men unzipped their parkas and removed their mitts, comfortable in the warmth provided by the exhaust manifold heater of the 450 horsepower radial engine.

McMaster extended his coffee thermos toward his friend. Banks took a deep breath of the waffling steam before refusing with a reluctant grin. No surprise. Brandy. Not long ago, McMaster had been the Yukon's most eligible bachelor. He was still eligible, a bachelor, and good-looking for that matter, but alcohol was already tracing its subtle marks of premature aging on his friend's face and physique.

Banks recalled the day the two had met eight years earlier, the very day he'd arrived in the Yukon after quitting what was not such an illustrious airline career with Canadian Pacific Airlines. He'd come to Whitehorse to fly with a new and struggling charter outfit called Arctic Air. The small operation had only two planes and a female owner named Kayla Jackson. Like everyone else in town, he took it for granted that Arctic Air would probably go belly up after the usual airline run of one or two years. But then neither he nor the citizens of Whitehorse had ever dealt with Kayla Jackson before.

Dale had arrived only a month earlier looking for a job. Any job, he'd told Travis, but preferably at the airport. The only job Ms. Jackson could offer was that of a loader. He took it, secretly confident that eventually he would sleep with his new boss. The new boss hired him because he could comfortably lift a 120-pound propane bottle over his head and onto an airplane. And for some reason mysterious to Kayla, he was willing to work for practically nothing.

McMaster and Banks had become instant friends and roommates, sharing a mutual love of raising hell around Whitehorse. In the course of their carousing, Travis learned just enough about Dale's life as a kid in Edmonton, Alberta, to realize why he felt intuitively protective toward him. His father, a strip miner, had been abusive and alcoholic, his mother cold and uncaring. Dale gave no details but the few things he'd said were enough for Travis to get the picture.

They'd partied for several years until Travis became sick and tired of being sick and tired. The older he became, the more abstemious he became. But Dale either didn't want to or didn't know how to stop boozing. Every now and then, they'd still get together for a bout of serious libation but the easy intimacy of their roommate days was over. It hurt Travis to see his friend beginning to go down the tube and become a bit of a joke in the local taverns. Maybe Dale was trying to work out his past the only way he knew how. Whatever he was trying to do, Travis was committed to helping him, if only by being there.

The pilot's musings were cut short by a touch on his shoulder. McMaster pointed ahead at the frozen shores of Alligator Lake, and raising his Nikon camera, aimed it at the front windscreen. A sprinting timber wolf was jumping off the icy shores and over the dead black pines strewn about from an old summer forest fire. With its naturally camouflaged earth-tone coat, the animal was visible only when it streaked over the patches of bright, deep snow. Even at that distance, the men could see its tail held high, the sure sign of a wolf's dominant position within a pack. It was the lead animal, breaking trail while the rest of a spread-out pack followed. Seconds later, two black wolves appeared in tow. With their tails down, they followed at precisely the same distance behind their leader's flank, combing the wilds for breakfast. Of all carnivores living in the wild, these graceful beasts were the most efficient.

The subliminal navigation system in Banks's head clicked on and he automatically banked the aircraft to the left, skimming over the rocky terrain of the Primrose Valley. As the aircraft turned the corner, the vast majesty of Mount Skukum filled the windscreen. The rocky peaks of the snowy mountain topped out at eight thousand feet above sea level and hovered over the Primrose Valley.

Banks flew just off the deck, skimming the stunted Northern pines. In the Primrose Valley, "just off the deck" put the aircraft fifty feet over the trees but 5,000 feet above sea level. McMaster raised his thermos and toasted two sheep bounding up the ledges of the gray and white mountain ridge passing off the left wing. Suddenly, the tiny body of frozen water known as Primrose Lake loomed at twelve o'clock.

"It's going to take a couple of tight turns."

McMaster responded by hollering with glee. He loved the low level reconnaissance flying, the chance it gave for a once-in-a-lifetime wildlife shot.

Banks rolled the aircraft sharply to the left. He picked up the southwest edge of the shoreline and followed it around to the trapper's cabin. Primrose Lake was tricky to circumnavigate. The small lake was three miles long, but only a quarter of a mile wide. He could hear the spinning electric motor on Dale's camera purring every few seconds as he shot everything in sight.

Banks could tell by the wispy remnants of ice fog over parts of the lake that surface winds were nonexistent. The northeast end of the lake, where the cabin was situated, was still dark and hidden in the morning shadows. The fog hung patiently, waiting for the sun to erase it from the landscape. The sunny south side of the lake would be where the trapper would work his traps this time of the morning. Travis dove the plane down along the brightly sparkling frozen shoreline. One ski flew over the frozen lake, the other over land. The airplane split the shoreline perfectly in half.

Dale screwed on his zoom lens and aimed it at the shoreline.

The nose of an approaching aircraft startled the man sitting on the birch stump next to the small fire on the west shore of Primrose Lake. He had been watching with deep enjoyment as the wolves fought over their breakfast. Now he instinctively leaped up, threw his metal cup of coffee on the small makeshift fire and cursed himself for doing so as a jet of frothy steam arose. It wasn't much but it could be seen from the air. He dropped to his knees and quickly packed snow onto the few remaining coals.

He continued kneeling, pressing his mitts onto the snow-packed fire, trying to imagine who would go to Primrose Lake in the middle of winter. He'd never considered the possibility that anyone might show up, at least not until the ground softened and the sun provided warm spring days. It couldn't be the police. He hadn't been the first to arrive and now there was more company.

He looked up toward the tree line. His snowmobile sat nestled in the brush and overhanging branches of short evergreens. Was it out of sight from the air? The arriving aircraft seemed to be heading away from the cabin and moving directly toward his position on the opposite shore. He didn't have time to cover the distance to the tree line without being seen by the approaching plane.

Covering himself in the shaggy animal pelts he used for protection from the cold, he crouched down to the ground. If he remained still, he might blend into the shoreline, which was dotted black and white with rocks, brush, and dead pines. He angrily eyed the aircraft as it stormed directly toward him, seeming only inches off the ground. For an instant, he could actually see the occupants as the machine approached. Two men. Both with headsets. One with a camera to his face. He covered his ears and watched the greasy belly of the Beaver thunder overhead in a steep turn. The one with the camera, on the right side, wheeled around and aimed toward the ground.

Immediately after the Beaver passed, the man plowed through the deep snow toward the tree line and the snowmobile. Once the loud radial engine was shut down, the metallic whine of his snowmobile would be heard for miles in the dead of winter. He had only a couple of minutes before the aircraft landed and taxied to a stop. It was enough. By then, he'd be long gone.

"See anything?" Banks asked McMaster.

"Nothing."

The dark murky end of Primrose Lake was approaching quickly. Banks pulled off his sunglasses and pushed the flap handle to the down position. It was time to slow the aircraft. He pumped the flaps down one notch. The Beaver slowed and nosed over slightly. He needed a tight radius to get the airplane the 180 degrees back out of the valley.

Finally, the gray outline of Ed Bellichek's cabin rose out of the dark fog. The two Beaver occupants immediately made the same startling observation. Dale spoke first, staring straight at the cabin's smokeless chimney.

"That's one very cold-looking cabin."

Banks quickly looked out the right window, sizing up the 100 yard distance he had between his right wing tip and the passing mountain. He rolled momentarily to the right to maximize every inch of airspace, then banked hard left into an almost wing-over-wing ninety-degree bank turn. McMaster hollered like a cowboy while grabbing the sides of his seat.

"See if he's out back in the drying shack," Banks barked.

The airplane leveled off and roared over the cabin all in the same instant. Travis made sure the cabin was beneath the right window for Dale to get a good look below. He didn't have time to look himself while navigating the dark end of the lake. The pilot longed to get back to the open sunny southwest shore.

"Anything?" Banks yelled.

"What the hell . . ." McMaster's voice trailed off as his head, straining downward, turned slowly, keeping an eye on a large object on the ground. He quickly reached between his legs and picked up the camera sitting next to his high-octane thermos.

"What?" Banks shouted over the loud rumbling of the radial engine.

McMaster fumbled with the lens cover and tried in vain to aim the camera. The aircraft was too quick. He lost sight of his target. He swung all the way around to face Banks.

"I'm not sure. But I think that weird son of a bitch got himself something big."

Travis didn't wait for an explanation. He prepared to land.

"There's a kill site behind the cabin. It's got to be thirty feet in diameter," Dale surmised.

A kill site that size made no sense. Trappers never moved large animals back to their campsite to dress them out. The airplane was slowly creeping back into the sunlight.

They skidded around quickly and made their final approach into the murky confines of the east end of Primrose Lake. After Banks pumped down the remainder of his flaps, retarded the throttle, and pushed the prop pitch forward, McMaster tapped him on the right arm and pointed to their two o'clock position. Below the lowest layer of fog, they noticed a half-dozen wolves a mile away sprinting back toward them and the middle of the lake.

"Why in the hell aren't those wolves running for the hills with the racket we're making?" Dale wondered aloud.

Banks thought he knew why. "We must have scared them off on the first pass . . . they're coming back now. They're probably starving." He eased off on the rest of the power and continued to shout over the engine's roar, "Bellichek takes a moose hide sometimes and buries half of it in the ice. Once it freezes, the wolves can tug and chew on it all day. It can't break loose. He sits on the shore with his rifle, takes aim, and gets his quota of wolf hides without ever leaving his shack."

Banks pulled back on the yoke and eased the Beaver onto the ice. Packed snowmobile tracks zigzagged across the lake in every direction. Carefully, Banks maneuvered to place one ski into the tracks heading toward the cabin. Once airborne, flying was generally smooth in the winter but taxiing on snow and ice could shake the aircraft as if it were coming apart, taking everyone's kidneys with it. This snow and ice were packed hard. The Beaver slid smoothly in the direction of the quiet cabin.

No smoke came from the chimney. A pack of wolves continued to play undisturbed in the middle of the lake several hundred yards in front of the trapper's cabin. Something was amiss.

Banks told McMaster to unpack the rifle and .44 from the survival kit. He spun the Beaver around and pointed the nose toward the small, dark figures jostling on all fours in the middle of the lake. The cabin stood seventy-five feet directly behind the aircraft. Banks pulled back the radial engine's gas mixture handle to starve the carburetor and then watched the Hartzell blade stop spinning in front of the aircraft's circular nose cowling.

Except for the crackle of the rapidly cooling cylinders and the yapping of the starving animals, the lake grew silent. Inside the Beaver, the two men watched the wolves tear the moose hide apart.

"Let's get the hell outta here," McMaster spoke. Unless it was last call for drinks with only one unescorted girl left in the bar, Dale wasn't the adventurous type.

Banks looked at his friend and stuck the muzzle of the Ruger .44 Redhawk out the window. He turned his head away from the impending blast and flinched slightly while firing three magnum rounds into the Northern Hemisphere.

The wolves quickly disappeared into the bush on the opposite shoreline.

"You coming?"

Banks opened the small aircraft door, hopped onto the snowy lake and, walking toward the tail of the Beaver, quickly surveyed the cabin. He called Ed Bellichek's name several times. Without looking down, the pilot emptied the three spent chambers of his gun onto the ice and slid three new home-loaded overcharged magnum rounds into the .44 handgun. His philosophy was simple. If he ever had to fire his .44 in close quarters, the Redhawk was so powerful that a direct hit wouldn't be necessary. Just a grazing shot could be fatal. He didn't care that the gun was illegal. He'd seen the aftermath of a grizzly attack, unlike the city-raised political tenderfoots who'd outlawed it.

Banks slapped the aluminum empennage of the aircraft's tail with his left hand and shouted at McMaster to get his butt out of the airplane. Dale peeked around the aircraft's right door. With trepidation, he lowered himself and the rifle onto the frozen surface of the lake.

The two men tentatively walked up to the cabin, occasionally taking a look across the lake. They listened intently for any unusual sounds. Absolute silence. The cabin was still enveloped in the cold shadows of the slow sunrise and the snow-laden branches of the surrounding pines.

Banks rapped on the cabin door.

McMaster stood slightly sideways, ten feet behind his partner with the butt of the .30-.30 rifle on his hip and the muzzle pointing back in the direction of the lake, where the moose carcass lay frozen in the ice.

Banks slowly pushed the door open with the muzzle of his gun. McMaster lifted the rifle and lined up his metal sights. He aimed over the pilot's right shoulder into the cabin's darkness. Travis stuck his head in first and then slowly disappeared into the cabin's shadows.

McMaster didn't alter his aim.

There was no sound.

"Travis!" The loader was getting worried and impatient with his friend's disappearance. "Goddamn! Banks?"

Finally, a voice from inside. "Nobody's home."

McMaster hesitantly lowered the Winchester and gingerly stepped up the slight incline to the trapper's residence. He went inside and looked around the cold, disheveled cabin.

"What a fucking mess!"

Banks smiled with memories of his ex-roommate's messy lifestyle. "Coming from you, that is an insult." He lifted the cover of the tin woodstove and placed his hand inside. It was cold.

"There hasn't been a fire in here for at least twenty-four hours," Travis dropped the lid back down. "The old man has either split camp or is in trouble."

"He didn't leave, at least not by snowmobile," McMaster said. "His double track is still hooked up to the sled behind the cabin. I saw it from the air. The only way out would've been by snowshoe and even that cunning bastard couldn't make it in this temperature."

Both men headed for the door. They split up and searched the surrounding area.

Behind the cabin, Banks eyed the drying shack. It stood silently under the pine boughs, half covered in roofing tin and perilously close to falling over. He propped open the door using a broken ax handle lying half submerged in the snow.

Inside, rows of wooden grids stood erect, covered in drying animal pelts. The freezing temperatures lessened the stench of rotting animal. Travis walked among the grids toward the rear of the shack, running his hands along stiff furs. The light from the door behind him grew less visible as he proceeded. He reached into the pocket of his parka and pulled out a watertight aluminum cylinder full of all-weather matches. He struck a match and slid it forward into the darkness that was swallowing him up. The match's tiny glow illuminated the dark rear wall. Various tools for processing pelts hung on the blood-stained wood next to several dozen leghold traps.

An empty Coleman lamp lay sideways on the trapper's dirty worktable. Banks attempted to light the rusted green lamp. The flame flickered to smoke as the lamp's white ashy mantle crumbled. Behind him, the ax handle fell from the shack's door. It swung shut. The darkness verged on absolute. Something moved over Banks's right shoulder. He spun around and raised the gun. Peering into the darkness, he fumbled for another match with his free hand. Using the denim on the back of his right hamstring, he quickly brought the match to life. A small Arctic fox with a frozen piece of hide darted across the floor underneath the rows of furs and scurried out the door. Travis exhaled and lowered the gun to his side. The light from the match lasted long enough for him to find daylight.

Banks saw McMaster slowly following a worn path into the woods behind the main cabin. The trapper's snowmobile was parked alongside the drying shack. Tracks shot off in all directions. Travis stood in the middle of a set of tracks with the unmistakable imprint of a torn tread; Bellichek's snowmobile must have needed a new track. Off to his right, there was another set of tracks heading to the middle of the lake. Unlike Bellichek's double track, these markings were of a single-track machine with metal lugs for gripping. A trail of two-stroke oil had left little holes burned into the snow both coming and going from the single-track markings.

Banks tilted the nearly empty forty-five gallon drum of gas, surprised to find he could do it with one hand. Even if Bellichek had tried, he wouldn't have had enough gas to reach civilization. Where the hell was he? Looking for clues, Banks lifted the snowmobile's seat cushion. Personalized trapping maps lay scattered about, stained with chewing tobacco. Several live rounds of ammunition, along with some empty shell casings, were rolled up on the sides of the seat locker. There was no sign of Bellichek's rifle inside or outside the cabin. Banks knew the old man probably slept with his antique rifle. If he could find the rifle, he'd probably find the trapper.

Next to the snowmobile's right front ski, something glimmered in the morning sunlight. The pilot bent down and pulled. A ring of keys popped out from the snow. He shook the ice off the frozen metal and rolled them around the palm of his mitt. It was odd for Bellichek to lock anything. Burglars didn't make it out this far and the old trapper didn't own anything worth stealing. One of the keys was made by a company Travis had never heard of. He slipped the keys into his parka. Maybe Bellichek had a lockbox in the cabin.

Banks was feeling the bitterly cold cylinders of the snowmobile's engine when McMaster shouted his name. He turned and crunched through the snowy trail toward McMaster's voice.

Travis pushed the last of the bushes aside and walked into the small clearing.

"See," Dale pointed and fired his camera at an area covered in blood, "that freak killed something big."

Banks looked around momentarily and then got down on one knee, removed his mitt, picked up some of the red-colored snow and squeezed it in the palm of his hand until it melted. He raised the melted bloody water to his nose and took a deep breath. He looked up at his friend.

"This isn't animal blood."

"What?" McMaster stood stock-still, his smoky breath rolling out slowly into the frigid air. "What's that supposed to mean?"

Travis took another whiff of his hand. The implication was obvious.

"Oh, that's great. Just fucking great!" McMaster snapped his camera case shut and headed back to the lake, mumbling something about flying away with or without any goddamn pilot.

Banks caught up to him as the two men reached the cabin. Travis tried to consider all the possibilities. They silently walked toward the aircraft. Its hot engine still billowed heat into the chilly atmosphere. Dale opened the left main door and placed the rifle on the Beaver's middle seat. He climbed in behind the rifle and squeezed into the right seat.

"I'm glad to see that you've finally come to your . . ." Dale stared at the pilot walking past the airplane toward the middle of the lake. He stuck his head out the window. "Hey . . . hey! . . . where the hell you going?"

Banks continued walking toward the moose carcass in the middle of the lake. He pulled the hammer back on his favorite handgun and shattered the pristine silence, firing once more into the air.

"Shit!" Dale pounded the dashboard. He reached behind his seat and pulled the rifle over his shoulder. He leapt back out onto the right ski and slipped on its aluminum surface, falling face first onto the frozen ice. He cursed, picked himself up, and followed.

As the two men moved toward the large dark fur stuck in the middle of the lake, they kept an eye on the opposite shore. The odds were remote that the wolves would show themselves but starving wolves in packs were unpredictable. Banks followed one of the snowmobile tracks pointing straight from the cabin to the carcass in the middle of the lake. It took ten minutes to cover a distance which looked much closer.

The pilot and loader slowed as they got closer. Travis cocked the gun and aimed it slightly ahead of his course. The large brown object was surrounded by blood. Ten feet away, they stopped and started to circle the hide. Dale hesitated and allowed Travis to circle the object alone.

The lake, surrounded by towering mountains on all but one side, was so still that the expansion and contraction of the two men's lungs seemed to echo in the valley. When Banks reached the other side of the carcass, he slowly came to a stop. He lowered the gun to his side and stood so still that Dale swore he'd stopped breathing.

McMaster circled the hairy, matted, frozen statue and joined his friend on the other side. He felt his stomach knotting. This was no moose carcass. The grotesquely disfigured image jutted up from the depths of the thick blue ice. It engulfed them both in an abyss of horror intensified by the unblemished silence of the frozen landscape.

"Oh, my God." McMaster's voice was barely audible.

The tattered remains of what closely resembled a human sat straight up, entrenched in a thick hole in the ice. It was as if the diabolical figure was standing on something a few feet below the lake's surface, frozen in place from the waist down. The arms and torso disappeared into the ice at the elbows. The bear skin parka with wolf trim had been torn and matted with blood from the victim's shredded face. Its ears, nose, and most of the flesh on the cheeks and neck had been stripped away by winter-starved wolves. There was no stench accompanying the obliterated human form. The frozen air robbed the atmosphere of the smell of death.

Banks finally turned away, keeping the gun pointed at the ice and slowly releasing the hammer. He deliberately walked in a small circle, eyeing the entire 360 degrees of the Primrose Lake shoreline. Travis didn't expect to see anything other than possibly a wolf. He simply didn't want to look at the image in front of him any longer.

"We've disturbed their breakfast." Banks pointed toward the shoreline. He was sure the wolves were hidden in the brush, panting and staring back.

"Is this thing Ed Bellichek?" McMaster continued to gawk at the macabre image.

"What's left of him." Travis turned to leave. He recognized the trapper's tattered thirty-year-old parka. "Let's get on the high frequency radio and get the Mounties. Wolves didn't dig this hole."

The bush pilot walked away with his friend fixated on the ghastly bust of the savaged Yukon trapper.

McMaster built a fire on the shoreline near the aircraft. It wasn't for warmth. Their parkas were designed to keep them relatively warm until the temperature fell to forty below zero. The fire focused their energies on something other than the dark figure frozen in the middle of the lake.

Dale crouched down, balancing on the balls of his feet and eyeing the western horizon for the inevitable arrival. He wiggled the tip of his tongue around the inside of his lips and fired a short little shot of spit into the fire. It wasn't easy to roll handmade cigarettes tight and these short spits removed the bits of tobacco that escaped into his teeth. He spat whenever he smoked, claiming that the habit was totally unconscious. He would probably do it, albeit unwittingly, even in the presence of royalty.

"Dale?" Banks snapped.

"What?"

"Do you mind?"

"Mind what?" McMaster responded, oblivious to the distraction.

"Would you stop that goddamn spitting? It's disgusting." Banks looked at him in disbelief. "Do you do that when you're screwing?" The frigid cold was beginning to wear down their patience.

"I don't know." Dale sat thinking. "I don't think so. No one's ever said anything."

Travis focused his eyes on Dale's left ear lobe and smiled at the thought of McMaster's usual bedmates. He pulled his parka on tighter.

"Somehow, I'm not surprised."

"What's that supposed to mean? What are you looking at?" Dale asked. He paused, angry at his friend's insult. "And stop looking at my new earring. You don't like it, do you?"

"It's beautiful." Banks tried to sound sincere. He didn't have the heart to burst Dale's bubble. He'd tell him one day it looked ridiculous. But only if they were both about to die.

The purring turbine noise in the distance ended their edgy conversation. The white and blue Twin Otter of the Royal Canadian Mounted Police quietly slid around the corner of Mount Skukum.

"It's about time."

McMaster spoke mostly to himself, looking up at the twin engine de Havilland Otter approaching the icy lake. He rolled another cigarette just to aggravate Banks. He lit the end with a stick from the fire, pushed himself up using his knees for leverage, and smiling, did one of his little spits into the fire.

Banks remained nestled in some evergreen shrubs near the fire with his back to the lake. He was in no hurry to greet Inspector Nick Radcliff, head of the Whitehorse RCMP detachment. Although they'd met soon after Radcliff's transfer to Whitehorse in the fall, they were not friends and Travis doubted there would ever be any rapport between them. The inspector was too taciturn and business-oriented to cultivate friendships outside of work . . . or even at work for that matter.

But that was only part of it. Radcliff seemed to be hell-bent on trying to bust Banks's passengers, especially trappers and miners who occasionally bent some obscure environmental law or regulation. He particularly loved to nail hunters who had spotted their prey from the air. This was impossible to prove because the only witness would be the pilot involved, and the pilot would have to incriminate himself to bust the hunter.

The truth was that most pilots did their best to prevent spotting from the air. They knew it wasn't sporting. Banks recalled how he'd handled a hunter the previous summer who had tried to spot from the air.

The two had flown around aimlessly for an hour trying to find some obscure lake that only the hunter believed to exist. After circling and passing numerous lakes, the passenger finally spotted the lake he claimed to have been seeking. A five-year-old bull moose with a huge rack happened to be eating dinner in the shallows of the far shore. After landing on the opposite end of the lake, the hunter actually jumped, loaded rifle in hand, into the water up to his waist before Banks even had a chance to secure the airplane. He then ran off into the bushes toward the animal, yelling instructions about where he wanted his supplies dropped off. He didn't realize how fast Travis could unload a de Havilland Beaver and taxi on water.

Within minutes, Travis was taxiing in the direction of the unsuspecting moose. He could see the delirious hunter crashing through the bush, cursing and swearing as he tried to get close enough for a shot. Sailing the floatplane quietly near the animal, Banks pulled the water rudders up and poured the coals to the 450 horsepower radial engine. The noise was deafening. Travis figured the moose didn't stop running until it reached a different time zone.

When Travis picked up the infuriated hunter a week later, he denied any knowledge of foul play. Even though Travis had saved the moose, Inspector Radcliff would have given both men a life sentence. In fact, Travis believed that, given half a chance, Radcliff would reinstitute the death penalty.

From the little Travis knew, Radcliff was a perfectionist with a gruff and unyielding manner. His perfectly groomed black handlebar mustache demanded either respect or ridicule. Either genetic predisposition or the North had hardened his looks by wrinkling the skin covering his once-chiseled facial features. His square jaw and upright countenance reflected the proud image of the RCMP Mounties. Rumor had it that the constable had no close friends. He never spoke of family and focused solely on his career. It seemed that no one had ever seen him out of uniform. He simply preferred to keep to himself.

Banks slowly unfolded his arms and turned his head in the direction of the arriving aircraft as it came to a sliding, bouncing halt.

Inspector Nick Radcliff hopped out of the twin-engine turbo prop before the blades had even stopped spinning. With light, bouncy steps, he propelled his athletic frame across the crunchy snow, covering the icy distance between his parked airplane and Banks before the accompanying constable/pilot and Staff Sergeant Leon Powell could catch up. Travis was thrilled to see Leon hop out the back door.

"Where is he?" Radcliff was always serious and spoke in a flat monotone. Things like this didn't happen often. This was sure to be one of the year's highlights in a district so void of true crime.

Travis stood up. "Top of the morning to you, too." No smile from the inspector. Travis pointed over Radcliff's shoulder toward the center of the lake.

The three officers stopped in their tracks and turned 180 degrees. Once the Mounties spotted the dark spot in the middle of the lake, they trudged toward the frozen remains of Ed Bellichek with McMaster and Banks in tow.

The officers spent the better part of the afternoon wandering around the end of the lake which had been Bellichek's neighborhood. The pilot and his loader explained in detail how and when they had found the body. Banks spent an hour scouring through the aircraft logbook, exacting dates and times of each trip into and out of Primrose Lake over the past several months.

Radcliff must have asked the same questions a hundred times. Travis responded in kind. No, he hadn't dropped anyone else near Primrose

Lake recently. No, he had not seen anyone by air on snowmobile traveling either toward Bellichek's cabin or away from it in the past several weeks. No, he hadn't found anything or taken anything. The inspector even rummaged behind the Beaver's aft bulkhead, inspecting Banks's survival kit and its contents. Radcliff pulled out the hunting bow and flaunted his strength by giving it a full unwavering pull that extended well behind his ear. The middle-aged police officer's skill was impressive. Banks's only retort to Radcliff's exhibition of strength was to jokingly mention the newer hunting bow he had at home that he could never fully draw back. Travis's lighthearted insult about Radcliff's strength was ill advised. The RCMP inspector tossed the expensive PSE hunting bow into the back of the plane and quickly grasped the pilot's rifle. He smelled the stock and barrel to see if it had been fired recently, as if Banks had suddenly become a suspect. Travis lightly hugged the .44 inside his parka.

As the day wore on, Banks finally had a chance to speak freely with his friend and racquetball foe, Leon Powell. Sergeant Powell walked out of Bellichek's shack toward the small fire Dale and Travis had barely managed to keep lit.

Leon was a bull in a china shop when it came to law enforcement. He was a stout ex-Marine from Montana who migrated to Canada as a young man because of his love of the wilderness. He had arms and legs like fire hydrants and could easily crush a man with his bare hands. After more than twenty years with the RCMP, only a touch of gray hair appeared on his balding head. On this day, a Denver Broncos football cap covered his shiny dome. The hair follicles had not yet abandoned Leon's eyebrows. They perched above his black piercing eyes and were so thick that a horse's currycomb could not have tamed them. The sergeant was the type you'd want on your side in an alley fight. He never played the politics required to become Inspector. He had made it to Staff Sergeant and that suited him fine. He was second in command in Whitehorse. He much preferred being in the field to riding a desk. Over the years, the two had done a lot of official business together. Whenever the RCMP needed to charter a plane in and out of small communities,

Leon would always request Arctic Air and Travis Banks. Travis paid Powell back by letting him kick his butt in racquetball and by taking Leon hunting with him each fall. In the past few years, their relationship had grown from professional to personal.

Radcliff had wandered back to the body, giving the bush pilot an opportunity to question Leon.

"Well, Powell, you guys are the experts. What the hell happened out here?"

"No idea, Travis." He eyed the lake while fumbling with the RCMP-issued camera in an attempt to load another role of 35mm film. "Never seen anything like it. It's hard to believe an animal could do such a thing."

"Fucking impossible!" Dale snorted to no one in particular.

"We don't know what happened here yet, Dale. And I'd appreciate if you kept quiet in town until we make some sort of determination as to the cause of death. We have to locate any next of kin." Leon struggled to hide his own suspicions.

But Dale wasn't going to let up. "I might not know what killed him but I sure as hell know what stopped him from having an open casket funeral. Those wolves over there are pissed off. We're playing with their dinner," he said, pointing to the other side of the lake and muttering about "tonight's dinner special," much to the annoyance of his companions. "McMaster!" Powell and Banks barked in concert. The day had worn their patience thin, and the ominous presence of the frozen figure had them both on edge.

"Travis," Powell began as he hunkered his chunky frame down next to the fire. "Inspector Radcliff wanted me to ask you if you know anything about Bellichek's private life?"

"Not friggin' likely," Dale interrupted. "You expecting to find out this guy kept a harem of beautiful women hidden somewhere?" He chuckled at the improbability of his hypothesis.

"Please, Dale." Officer Powell looked at the ground in frustration. "Travis? Anything?"

Banks stared at Powell, trying to think of something that might be pertinent to the life of Ed Bellichek. Nothing came to mind.

Powell continued, trying to unlock some seemingly inconsequential recollection that Banks might have parked in the recesses of his memory.

"Did you ever spend anytime just talking to him when you flew supplies in during trapping season?"

Travis smiled at Powell, hoping he'd see the absurdity of his question. "You mean, like, sitting around the fire with my good buddy Ed Belichek just shooting the shit, talking about how many wolves he's screwed out here?"

"C'mon, Travis, you know what I mean." Powell angrily tossed a stick he'd been playing with toward the frozen lake.

"Look, Leon, I'm sorry. It's just that there isn't much to say. The guy was a loner. He was a strange cookie, that's for sure, but I can't imagine anybody doing anything horrendous enough to end up like that." Travis pointed to the middle of the lake. "I honestly don't think anybody knew the man. He certainly wasn't the most gregarious fellow I've ever met. Most trappers we outfit with supplies let us use their cabins during the fall moose hunting season. As long as we clean up our mess and replace any used firewood, we're invited back the following year. Not Mr. Belichek. I thought that after flying him around a few years, I might have finally gained his trust. No way. I broached the subject once about possibly using his cabin and received an unconditional refusal."

Dale had grown weary of the friendly interrogation between the pilot and sergeant and wandered off toward the frozen shore to take a few pictures of Radcliff and his crew scurrying around as though auditioning for an episode of "NYPD Blue".

Banks sensed that Powell was listening to him but was more concerned with his next question. Powell's piercing eyes bored into Banks, picking the locks of the bush pilot's memory.

"Who would pick him up when you brought him out each spring at the end of the trapping season?"

It was a good question. Skilled police officers have the knack of soliciting a response from subjects who honestly believe they have no valuable information to offer. Leon Powell was both accomplished and patient.

"You know, there was this fellow, a little guy." Banks looked in

Powell's direction trying to extract the image from his mind. "I have no idea who he was, but on several occasions he would pick Bellichek up right at the airplane on the ramp in Whitehorse. Introductions were not the order of the day around Bellichek. He never mentioned who the guy was and I never asked. Bellichek didn't come out of Primrose Lake until the end of each season. He'd take several R & R's during the winter. Get smashed, tie one on for a weekend, then call Kayla wanting to get back to his trapline." Something else clicked in Banks's head and he looked over at Dale standing behind his camera 30 feet away.

"Hey, McMaster, didn't Kayla ask you to drop Bellichek off somewhere downtown last year when we flew him to Whitehorse? It was a nasty day. Snowed like hell all day. It was around Rendezvous, almost a year ago?"

"The Regina," Dale answered confidently without taking the camera away from his eye. He rotated the short zoom lens and focused on something in the middle of the white lake. Travis had asked him to take several specific pictures and he continued to carry out the assignment.

Powell was deep in thought. He thanked Banks as if they had just met for the first time and turned away, heading toward the shack. He aimed his government-issued camera at the ex-homestead of Ed Bellichek and took one last parting shot.

It was getting late, dark, and cold. Dale was beyond agitated. His thermos had been empty for hours and the Klondike tavern was beginning to consume his thoughts. He had tried to sneak into the dark home of the dead trapper and steal a tug from Bellichek's private stock of libations but was caught and severely reprimanded by Radcliff for tampering with evidence.

Travis was beginning to sense that the RCMP pilot took some comfort in his presence. There was no apparent reason to detain Banks and McMaster any longer. The young pilot did not have the experience that came from flying in the bush full-time. Radcliff might keep his pilot alive in the wild frozen North but he couldn't fly a Twin Otter. RCMP pilots normally flew asphalt-to-asphalt during the day under "IFR," or instrument flight plans. In essence, they weren't true bush pilots. Most young officers of the RCMP Northern detachments came and went as soon as their apprenticeships were up. This pilot was no different. If his new and shiny turbine toy didn't start, he would probably survive, but only because of Bellichek's cabin and Powell's experience. Nonetheless, it would, likely be the most miserable experience of his life. Having Dale and Travis stick around was an insurance policy. One that was about to expire.

"Excuse me, Nick?" Banks politely caught Radcliff's attention as he returned from the body with tiny bags of evidence.

"Sorry . . . Constable Radcliff . . . look, I don't have an instrument-equipped turbine-powered airplane. I've got a twenty-year-old aircraft with a piston radial engine designed about the time Babe Ruth was in the minors. It's getting late. You're down to two choices. You either let Dale and me get the hell out of here now, or you shoot us." Travis cracked a smile.

"Don't tempt me, Banks," came Radcliff's unsmiling retort. He looked up from the little bags he was tagging and arranging in the doorway of the Twin Otter. "Keep an eye out for any signs of wildlife that may be involved. Let's get started on the body." He motioned at Powell.

Banks couldn't believe his ears. Wildlife? They might as well have said Elvis killed Bellichek.

Dale jumped in incredulously, "Excuse me! You don't think this was done by some overly zealous, hibernating Yogi Bear, do you?"

He wanted to mention what he and Travis had been quietly discussing earlier. But seeing Banks slice his forefinger across his throat, he decided to yield the floor.

Travis added to Dale's remarks with caution, "Nick, this wasn't done by a bear. I'm not familiar with the species of bear that places their dead in frozen lakes . . . vertically!"

Radcliff ignored Banks's remark.

"By the way," Travis hesitated because he knew Radcliff would not want to hear what was next. "There's something about Bellichek's body you should know about." Travis sounded like a child about to confess to a parent.

"And what's that?" Radcliff practically growled with impatience.

"Can I borrow a sectional or WAC chart from your pilot?" Banks was angry with himself for not remembering the RCMP pilot's name.

The young pilot rifled through the seat back on the captain's side of the aircraft and produced WAC-16. It included not only navigation routes, but also the geographical outlay of most of Canada's Yukon and part of Alaska's southern panhandle. He handed it to Banks without ceremony.

The Arctic Air pilot unfolded the chart and spun it around a couple of times so that north pointed up.

"If you look here, you'll notice that Primrose Lake, Bellichek's trapline, and his cabin are here," Travis pointed to the small lake on the map.

"So?" Radcliff was uninterested.

"Well, I'm surprised your pilot didn't notice this, but do you see the shaded dashed line going through the middle of Primrose Lake?"

"Yes, he did notice it. What's your point? He said it's a line of magnetic deviation. Forty-two degrees east. So?" The possibility of Banks pointing out a flaw in the RCMP pilot's aeronautical knowledge rankled him.

Travis opened another fold of the map and pointed to a similar dashed line.

"I'm afraid it's not deviation. Do you see the length of the dashes in this line? They're long. *That's* a line of magnetic deviation on a WAC chart. Now, look at the dashed line crossing Primrose Lake." Travis folded the map back. "They're short dashes with dots in between. It's also shaded."

The RCMP pilot quickly looked at his aviation counterpart from Arctic Air, then back to Radcliff. Powell steered clear, knowing the smart money was on Banks. The young pilot/constable who had obviously written his aeronautical exams fairly recently knew where Travis was going and dropped his head.

Radcliff stared at Banks waiting for an explanation.

"It's the border." Banks softly touched the chart without looking at the map. "It's the U.S.-Canada border."

Radcliff looked out across the darkening lake. "What are you saying, Banks?"

"I'm saying Ed Bellichek might have been killed in Canada but he is definitely stuck in United States soil. Or, in this case, ice. I would say he is at least a quarter of a mile within the U.S. border. Maybe more, but definitely not less. By the letter of the law, his death might be outside Canadian jurisdiction. If we move the body, we might be tampering with evidence in a U.S. murder investigation."

One glance at the two faces of his detachment members told Radcliff they concurred with Banks's geographical evaluation. The oversight by his hand-picked pilot infuriated him. He raged silently and struggled not to show it.

"Leon. Get the axes. I want the body on board in ten minutes." He controlled his disgust in amazing fashion. "Banks, you're not a cop. You fly airplanes and leave law enforcement to me." He flipped his forefinger in Banks's direction. "Go home, I'll contact you tomorrow. Don't say anything to anybody. I'm not interested in people flying out here looking for Bigfoot."

Banks had the de Havilland Beaver airborne before the Twin Otter began to taxi. He buzzed the lake once to confirm that both blades of the RCMP aircraft were spinning.

Several minutes later, at 2,000 feet above the trees, the Twin Otter crept up along the right side of the slower Beaver. The two airplanes were so close that Dale could make out the faces of Leon Powell and the pilot police officer in the glow of the cockpit lights. The pilot smiled at McMaster, savoring the moment as his plane sped past the rumbling Beaver. Banks imagined that Powell would much rather have gone home in the slower Beaver.

In the back of the RCMP Twin Otter were two men, a dead trapper and an RCMP inspector who was a mystery to all who knew him.

Upon returning from Primrose Lake, Banks closed his flight notification with the tower and quickly headed for home. Nick Radcliff had issued a gag order and would not hesitate to incarcerate Travis if he ignored it. Kayla was aware of the situation because she had been the only one in the office when Banks called for the RCMP on the HF radio. The tired pilot filled in the rest of the details and warned Kayla about Constable Radcliff's insistence of silence until the investigation was complete. As soon as she was briefed, Ms. Jackson began rummaging through her files to see if Bellichek owed her any money. Business was business.

Travis quickly drove into town via Two Mile Hill. He needed a few groceries and soon found himself in a snake pit called Woodward's Food Store. He chose a checkout line that appeared to be moving along quickly but, as usual, it slowed to a crawl. The express lane. Ten items or less. The woman ahead of him, clad in curlers, untied boots, and puffing on an ash-laden cigarette butt, had a third-party check and was waiting for an act of Parliament to approve its cashing.

Banks eyed her basket. She had more than just ten items. He imagined starting a new law enforcement agency—Express Lane Police. On top of the woman's illegal number of items, her basket contained a bikini wax kit. He looked at the woman from head to toe and became nauseous at the thought of her applying it to whatever was hidden below her protruding belly. After fifteen minutes in the "express" line, he made it back to his truck and headed for Hillcrest.

Hillcrest was a small neighborhood north of the airport. It consisted of about thirty single-family dwellings and an equal number of old military duplexes. All were about fifty years old. They were simple two-story wooden structures with minimal shrubbery and short driveways ending in open-covered carports. Like the Arctic Air hangar, they'd been built for the Army constructing the Alaska Highway in 1942. The duplexes were the off-white enlisted housing you could find near any military base in North America. They were located toward the back of the neighborhood. One had to pass the single-structure homes first.

The zone between the two architectural styles contained a gray stone residence that was unique to the neighborhood. It was the place that Banks called home. He occupied the right side of a plain fifteen-year-old duplex. Unlike the military version, his had two stories, the only one like it in Hillcrest. The cold hardwood floors were comfortable in the summer but necessitated slippers over wool socks in the winter. The small kitchen and living room were downstairs, the two small bedrooms were upstairs. Travis used his spare bedroom as a part-time office and refuse container. It had a desk hidden somewhere under piles of clothes, unopened boxes of books, and an array of unclaimed junk from several overnight moves. The entire house was tastefully decorated from yard sales and hand-me-downs. It looked like hell, but it was all his.

The shale stone duplex had been uniquely modified years earlier. At some point in time, the two halves of the duplex had been joined by knocking out the living room wall and connecting both living rooms. In their place, a large atrium was built. Years later, a developer seeking income from both units restored the original duplex by adding two large, windowless double doors in the middle of the atrium. Once again, there were two separate living rooms, each with its own doors and locks on each side. When all four doors were opened, both residences could be joined with the large hardwood-floored atrium.

It was a chore the first time Travis attempted to open the doors. Years of over-painting made it nearly impossible. When the doors finally creaked and splintered open, exploding ridged paint, there standing in front of the stunned pilot was a wiry little Englishman in baggy boxer shorts. He was wearing an open smoking jacket and puffing rapidly on a pipe. He was not pleased by this intruding neighbor. Yet it was almost as if he had been waiting for Banks to break through. When Banks had asked him why his doors were already opened, he barked it was none of his "bloody" business and demanded to know if Travis drank his Guinness Stout at room temperature.

Banks surmised that the real estate agent must have paid Monty to stay hidden indoors on the day he had purchased the duplex seven years earlier.

The better half of Banks's building was the residence of Lieutenant Winston Montgomery. Most called him Monty. Travis occasionally used Lieutenant out of reverence. The Lieutenant had more flying experience than any other pilot in the Yukon.

When Travis pulled up the driveway, Monty was outside dressed in his favorite red flannel jacket and black cotton toque. He was eyeing a piece of dry firewood sitting on the chopping block. With a mighty blow from the small man who was more than twice Banks's age, the elongated section of spruce split, flipped through the air in opposite directions, and landed in the snow. The sprite old man carefully put down the ax, retrieved the hidden firewood and placed it precisely on his immaculate pile of split firewood. Taking a sip of Guinness Stout, he placed the mug on the steps leading to his front door, picked up the ax and selected another section of spruce to repeat the process.

Monty was a proud World War II Royal Australian Air Force veteran from Maryborough, Queensland, Australia. As a child, he had moved to Cirencester, England. Years later, during the war, he'd met a Canadian nurse from Whitehorse named Mindy Allan, at an RAF dance in Lichfield. They instantly fell in love. After the war ended, they wed and settled in the English countryside. Soon, they moved back to the Yukon when his mother-in-law became terminally ill. Not long after Mindy's mother died, Mindy herself was diagnosed with Hodgkin's disease and passed away. Monty had worshipped the ground she walked on and would never consider "blemishing" their love by remarrying. With no surviving relatives abroad, and no children, he elected to remain in Canada. Though he was content as a loner, the other neighbors found him aloof and difficult.

Over time, Banks found the opposite to be true. Monty could be arrogant, stubborn and unyielding, but, to his few friends, he could also be generous to a fault. The atrium doors separating the two homes had long stopped being locked. They were open far more than closed. Other than Banks, the only friends Monty had were old RAF pilots who kept in touch by letter. The two neighbors chided each other constantly, but Travis never forgot who was the elder statesman and, with that in mind, treated Monty with respect. The Lieutenant's experiences in aviation were something Banks had only read about in history books.

Occasionally, Travis would come home from the airport and find the old soldier sitting in front of a roaring fire with a letter in one hand, a brandy snifter in the other, and a tear in one eye. Another old RAF buddy had passed away, reeling him in closer to the unpleasant reality of his own mortality. Travis would stay up with him, get drunk on brandy, and listen to his reminiscences about the fallen comrade. Not many of Monty's friends had survived the air war over Germany.

And the few he had left were his only tie to the past.

The war had ended early for Flight Lieutenant Winston Montgomery.

He had been assigned to 460 Squadron, Breighton in Yorkshire. In 1942, he flew Wellingtons and then Halifaxes. Both aircraft proved unpopular and, in October 1942, the squadron began flying Lancasters. The following spring, 460 Squadron moved its operation to Lincolnshire, then Binbrook. Winston Montgomery had completed twenty-eight missions over Germany by January 1944. Thirty missions meant going home. Most airmen were lucky to survive half that number. The Squadron had quite a reputation as the first unit in Bomber Command to complete 1,000 sorties—all in only eighteen months. But that record took its toll. Ten to twenty percent casualties per mission was not uncommon during the peak of the air war over Europe. Simple statistics meant a crew's number was up after five missions.

Monty's final two missions took place in January 1944. He successfully bombed Berlin on the 20th. On the following night, January 21, 1944, he was to fly his final mission and bomb industrial sights at Magdeburg, Germany. The young commander, Lieutenant Montgomery, launched into the Binbrook sky that evening to join nearly 600 bombers and God knows how many fighters. At last, his final sortie! He had completed his bombing run and was turning toward home in a sea of flack when 'Miss Mindy' was struck by a falling allied bomb and lost part of a wing. He had made it through nearly thirty missions and here he was spiraling to the ground because of an allied bomb tearing off a section of his wing.

Somehow, he and two other crew members managed to overcome the G-forces and parachute from the crippled Lancaster. They desperately tried to locate and assist the other wounded airmen on board before jumping, but once the Lancaster was crippled by the errant bomb, it had been riddled and strafed by German JU 88s and ME 210s. The drifting airmen watched 'Miss Mindy' lazily circle and corkscrew below them like an autumn leaf falling from a tree until it struck the ground in an exploding ball of flame. The men held their parachute straps and wept for their comrades. They could only hope and pray that the other crewmen were dead by flack or gunfire before they struck the ground.

German solders waited for the falling airmen and Winston was taken prisoner at Raines-Glinde, approximately ten miles southeast of Magdeburg. That's how his last mission ended. He finished the war in a POW camp and was reunited with the real Miss Mindy in 1945.

The backgrounds of the two neighbors gave them a common interest that was the foundation of their friendship. That friendship had been severely tested when Monty found out that Travis was born in California and lived in the United States during his early childhood before moving to British Columbia at the age of 15. The Aussie was convinced that the "Yanks" had nearly lost the war for the Brits. Though his logic had always escaped Banks, it was fun to hear him rail against the U.S. military, especially its substandard pilot training. Banks occasionally took Monty with him on test flights and other non-passenger charters when the customers didn't object. To everyone with business at Arctic Air, Lieutenant Montgomery was treated as family—Travis's Uncle Monty. The old man was in better shape than anyone Travis's age and it seemed he would live for another ninety years.

Banks parked his truck in the driveway and jumped out. "You ready for some help?" Travis knew Monty would scoff at the offer. "The day I need help from a Yank, lad, nip in behind me and club me on the noggin with this ax, would you please?"

Monty balanced his next victim on the chopping block, fully planning to show off in front of Travis. The blow came hard and sent two pieces of spruce flying through the air. He collected the wood, stacked it, and took a quick breath as he looked Travis in the eye with a smile. "So, Mr. Banks, you managed not to kill yourself again today?"

"Just barely, Lieutenant." Travis forced a smile, paying his once daily homage to Monty's rank. Banks took his headset and the small bag of groceries from the passenger side of the truck and headed across the small snow-covered yard to his carport. Monty saw the expression on the pilot's face and placed his ax on the woodpile before disappearing into his half of the duplex. A moment later, he appeared at his front door with a freshly poured creamy Guinness Stout.

"Come on, lad, are you going to come in here by the fire and drink this or sit out there and freeze your tush?" The Lieutenant knew Travis too well. He saw something in the bush pilot's deportment that Travis thought he had concealed. They went inside and sat by the elder statesmen's perpetually roaring fire.

"O.K., son, tell me what happened." He crossed his legs on his old brown leather ottoman and ran his pipe's large cherry wood bowl through an unzipped leather pouch of sweet-smelling tobacco.

Travis raised his eyebrows and tried to look puzzled.

"Travis, on more occasions than I care to remember, I've seen pilots come home from having been face to face with the grim reaper. You have that look about you. Unless my senses have finally failed me, something happened out there today, lad. You don't have to tell me if you'd rather not but, believe me, it helps to talk about it." His cheeks collapsed as he sucked the flame of his old RAF wick lighter into the bowl of his pipe. Enormous clouds of smoke swirled around his head. The sweet aroma of his favorite pipe masked the musty smell of the old furniture. He stared at Banks without saying another word.

Travis had come to trust the Lieutenant as much as he trusted Dale. Radcliff's gag order would have to take a backseat to his belief in Monty's integrity. Travis explained, in detail, the events of the day.

"Sounds rather gruesome," Monty said matter-of-factly. He exhaled smoke nonchalantly, his English accent making the discovery at Primrose Lake sound more like a nosebleed than the remains of a ripped and tattered frozen corpse.

"Now what?" He warmed his fingers by rolling them around the bowl of the pipe.

"I don't know, Lieutenant. I guess we wait for an autopsy and go from there. The autopsy can't possibly conclude that this was an accidental death. This was no accident."

The two shared one more Guinness together and discussed the rest of the day, avoiding further talk of Ed Bellichek. They agreed to talk more later about the gory discovery at Primrose Lake. Travis thanked Monty for listening, excused himself, and slipped through the atrium doors. He had to be downtown within the hour.

The blinking light on the answering machine flashed out Morse code for "get another beer and have a seat." A few of the calls Banks had to return. Specifically, the RCMP. They had phoned several times while he was next door. It seemed Radcliff had a new question every five minutes about Banks and McMaster's complicity in the grisly discovery at Primrose Lake.

Travis's sister had phoned and left a message from Anchorage about getting together for Easter. She worked in a lab for the FBI and was all the family Banks had left. The idea sounded great. There was a recurring theme to the visits from his sister. He would phone her and offer to buy her a ticket to Whitehorse. She'd gush into the phone graciously and politely refuse, pointing out, gingerly, that she made twice as much money as he did and had no need of his generosity. He'd try again and buy it anyway.

One of the blinking message lights was Dr. Michelle Baker, who had told Banks repeatedly not to call her at work. She would often call and remind him of that fact. Travis marveled at such perplexing logic. Phone to tell him not to phone? What did women do before Alexander Graham Bell invented the device? It seemed to Travis that witchcraft ended at about the time the phone was invented.

Banks had first exposed himself, literally, to the good Dr. Baker during his first winter back in Whitehorse after leaving the airlines.

Travis had taken off from a small frozen lake near Atlin, British Columbia and encountered "whiteout"—white ice, white horizon, and white snowfall. Pilots compared it to flying inside a Ping-Pong ball. It was difficult to know which way was up. Before he was airborne, the bush pilot's right ski had been torn off by a deftly hidden pingo. A pingo was an ice upheaval normally found on the Beaufort Sea. Unfortunately, they were not exclusive to the Arctic Ocean. They could range in size from a few inches to more than 100 feet tall on any moving glacial lake. The big ones were easy to see by day. It was the little ones that struck in clandestine fashion.

Banks managed to keep the crippled aircraft flying and, knowing it would be a night landing with marginal runway lights, he elected to attempt the maneuver back at the Whitehorse Airport. It was equipped with relatively up-to-date crash, fire, and rescue facilities. Except for a distinct yawing to the left, the aircraft flew remarkably well. With a little rudder trim, the missing leg was hardly noticeable until he attempted to land. He flew the Beaver as inefficiently as possible—mixture rich, prop pitch forward, one ski down, flaps slightly extended. He needed to arrive at Whitehorse with only enough fuel to land, not to be cremated. The awkward landing on one ski didn't cause any bodily harm. It was the cartwheeling and sudden stop that forced Banks to come face to face simultaneously with Dr. Death and Dr. Baker. There were moments during their tumultuous relationship when Travis was convinced that the two doctors were one and the same.

Michelle Baker was the doctor on duty when they wheeled Travis into the emergency room. She was also the local coroner. Her responsibilities were preliminary autopsies. The more complex forensic procedures were performed at the morgue in Vancouver, B.C. On this night, Banks was relieved that her duties as coroner were not going to be required. He was slightly bent but not broken.

She quickly sheared off his trousers. She claims it was to check for any broken bones. He'd always insisted that she had been unable to control her curiosity. Either way, the pilot suffered only minor cuts and bruises and was discharged the following day. Travis had never been able to pinpoint the reason for his insatiable quest to see the doctor after his discharge. Maybe he was grateful and felt an indebtedness. It might have been her independence. She was not a classic beauty. Michelle had a small, appealing, athletic figure like an Olympic gymnast, with short brunette hair and soft linear facial features. Unless she was careful, her long hours, poor eating habits, and intermittent sleep would soon exact a toll on what many considered an attractive woman.

Dr. Baker was a welcome change from women looking to settle down and have babies on the third date. She was intelligent, attractive, self-sufficient, and made four times a bush pilot's salary. She would make someone a perfect wife if she could only learn to enjoy a football game and put jalapeños on her nachos. Travis kept seeing her because he felt that she had no plans to quit working anytime soon and have a louse like him try to support her.

Banks sent her flowers every day for a week after the accident. When he finally phoned, she insisted that seeing patients was not ethical or appropriate and it broke some obscure, unofficial medical rule. A few candlelit dinners later, all medical ethics were shelved.

They had their ups and downs. Both of them were tenaciously independent, which made a long-term commitment difficult. It suited Travis fine that they remained "significant others." Her pretense of independence was a double-edged sword. It attracted Banks, but might also prevent them from ever getting closer than they were. Neither of them had ever spoke of what tomorrow would bring. It was an odd but passionate relationship. Passionately hot some days and just as passionately cold the next. According to Michelle, there were no restrictions on dating other people. Banks knew that was bullshit. He knew that meant it was not a problem as long as she didn't know about it. He felt that she didn't want him too close or too distant. To be honest, he'd given up trying to figure out what she wanted and played it day by day.

At some point, he was going to have to approach her about his impending "platonic" date with his boss, Kayla Jackson. It could wait. The day had already been too full of surprises.

Dr. Baker had made it clear that she didn't like being called at work but Banks had to call to get information on Ed Bellichek. Canada's socialized medical system made the medical profession a wealth of knowledge. He would clean up first.

Travis showered, changed, and attacked the mess in his small bungalow. The kitchen was a disaster. Pratt and Whitney, his two alley cats of no discernible pedigree and a recent gift from the good doctor, had torn up the garbage. Now would be a good time to call her at work. If she was angry, he could always bring up her damn cats.

He knew better. She was always on edge working the evening shift in the emergency room. She didn't understand his profession. Likewise, he couldn't comprehend spending weekend nights sewing up the bodies of bar fight victims who were half-dead of exposure.

Although pleasant and warm, she began to question his phone call but fell silent as Travis explained the discovery of Bellichek's mutilated body.

The body, he explained, should already be at the hospital. When she finished her examination, would she please let him know the exact cause of death?

After the normal lecture about the right to privacy, she agreed to accommodate his request once the autopsy was complete. She would also look into hospital records for any medical history on Ed Bellichek or any living relatives in Whitehorse. She planned to meet Banks after work for a drink at the Klondike Inn. He was glad he had called.

Banks turned left off the Alcan Highway at one of only three traffic lights in Whitehorse. The sun had set several hours earlier, destroying the high temperature for the day of minus twenty-four degrees. The mercury was back down in the minus thirty range until the next sunrise.

Winter would last several more months. Spring was always welcome in May after eight solid months of freezing temperatures. The cold permeated every aspect of a person's life in the far reaches of the North. People didn't worry about fashion. Warm clothes were always in vogue, regardless of how they looked. The designer of a parka was not nearly as important as its thermal rating. If your parka kept you warm at forty below, no one gave a rat's ass if the label said Calvin Klein. A forty-below parka would turn heads at the most sophisticated parties.

All exercise and sporting activities had to be done indoors. Curling clubs were as common in the North as bowling clubs were in the South. Even with all the snow, cross-country skiing was abandoned in the heart of winter due to the crippling temperatures. Deeply inhaling a good wallop of forty-below-zero air could burn the lungs and bring you to your knees. Fortunately, one of the Yukon's most celebrated sports, drinking, was not affected by the sub-zero temperatures. It was an all-weather sport. Banks was sure Dale, his occasional drinking partner, had begun the evening's competition without him.

Travis slowly negotiated the treacherous and icy descent down Two Mile Hill toward Dale and the town that was reputed to have the most bars per capita of anywhere north of the 49th parallel.

There were only two accesses to the small downtown community of Whitehorse, which nestled itself between the airport on the western ridge of the city and the Yukon River to the east. The two routes were Two Mile Hill and the south access road. Ninety percent of the local traffic went via the steep Two Mile Hill.

Banks followed the milky exhaust and single taillight of a rusted-out Ford pickup. It was rare not to have some rust and a cracked windshield living in the Yukon. There were those who already had a glass spider in their windshield and those who soon would. It was a rite of residential passage.

The Klondike Inn and the familiar surroundings of its pub were only minutes away. Banks was to meet McMaster and Constable Powell by 8:30. The sight of a shredded Ed Bellichek had rocked even the normally impervious McMaster. The two men had not said much to each other on the flight home from Primrose Lake. Travis assumed that Dale was probably at the pub within thirty minutes of landing. Banks was curious to learn how Powell's flight back to Whitehorse with Radcliff had gone.

Travis parked his truck and plugged in all the heaters. Almost every public parking spot in Whitehorse had electrical outlets for vehicles to plug into during the frigid winter months. The bars had two last calls, fifteen minutes apart. One to go outside and start your car and one "last call for alcohol." By the time they threw you out, your car was warm and ready to roll.

Banks had one short extension cord connected to four heaters–the engine block heater, the circulating water heater attached to the radiator hose, the battery blanket, and a car heater inside the car. Together, they kept the car ready to drive on even the coldest winter nights. Within three minutes, Travis was inside the smoky warmth of the boisterous tavern.

The bar was starting to fill up in direct proportion to the drop in the temperature outside. When the mercury bottomed out, the Klondike dance floor would be full. The same band that had been playing for an eternity plucked away at a twangy country version of Juice Newton's "Angel in the Morning." The smoky haze settled on the red velour, brass, and oak surroundings, limiting Banks' vision. The obstructed view prevented him from quickly spotting his friend. Sometimes it was easier to wait a few minutes until a woman hidden in a dark corner screamed "No!" and slapped his handsome, half-pickled cohort.

McMaster's exploits with women were legendary. He proudly compared himself to the Fuller Brush man. If he knocked on ten doors, he'd sell one brush. He always asked a woman within several minutes of their initial encounter if she was interested in sex. Nine out of ten times, he was unceremoniously slapped in the face. The operative word is nine out ten times. He was a believer in statistics and odds. He lived for that ten percent.

The only facet of Dale's exploits that Banks had grown weary of occurred when they were roommates. McMaster had the infuriating habit of giving away clothes to strange women on the morning after their encounter. Usually, it was Banks' clothes that were given away. Travis had inquired many times as to the logic of this "door prize" mentality but had never received an acceptable response. The only thing he could attribute Dale's "Monty Hall" generosity to was that Dale, in the heat of passion, had either lost or destroyed his date's clothes somewhere between the initial meeting and his bedroom. It wasn't intentional. Dale had claimed he would have given his own clothes away to the stray encounters, if only he had any clean ones. During the ensuing warmer months of summer, Travis would be wandering downtown Whitehorse and pass a strange, usually unattractive woman wearing one of his more expensive shirts. Banks wanted to say something and get his shirt back but it was a difficult matter to broach with a stranger. What could he say? "Hi! You don't know me but you're wearing my clothes."

"Ace!" The familiar voice came from a booth hidden in one of the darker recesses of the noisy bar. Dale was sitting next to the off- duty police officer, Leon Powell.

Banks wandered over and threw his parka and mitts on the table next to them before sitting down.

"Good evening, gentlemen." He elbowed Dale. "Aren't you in heat yet? There are two classy women at the bar shooting tequila. They might buy something from the Fuller Brush man."

"Very funny." Dale was not his jovial self. He tumbled his hand-rolled cigarette along the edges of the pitted black plastic ashtray.

"What's eating you?" Banks was looking for the barmaid.

"What the hell happened to Bellichek? Powell, here, is not talking."

Powell piped up, "I don't know anymore than you do. We still have to find next of kin and get the lab results before making any public statements." He swallowed the rest of his soda water and lime.

His decision to quit drinking had saved his marriage and his career. He had not consumed any alcohol in six years, ten months, two weeks, and one day. They got an update daily. He was worse than a reformed smoker. But it became clear early on that he was not to preach to Dale. He obliged. The only reference to drinking he made was that if Dale and Travis couldn't drive him to drink again, nothing could. He located their waitress and twirled his finger in the air, ordering another round for their table.

Dale mumbled in Powell's direction as smoke exited his nostrils. He hated police protocol. He wanted answers about their discovery without all the procedures that Powell was required to follow.

"I don't know what happened," Powell continued. "Radcliff will get to the bottom of it."

"Not if he thinks Bellichek was turned into a bloody popsicle by some goddamn acrobatic circus bear." The alcohol began to make Dale unusually truculent and argumentative. The events of the day had left him noticeably shaken.

"A bear that can drive a snowmobile," Banks added.

Powell looked up, surprised. "What do you mean?"

A group of inebriated diamond drill operators, who had probably been in the bush for weeks, staggered by their table laughing. They eyed the girls on the dance floor and bragged, like most men, that they could "show them girls what a real man could do." Travis waited until they passed. "I'm amazed Radcliff didn't notice the tracks."

"What tracks?" Powell queried.

"Snowmobile tracks."

"He did. Hell, they were everywhere. How could you not notice? There are traplines all over Primrose Valley. I'm sure Nick figured another trapper visited, that's all. Those tracks could have been there for weeks."

"Not the tracks I'm referring to."

"Well, hell, I don't know Travis, that's what Radcliff told me when you guys were warming your sorry backsides in front of the fire. Look, we're flying back tomorrow. We'll check out the immediate vicinity and see if anyone local dropped by." Powell actually sounded as though he was defending Radcliff.

"Oh, he had visitors all right," Banks paused. "*After* he was killed."

Both men looked at the bush pilot. Everyone always accused Travis of surreptitiously pointing out obvious facts a little too late. It wasn't that. He simply liked to be sure of something before opening his mouth. He should have prefaced his next remark to Constable Powell with a warning to ensure that Powell wouldn't pass the information onto Inspector Radcliff. Banks didn't need Radcliff on his case any worse than he already was.

"Dale and I can prove it, Leon."

"We can?" Dale was shocked.

"Some of the pictures I asked Dale to take show blood under a certain set of tracks. Blood frozen in the snow before the tracks were made."

"They do? They do." Dale was bewildered. Earlier in the day, on Primrose Lake, Travis had asked him to take some close-ups of a certain set of tracks around the cabin. At the time, McMaster shrugged his shoulders and did it. Now he wanted to know why. He looked at his ex-roommate, hoping Banks would explain to him what he was already supposed to know.

Travis continued. "Tracks, or any markings, put into snow show their age. Even at freezing temperatures, snow slowly evaporates. The wind eats away at it. After a day or so, the edges of any disturbance begin to round out. Those tracks were sharp, less than twenty-four hours old."

Powell sat up and squinted his bushy eyebrows. "What are you saying, Travis?"

"I'm saying it's extremely probable there was a snowmobile on Primrose Lake riding around after Bellichek was killed."

"Go on."

"It was a single track with metal lugs, a fast machine. The spray coming off the track gave its speed away. Then you look at the large turning radius and the minimal depth of cut the tracks made in the snow. It also was oil-injected. Most two-stroke snowmobiles run on gas mixed with oil. This had a leaky oil tank. There was no gas in the oil I found in the snow. There were spots of oil all over the place. You had to look closely."

Powell was very interested in the pilot's observations. "Is there any way of knowing what type of machine it was?"

"Not really." Travis hated not being forthright with Powell but he had already said too much without more facts. He also realized that anything he said would, more than likely, get back to Radcliff. Travis didn't trust Radcliff nearly as much as Constable Powell. For the time being, he was going to keep much of his theory to himself.

There weren't very many quick, oil-injected, lugtracked snowmobiles. The only one Banks knew of was the Polaris 440 cc. There was one person in Whitehorse who would know if anyone owned a Polaris 440. He'd phone him when he got back from Yellowknife.

"Anyway, even if I'm right, whoever showed up might not be involved. His timing might stink is all." Banks lifted his shoulders and hands, feigning innocence. "He shows up to have a drink with Bellichek, finds the body and hightails it out of there." Travis's skepticism at this hypothesis must have been obvious. The other two men at the dark table eyed him warily for suggesting such a ridiculous theory. Banks might well have said that a Martian was spotted on the knoll in Dallas the day Kennedy was shot. The odds of Bellichek receiving visitors were remote at best.

"If there was anybody on Primrose other than us, we'll find out tomorrow." Powell began to smile. "Did you see the look on Nick's face? It nearly killed him, Travis."

"What?"

"When you mentioned the U.S. border. You're on the top of his shit list for a while."

Dale reached into his jean jacket and pulled out his pouch of Players tobacco and Zig Zag cigarette papers. The memory brought a smile to his face.

"He'll get over it," Banks said.

Travis's mind was on something else. Something had been nibbling away in his stomach since they discovered Bellichek's mutilated remains.

"Leon, where did Radcliff come from?" Travis had never asked before.

"The Vancouver B.C. detachment via Edmonton, I think. Before that, I don't know. He's got an impeccable background. He could name his jurisdiction. He wanted Whitehorse."

"That's what doesn't make any sense," Banks responded.

"Don't read anything into that, Banks. Take me, for example. I could have picked anywhere I wanted to go and I chose Whitehorse."

"I thought when you guys left training in Regina, whatever province you were assigned to, that was it. There was no choice. You stayed there for the rest of your career."

"Usually. But if you choose a *Northern* detachment, after several years of misery for most new constables, you can pick the province of your liking. A big benefit if there's a specific place you want to go. Like for family or whatever. You simply have to put up with the North for a few years."

Dale wasn't listening. "Did you phone Michelle?" He was making his plans for the night.

He always tossed her name aside. As much as Dale had wanted to be friends with Michelle, it was apparent every time he mentioned her name that he believed she was one of the reasons why he and Banks were no longer roommates. The strained feelings went both ways. Dr. Baker felt it was time for Dale to sober up and get a life. She was never enthusiastic when Travis met Dale socially. It meant beer breath, snoring, and often Dale on the couch if he didn't sell a brush.

"She's looking through hospital records as we speak. Once the autopsy's complete, she'll let us know what killed him."

"Shit! How can they tell?" Dale shook his head after downing the remnants of his drink. "Christ, he could have froze to death, been eaten alive, been shot, who the hell knows what actually killed him?"

Powell shook his head in disbelief. "Travis, for Christ's sake, you can't have Michelle passing confidential police information to you during an investigation. Listen, I don't want to hear anymore about what information Dr. Baker is or is not giving you. This is a police matter. We'll do our job."

"Sorry, Leon. I can't help it. I'm partial to cops. My sister's a cop..."

"She's an FBI police psychologist," Powell interrupted.

"Curiosity runs in the family."

"It also killed the cat."

"Michelle will figure it out," Travis continued. "She's often told me that one of the benefits of our cold climate is, once the heart stops pumping, the cause of death is sort of 'frozen in place.' Regardless of what happens after."

"She's meeting you later?" Dale wanted to know.

"It's a possibility." He smiled.

"Well, I'm not interested in cramping your style tonight." The barmaid interrupted Dale by placing a clean ashtray on the table. He used the interruption to order one more drink for the road.

"Travis, you go study the good doctor's anatomy. I'm heading to my apartment. I'm not in the mood tonight."

Banks was sure McMaster had consumed quite a few drinks since they'd returned from Primrose Lake. But Dale appeared to be amazingly under control. The memories of the day had drowned Dale's desire to party and dampened his desire to drink. He wasn't avoiding Michelle, he simply wanted to have a drink alone at home if Travis was having company. Banks knew his old roommate well.

Dale's drink, along with the bill, was dropped off. From habit, he swept them both up. It was a trick he used when he had been knocking back the Scotch. It was the destruction of evidence. He paid the barmaid so no one knew how drunk he was. He pounded back his last drink and got up to leave.

"Give my regards to Dr. Baker and I'll see you guys tomorrow."

"You coming to Yellowknife with me?" Banks always felt sorry for Dale when the loader tried to hide his loneliness.

"I thought it was people. I don't load people."

"They've got lots of bags, and besides what else are you going to do tomorrow?"

"Kayla's always got some pile of shit for me to move around the hangar. She'll find something for me to do." He zipped up his parka and slid on his mitts.

Travis tried one last time. "We'll be back by early afternoon."

"We'll see." Dale started walking away and then turned, grabbed his crotch, and winked at Travis. "May the force be with you tonight, buddy."

He really was the crudest creature Banks had ever met. It was a limitation. But along with Monty, he was also the most reliable friend Travis had ever known.

"I've got to go as well," Powell started getting up. "Be careful sticking your nose into this Bellichek thing, Travis. Radcliff would love to hang your ass on some trumped-up obstruction charge."

"I'm just doing what the boss asked." The bush pilot stretched the truth. "Kayla needs next of kin info for billing reasons."

"Right." Powell almost knocked over the table maneuvering his large torso out of the booth. "I'll see you on the racquetball court. Do you want to come over for dinner tomorrow? Mrs. Powell invited you, not me." He smiled.

"Thanks. It depends on when I get back. If I can make it, I'll call."

Powell disappeared into the shadows.

Before Banks could finish his beer and leave, the weak public address system scratched out his name. He had a message at the bar. Travis wandered over and read the message with a frown. Dr. Baker was tied up at the hospital and would be unable to meet him.

Banks flipped the message back on the sticky oak bar. He really didn't want to catch up to Dale just to drink. Tomorrow would be a long day. Seven hundred miles in a DC-3 with no autopilot.

He finished his beer leaning against the brass trim of the bar and watched the band start "Mammas, Don't Let Your Babies Grow up to Be Cowboys." He had heard the band's rendition of the song a thousand times. It was time to go home. He needed some fresh air. Maybe there would be something on the boob tube. Banks picked up his gear and exited through the hotel lobby.

On the way out, the slightly intoxicated pilot noticed a familiar hairdo and the faint aroma of lilac in the empty lounge of the Klondike Inn's hotel lobby. It looked as if Kayla Jackson was sitting alone, having what appeared to be an alcoholic drink. Impossible. No one had ever seen her leave the office before midnight, let alone drink in a bar.

Banks cautiously approached the figure so resembling his boss. He was all prepared to apologize to the stranger and head home. When their eyes met, he was stunned.

"Hi." She was very subdued and looked up only for an instant. "Have a seat. Where's Dr. What's-her-face?"

She didn't even try to hide her sarcasm. Her whole world seemed bummed out.

"Excuse me, it's just that you look like someone I once knew in the Yukon. My dictatorial and imperious boss. A real pain in the ass, but a nice gal once you got to know her."

Kayla Jackson barely managed a smile.

"I don't mind saying, Ms. Jackson, this has been a very strange day indeed." Travis gently took a seat. He noticed three empty glasses in front of her. No need to get hung up on formalities. Banks motioned the bartender to bring him whatever his boss was drinking, a lame attempt at protocol.

"First thing this morning, you asked me out on a date. Then I find a butchered trapper stuck in the middle of a frozen lake on the U.S. border. I've been verbally spanked by the RCMP for trying to help their cause. I've just been stood up by a usually reliable member of your own species. And to top it off, Dale McMaster does *not* want to drink tonight, but *you* do. There must be a full moon." He tried to sound cheery.

She paid no attention. The waitress dropped off a copy of Kayla's drink—bourbon. Travis's stomach rose. He hated bourbon. The only time he used bourbon was to clean his carburetor.

"Banks, have I ever mentioned the name Kitch Olson to you?"

It was hard to believe after all these years, he was actually sitting in a bar about to have a drink, albeit bourbon, with the aloof Kayla Jackson.

"Sure. He was the Air Canada old-timer who instructed you throughout your commercial license?"

She was totally despondent. "He was a lot more than that. You might say a mentor. He pushed me harder than anyone, including my own family. He was the impetus for me believing in myself. He convinced me, when no one else could, that a woman, specifically me, could buy and operate her own airline." She paused and took a deep breath. "He's the real reason Arctic Air exists." She was looking in all directions other than at the employee sitting across from her. Her mind was conjuring up some very warm memories. "He always acted like such a tough son of a bitch. He was a pussycat. I owe him everything," she said more to herself than to Banks.

Travis felt like he was intruding on some private journey into the past. He was inherently uncomfortable with the direction the conversation was going. Travis had been here before. He waited politely, expecting some explanation to accompany this trip down memory lane.

"Kitch was killed today." Her eyes began to turn red and glisten. This was probably the first time since hearing the news herself that she had said the words out loud. The sound was devastating. She discreetly turned and dropped her head before sobbing.

Banks had never seen Kayla Jackson lose control. He desperately wanted to console her, knowing she had no one in Whitehorse to share the tragic news.

"I'm sorry, Kayla." His feelings were genuine. She had often spoken of Kitch's influence on her life and career. Travis had long since stopped trying to find the perfect reply to the news of another dead airman. He switched seats, slid next to her, and gently placed his hand on her back. Silence was the best response.

Eventually, she regained her composure and, without pulling away from their touching shoulders, wiped her red swollen eyes and outlined her understanding of the accident.

"He was in the middle of a multiengine check ride. It appears the student got into a flat spin during a V-1 engine cut. Kitch couldn't recover. They were in an old Piper Navajo. One thousand feet into the Strait of Juan de Fuca. I don't know what could have happened. I just can't believe he lost control of a light twin."

The two sat for a while without saying a word. Kayla occasionally pressed her napkin to her eyes and even laughed once or twice when the conversation slid downhill into a Dale McMaster exploit. They spoke of all the people who had influenced their insignificant careers. It was the first time Banks had ever seen the personal side of his boss. It was the first time she allowed him to see that side of her.

Kayla looked at Travis several times in a manner he was unfamiliar with. Her vulnerable side was not only new to the single pilot but also intoxicating. He felt drawn to her in a way that would have seemed incomprehensible only hours before. Banks wanted to hold and console her. He saw a beautiful, compassionate woman in need of help. Travis gently slid her blonde hair back behind her ear and exposed the elegant nape of her neck, releasing the fragrance of sweet lilac. Instantly, his grandfather's dictum regarding "dipping one's quill in company ink" ruined the moment. The long pause gave her the opportunity to ask the ex-airline pilot a question and get his hand off her back.

"Travis, what would possess you to quit the airlines and come back North?"

The question made Travis recoil in his seat. It was a subject he was reluctant to discuss. He quickly took a hard deep swallow of his drink. Shit. He forgot it was bourbon. Sipping this crap was bad enough, guzzling it was suicidal. His whole stomach lit up like a flaming Christmas tree. Banks refused to become ill on his boss's lap while she confided in him about the death of her mentor. The burgeoning sweats and his stomach's desire to repel the invasion of drain cleaner weren't passing quickly enough and he pretended that the unexplained interlude stemmed from a deep desire to concisely answer her question, not the fact that he'd throw up if he opened his mouth.

She noticed his discomfort. "Is everything all right?"

"Fine." Banks managed to squeak out without tossing his cookies. His organs finally calmed down enough to address Kayla's question.

It wasn't that he was reluctant to explain his reasons in leaving the airlines to her. The problem was that she wouldn't be able to understand what he was saying.

Kayla had asked a valid question, one Travis had never fully explored himself. His lack of candor over the years with his Northern friends could have stemmed from a desire to shield himself from his own doubts. Rational pilots do not do what he had done. Once on with a major carrier, you stayed there until you died or retired. Whichever came first. Quite often, it was the former. The job was not conducive to longevity. Too many nights eating and drinking in the finest hotels on the planet. What attracted Banks to the profession was nearly gone by the time he made the scene. In recent years, things had begun to change for the worse. It had become a highly stressful profession for reasons beyond the pilots' control.

In the early days of airline flying, the job demanded respect and the benefits went hand in hand with such respect. When you pushed off from the gate, you called your own shots and were essentially your own boss. Most airline pilots had come from World War II, Korea, or Vietnam. They had spent their formative years being shot at and were hardened by the experience. They felt that, having survived dogfights and bombing raids, they were entitled to a little deference. They didn't take much shit from underlings or management. When the day was over, they didn't worry about having to pee in a bottle to prove to some overreacting political sycophant that they weren't drunk, or hadn't been mainlining heroin on layovers. Stewardesses, or flight attendants as they are now called, were required to be young and single, which now causes political discord. Amazingly, back then, it didn't prevent multitudes of women from applying for and enjoying the job. Layovers were a social event and what transpired was none of the government's damn business. The crews were responsible and did what they had to do to fly a safe ship and get the people to their destinations on time.

But times change, sometimes drastically. The government was becoming more and more involved. A plethora of people, from local and federal aviation authorities, dispatchers and inept money-hungry CEOs with useless degrees in bean counting to legislators who looked upon airlines as buses now made the decisions, and the only time they gave pilots responsibility was when something went wrong. Banks always found it interesting that, when a pilot was dead after an accident, it was pilot error. If the pilot lived and told the authorities what actually happened, they had to come up with another scapegoat.

Travis spent several years flying the Boeing 737 domestically and

B-767 internationally and realized that flying in a radar environment to the same dozen airports was going to bore him to death. He wanted the freedom he had found in bush flying. To his peers, he was the quintessential aviation idiot. Quitting the airlines and coming back to the low pay and hazards of Arctic flying was unheard of and considered one of the first stages of aeronautical mental retardation. What he knew and they didn't was just how monotonous the airline grind was. Travis felt satisfied and confident that he had made the correct decision and had found little desire to explain himself to people speaking from lack of knowledge. To Dale's credit, he was the only person Banks knew who supported his move from the first moment they met. Travis wanted to explain these reasons to Kayla but, to someone who hadn't been there in the profession's heyday, it was an impossible task. He needed to give her some type of answer. He just didn't have enough of the answer himself.

"Didn't Kitch ever tell you why I quit?" Travis spoke softly.

"He didn't even know you."

"He didn't have to. He spent long enough in the profession to know why I quit." Banks paused, looking for a clever explanation. There was none. "Kayla, the airline business no longer exists the way you and I imagined it as youngsters. You may not understand this, but what you've got in Arctic Air is twice what any airline pilot will ever have. That's the best answer I've got. If I can ever fully explain why I quit, I promise you'll be the first to know."

Banks realized it was time to leave. Kitch's death had been a terrible blow to Kayla Jackson and only time would soothe the pain. There was nothing he could do other than lend a sympathetic ear. And he'd done the best he could.

The tired pilot had misgivings about letting Kayla drive home. It had become obvious that her tolerance for alcohol was minimal.

"I'll give you a ride, Kayla."

"I'm all right, Travis," she smiled, reverting back to her independent self. She scooped up her keys as if they were a pair of hot dice at a craps table.

"You do whatever you want. But try to drive home in this shape and you'll be running your company from the slammer."

She stared at him momentarily while he put the parka around her shoulders.

"No funny business?"

"I'm taken. Remember? Dr. What's-her-name." Travis gently removed the keys from her hand. "Let's go."

They said little on the way to her place. It was a quick ride. No more than five minutes. She was staring out the window, still thinking about the childhood crush she had on Mr. Olson.

Banks had driven to her place on business several times over the years. She lived in Riverdale, a population of a couple hundred. A middle-class neighborhood too rich for Banks' blood, Riverdale was located on the eastern side of the Yukon River. A small bridge near the hospital went straight into the community rooted below the rolling slopes of Gray Mountain. The streets were tree-lined and most of the lawns were well manicured in the summer months. In the winter, it was just another snow-covered residential neighborhood. Travis made it to this side of town only when Leon Powell invited him over for a butt-kicking at the community's racquetball club.

Banks spotted her red, cedar-sided ranch house. It could not have been more than 1,500 square feet inside. More than enough room, considering she was never there. The trim was white but cracking and in sore need of painting. The once oval evergreen bushes lining the front walkway were growing in every direction but up. They needed trimming but were owned by someone who didn't have the time or the inclination to develop a green thumb. The front porch stoop was lined with an array of wind chimes, which probably fell mute during the still, silent Northern winters. The tires on her car attacked the snowy driveway with a chalky crunching sound as Travis turned toward her cluttered, covered carport. He had to dodge a display of Arctic Air airport paraphernalia in order to park. There were old airplane heaters, ore sample boxes from diamond-drilling customers, moose horns, and even a Cessna 172 Lycoming engine in dire need of a tune-up.

Banks jumped out and quickly ran around to open her door. She was so tired, she allowed him to carry out this chivalrous act. He helped her out of the passenger side of the car and then up the walkway to the slick stairs at the front door. Travis unlocked it, handed her the keys, and pushed it open.

"Can you make it from here?" he teased.

She looked down at her purse, fumbling to find a spot to put her keys. "Would you like to come in for a minute?"

It was times like this when Banks hated his grandfather. Years before it would make any sense to him, Grandpa Banks, the family patriarch, would give advice to the young Travis. One of his clever lines would always pop up at the most inopportune times. Like right now. "Travis, my boy, don't ever dip your quill in the company ink." The old man could be obnoxious and rude. Yet years later, his advice always turned out to be remarkably apropos.

"Kayla, you're forgetting. I've got to make you rich tomorrow. Those people going to Yellowknife don't want an exhausted, hung over pilot with bloodshot eyes flying them across hundreds of miles of uninhabited wilderness." He did his best to politely deflect her invitation. He couldn't believe his own ears. Every male pilot in Whitehorse had imagined himself being invited into this woman's home. Here he was saying no.

Travis's refusal seemed to surprise Kayla.

"Look, Ms. Jackson," he said, gently placing one hand on her shoulder. "I honestly can't think of anything I'd rather do right now than 'come in for a few minutes.' But not like this. You've just lost one of the most important people in your life today. I suspect you've had more to drink tonight than you've had in years. You need some rest."

"I didn't ask you to sleep with me," came the curt reply. "I was simply going to get you a cab." She looked straight into his eyes for the first time.

Travis felt like an idiot. Maybe she was telling the truth. Did he totally misread her? It certainly sounded more like the Kayla Jackson he'd known over the years.

"Thanks, but . . . uh . . . I think I'll walk. I love walking at night. The colder, the better. It won't take much longer than driving." Banks felt the need to run. Damn these creatures called women! They were harder to figure out than the electrical system of a British car. He now understood how surprised the male black widow spider must be when, after mating, he is eaten by the female.

The mixed signals were not over yet. Kayla took one step toward him.

"Are you sure I can't get you a cab?" She placed one hand on his chest and gently kissed him on the cheek. At this moment, he really hated his grandfather.

Banks found it hard to enjoy the kiss. He expected to be eaten any second.

"I needed a friend tonight and you were there. You're a very honorable and sweet man, Travis Banks. Thank you." She turned, went inside, and slowly began to close the door. "I'll see you tomorrow. Good night." She was gone.

The freezing pilot stood motionless under the porch. The door light illuminated his breath momentarily until the light extinguished, bringing to life a million stars in the Northern sky. Banks wiped his half-frozen nose and began walking back to the Klondike Inn.

Halfway down the block, he turned toward Kayla's house. She was looking at him from the upstairs window. He didn't know whether to wave or not. It almost looked as if she blew him a kiss and closed the curtain. Impossible.

It was midnight.

By 1:00 a.m., the Fifty Below Zero Tavern on First Avenue was reaching its nightly crescendo of raucous behavior. It was the "Queen of the Fleet" in terms of seedy bars, impressive in a town whose embarrassing claim to fame was more bars per capita than any other community north of the 49th parallel. It was by far the shabbiest drinking hole in town. Situated along the Yukon River one block from the old White Pass railway station, the joint was totally dilapidated. There was no obvious entrance point. To get inside, you had to crawl down an old, icy, concrete stairwell hugging the outside wall of a condemned building. The inside was as small and disgusting as the outside. The tiny tables were covered in stained, putrid terry cloth towels. It was too dark to truly appreciate its obscene decor. Even during the day, the revolting and cavernous interior was protected by the cover of darkness.

Only regulars would venture into the washroom. There was no stall around the toilet. Cigarette burns decorated the plastic seat with jagged brown circles. The chlorine-laced urinal was nothing but a cracked white tile wall with a leaking hose and drain partially clogged with cigarette butts and vomit.

The clientele was not hard to imagine, considering it was the last bar open in Whitehorse every night.

Dr. Michelle Baker received much of her business from the late-night antics of Native Indians and Aleuts who spent too many hours at the Fifty Below Zero Tavern. Tonight would be no different, just more severe.

The unruly patron with the weathered face shouted at the bartender for another drink. He had spilled most of his drink trying to find his lips. He was extremely drunk and looking forward to someone crossing his path. He liked being bold when his big brother wasn't around. He could do it only when he was drinking. He missed his brother. They did everything together. He especially liked getting drunk with his big brother. Soon, the trapping season would end and they would be together for the summer.

Watching the bubbles rise in the yellow light of the old jukebox was making him sick. He staggered through the crowd, using drunk, dancing bodies to negotiate his trek to the washroom. He wobbled up to the urinal, held a rusted pipe with one hand for support and opened his fly with the other. He was too drunk to even look down at the direction of his task. His head oscillated back and forth seeking the source of fresh air. A small window high up on the wall was wide open. The steamy urinary stench of the washroom emptied itself into the Yukon night air. Bitterly cold, dense air came pouring in like a thick fog, replacing the foul atmosphere of the decrepit underground saloon. The only view afforded by the small window was the Arctic permafrost and the large treaded tire of a parked truck.

The unemployed miner spat several times toward the wall but only managed to dribble phlegm onto his own chin. He wiped the viscous substance onto his oily sleeve and reeled backward, bumping the opposite wall. He teetered out into the crowd without pulling up his zipper and tried to focus on where he had been sitting. He had no idea. Did he owe any money? Screw 'em. He found his jacket on his back. He wanted to lie down someplace and sleep. It would take only a couple of minutes to walk to the one-room dive he and his brother rented two blocks away. He did the trip drunk most every night.

It took more than one attempt to finally scale the left side of the icy concrete staircase. The heat from the downstairs waffled out of the club and up the steps, turning some of the icy snow into slush. Twice he slipped and had to start over. He was doing it the hard way. Once at the top, he looked down and realized he had avoided the bare, salted, and less treacherous right side containing little ice. He hiccuped and chuckled to himself.

The freezing night was invigorating. He took several large gulps of the Arctic winter air. It was so biting in temperature that he bent over coughing and tried to take shorter, warmer breaths. Several parkas with little or no face exposed through the fox-fur lining stood around the warm hoods of running parked cars.

Many people simply left their cars running, especially those with diesel engines. Everyone carried an extra set of keys. You could lock your car with it running and it would be warm when you returned. You didn't even need to lock it. Nobody stole cars in the Yukon. Where would you go? It would take days of treacherous driving on the Alaska Highway to find another major city. The police would be bored waiting for you by the time you arrived. The only "chop shop" under the Northern Lights cut up moose carcasses.

The drunk stared wantonly at the Yukon Jack whiskey being passed back and forth by the patrons in the parking lot. They gazed with disdain at the fifty-year-old man who acquiesced, straightened up, and started to walk down the street in a clumsy, stilted fashion.

From across the street, a shadow emerged, eyeing the small crowd of people milling around the entrance of the vile little club. The figure slowly glanced up and down the otherwise deserted First Avenue.

There were only two streetlights between the club and the drunk's boarding house. One was in the parking lot across from the Fifty Below

Zero; the other was the boarding house itself. The block in between was pitch-black.

The drunken miner, hands in pockets, focused his attention on the small hotel he called home and began crunching through the dry white snow in his tattered boots. The lights and noise of the bustling bar slowly faded. He crossed the first intersection haphazardly looking both ways. Learned behavior. He had little recollection of his mother but one of his vivid memories was being slapped viciously from behind whenever he stepped into the street without looking in both directions. No wonder he thought she was a bitch.

To the left, the few lights of downtown lit up the ice crystals drifting and swirling in no particular direction. Less than a block to the right, the frozen dark abyss of the Yukon River separated the downtown section of Whitehorse from Wickstrom Road to the east. No one ventured into this part of town at two in the morning. The only sound now was his quick short breaths and the methodical crunching of the snow beneath his feet.

Yet, instead of only two feet crunching, there was an echo, almost as if he had four feet. He instinctively looked over his shoulder while barreling forward. There was no one behind him. He could still see several people huddled together in front of the tavern a block away but could no longer hear them clearly, just an occasional burst of drunken laughter. Less than a block from the Regina Hotel, the need to pee once again became unbearable. He couldn't make it all the way.

Ahead and to the right was a small alley full of empty fuel drums. Turning the corner, he recognized the pit stop. It wasn't the first time he had stopped here for the same reason. Several wooden pallets were thrown recklessly into a splintered heap along the chain-link fence at the back of the alley. There wasn't much room to negotiate. The small lane was bordered closely by two large concrete office buildings. He pressed his rump against one of the barrels and urinated onto the frozen chain-link fence. The clear discharge froze almost immediately upon striking the fence. The little urine splashing through the fence burrowed a small hole in the snow. During the summer, he had insects to shoot at. There were no live targets in the winter.

He turned to leave, trying to find his zipper. Between him and the street stood the dark outline of a parka-clad shadow. The vague lights behind the image prevented seeing any features other than the silhouette. The figure didn't move. It just stood there breathing slowly. Its legs were slightly apart and covered with mukluks up to the knees. The mitten-covered hands hung down at its sides. The image was stoic. Only the frosty white, rhythmic breathing gave indications of life.

The miner looked around the alley, trying to survey another exit. There was none. He had to pass the form to leave.

"What the fuck do you want?" The miner tried to sound belligerent and hide his concern. He stumbled slightly, bending over to package up his goods. Nature's cold hand was a stark reminder to zip up.

He couldn't decipher what was happening. He felt threatened. This was not what he had in mind when wishing for someone to cross his path.

The silhouette remained steadfast.

The drunk cautiously moved toward the black outline. He headed for the gap between its left shoulder and the wall of the alley. His chest filled with air and adrenaline. Although much smaller in stature than the frame facing him, the alcohol made him feel huge. He readied himself for a confrontation. As he approached, his bravado could not control his innate sense of danger. He knew this meeting was unnatural. The unemployed miner instinctively cringed slightly as he passed to the left of the stranger. His heart raced and his breathing stopped. He slipped by.

Having apparently dodged this odd encounter, he was overcome with relief. The miner tried to act confident and self-assured. He casually blurted several obscenities and laughed out loud. He wondered, "Who was this asshole?" He turned to see the reaction and the face of the image he had humbled. Momentarily, like a flash on a camera, the face was in the glow of a distant streetlight. Moving. Swinging. The image was clear. He knew the face. Just as suddenly, another image appeared. Circles. Brown oblong ovals. Rusted. The drunk heard a metal crashing sound. Like the sound marbles make when rolled together. The sensation engulfed his head. He reached up to remove the increasing weight and fire burdening his shoulders.

The physical pain was increasing but was not as terrifying to the man as the sensation of losing mobility and entering darkness. He had always feared small enclosed places. He thrashed about wildly, scratching and pulling at the rough and rusted constraint encompassing his head. His arms and legs were free to move but his face was in darkness under enormous pressure. Within moments, all he could see were little slits of light through the brown ovals. His head was encased in yards of rusted chain. He tasted blood in his mouth but could not cry out. His jaw was locked shut. He reached out and tried to grasp the force in front of him. He was being pulled forward and away from the alley.

A block away, the drunks in the parking lot at the Fifty Below Zero looked down the street. For an instant, they saw the image of the little drunk stumble around the corner and disappear.

The attacker struck him again from behind. The miner tumbled to his knees with the shattering explosion of searing pain on his back. He tried to regain his footing but collapsed in the snowy street. The end of the chain encircling his head was dropped in the snow in front of him. It lay there like a dog leash. His feet rose slightly off the ground and were then bound together. A violent tug on his hands and they were fastened to his ankles.

He lay in the frozen street teetering and rocking on his stomach. He tried to stir up an untapped source of strength, which might free him. He had none. The booze and quick struggle had depleted all his energies. His sweaty cheek lay on the convex curves of the chains, slowly freezing his flesh to the metal. Blood trickled through his eyes, down the bridge of his nose, and into the snow. Through the many orbs of rusted rings obstructing his burgundy vision, he could see the figure walk forward, pick up the chain, and begin dragging him several yards along the dry, slippery snow. The large shadow stopped at the back of a snowmobile. With a whipping motion, the chain was securely fastened to the rear hitch of the winter vehicle. The drunk looked up and mumbled something to the silhouette mounting the snowmobile. The little life that still coursed through his veins was filled with panic. This was how dead wild game was transported through the Arctic tundra.

The big black rubber treads of the snowmobile had packed snow lodged inside its tracks. As the electric motor whirled to start the engine, the vibration rattled off the loose snow. Slowly, the accelerator wound up and the large tread began to spin. It kicked snow into the face of the miner. He began to feel his body move over the icy ground. At first, the smooth surface offered no resistance. As his speed accelerated, the mounds of snow and ice pounding against his body became more frequent and punishing. Racing down the street, he rolled violently from side to side. Turning to parallel the Yukon River, the snowmobile purposely cut one corner too close. The iced curb shattered the right collarbone of the bound man spiraling behind the squealing Yamaha. The drunk began to fade. He looked up one last time. The parka-clad driver turned momentarily, getting the attention of his terrorized passenger. He pointed ahead and to the right as if giving directions to their final destination. There was a gap along the street where the snowmobile could jump the sidewalk, fly several feet, and plunge into the pitch-black chasm of the frozen, thousand-mile-long Yukon River.

The machine turned and fishtailed slightly, aiming at the point along the street. The blackness rushed forward with hyperspeed. He tried to scream. Snow and ice pummeled his face. With a silent gasp, the man saw the snowmobile launch itself into the dark Yukon night. Almost instantly, he felt the punch of the curb as he flipped up and flew into the darkness himself. The lights of the sleeping city climbed for what seemed like minutes. The screaming engine of the snowmobile accelerated wildly without resistance on its track. Yet he could barely hear it. He felt the frigid air rush through the chains around his face. His body twisted and rolled in space. He could see and hear only an instant of the snowmobile's landing; sanguine moment frozen in time.

DAY 2

ONE EYE WAS OPEN and working. Banks' mouth was ajar just enough to allow some drool to slither out onto his pillow.

The steam from the Schwatka Lake Dam billowed into the dark morning over Whitehorse. It was dark when he went to bed and it was still dark. That's the way it was six months of the year. The groggy pilot suddenly noticed the alarm clock on the dresser far across the room. He put it there when he knew waking up was going to be a problem. It must have gone off as planned. Travis had a tendency to strike things that woke him if he had been drinking the night before. It was smashed into several pieces on the dresser. He looked at his watch. 6:20. The charter to Yellowknife was scheduled to depart at 8:30. If the mechanics had done their jobs, the DC-3 would have been either in the hangar or being heated since 5:00. Without pre-heat, the blades on the Pratt and Whitney 1830 engines wouldn't budge.

His adrenaline gland purged itself with the piercing ring of his phone. Travis knew who it was before he knocked the phone off the cradle and onto the floor. He fumbled for the receiver with one hand. His other pushed on the soft mattress, striving to get his head elevated above the rest of his body before the cranial pressure exceeded its design limits and ruptured a blood vessel in his brain.

"Banks? Banks? I know you're there." The caller would soon be agitated.

Travis propped some pillows under his aching head before putting the phone back to his ear.

"Yeah." He cleared his throat and rubbed his tongue around the dry cavity of his mouth.

"Rise and shine, Travis," the caller chuckled.

He'd guessed wrong. It wasn't Doc Baker. The once despondent Kayla Jackson was looking for a DC-3 captain.

Banks mumbled into the phone, "I'm sorry. The party you wish to speak to is unable to come to the phone right now. If you would care to leave your name and . . ."

"Travis!" Kayla abruptly cut him off and then sweetened the tone of her voice. "Are you still planning to make both of us some money today?"

"You're the only one making money. What I make simply prevents me from qualifying for government assistance." Little shots of light fired in his eyes as he gently placed his face back into the pillow. "I'm just getting out of the shower," he lied.

"I'll bet. Then it shouldn't take you more than a few minutes to get here." She was finding this all very amusing.

"I was up late last night taking wayward women home who were too inebriated to drive."

"About last night . . ."

"Forget it." Banks wanted to. A night's sleep fortified his grandfather's assessment. There's no future in snuggling the boss on cold winter nights.

"No, I won't forget it," she paused. "You were a gentleman. Not many of your testosterone-rich, dysfunctional peers would have had the decency to conduct themselves the way you did. I was impressed."

"Don't be. I was down a quart of hormones. Next time, you won't be so lucky."

"I hope Saturday's still on," she said, leaving him no time to respond. "I'll see you shortly." She trailed off, then casually remembered, "Oh, by the way, your doctor friend phoned here a few minutes ago looking for you. Said there was no answer at your house. Naughty, naughty."

Banks remembered the ringing a little earlier. He thought it had been just another bad dream. Assuming he was going to qualify, he prayed God wouldn't allow phones in heaven. At least not ones that ring before 6:00 a.m.

"Thanks. I'm walking out the door." Travis kept the receiver to his ear after Kayla hung up and aimlessly flailed away at the cradle until a dial tone sounded. Breakfast with Dr. Baker would give him the opportunity to disclose his actions from the previous evening. Whitehorse was a small town. She would hear about his rendezvous with Kayla sooner or later. He'd rather explain in person that his encounter with Kayla the night before had been by chance and strictly platonic.

Michelle was just about to leave the hospital when the nurse put Travis' call through. They spoke for only a minute. He didn't want to give her a chance to grill him about the previous night over the phone. He'd tell her the truth over breakfast. The truth? His boss was drunk and he drove her home. What's immoral about that? Nothing except that he was relating this story to another woman. All bets were off.

Banks had yet to meet a woman who didn't have an inherent distrust of men. For good reason. He knew in advance that once Michelle faced him in person and he told her "the truth," she would figure out a reason why his actions were inappropriate and dispense some horrible psychological punishment that only another woman would understand and appreciate. And because he wouldn't be able to understand her strange double-X chromosome logic, he would have to just smile and nod his head politely. Then she'd smirk, saying he was typical of all men because he obviously didn't care about their "relationship." He was convinced that the statistical life expectancy for men is a decade less than for women because men simply give up. Death was easier. It might be a cop-out but at least the nagging and head games stop. Michelle wouldn't pry into Travis' whereabouts over the phone. That might blatantly show that she cared. History indicated that she would prefer to systematically dismember him in the flesh at a later date. That way she could see him squirm in person. Then she would flippantly remind him they were both independent and were not required to explain their time away from each other. He knew that was bullshit. He would pay one way or the other.

"Good morning, Doctor, did you miss me last night?"

"I'm sorry, Travis, we were swamped." The uncharacteristic short pause gave away her instinctual distrust. "So, what did you do last night?"

He was doomed. “Oh, nothing. I met Dale and Leon for a beer and went home.”

“Straight home?” She started boring in.

“Almost,” came Banks’ pitiful reply. “Look, don’t worry about last night. I’ll tell you all about it over breakfast. They’re pre-heating CUG and I’ve got thirty minutes to buy my favorite physician breakfast. How ’bout it?” His perkiness was only a stay of execution.

“I’ll see you at the Chalet in ten minutes.” Her hoarse voice cracked as she sighed with fatigue. She wasn’t overtly jealous. It was a well-rested emotion she rarely exercised. Travis jumped up to have a quick shower.

He glared into the mirror while shaving and stopped for a moment. It was the image of a stranger. The face was almost unrecognizable. He used to be young. The shaving cream hid the lines around his face but didn’t hide the crow’s-feet branching from his eyes. A permanent brown skin had evolved through a combination of genes and flying above the clouds near holes in the ozone. His old girlfriends in college would lie to him and coo that he looked like a young Gene Kelly. The mirror didn’t lie. Not anymore.

It reminded him of his fear that Michelle might start hearing her biological clock tolling soon. Marriage was so damned frightening. Hell, it was to any man with half a brain. Women invented it. Men didn’t “settle down,” they surrendered. Men just went along with it because they needed sex and didn’t think much else about it. If men gave marriage and its consequences even an iota of thought, they’d obediently fall in line behind the lemmings and hurtle themselves into the ocean. Maybe it’s children who make marriage tolerable to men instead of the accepted belief that it’s the other way around.

Travis peered into the mirror. Was he too old to have children? Did he even want them? Would they want anything to do with him?

Checking his thoughts, he looked at his watch and dialed Dale’s number. Damn, he was late! When he heard the phone ring at the other end, he placed the receiver on the table and jumped into the shower.

The Airport Chalet was the airport's oldest hotel. Considering there were only two, it was an easily marketable claim to fame. The dark cedar siding encompassing the entire single-story, twenty-unit complex was weathered and showing signs of its three decades of existence. The hotel catered mainly to weary travelers who had endured the 1,500 miles of the Alaska Highway. It sat directly across from the airport's main entrance. It was close enough to the Alcan Highway to see the beleaguered look of drivers desperately seeking a road sign indicating an end to their arduous voyage.

The Chalet coffee shop was a favorite eatery for the airport's pilots, who usually needed morning nourishment following a protracted evening of war stories in the Chalet's lounge.

The hotel was owned and operated by a delightful Aleut couple who had permanent smiles emblazoned on their faces. Betty Frost, a smiling, cherubic-faced native, and Charlie Charlie Frost, her tiny, two-first-name husband. In all the years Banks had been in the North, no one was able to explain to him the native habit of calling some men with two first names. That's just the way it was. Charlie Charlie himself couldn't answer the question, other than to say that his father, Jonny Jonny, never told him either.

Betty treated all the local pilots as family. Travis was her favorite adopted son. She also made the best moose hash and scrambled eggs known to man. Charlie Charlie ran the lounge with the exuberance of a child. He wanted every happy hour to stretch the boundaries of a good time. If anyone left before last call, according to Charlie Charlie, you needed more practice drinking and he was always willing to tutor you for only the nominal cost of supplies. The entire airport staff was convinced the Frosts would even welcome Mussolini with a smile.

The remainder of the hotel staff consisted of the numerous daughters Betty and Charlie Charlie had raised over the years. There were no sons. Every time Travis entered the coffee shop, Betty would pull at his cheek, tell him how cute he was, and insist that one of her daughters would make him a perfect wife. The problem was that she mentioned a different daughter each time. Banks had no idea how many daughters there were, all told. Travis wasn't sure if the parents knew for certain.

Betty gave her favorite pilot a pinch on the cheek and stern nuptial advice before letting him sit down. Travis requested his normal breakfast with a smile. Michelle couldn't have arrived much sooner than he had. When Banks sat down, she was still unwinding the maroon scarf he had given her the previous Christmas. The presence of her green surgical fatigues announced that she had been too tired to change after her shift.

"Bad night, Doctor?" Travis stroked her hand across the table.

She offered a weary smile. "I'm sorry if I was short with you on the phone, Travis. Socialized medicine is great for the consumer but hell on doctors. We need more physicians. Three double shifts in a week are too much. My intern days are over."

"Sorry." Banks tried to think of something soothing to say. "You need to get a bite to eat, have a hot bath, and go to bed."

"Is that an invitation?" Her smiled widened.

"I can't think of a more pleasant thought . . . if I wasn't on my way to Yellowknife." He was titillated by her aggressive remark. Normally, he had to do the chasing.

"Travis," she said, suddenly sitting up and became far too serious in her deportment. "What's happening with us?"

Damn, he thought. Why did women do this? A perfectly good four-dollar moose hash and egg breakfast down the tubes. By the time he tried to satisfactorily answer this question, Banks' breakfast would arrive and become cold before he had a chance to even taste it. He was forty and fit. But if he ever decided to stop eating and lose weight, he would eat all his meals with an emotionally and physically exhausted female emergency room physician. Banks wanted to state flatly that nothing was "happening with them" but knew she'd pounce on any such statement like a lion after a bleeding zebra. No, if he was to have any chance of getting to eat a hot breakfast, he had to come up with a response that was both sensitive and compassionate.

"What do you mean, Doc?"

The mundane answer dribbled out of his mouth before he had a chance to intercept the movement of his lips. His mind was attempting to deal with both the need for a response and his impending "date" with his boss. The look in Michelle's eyes indicated that, no matter what he said, his breakfast was going to end up as a take-out.

"Travis, we're both getting older."

"Isn't that the truth?" He smirked and paused, praying for more pause. He thought the pause was long enough to escape and he continued, "Except for climbing into the garbage, Pratt and Whitney are doing great."

"I'm serious!" Like a pit bull, she held on. The Doc was delving into new territory for both of them.

"I know you are," Banks spoke warmly, "but we both agreed to take this slowly."

"That was three years ago!"

"Has it been that long?" He feigned shock. Now was definitely not the time to mention his date with Ms. Jackson the next night.

"Yes, it has," she calmed down slightly. "I know we agreed to be independent and noncommittal but for how long?"

He held his tongue. Twenty-four more hours would be a good start.

"Michelle, you know I care about you very much, but you also know why I don't want to make a commitment. You were the one who pointed out that, in the past five years, out of the forty or so pilots based here in Whitehorse, I've had to bury eight of them. Those are lousy odds to plan a family around."

"I wish you'd never quit the airlines," she said, frustrated. Along with the boredom, airlines offered higher salaries and better life expectancy than a bush pilot could ever hope to achieve.

"I don't." He was about to upset her. "Look, if I hadn't quit the airlines, you and I would have never met."

They both sat quietly, knowing there was no easy answer to their situation except a compromise. Which, translated, meant he would do whatever she demanded. She wasn't sure what she wanted anyway. If he asked her, right here, right now, over moose hash, to marry him, she'd laugh all the way home for two reasons. First, she wouldn't believe him and, second, she didn't want to herself. Michelle wanted to know that he was always going to be there. Especially after long traumatic shifts in the emergency room. It was a promise Banks couldn't make.

She patted his hand and half smiled. Travis had no idea what she was thinking. They sat quietly for a few minutes.

"Speaking of Yellowknife," she perked up and changed gears, "I was hoping you could do me a favor when you get there."

Banks smiled. "Anything."

"I received a fax from the coroner in Yellowknife, a college friend of mine, Dr. Blain Askew." She added more cream to her coffee. "An exploration company recently found the remains of a teenage girl. He's searching dental records for a positive ID. The remains are about twenty years old. They found her somewhere north of Yellowknife. I want to see the file. There was a girl from Whitehorse who disappeared about the same time. It's an open case that's been in my filing cabinet since I've been coroner. The girl was never found. I can't help but wonder if it might be the same girl." Michelle slowed her chewing and let her mind wander for a moment before suddenly coming back to earth and stabbing at her food again. "She was a thirteen-year-old native youngster from Takhini. I have no idea how a teenage girl can go to school one day in Whitehorse and end up in Yellowknife but stranger things have happened. Anyway, I'm the coroner. It's my job to check it out. Dr. Askew's office isn't too far from the Yellowknife Airport. If you have the time, would you mind swinging by and getting the file?"

"Why doesn't he just fax you the material?"

"He has some Polaroids and X-rays. But they don't scan well. I'd rather see the originals."

Travis was perplexed. "Why would the RCMP, or your office for that matter, want to spend resources on a twenty-year-old case? Aren't you opening some sensitive wounds for somebody?"

Dr. Baker began one of her lectures. "Travis, first, there are no limitations on kidnapping or murder. Second, little girls just didn't disappear from these small communities in the '60s. Of all the distasteful tasks my job description contains, the worst assignment is having to let parents view their dead child. The worst task the police have is telling parents that their child is probably dead but we don't have a body to prove it. They live their entire lives with the hope that one day, the child will walk through the front door. It rarely, if ever, ends that way. They need closure. They need to bury the child. If I can help the process, regardless how unpleasant, I'll do it. I have no idea if the parents are alive, but if we can ID the remains, I'll try to find out."

Banks didn't have children but wondered about the agony and helplessness those parents must feel who lost kids for one reason or another.

"What would possess anyone to take a child?" he thought out loud.

"We lose a few kids every year in the North. Usually, it's from abductions. Nine out of ten times, the child knows the abductor. It's a family member or someone close to the family. But as they get older, especially teenagers, they disappear for other reasons. They get drunk, lost, unconscious in a car wreck, whatever, and end up dead of exposure. The reason I want the file on this girl is, according to Dr. Askew, she experienced some trauma before death. Doesn't sound like an accident. It might be a homicide."

"I'll get the file," Banks agreed, wanting to change the subject. Dr. Baker was unusually introspective this morning. The aftereffects of a long night shift.

"I'll let Blain know you're coming. You'll have to sign a release. You're acting as an agent for the Whitehorse coroner's office, so behave yourself." She leaned back, allowing Betty to place two steaming plates of breakfast in front of them.

"Be prepared. Dr. Askew is . . . how can I say . . . well, let's just say he's different. A little high-strung. Maybe hyper would be a better word. But don't be fooled by his appearance. He's one of the best forensic pathologists in the country."

Travis nodded. "Any news on Bellichek?" The hash looked better than ever.

"I did him early this morning. He didn't die a happy man." Banks could tell she was enjoying her breakfast. Normally, she stayed away from meat. But moose meat was leaner than the fittest chicken.

"Go on."

"Well, the obvious trauma of severe lacerations caused by the wolves didn't kill him." She took her napkin and wiped the corners of her mouth. "Bellichek died from hypothermia."

"Hypothermia? What about the wolves?"

"What's even more interesting is that I found rusted metal fragments lodged in the exterior side of both tibias and fibulas."

The pilot hated when she forgot he wasn't a doctor. "Excuse me, Michelle, I'm sorry, but they didn't teach me the ins and outs of autopsies in flight school. In English, please."

"His ankles were shattered." She looked up, dribbling food out of the corner of her full mouth. "It seems as though he suffered severe contusions and lacerations by a sharp metal object with teeth," she swallowed and continued, "possibly several blows from a sharp metal tool, but more than likely a large animal trap. The muscle and soft tissue were pulverized. I found evidence around both ankles." She began to poke ravenously at her breakfast again. The sordid conversation didn't faze her a bit.

"He experienced a massive amount of blood loss. One artery on the left leg was nicked, but not enough to kill him. He may have bled to death if it weren't for the fact that he was stuck in the ice. The bleeding at the ankles had slowed to a crawl."

"How come you're so sure about the cause of death?"

"It's my job to know," she stated proudly. "The hypothermia was the primary cause of death." She put her silverware down and leaned toward Travis, lowering her voice. "If he was dead when the wolves got to him, there wouldn't have been any signs of vital tissue reaction . . . and there were." She could see Banks needed more help understanding. "As soon as you tear skin, the body immediately begins to heal itself by sending white blood cells to the damaged area. In other words, his heart was still beating when he was stuck in the ice. There were white blood cells on Bellichek's face and hands." She raised her eyebrows in the pilot's direction, trying to get him to think. "You know? The clear liquid you'll see on a cut or wound. I found it all over his facial lacerations."

"Jesus. Are you saying he was alive when the wolves got to him?"

"Well, I would guess that he was in a severe state of neurological shock. I doubt he was cognizant of his surroundings, though. If he did regain consciousness, it wasn't for long. I suspect having wolves eat you alive while you were frozen helplessly in place, well, it would probably cause enough trauma to induce unconsciousness. Don't you agree?" Her eyebrows shot up.

"With broken ankles, how could he..."

"He couldn't," she interrupted. "He didn't walk to the middle of the lake and accidentally fall in a hole in the ice."

Banks lowered his voice. Radcliff had not yet informed the media of his discovery and he didn't want the locals to overhear their conversation. "You're saying he was murdered? A person had to do this, right? Not an animal?"

"Yes, a person. Either that or a very intelligent and nimble Bullwinkle."

"What about time of death?"

"You were close. Approximately twenty-four hours before you found him. If what you said was true, that he usually ate wild meat jerky and spiked coffee for breakfast, well, that's exactly what I found, nearly totally undigested, in his stomach. He died soon after his breakfast and he was frozen solid when you found him right after breakfast. Had to have been the day before. One more day with those wolves and nothing would have been left but polished bones."

Radcliff would have a hard time ignoring Dr. Baker's autopsy.

They finished breakfast and Travis walked her to her car in the frozen, open-air parking lot. Cars and trucks roared by on the Alaska Highway, blowing snow and gravel into the side of her small car. He gave her a kiss and told her he'd call her later. It was hard to tell if she wanted him to or not.

He'd forgotten to tell her about his date the next night with Ms. Jackson. He tried to get her attention by waving into her rearview mirror as she drove away but, luckily, she didn't see him.

The information Dr. Baker had passed onto Banks about the trapper's death was gruesome but not altogether unexpected. Banks had known it wasn't an animal. So that left the questions who and why? Neither question seemed of concern to Constable Radcliff.

Ed Bellichek's government medical records had been transferred from Yellowknife years before. Travis would be in the Northwest Territorial capital in a few hours. Looking into Bellichek's sordid background in Yellowknife might give him something to do.

Banks thought about the little girl, a name printed in the newspaper more than twenty years ago. Just a name. Someone else's tragedy. There are some wounds time refuses to heal. Burying a child must be one such wound. Even without having children, the concept of closure began to make sense to him. Travis assumed it was an unwittingly part of the package when a person takes on the responsibility of becoming a parent. He didn't know if he was ready. Hell, he couldn't imagine ever being ready.

Bellichek had been a child. He must have had a family. As vile as he was, he probably didn't deserve to die the way he did. His family probably didn't need closure over his death. But that wasn't for Banks to decide. Although he didn't know Ed Bellichek all that well or even like him that much, Travis was probably the closest thing to a friend Bellichek had. If Dr. Baker could find the little girl's family, Banks could try to find Bellichek's.

A glow across the eastern skyline illuminated the silhouette of the Big Salmon Mountain Range and announced the arrival of another winter day in the far North.

The bright orange and white DC-3 parked on the Arctic Air ramp looked like a postcard from the fifties. The background of the dawn picture was filled with snowy white and the evergreen trees of Gray Mountain.

A hive of activity buzzed around the old Douglas airplane. The secretary, Peggy Rand, who subbed as a flight attendant in the winter months, scurried up the small portable stairs of CF-CUG. Sliding up the small aisle toward the galley behind the cockpit, she carried a large box of half-frozen cinnamon rolls and three or four cartons of orange juice. The hot coffee would be boarded last, after the passengers. Timed perfectly, slightly warm coffee would be served just after liftoff.

The mechanics were finishing up pre-heating the cold airplane when Banks arrived. There hadn't been enough room in the hangar so the aircraft had spent the frigid night on the frozen ramp. Numerous heaters were plugged into the modified military C-47. Black extension cords snaked through the snow in all directions. In order to prevent tripping all the circuit breakers in the small Arctic Air hangar, each cord had to be plugged into a separate circuit. Each engine had its own oil strap heater warming the oil pan. A set of car heaters was bolted onto small sheets of plywood and placed in the cowling intakes of the Pratt engines. Fitting like a snug jacket, a large canvas tarpaulin was snapped around each engine to keep in the injected heat. The cabin and cockpit were heated by a combination of Herman Nelson and blast heaters. This combination had the skin of the old bird radiating heat within a couple of hours.

Banks filed an instrument flight plan in one of the small offices adjacent to what was generally considered Operations—a small area with seats, a montage of Arctic Air pictures, several uncomfortable chrome chairs, a table, and a coffee machine. The two small offices connected to the area belonged to Arctic Air's chief pilot, Frank Flemming, and the company's chief mechanic, Ralph Michaels.

The weather en route to Yellowknife was clear and only a few patches of icy fog were expected upon their arrival. Banks picked up three low altitude Jeppesen Revisions in an effort to have any and all updated aeronautical information for Yellowknife. There was not a more unsettling feeling in aviation than to shoot an approach down to 200 feet in a snowstorm on the basis of an out-of-date approach chart.

Flemming was sitting around in a foul state trying to drown his liver with coffee and exorcise the alcohol from his system.

"Why in hell are you the captain going to Yellowknife?" His scowl was intense when he looked up from his desk.

"Orders from the boss." Banks smiled. He longed to tell the old fart he would soon be looking for another job.

"Well, aren't I the goddamn chief pilot around here?"

"I don't know, Frank. Are you?" Travis couldn't resist.

"Screw you, Banks!" Flemming glared at the younger pilot before continuing. "Why doesn't someone tell me what the hell's going on around here?"

"Frank, I truly don't know. Why don't you walk down the hall and take this up with Ms. Jackson? I'm a little busy." Flemming's suffering added a short-lived smile to Banks' face.

"As a matter of fact, Banks, I already did that."

Flemming knew something Travis didn't and the chief pilot liked what he knew. A smile crept across Frank Flemming's face. Travis sensed he'd stepped into a trap.

"And guess what? You're due for a line check. I'm going with you today and acting as a check airman/first officer."

The color drained from Banks' face. He didn't want to spend the better part of the day rumbling across northern Canada stuffed in a 1936 cockpit the size of an outhouse with this prick. Nobody did line checks in the North. Line checks were only administered at airlines as an annual legal requirement to pacify the federal government. A designated check airman from the airline or government sat in the jump seat observing your skills during an actual revenue-generating passenger trip. Simulators were designed to assess your ability when everything went wrong. Line checks reflected your composure when everything went right. It was in the Operations Manual of Arctic Air but never practiced. The Ministry of Transport inspectors came up from Edmonton, Alberta, to Whitehorse twice a year to administer check rides. It was the only requirement to remain current as captain. This was Frank Flemming's way of pissing Banks off and making a few extra bucks to buy another bottle of Scotch. Travis had assumed Kayla would have paired him up with one of the regular first officers.

A quick visit to Kayla's office offered no relief. She asked Banks to put up with Flemming for just a few more weeks and gave a brief reason why. The whole DC-3 operation, including Travis' paycheck, would suffer if they had to replace Flemming before the spring when they changed over from skis to wheels. The sullen Banks managed a teeth-gritting smile and told the old bastard he'd meet him at the airplane. Travis' only hope was that Dale would show up. Then the two of them could split from the Yellowknife Airport and abandon Flemming for the three hours they were scheduled to sit on the ground there. There'd been no news release about Ed Bellichek's murder and Travis wanted to dig into his background in Yellowknife without having to explain his actions to Frank Flemming.

Before heading out to the ramp, Banks made a quick call to "Northern Tracks," the best garage in town for fixing any small engine. Their specialty was snowmobiles and ATVs. The owner, Rick Meyers, a surgeon when it came to snowmobiles, answered the phone.

"Rick, Travis Banks."

"Hey, flyboy, what's up?"

"I'm looking for some information."

"Shoot."

"I'm trying to find out if you know anybody in town who owns a Polaris 440, oil-injected lug track."

"Why? You want to buy one? They're not very common. I've got a great deal on an Arctic Cat."

"No thanks, Rick. Just looking for some information on a Polaris 440." Travis had to speak over the scream of a small engine being bench tested in the background of Rick Meyers' shop.

"What'd you want to know? The Arctic Cat's better." Rick had a hard time simply answering a question without trying to sell something.

"Do you know someone who owns one?"

"Well, let's see." It sounded as if he was flipping through a Rolodex. "I had a trapper in here last year with one. But he had all sorts of problems with it. I think he sold it."

"Do you know who bought it?"

"No idea."

"O.K. Thanks, Rick. If you hear of anything, would you let me know?"

Banks could sense Rick was being distracted by something on the other end of the phone.

"Hang on. Here we are. I just ordered a new oil tank for a 440 two weeks ago. . . . Yep . . . Polaris 440."

"Who ordered it?"

"That's privileged information between me and my client." Meyers laughed into the phone.

"For Christ sake, Rick, who was it? I promise. I'll buy my next machine from you." Ralph Michaels came into the office, mouthing the words that Flemming was about to leave without Banks.

"John Smith."

Although a common name in the rest of the world, Travis had met most everyone in Whitehorse over the years and had never heard of a John Smith. It was the type of name used checking into a hotel for a clandestine sexual encounter with a married woman.

"What's he look like?"

"Don't know. It was a phone order. I've got the part. He just hasn't picked it up yet."

"Do you have a phone number?"

"Nope. The order says he'll pick it up."

"Do me a favor, Rick. When Mr. Smith picks it up, can you call me or get an address, phone number, some type of ID.? Especially if it's paid by check. Say it's a company return policy. I need to find this guy. But don't tell him I'm looking for him."

"Travis, what's this about?"

"Can you do it for me? I'll explain later. I've got to go. Thanks, Rick." Travis hung up the phone and hurried out through the hangar side door, dreading a ten-hour day with Frank Flemming.

Walking to the old DC-3, Banks heard the free-floating PT-6 turbines of the Royal Canadian Mounted Police (RCMP) Twin Otter take off in a southbound direction. The humming Pratt and Whitney turbo prop climbed several hundred feet and turned west. Radcliff and Powell were headed for Primrose Lake to finish their investigation.

It took only several minutes to unplug the heaters and board the twelve government officials from the Department of Wildlife and Game Management.

Banks was curious to see how Miss Rand would handle one of Arctic Air's most lucrative customers, the Yukon government. She didn't get many opportunities to act as a flight attendant, only the odd winter trip when the part-time summer flight attendants were back at college. She relished the experience. Unfortunately, she had a habit of unwittingly terrifying the passengers with her intricate knowledge of all the horrible things that could happen during a flight on a DC-3. Travis had tried to teach her the subtleties of handling people who were familiar only with jets. The vast majority of their passengers found themselves climbing onto an airplane they hadn't seen since watching black-and-white footage of the Berlin Airlift. She desperately tried to follow Banks' instructions but found that, once on board, her nervousness took over and she would revert back to her terrifying tales. Peggy would greet her passengers with a smile, quietly seat everyone as assigned and then, forgetting everything Travis had told her, take them on a terrifying historical roller-coaster ride through the DC-3 and its colorful history. She thought she was being informative when, in reality, she was scaring the crap out of everyone, including the captain, Travis Banks. She elaborated on how many DC-3s crashed, were shot down, or simply disappeared from radar screens and were never heard from again. Finally, she would move on and deftly explain the few safety features the converted C-47 had to offer by unintentionally glorifying, in great detail, old accidents in which the only people who died were the ones who had not listened to the flight attendant during her safety briefing.

Banks had to admit it got their attention. Looking back during preflight checks, he could see passengers with their jaws open, staring forward, pawing at safety briefing cards, ready to sprint to the nearest emergency exit at the first unusual sound. And this was all before Travis had even started the engines. The one part of her briefing he had specifically requested her to skim over or completely bypass was her graphic explanation of what to do in the unlikely event of "an unscheduled water landing." He had explained to her, on many occasions, that there was no such thing as a water landing. Pilots are not trained in any such maneuver. It should more aptly be referred to as "crashing into the ocean." Seeing how there were no oceans between Whitehorse and Yellowknife, only frozen lakes, it would not be wise to unduly upset the passengers about a situation they couldn't possibly encounter. She insisted that she was required to brief her passengers on water landings and "her hands were tied," according to the air navigation orders and federal air regulations located in the chief pilot's office. Passengers spent the first hour of charters involving Peggy Rand fumbling with crucifixes, quietly praying, and staring out the window looking for large bodies of shark-infested water.

Not long before the door was shut, Dale McMaster climbed onboard and made himself comfortable on the jump seat. Usually, the charter customer had to be consulted about additional company personnel flying on the charter. But after Miss Rand's disturbing briefing, they all looked petrified and eyed the muscular Dale McMaster as if his corpse could provide weeks of food after their inevitable crash into the Andes Mountains—the site of another famous DC-3 accident which Peggy had described in excruciating detail.

Flemming noted Dale's arrival with displeasure. They tolerated each other because they were often the only two left in the bar at last call. And there was always the hope that one would buy the other copious quantities of liquor. His presence on this flight, however, promised only one thing—hours of playing solitaire upon reaching their destination. On this morning, Dale was surprisingly well rested and his pupils were actually encircled with white instead of the customary red.

"Glad you could make it." Banks turned to face him as he buckled in. "You look well rested today."

"Don't let it fool you. I'll be sleeping the entire way. Had an unexpected visitor last night when I got home." He fumbled for his shoulder harness. "Remember that girl from Ross River . . . "

Travis thought for a moment. "You mean the one you gave my only navy blue Polo golf shirt to?"

"Right. Well, she knocks on my door at midnight. It was the first time in ages I was sober during sex. It wasn't pretty. I lasted only a minute," he said, looking disgusted. "Was I embarrassed! I needed an excuse to get out of the house and you were it. She's sitting there right now, in bed, thinking I'll be back any minute with breakfast. I couldn't do it. Hell, if it wasn't for your shirt, I wouldn't even have recognized her."

Even Flemming had to chuckle.

The two pilots completed the "Before Start Checklist," primed the engines, turned on the magneto master switch, spun the electrical starter, and engaged the start switch. Flemming counted seven blades on the right side. Travis engaged the number two magneto switch counter clockwise, placed the mixture lever into auto rich, and the Pratt and Whitney 1830 spat, backfired, and came to life. Even with pre-heating, the oil pressure needle pegged itself off the gauge somewhere beyond 180 PSI. He kept the rpm's down at 800 until the temperatures began to rise and the oil pressure came back into view. Travis took pride in never having blown an oil cooler and he didn't want to start in front of Flemming with his silly line check. With both engines started and warmed, he unlocked the tail wheel, waved off chief mechanic Ralph Michaels, and taxied to runway eighteen.

The temperature was close to thirty below and they never got the cylinder head temperatures into the green during the 1800 RPM run-up. They would finally reach the green arc on the second segment climb. Banks cycled the props several times, filling the prop hubs with warm oil. Travis knew Flemming would want to see a full cycle on the auto feathering system. If they lost an engine on the gooney bird, their only hope was to get it feathered right away. Otherwise, the dead prop would act like a sheet of plywood, creating more drag on one side than the good engine could overcome. The system functioned as designed, and moments later, the tower cleared them for takeoff.

The routing Banks chose would take them from Whitehorse to Yellowknife over Watson Lake and Fort Simpson via nondirectional beacons or NDB airways. NDBs were in the frequency range of AM radio stations. It was simply a needle that pointed to a signal. Many lost pilots had found their way home grooving to the oldies. The primary airway departing Whitehorse would be Alpha Two. The trip was about 500 miles and VHF or Omni directional beacons, the preferred navigational instrument, did not have the range of NDBs. Their signal was stronger but limited to line-of-sight transmissions.

After an hour, the aircraft lost the Whitehorse NDB signal. They had calculated wind drift and kept a steady heading knowing eventually the Yellowknife signal would strengthen and point their NDB needle toward Yellowknife, the heart of the Northwest Territories.

The flight would take just under three hours. Flemming and McMaster tried smoking Travis out of the cockpit the first half- hour. Peggy, believing it was an electrical fire on the flight deck, wanted to discharge a fire extinguisher in the cockpit and then evacuate the aircraft at 10,000 feet. Banks finally cracked open his window, creating a vacuum that instantly rid the cockpit of smoke. At 145 knots, in minus forty degree air, it didn't take long to get their attention. They behaved the rest of the way.

The weather was perfect. In aeronautical circles, it was described as "severe clear." Banks and Flemming would be able to see Yellowknife by the time they picked up the Yellowknife NDB signal.

Finally, the magnificent Mackenzie River came into view. It stretched from Great Bear Lake to the Arctic Ocean and was now snaking off each wing tip, disappearing off into the horizon in both directions. Next to the Mississippi-Missouri, the Mackenzie River was the longest river in North America, stretching more than 2,600 miles.

Thirty miles from the airport, the city of Yellowknife, situated on the northern shore of Great Slave Lake, filled their field of view.

Flemming handed Travis the ATIS, or automated terminal information weather report. Every hour, on the hour, it was updated and renamed by the next letter in the phonetic alphabet. All transmissions in aircraft were enhanced by using this alphabet: Alpha, Bravo, Charlie, Delta, and so on. To just say the letter "P" instead of "Papa" can be confusing. P sounds like T, D, E, C and many other letters. The alphabet prevented erroneous and possibly fatal transmissions with air traffic control.

The current ATIS was information "X-ray." The observation was taken at 18:55 Greenwich, just minutes earlier: ceiling 25,000 thin scattered, visibility fifty miles, temperature minus twenty-seven degrees Celsius, dew point three degrees, wind 180 degrees at four knots, altimeter 30.03 inches of mercury. The Edmonton air traffic control center cleared the DC-3 for an instrument approach to runway twenty-seven and advised them to contact the Yellowknife tower on frequency 118.3 VHF. The icy fog had burned off in the morning sun and the visibility seemed endless. It was a beautiful day in Yellowknife.

"Yellowknife Tower, good morning, this is Douglas Charlie Uniform Golf. We've got X-ray, out of 3,000 feet, and have been cleared for the ILS to 27."

"Roger, Charlie Uniform Golf, this is Yellowknife Tower, good morning. You are cleared for the approach and are currently number one for runway 27. Check gear down and you are cleared to land."

The voice on the tower frequency was that of an old friend of Banks, an ex-controller from the Whitehorse ATC facility named Doug Smiley. Doug was a good hearted fellow with a voice that led you to believe he was six-and-a-half feet tall and weighed 300 pounds. He was the tiniest human Travis had ever met. Back in Whitehorse, the joke had always been that Doug controlled aircraft from a high chair in the tower.

"Is that you, Doug?" Banks smiled into the small boom mike of his David Clarke headset.

"That's affirmative, Charlie Uniform Golf. Aren't you a little far from home, Banks? You must be out of bread crumbs by now. How are you going to find your way home?" The radio chuckled back into the gooney bird's cockpit headsets.

"We could see you a hundred miles away, Doug. Tell you what; we'll cancel IFR."

"Very good, Charlie Uniform Golf. IFR cancellation received. Squawk 1200, check gear down, and you are now cleared for the *visual* approach to runway 27. When you get on the ground, Travis, swing by the tower cab."

"Wilco, and Douglas Charlie Uniform Golf is now cleared for the visual approach to runway 27. See you shortly, Doug."

The approach and landing into the small airport went smoothly considering that Banks had Dale in the jump seat and Flemming in the copilot's seat making cracks about the awful landing he was about to make. They had radioed ahead with an ETA and arrived ten minutes early at 11:30 A.M.

Their passengers' hosts were early as well. They drove standard government green and yellow Ford extended cab pickups with Game and Wildlife logos on each door. The government drivers cautiously navigated the long trucks toward the small stairs on the left rear of CF-CUG.

By the time McMaster and Flemming had put the control locks on the elevator, vertical stabilizer and ailerons, the government officials had left in a cloud of unleaded exhaust. Dale and Travis were able to slip away from Flemming when he insisted on solid food. McMaster and Banks claimed not to want lunch. The consensus was to meet back at the airplane at 3:00 o'clock for a 3:30 departure.

In the control tower, Doug was doing solo duty and buzzed his two friends up to the tower cab. Doug was one of the few short men Banks knew who was proud of his slight stature. They shook the controller's hand and immediately teased him about being vertically challenged. Doug responded in kind, laughing and slapping McMaster's stomach, insinuating that it was protruding a little more since their last meeting. Doug hadn't changed much in two years. But a large beard had turned him into something resembling one of the furry little canvas-clad bears in the *Star Wars* movies.

Doug closed their flight plan with Edmonton Center and chatted about his desire to get back into the Whitehorse tower one day. The three men spent a few minutes reminiscing about old days in the Yukon before Doug generously offered Banks his car for the afternoon if the two men wanted to go into town. Doug Smiley's shift in the tower ended at 4:00 P.M., which gave McMaster and Banks ample time. They gratefully accepted. Within twenty minutes of landing, Travis and Dale were headed for the first of their two stops. Although hungry, they decided to wait until they returned to the airport to eat in case they ran short of time.

Banks found Doug's old AMC Ambassador in the Ministry of Transport parking lot. He quickly removed his Arctic Air epaulets and tie and tossed them into the car's disintegrating backseat. They had only three hours to pick up the autopsy report Michelle Baker had requested and to find any information on the family of Ed Bellichek.

The Yellowknife Public Library was in the middle of town and would have to wait. Dr. Baker said the autopsy report was with a colleague at the hospital.

The drive to the Stanton General Hospital in the community of Frame Lake South would take less than ten minutes. The pilot and loader followed Old Airport Road past several small industrial parks and found the hospital before figuring out how to work the twisted seat belts in Doug's antiquated jalopy.

The hospital was less than ten years old and had not been discolored by the vast seasonal changes, which mark buildings after several years in the North. It sported the organic architecture currently in vogue with new medical facilities. Several floors of waffle-iron concrete and long windows recessed just far enough to prevent getting a decent view in or out. Banks parked in what seemed to be the only general parking area near the entrance.

The maternal-looking nurse on duty inside the automatic glass doors still wore one of those little white hats from years past. It was pinned to her gray hair, perfectly centered on the top of her head. Her white name tag, meticulously displayed above her immense left breast, said "RN Thatchet." Ironically, the name—and, as it turned out, the personality were remarkably close to that of Ratchet—as in Nurse Ratchet of *One Flew over the Cuckoo's Nest* fame. Nurse Thatchet was slightly older but just as cantankerous. Defying gravity, her bifocals managed to hang onto the last cell of tissue at the end of her nose. It must have hurt her eye sockets to stare up at the two men and converse without raising her head. Her eyes danced suspiciously. She kept looking behind McMaster as if he were hiding a hundred sausage pizzas with extra cheese destined for the coronary unit. Banks finally stretched the truth, telling her they were from the coroner's office in Whitehorse on official business and, if she had a problem, to contact Dr. Michelle Baker at the Whitehorse General Hospital. The testy nurse begrudgingly acquiesced and gave them directions to the cavernous, antiseptic-smelling basement which housed both the morgue and Dr. Askew.

Dr. Blain Askew was not hard to find. He was the only living being in the hospital's basement. He reminded Banks of a mad scientist with his spindly arms and legs and disheveled hair sprouting in all directions. It was impossible to ascertain his age beyond the fact that he was somewhere between thirty and sixty. He ran around in circles like a wound-up toy and seemed to accomplish nothing. Dale and Travis both tried to introduce themselves with a handshake, but to no avail. Askew simply nodded his head and wouldn't stop hopping around long enough to make physical contact.

"So, how is Michelle Baker these days?" He stopped momentarily, looking into space, as if he had just figured out why lightning hadn't brought one of the clients in the stainless steel drawers surrounding Banks and McMaster back to life.

"Fine, she sends her . . ." Banks began.

"She was a real devil in medical school. Let me tell you!" he interrupted with a creepy, lascivious smile. Travis couldn't imagine that the doctor was alluding to some romantic tryst he and Michelle had shared in the past. "I was about to intern when she entered first-year. I made a point to always be available to tutor those cute little first year med students, if you know what I mean." He finally looked at McMaster and winked.

It was obvious that Askew was harmless, but Banks would have preferred if Michelle had remembered to mention that he was a pervert.

The doctor went back into high gear. "Anyway, Dr. Baker has a twenty-year-old case involving a missing native teenager and she wants to know if my Jane Doe might be her missing person. Right?"

"Yes." Travis' eyes had to chase him around the room.

"Well, I've got good news and I've got bad news for Dr. Baker." He bounced out of the room and out of sight.

Dale couldn't take much more. "Jesus Christ, this guy's sniffing too much formaldehyde. No wonder he works down here alone." McMaster surveyed the walls stacked with drawers and pointed. "Probably full of old assistants who finally whacked themselves. Can you imagine working with this guy every day? Someone needs to slip a Quaalude in his coffee . . ." Dale clammed up as a whirling white lab coat blew into the room and Dr. Askew continued as if he had never left.

He tossed a small stack of papers, X-rays, and several photos on a gurney next to Dale. "The bad news for Dr. Baker is I don't think this is her Jane Doe. She's missing a native girl. The facial bone structure of my Jane Doe is definitely Caucasian."

"What's the good news then?" Dale eyed the stack of papers but refused to touch them in case Dr. Askew's problem was contagious.

"I think I know who the Jane Doe is." A cocky smile twisted one side of his face. "This is why I get the big bucks!"

Dale and Travis said nothing.

"Well, anyway, I've got a preliminary finding on the remains found at a small lake fifty miles north of Yellowknife. . . ." He glanced at his stack of papers. "Where is it . . . here it is . . . Tetcho Lake. I've had it a couple of months. I was pretty sure who I had the day it was discovered. It's an old case. I let the police know but told them to hold off informing the family until I'd confirmed it with conclusive physical evidence. A diesel mechanic uncovered the remains. Can you imagine?"

Dr. Askew became instantly motionless and poured a red opaque liquid from one lab beaker into another. "Besides the body, the shallow grave contained clothing fragments consistent with a missing persons report filed with the RCMP twenty years ago. Same dress, socks, even found the little blue bow mentioned in the report, stuffed into a small pocket on her dress. Anyway, I finally found the dental records to confirm the remains in number twelve," he pointed somewhere in the room so quickly neither Dale nor Travis knew where. "It's of a missing girl named Kelly Margaret Radcliff."

McMaster made a gagging sound. Banks leaned against the gurney for support. The only Radcliff Travis knew was the RCMP Inspector who had nearly arrested him the day before at Primrose Lake.

The silence in the room was shattered when a phone began to ring somewhere. Dr. Askew knew where to look, on a cluttered table below a series of windows. It was flashing under a stack of papers. The doctor hurriedly picked it up and pounced on the pulsating orange button. It was Frau Thatchet calling from her guard post upstairs. She actually had the nerve to phone Whitehorse and check Banks' story. Unable to reach Dr. Baker, who Banks assumed was still sound asleep, the nurse was reporting to Dr. Askew that they should be arrested. He was brusque on the phone with Nurse Thatchet and, it seemed, got an equal earful back. Luckily, he did corroborate their story since she apparently ran a tight ship. Blain Askew was not one of her biggest fans.

"God, I wish euthanasia were legal." He slammed down the phone. "I'd have that creature strapped to a gurney in a New York minute." He headed back to his beakers.

Dale managed, "Excuse me, did you say . . . Radcliff?"

"That's correct." The doctor spun around and opened a drawer. He nonchalantly unzipped a long black body bag as if a tuna salad sandwich awaited him.

"She disappeared over twenty years ago. Of course, I wasn't around but the local folks say it was awful. Tore the whole town up. Nothing like it had ever happened before. A few times since then, but never before. Kind of a disgusting first." A little passion crept into Askew's voice.

McMaster and Banks thanked Dr. Askew for his time, scooped up the Jane Doe file, and quickly found their own way out of the hospital. Banks doubted if Askew even noticed that they had left. Nurse Thatchet gave them a cold smile, like a hunter who had his prey in the cross hairs—but it wasn't hunting season yet.

Once in the car, the two men discussed the odds on how many Radcliffs lived in northern Canada. Dale drove so that Banks could dig through the manila envelope containing the coroner's report Michelle had requested. Travis flipped through the pages trying to find a name. A parent's name.

"There's no way this girl is related to Nick Radcliff?" Dale was looking for reassurance.

"I doubt it." Banks mused. "That's something that would follow you around. You'd think we would have heard about it in Whitehorse."

Dale added, "Maybe not, considering he just moved to Whitehorse this past fall. I don't know if anyone knows where he was twenty years ago. Hell, I can hardly remember where I was twenty minutes ago."

They spent the rest of the drive downtown quietly considering the possibilities. Travis knew there had to be more than one Radcliff in northern Canada twenty years ago. Maybe the library would have the answer. They were on their way there anyway to look into Bellichek's family. Checking out Radcliff's family wouldn't require much more time.

Doug's directions into town and to the library were flawless. Except that he assumed they would be starting out at the airport, not at the hospital. McMaster became hopelessly lost and decided to backtrack the five-minute ride to the airport and start over.

They finally turned onto New Airport Road and passed Max Ward's Bristol Freighter Monument. Within minutes, they drove by the Prince of Wales Museum and the Explorer Hotel. According to Doug's scribbled map, they were headed in the right direction. Banks looked at his watch. The Dr. Askew visit had taken longer than expected. It was after 1:00 P.M. They had less than two hours to get to the library and back.

The drive into downtown took only fifteen minutes. The barren landscape made Banks appreciate the beauty of Whitehorse all the more. The terrain in the central part of the Northwest Territories was blasé compared to the mountainous majesty of the Yukon, as different as Kansas is from Colorado. The vegetation was scraggly, the birch and spruce trees dwarfed, by repeated frigid slaps of winter. Seeing it at this time of year didn't help. But even copious amounts of spring foliage wouldn't bring Yellowknife anywhere near Whitehorse's beauty.

The library was part of a gaudy pink ten-story building connected to the Yellowknife Inn and a small mall situated at the corner of Franklin Avenue and 49th Street. They had to enter the mall and take the elevator up one flight. When the door opened, they were standing in a library so modern it verged on opulence—a stellar example of the ridiculous amount Canadians paid in taxes.

McMaster and Banks passed through the theft detectors and quickly made their way to the front desk. An attractive young librarian with brunette hair met them with a smile. She was no more than twenty. Her delicately painted lips drew a similar smile from Dale. After the unpleasant episode with Nurse Thatchet thirty minutes earlier, the face before them was a welcome change. She was as helpful as she was attractive.

"May I help you?" She asked in a soft, sexy voice, nearly crippling Dale.

"We're looking for your genealogy section, if you have one," said Banks.

Dale's eyes were working, but not his mouth.

"Not only do we have one but it's the most modern genealogical computer in the North. It's tied into the Internet. It will access and cross-reference back copies of Canada's 10 largest newspapers for the past forty years. It will also search any Canadian phone directory. It's quite a technological marvel."

"So are you," Dale couldn't resist saying. "Could it find your phone number?"

Surprisingly, she didn't seem offended by his remark. She smiled at him and continued, "It's in the far corner." She pointed over Dale's painfully expanded chest. "Anybody specific?"

Banks said, "I doubt whether you would know or want to know who we're looking for, but thanks." The two began heading for the corner of the library.

"You never know," she insisted. "This is a small community."

"The fella we're looking for probably hasn't lived here for decades. He's an old . . ." Travis searched for a better word than creep ". . . ill trapper named Bellichek and we're simply looking for any surviving family."

"You're kidding," she answered with a youthful exuberance that gave away her age. "I mean, you're right, I don't know him. But someone else called this morning looking for information on that name. It's an unusual name. Was it you who called?"

Travis looked at Dale momentarily. "No." The pilot turned back to face her. "Do you mind me asking if you know who called and if you found any information?"

"Julie took the request, not me. I overheard Julie referring the caller to the mining recorder's office. But I have no idea who it was, we usually don't ask. It's not required. It's a free service."

"I see." Banks thought for a second. "Is Julie here?"

A look of disappointment crept across her face. "No, I'm sorry, she had to leave early today and won't be back until next Tuesday. But if it makes you feel any better, I know she didn't find anything."

"Well, thanks, we'll give it a shot anyway."

Dale had that Fuller Brush look in his eyes and Travis quickly led him away.

As soon as they were out of earshot, Dale piped up, "Who do you think beat us here? And why mining deeds?"

"I don't know. I assume it had to be the RCMP. No one else knows

Bellichek's dead. It's no big deal. They might be having problems locating next of kin. And it doesn't really matter anyway, does it?" Travis smiled at him. "They didn't get any information. Maybe we'll have better luck looking in person."

There were many stacks of books for a community with only 15,000 people. Old gray metal stacks full of books were the only holdovers from the former library. Everything else looked new. The floor was tastefully covered with navy blue carpets and modern oak furnishings. The entire facility was alive with the soft but bright dispersed glow of new fluorescent track lighting. The vast exhibition of new electronic services was amazing. Obviously, Banks needed to spend more time in the Whitehorse Library. He hadn't been in a library since he had studied for his last university exam nearly twenty years earlier. There were stacks of books recorded on tapes and computers with multitudes of CD selections. To their surprise, the library had an entire room dedicated to genealogy. It was located back in the corner near the washrooms and a reading room. The small computer room apportioned for the study of family lineage looked like a glass and cedar birdhouse with bay windows. Three sides of the room faced the stacks. The records were kept both on microfiche and computers.

Once inside their private room, the two men split up because the computer couldn't access smaller newspapers. Dale searched on microfiche for local newspaper stories on the death of Kelly Margaret Radcliff. He began his exploration on the approximate dates Dr. Askew had given them regarding the disappearance of the little girl, around the end of the 1950s.

Travis rummaged through the computer's hard drive for a family tree by the name of Bellichek. Banks simply inserted "Bellichek" into the blue flashing cursor space on the genealogy software and pressed "Enter."

The hard drive was part of a new system that must have possessed a million gigabytes of something or other. The mother board clicked away, flashing the C-drive's green light, pleading for Banks to be resolute. It took several minutes before the screen flashed "NO DATA: BELLICHECK."

Travis spent an hour trying every variation of his name. One "L" instead of two. Each time he waited for the newest in computer technology to surf the net and cross-reference God knows what. Unfortunately, every time he hit "Enter" the electronic marvel came back to inform him he didn't know what the hell he was talking about. Impossible. This IBM Goliath couldn't find one reference to a bum named Bellichek in all of Canada. It didn't make sense.

Dale was coming up with goose eggs as well. Every angle that each of them explored proved futile. There had to be a record of the Bellichek's family in Yellowknife. Michelle had government medical records indicating that he was from the area or at least spent some time here.

Travis checked his watch. It was time to leave. It didn't look like either one of them was going to have any luck.

"C'mon, Dale, let's get out of here. We've still got time to swing by the Social Security Administration office. They might have a line on this guy's family." Banks started to gather up his parka and shut down the computer.

"Bingo." Dale sat up and looked into the grainy magnified image starring back at him from inside the microfiche projector. He stopped the rotation of the little handle, bringing the whirring film to a stop. He slowly backed up the film to a spot he had passed several seconds before.

"What have you got?" Travis whispered unnecessarily. They were alone in the room.

"Come here." Dale didn't look up. He was zeroing in on whatever he'd seen.

Travis sat down in his chair again and wheeled it toward McMaster's desk. He peered over Dale's shoulder, trying to focus on each passing screen.

"There, right there!" He stuck his tobacco and diesel-stained finger on a headline behind the glass screen. "NO BODY, NO JUSTICE."

Banks said, "Other than the headline, I can't read anything."

"Hang on." He turned another knob and the front page of the *Yellowknifer* dated June 13, 1960, came into focus.

"You can read that?" Travis squinted.

"Yes I can. Why? Can't you?" Dale looked up concerned. "Shit, Banks, you're a goddamn pilot. Maybe I should take a cab back to Whitehorse."

"It must be the angle I'm at."

"Yeah, right." He looked down and brought the picture into perfect focus. "Don't worry, just promise me that when you get your Seeing Eye dog, you'll retire from aviation."

Dale leaned closer to the screen and started to read the front page article. "Let's see . . . blah, blah, blah . . . okay, here it is, 'the body of young Kelly Radcliff has yet to be found . . . been missing since April 1 . . . presumed kidnapped . . . little hope of finding the girl alive . . . police are still following up leads . . . blah, blah, holy shit, Banks . . ."

Travis had almost caught up to Dale and was only a sentence behind.

". . .the father of the little girl, *RCMP Detective Simon Radcliff*, . . . has sworn vengeance to the people responsible." Dale turned and glared at Travis.

"*Simon* Radcliff?" Banks probed.

"That's right." Dale pointed at the screen. "Do you think he's related to you-know-who?"

"Keep reading," Travis prompted Dale, unable to squint hard enough to read the old newspaper image.

McMaster continued, ". . . the mother has been in shock and heavily sedated since the incident began . . . the investigation is currently focusing on several miners residing north of Yellowknife. . . . "

Banks looked closely at the old photo accompanying the front page article. It was a poor image compared to modern newspaper photography. Several people were leaving what looked like either the Territorial courthouse or a police station. Some were police in uniform, some were obviously suspects. Several names were listed below the indistinct picture.

"Dale, look at that picture . . . what do you see?"

He stared intently without speaking.

Travis sunk back in his chair. "Do you see it?"

Dale looked at the screen again. "No."

Travis pointed. "Look at the third guy on the right. In the group of four. The one to the far left of the business suits. What do you see? Who is that?"

"Christ, Banks, I don't know who . . . hell, two of them look alike."

"They are. They're brothers. Put a beard on the taller one and tack on a couple of decades, who do you have?" Travis stared at the back of Dale's head, waiting for the lightbulb to finally illuminate.

"It's Ed Bellichek." His voice trailed off to a whisper. "I'll be a son of bitch. That might answer why our mysterious caller to the library wanted mining deed information. Bellichek was once a miner."

McMaster mumbled, focusing intensely on the image in front of him. "There's kidnapping suspect Ed Bellichek, over two decades ago, standing next to a cop named Simon Radcliff whose daughter was abducted." He paused. "C'mon, Banks, what are the odds these Radcliffs are related. And assuming they are, why in the hell didn't Nick Radcliff mention this at Primrose Lake that Bellichek was accused of kidnapping his niece?"

"Hasn't he always denied having any surviving family?" Travis stared at Dale, mulling over his observations. It was a possibility. He looked at the film again.

Banks had no idea what any of this meant and continued thinking out loud. "It's not just the fact they might be related or knew Ed Bellichek. It's the circumstances." The two men jockeyed for position in front of the screen.

Banks continued. "It says here, Bellichek was one of four miners from some lake, where is it . . . here it is, Tetcho Lake, questioned about the girl's disappearance. No evidence. It mentions two of the other miners' names—William Watt and Mike Jansen. Who's the fourth guy?"

"What Lake did you say?" Dale rifled through the papers Blain Askew had given them at the hospital.

"Tetcho Lake."

"Here, that's the lake where Dr. Wing Nut Askew said they found the body."

"You're right."

Dale studied the front page some more. He was trying to find any tie between Simon Radcliff and Nick Radcliff.

"It doesn't mention Nick at all. But look at this guy here. That could be a young Nick Radcliff . . . wearing . . . what looks like gold striped RCMP trousers," he pointed to the background of the obscure picture, "damn, it's hard to make out the face."

"It's too hard. It could be anybody, Dale."

"This is all one hell of a coincidence." He closed in, almost touching the screen with his nose.

"Wait a minute." It suddenly dawned on Travis while he was looking at Dale's screen that there was a misprint on the caption under the photo of the suspects on the police station steps. A reporter had spelled Radcliff with a "ck." Radckliff. Banks spun around and wheeled back to the computer. "I've been asking this computer to find a Bellichek spelled with 'ck' at the end."

"So what? That's how it's spelled."

"Nope."

"That's how it's spelled in the paper."

"I know. Because they made the same mistake I did. I just remembered something. And I'll bet whoever phoned this morning didn't know what I learned years ago."

"What's that?"

"When I met Bellichek and handed him his first charter ticket," Banks said, pushing buttons on the computer's keyboard until the hard drive began to grind once again, "he gave me grief over the spelling of his name. Said everybody screwed it up. I forgot about his lecture and kept spelling it 'ck.' But he said it was properly spelled with just a 'k..'"

Dale watched Travis' flurry of activity. "You might be going blind but I'm impressed with your memory, Banks. This fancy computer should've figured it out and given you all the possibilities."

"Not necessarily. Garbage in, garbage out. I'm sure you have to be specific or a million names would come up every time you hit 'Enter.'"

The genealogy program was still up and running. Travis typed in the new spelling and hit "Enter." Moments later, the screen lit up with the very short family tree of Edwin James Bellichek.

"Well, well. I think I just found our missing miner."

Banks hit the print button and read from the screen, "Ed had only one surviving family member. A younger brother named Brock. Last known city of residence was in Whitehorse, Yukon Territory. According to this, he's still alive. Neither men have any children."

He didn't wait for the computer to finish printing before entering the name "Radcliff" into the flashing cursor line. Moments later, the screen fell dark for a split second, then came alive with the Radcliff family tree.

"Here we are. Nicholas Brian Radcliff. No address. Date of birth, July 1, 1932." Banks turned to McMaster. "He was born on Canada's Independence Day, no wonder he's such a patriot." He continued, "Father: Charles William Radcliff. Mother: Kelly Anne Savard. Both deceased. One older brother: Simon Pierre. Born November 13, 1930. Lived in Norman Wells, NWT with wife Patricia."

"Lives or lived?"

"It says Patricia died nearly fifteen years ago. No cause of death. She would have only been in her late thirties. Simon Radcliff . . . doesn't say. A younger sister, Solange, died in 1945. Cause of death unknown. She was only a kid." Banks slumped back in his chair wondering aloud.

"Must have been an accident or illness." Dale listened while printing everything the projected edition of the *Yellowknifer* had on the investigation and disappearance of Simon and Patricia's daughter, Kelly.

"Nick Radcliff wasn't lying. He doesn't have much family left, other than a brother. That's a lot of misery for one guy." Travis thought of the horror Simon Radcliff must have suffered losing his child.

"Why don't we just ask Nick Radcliff what happened to his long-lost brother and sister and the rest of his whole friggin' family tree?" Dale suggested in an almost offhand manner.

"Right. Everything we've figured out today, he's known for a long time. Before you go off half-cocked demanding an explanation from the Inspector of the Whitehorse Royal Canadian Mounted Police detachment, you might want to ask yourself, why *didn't* he say something sooner? He certainly had the opportunity yesterday."

"He might have thought it was none of our business."

"An hour ago, I would have agreed." Travis sat in the swivel chair with his hands cupped behind his head staring at the new library's textured ceiling. It was odd that the information they had found wasn't known in and about Whitehorse. Family secrets were a rarity in small Northern communities.

"I started out to get some information on Bellichek's family, not Radcliff's." Travis sat back up in the chair. "I'm sure Constable Radcliff has a very sound reason for not clueing us in on his family's past. I think we ought to find Brock Bellichek. He might be able to answer some questions about both families. I also need to see if Michelle can shine some light on what happened to everybody in this family."

Dale warned, "And maybe Brock Bellichek had something to do with this girl's vanishing act and is not interested in reminiscing about old times with two complete strangers."

Banks waited until it was safe to turn off the computer and then switched it off. "We won't know until we ask, will we? Let's photocopy everything we've dug up. There's a lot of people who aren't going to buy this if all they have is our word."

They gathered up their belongings, photocopied their findings, and headed back to the airport. Travis Banks had a lot on his mind but had to focus on aviation for the rest of the afternoon.

Banks could only assume he passed his line check. As Ralph Michaels was securing the airplane, he was almost bowled over by Frank Flemming, desperate to get out of the airport and into a bottle at the Airport Chalet bar ASAP. It was long past "Miller Time." On the trip back from Yellowknife, it seemed that Flemming's nose had become redder and redder with a burgeoning cauliflower physiognomy.

As soon as the DC-3 CF-CUG, was plugged in and put to bed on the white frozen canvas of the Arctic Air ramp, Travis phoned his racquetball foe, Sergeant Powell, who was already back from Primrose Lake. They had planned to play a game of racquetball and possibly have dinner. But Travis was running behind and asked Powell to meet him at the Airport Chalet lounge in thirty minutes.

Travis was curious as to what, if anything, they had discovered on their second voyage to the site of Bellichek's murder on Primrose Lake. He was equally interested in the disposition of Powell's superior, Nick Radcliff. He desperately wanted to share with Powell the discovery they'd made in the Yellowknife Library but had misgivings. Powell's inexorable respect for Radcliff was based exclusively on the inspector's personnel file. RCMP officers were like doctors. They might bitch 'til hell froze amongst themselves but never publicly. Travis had flown in the airlines with military pilots who suffered from the same affliction. It's hard for a pilot in the military to objectively evaluate other military aviators. They are blinded at a professional level by a human resources dossier stating how many hoops they've jumped through and what respect and rank they should command. That's why the best pilots come from the military . . . and also the worst.

Travis just couldn't risk telling Powell everything yet. By ignoring the U.S.-Canada border when they discovered Bellichek's body, Radcliff had demonstrated his willingness to decimate his entire exemplary police career for nothing, which didn't make sense. Unless what Banks had learned in Yellowknife was tied in somehow.

Travis couldn't make it out of the hangar before the still despondent Ms. Jackson called him into her office to discuss how the charter to Yellowknife had gone. She haphazardly looked over the charter billing ticket Banks had submitted for the trip. The long day had worn her down and depleted her defenses, which had been impenetrable earlier in the day. It was obvious by her deportment that the death of her mentor, Kitch Olson, was still on her mind.

"Travis, I've got a Beaver trip for you tomorrow morning at 8:00. Finlayson Lake. Just some groceries for the Rylance drilling crew. You'll be back by noon." She paused before hedging. "Plenty of time to clean up for dinner."

Banks had temporarily forgotten about the Rendezvous Chamber of Commerce dinner the boss wanted him to "escort" her to.

"Have you thought about tomorrow night?" Kayla didn't look up.

"I'm sorry, I hadn't given it much thought with all that's been going on the last couple of days. Let me mention it . . . ah, what the hell, it won't be a problem." He lied. Doc Baker was not going to like his new "escort" service, even though she would never let on. This would be a test of his freedom and independence.

"Is that a yes?"

"Sure. I'd enjoy it. What time can I pick you up?"

There was actually a bright spot of anticipation in his boss's eyes.

"How about 7:30? Don't forget. Something resembling a suit and tie."

"Can't wait." Travis headed for the door.

What in the hell was he going to do? He didn't own a formal dinner suit. He wasn't sure he still owned any type of suit.

"By the way, Ms. Jackson, am I required to dance tomorrow night? I'm not much of a dancer. In fact, I might get one or both of us hurt if I attempt to cut a rug."

"Don't worry. I won't ask you to do anything you're not comfortable with." She smiled, looking at the papers on her desk.

As much as Banks was looking forward to the evening, it was making him somewhat uncomfortable.

"Anything new on Bellichek?" Her fingers began dancing on her calculator once again.

"No. Nothing important." Travis was growing weary of lying to those closest to him. In the past twenty-four hours, he'd perjured himself to everyone but Dale. He was convinced he was protecting someone. After what Travis learned in Yellowknife, he wondered if he was simply protecting himself.

Before leaving the pilots' small crew room, Banks slid into Frank Flemming's messy office and dialed Dr. Baker's residence in Porter Creek. He fully intended to notify Michelle of his intentions to "escort" Kayla Jackson to the business dinner the following evening. Once the phone started ringing, he realized he might as well have phoned "Dial-a-Fight." She would be about to walk out the door on her way to the hospital and if his news upset her, it might transform all her evening patients into victims.

Banks panicked and decided to abort the call halfway into the second ring.

He wrote a note instead. He included it with the coroner's report he was going to drop off. Travis asked her to dig into her computer at the hospital. He was hoping she might find some government medical information or at least a current address on Simon Radcliff. He wanted to know if Simon still resided in Norman Wells. If he did, Travis could easily make a trip there to ask him about Ed and Brock Bellichek, about his own brother, Inspector Nick Radcliff, and what killed their younger sister, Solange. They were all sensitive subjects, especially considering the news that Dr. Askew had just confirmed having the remains of Simon's own daughter, Kelly Margaret Radcliff. Banks assumed Michelle was right and Simon might seek closure to the tragedy.

Travis knew Michelle would honor the request. But he also accepted the fact that he would get the normal lecture regarding doctor-patient privilege. He put the note—which failed to mention his "escort" service the next evening—together with the coroner's report and headed to his truck.

Night had settled in over Whitehorse. Travis left the airport and turned right. Normally, a left turn took him home to Hillcrest but he had the coroner's report to drop off at the hospital. It would take only fifteen minutes to run it over to Michelle Baker, return home, shower, change, and meet Leon Powell and Dale for a well-deserved beer at the Chalet.

Banks accelerated onto the Alcan Highway, passing the Canadian Pacific Airlines DC-3 perched nearly ten feet off the ground at the airport entrance.

It was one of the original gooney birds flying in the North. It had made the unforgivable mistake of losing an engine on takeoff and stumbling into the frozen Arctic morning air, barely making it back to the airport, landing gear up and skidding into the side of a hangar. It was a fate suffered by many aircraft that had tried to call Alaska or the Yukon home.

As aviation grew into larger four-engine props and eventually to jets, yesterday's workhorses became today's garbage. The DC-3s, Lodestars, C-46s, Beech 18s, the remnants of 1930s aeronautical technology, became a nuisance across the nation's airports the first time they failed to start or broke a leg landing. They weren't worth the time, trouble, or money to fix and most landfills said no. They were destined to travel the familiar historical journey of all successful mechanical technology, a trek that spanned from being christened "incredible creation" to becoming classified as "magnificent antique." In between are many years of being labeled "obsolete piece of junk."

The proud Douglas DC-3 airframe passing out his right window had originally been cannibalized by the mechanics of Canadian Pacific Airlines for the engines and any other salvageable parts. The rest was left to rot. They had towed the remaining airframe from one grassy spot at the airport to another for the past thirty years.

Fortunately, no one had yet created the mechanic or tool able to dismantle the character or soul of the greatest and most influential aircraft ever built. Years later, when the old CP Air DC-3 finally graduated to "magnificent antique," a restoration project reconditioned the exterior of the aircraft and the city mounted it off the ground on a swiveling foundation and turned the proud ship into the world's biggest and most beautiful windsock.

Discretion was the better part of valor. Banks would drop Askew's report off at the hospital front desk and not risk a confrontation with Dr. Baker. He knew Michelle might arrive any minute to start her shift in the emergency room. Not her favorite shift and certainly not the best time to inform her of his "platonic" date with Kayla Jackson. Surprisingly, he was actually looking forward to the evening with Kayla. Not the part about wearing a suit or the dinner. He couldn't care less about the Chamber of Commerce. It was, he had to admit, her company. The night before, she'd been positively intriguing. Something had transpired between them. He had no idea what, but it certainly seemed genuine and unforced. He simply had to exorcise the little gremlin his grandfather habitually perched on his shoulder to offer sexual advice.

Travis dropped off the report and was on his way home within ten minutes.

It was almost 5:00 P.M. and pitch-dark when Banks turned the corner into Hillcrest. The sun had long since slid back below the surrounding mountains. His headlights lit up the neighborhood in a brilliant white light of snow-covered houses, lawns, and streets. It had snowed off and on all day in Whitehorse after they left for Yellowknife. Now it was a picture postcard, made more attractive from the warmth of his truck.

Lieutenant Monty was sweeping a dusty layer of icy crystals off his driveway when Travis pulled up. It was a waste of time. A gust of wind would remove it all and another gust would put it all back. It was a make-work project until 5:00 P.M., when he could justify several Guinnesses in front of the fire. It was terribly important for Monty to show the world he was still vital.

Wet snowfalls usually occurred only once or twice a year, usually in the early fall and late spring when the temperature was near the freezing mark. Once the temperature plummeted into the minus twenty and thirty range, precipitation came in the form of ice crystals. It was nearly impossible to make a good snowball, or any snowball for that matter. It was like trying to make a ball out of sand. You'd have to add water to the powdered sugar like snow to create a good sphere. Neighborhood kids often did just that and would nail Banks driving home. Most Northern children didn't concern themselves with the snow anymore than Hawaiian children worried about their tans. Travis had seen only one snowman in all his years in the North. It was last winter when a family from Arizona had moved in down the street. They moved North to "get back to nature." By the time the little girl had finished her first snowman, Banks and Monty had to rush her to Michelle at the hospital to be treated for frostbite. Travis hadn't seen the little girl play outside once this winter. There were rumors floating about that the family might be heading back south soon. They found Mother Nature unforgiving and the North too cold. The wife missed tennis lessons, the daughter missed the malls, and the husband's golf handicap was back to double digits. Banks had mentioned to a few people that there was going to be a good deal on a house in Hillcrest soon.

As soon as Monty knew Banks had seen him working, he quickly threw the broom and shovel into the carport and waved at Travis to join him in the house. Monty could mime sipping a Guinness better than anyone. The English call it afternoon tea. Travis called it "Miller Time."

The furnishings inside the Lieutenant's half of the duplex spoke of a very tasteful woman's touch. The living room, with its classic dark antique oak and mahogany Georgian furniture, had a gracious and inviting atmosphere. A statuesque Victorian clock near the door chimed away every fifteen minutes. A beveled oval mirror hung over the fireplace and a Queen Anne's tea set and a silver stand was placed on the sideboard next to Monty's ox-blood red leather chair. Next to the tea set were three crystal decanters containing Scotch, port, and his favorite brandy, all three within arm's reach. Only the plants, fitfully watered by Monty in his wife's memory, had seen better days. Banks could almost feel his blood pressure dropping when he spent time in the Lieutenant's home.

"How'd the ol' gooney bird handle today, Banks?" Monty threw another log on the fire.

"Fine. Just fine."

The Lieutenant rubbed his cheeks and scurried into the kitchen to fetch his favorite dark elixir. He was excited to have Travis home. The younger pilot had begun to realize that he was an important part of Monty's life. Winston Montgomery had let slip once or twice he had wanted children. Mindy's Hodgkin's disease had ended the dream. He would have been a good father. Travis enjoyed being a surrogate son. One of Banks' favorite pastimes had become watching old movies with Monty one night a week. They alternated each week in picking movies. Monty always picked old black-and-white flicks and the next week Banks would force the Lieutenant to sit through a film developed in color with sound. It always created lively debate afterward. Today versus the "good old days."

"Lieutenant?"

"Yes, lad."

"What would you do if a very attractive coworker asked you out for dinner?" Banks searched for an accurate description of the upcoming evening. "Under the premise it was a platonic date?"

Monty handed Travis a room-temperature Guinness, raised his glass, and like a true English gentleman, slowly lowered himself into his evening chair.

"How attractive?"

"You're kidding, right?"

"Listen, lad. If she's a real beaut, you're not going to take my advice anyway. The smart money is on keeping your pecker out of the payroll."

He was beginning to sound like Banks' grandfather.

"Don't bullshit an old man, Travis. Everybody at Arctic Air is a man. Except your boss and the charming but undesirable Miss Rand. This wouldn't happen to be the vivacious Ms. Jackson asking you on a date, would it?" He leaned forward in his chair.

"Yes."

"Jolly good. Hear! Hear!" He took a deep gulp of Irish stout. "Absolutely. You have my blessing. Now, there's a woman worth getting fired over." He raised his glass and let out a hearty laugh.

It was good to hear Monty laugh. Travis smiled and toasted him back.

"Does the good doctor know?"

"No." Banks stared into his mug.

"C'mon lad. Be a man. 'Fess up. Women know these things. If you don't tell her, she'll see it in your eyes anyway and then you'll be up shit creek. Lying to a woman is as dishonorable as cheating."

"Lieutenant, it's just a date."

"Poppycock! Either you're lying to yourself or you're a bigger fool than I thought. Or maybe both. That Kayla Jackson is too good looking for 'just a date.'" He puffed out his chest a little. "Hell, if I had a little more spark in the ol' furnace, I'd be down there at her office right now stoking it."

"I'll tell Michelle tonight. Thanks for the Guinness."

"You hardly touched it."

"I found out some interesting news today in Yellowknife. As soon as I know what it means, I'll let you know. I've got to meet Dale and Powell."

Banks quickly ran next door and changed. He needed to find the murdered Ed Bellichek's brother, Brock Bellichek. Travis was hoping Brock would shine some light on a very foreboding theory that was troubling Banks' conscience.

Charlie Charlie, the social ringleader and manager of the Chalet bar, was in a priceless mood. Betty Frost, his adorable, matchmaking wife, had given up years earlier being embarrassed by her husband's antics. It was only 6:15 and Charlie Charlie was doing a happy jig in the half-full lounge of the Chalet bar, professing that today was Friday and might be the last day before Armageddon.

Time to drink up!

The lounge at the Chalet was a dark, split-level, rectangular-shaped room with the bar at the inside far end. It held only fifty people. The walls were two-toned with wood paneling on the bottom half, red velour wallpaper on the top half, and four inches of wooden trim separating the two. There was always a warm fire crackling in the raised open fireplace topped with a black flue and surrounded with a wire curtain. The fireplace sat on the upper level and was surrounded by a half-dozen chairs . . . select seating if you were on a romantic quest.

Flemming was just getting loose. He was half in the bag and wandering around the bar, spouting an absurd tale about how Banks had almost killed all of them on the way back from Yellowknife. He sought out any patron willing to listen and explained how he had to finally take control of the DC-3 and save everybody. He was a true abomination to the flying profession. Decorum dictated that Travis have one drink with him, as Dale and Powell hadn't shown up yet. No problem. Banks would have a clandestine toast with Flemming about the old fart's impending pink slip.

It was easy to dislike Frank Flemming but impossible to hate him. Most people simply felt sorry for him. He meant no harm. Simply put, he was unsophisticated and unwittingly rude. He had the grace of a pig on stilts. No emotional guidance. His wife had left him years earlier. Banks could certainly understand why. An alley cat had more redeeming qualities. Flemming now divided his time between Winnipeg, Manitoba and Whitehorse. Travis assumed Winnipeg was because that was where Frank's ex lived. Banks knew the chief pilot had children but he didn't know anything about them. Flemming never spoke of his kids other than to say they were long gone and "good riddance." Travis had no doubt that the kids left at the first opportunity. He couldn't imagine the nefarious type of relationship that must have existed between father and children. It made him think of his own parents often.

Banks lost both his parents in a car accident soon after he enrolled in college. A drunk hit them head-on. They never really left and they never would. They had been taking their first real vacation after twenty years. All their money had gone toward tuition for his sister and himself. At the time, Travis felt angry, robbed of time, and denied the chance to prove to them what he could do. More than anything, he wanted to show them that all their hard work and sacrifice had been worth it. He felt robbed of his biggest dream—to be the pilot on their first flight.

As Travis grew older, the anger turned into regret. His mother had always insisted he would be a success, no matter what field he chose. Banks took solace in her confidence. She was a saint, a hard-working housewife who thought raising children was more important than a paycheck and a second car. An odd concept in today's thinking. She put both his sister and himself at number three on the all-time hit parade, with only God and his father ahead of them. People who thought that being a housewife was, in some way, inferior to "working" for a living didn't know women like his mother. She'd worked harder than anyone and all without an ounce of acknowledgment. He had never met a "professional woman" who didn't pale against her shadow. Her reward, she felt, was that her son and daughter were resounding successes. A pilot and a Ph.D. in Psychology. Travis wasn't a devout religious man but if there was a heaven, he knew his mother was there.

His father was a longshoreman. Travis often thought that if the use of foul language precluded entrance through the pearly gates, there'd be a lot of question as to whether his father had joined his mother. A tough stevedore whose big hands moved thousands of pounds of freight during the day and rocked Travis to sleep at night, he was the archetypal "hands-on" father thirty years before it was in vogue. Once you understood what was expected, life was good. But don't ever forget what was expected. Banks Sr. could be as tumultuous as an erupting volcano and as gentle as a kitten. He joked about never receiving a formal education. He'd rib Banks' sister once she enrolled in college by telling her he thought a serial killer was someone who ate Rice Krispies. He was a very intelligent man who wasn't given the opportunity to attend college. He insisted his kids get a university education to ensure that they never had to load half-a-million cubic tons of grain onto a Liberian freighter just to survive. And if they didn't like college, too bad, they were going anyway. He didn't read in any child-rearing guide that his kids had to like him, just pay him mind. Travis often wondered if time or the tragedy of their deaths tainted his memories of his parents. His sister, the police shrink, always reassured Travis they were blessed with extraordinary parents.

To sit now and listen to Frank Flemming rail vociferously about his three estranged sons and what louses they were made Banks ill. Travis knew Flemming was the problem and unless Frank had trained them not to be like daddy, it was too late now and they all deserved one another.

What Banks would do if he could have just one hour with his big, boisterous volcano of a Dad.

Travis had always assumed Flemming's antagonism toward him stemmed from some defense mechanism he'd developed to cope with his own numbing failures. He would be gone soon. Cheers! Travis decided to drink to that.

Banks had taken only one sip from the frosty Labatt's Pilsner in front of him when Charlie Charlie came cavorting up to the table and told him that Dale had phoned. Banks was to call McMaster at his apartment immediately.

The price to use the phone at the front desk was a hearty facial pinch from Betty and an assurance from Travis that he would take a peek in the kitchen at the next daughter coming of age. Banks often felt that this whole breeding ritual would make an interesting *National Geographic* special.

Dale picked up the phone before one full ring.

"What's up?" Banks said while dishing through the "B" section of the thin Whitehorse phone book.

"Someone busted into my place!" He squealed into Banks' ear.

"What place? What are you talking about?"

"My fucking apartment! Someone broke in. Jesus, what a mess."

Banks put down the phone book and thought about McMaster's

disheveled residence. "Calm down. How can you tell?"

"Travis, I know this apartment's never going to make the cover of *Better Homes and Gardens*, but I know my own fucking mess. Anyway, it's my darkroom. It's been busted into."

"Is anything missing?"

"All the film I was developing," he said in exasperation, looking around the room at his stereo and TV, "the rest of the place is normal."

It hit Banks like a slap across the head. "The film, Dale. The rolls of film from Primrose. Where are they?"

"They're gone. At least the negatives are gone. Hell, every negative in my darkroom is gone."

Travis cursed under his breath into the phone.

"Don't worry, Travis. After I left you and Powell at the Klondike last night, I picked up some photo chemicals at the float base before coming home and making a set of prints. I keep most of that stuff down there in the winter. It's good and cold. I made a set of prints. Actually had them in my pocket today going to Yellowknife. I forgot to give them to you. But there's nothing on them. I already looked them over. I left a couple of rolls of film from Primrose at the float base. What have they got to do with anything? The only people who knew about those pictures are you, me and Powell."

"As far as we know. Last night at the float base, where did you put the rolls of film?"

"On the top shelf in the storage room."

"Do me a favor, Dale, bring the prints by the Chalet. Powell will be here in a few minutes to meet you."

"Where the hell are you going?"

"I'm going by Schwatka Lake and get the film. I'll meet you back at the Chalet."

"Banks, this whole thing's getting a little out of hand. I'm an aircraft loader. Not Charlie Chan."

"Bring the prints, Dale. I'll see you in thirty minutes."

Banks didn't have a clue if there was something more to the bizarre death of Ed Bellichek. But if there was, he felt they were becoming involved. They needed insurance. The film was a start.

The phone book still lay open to the "B"s. Staring up at Travis was the name of Brock Bellichek, incorrectly spelled with "ck" at the end. Even the phone company had it wrong. He dialed the number and got the desk clerk at the Regina Hotel. Banks had found Ed Bellichek's brother. If Brock had not been told of his brother's death yet, Travis didn't think it would be appropriate to do it over the phone. He hung up the phone before the desk clerk put his call through to Bellichek's room. A minute later, he was in his truck on the way to the deserted float base office.

Banks turned his Chevy truck right off the South Access road next to the Schwatka Lake Hydro Dam and onto Schwatka Lake road. The power station was roaring with a full head of steam, providing Whitehorse with its electrical needs.

The float base was a hive of activity in the summer months when Arctic Air was busy flying floatplanes to supply hunting outfitters and mining companies. But exploration in the cold winter months was almost nonexistent. The effort to drill for ore samples during the winter was tedious and too costly. The little flying that was required was done using skis from the main airport. Nobody ventured to Arctic Air's summer facility in the winter. There was no need. It made an ideal location to hide something.

It was a drive Travis loved. He could do it in his sleep. A few times, he practically had. He'd always felt that flying floatplanes should be the height of any pilot's career. The DC-3 paid more but flying under instrument flight rules handcuffed the true freedom found in float flying. Float pilots were the closest things to human birds. Seven-tenths of the earth was water, all of it a runway for a float pilot. You never bothered talking to control towers. Never needed permission to land at some isolated lake in the wilds of the North. If the water looked deep enough and long enough, a float pilot crossed his fingers and landed. Airlines corralled your aviation spirit, floatplanes set you free. Float flying was the ultimate in aeronautical liberation.

Whenever Kayla was short a pilot at the float base, Banks would always volunteer his services. It kept him away from the main office and hangar at the airport where Flemming consumed his days finding new ways to aggravate people. Banks thought about the spring. He couldn't wait to arrive at the float base, open the office, turn on the radio, and then sit on the vinyl recliner outside, soaking up the warm Yukon sun. It was a sun that spent twenty hours circling the horizon. Even the sweet smell of old moose blood on his overalls was a welcome memory. It was the smell of victory against the rat race of the main hangar and office. The sounds, smells and feelings of the float operation. Just a few more months.

The float base had been closed since October and the road had been plowed only once or twice. Except for a few floodlights dispersing a negligible amount of light in his rearview mirror, it was pitch-black. Banks spun his all-season radial tires over the tracks left by Dale the night before. The little summer Arctic Air office and dock slid into view.

The dark frozen lake gripped the small L-shaped dock jutting from the shore. A few snowmobile tracks wandered off in different directions, a sign that P.T. Barnum was correct. A sucker was born every minute. The ice was thick enough in midwinter to support most any vehicle. But Schwatka Lake's hydro station drew thousands of gallons per hour from beneath the lake's northern shore. This caused unpredictable ice movement and breakup. If you were unlucky enough to be on the ice at the wrong time, your reward would be getting a close look at one of the hydro station's intakes submerged 100 feet below the lake surface. Banks had spent several days the previous summer looking for a tourist who, in order to relieve himself, had ventured too close to the edge of one of the city's tourist attractions, the Schwatka Lake Miles Canyon Bridge. They found the body several days later, zipper down, caught in one of the intakes. Travis wondered what was written on the poor fellow's headstone.

Banks parked the truck but left it running with his headlights on high beam. He negotiated the slippery and twisted frozen two -by-twelves that made up the office walkway. The Arctic Air float office had only two rooms, a tiny outer office with an antiquated desk, torn diesel-soaked love seat, and a woodstove used in the fall; and a larger back room containing several rows of shelves that stored tools, engine parts, and anything else that needed to be kept indoors during the winter.

The Arctic night was still and quiet. The only noise was his idling truck and the hydro station purring in the distance. He turned around to catch the headlights, fumbled for the key that would unlock the large dead bolt on the office door. His foggy breath swirled in the beams of the headlights as the electrical radiator fan kicked on. He swore and removed a mitt to finally select the right key and stumbled toward the door. He tried to keep a small shaft of his headlights in front of him for guidance. The lock . . . it was gone! The lock was not on the door or the latch. Thank God Kayla hadn't come by for some obscure reason. She would have had a fit.

Banks pushed the door open and felt along the walls as if blind, looking for the light switch.

When the cold shack lit up, he stared in disbelief. It looked as if it had been hit by a hurricane. All the drawers in the ancient desk had been emptied onto the floor and couch. The dirty linoleum floor was covered with old charter tickets. The aeronautical charts had been opened or torn off the walls and tossed into the surrounding mess. He rummaged through one of the drawers sitting on the floor and found an old flashlight. The batteries were on their last leg and he fired a dim yellow beam into the back storage room. It looked untouched.

Every winter, they experienced at least one break-in. Usually the only thing touched was the phone. Young kids getting their jollies by phoning Luscious Lucy on a 1-900 number. Travis picked up the phone. Dead. It had been torn from the wall jack. This wasn't the adolescent porno gang's normal method of operation.

He shook the flashlight and temporarily revived the dying yellow beam. There was no door or electric light in the back room. With twenty hours of daylight in the summer, it was never a pressing concern. A two-foot-square window on the back wall of the storage room offered only a scant ray of light from one of the floodlights perched high above the Schwatka Dam. He inched forward through the doorway. He silently vowed that this was the year he would get one of the mechanics to wire lights in the back room.

To the left, he could barely discern the rack cluttered with overalls stained with moose blood and diesel fuel. To the right were banks of dark-stained shelves. On the first row of shelves sat various aviation motor oils for the aircraft. Travis knew little of the old airplane parts and assorted other junk that sat on the other shelves recessed in the darkness at the back of the room. He rarely found cause to venture into the back shadows. There was no need to. There was nothing of any importance.

The old flooring creaked. Banks stood motionless. He hadn't moved. The sound seemed to emanate from somewhere in the dark shadows in the back. He had been on edge since the discovery of Ed Bellichek's body at Primrose Lake and smirked inwardly at his overactive imagination. He started to straighten up when the old flooring creaked again. He stopped breathing and strained his ears until they hurt, trying to zero in on the location of the noise. Continuing to stare into the darkness, he allowed his mental inventory of the building to direct his hand near the doorjamb and grasp hold of a spare Cessna 185 EDO paddle used in the summer to direct the float airplanes in tight confines. His sense of panic began to grow. The flashlight had to be shaken every few seconds to stay alive. The weak yellow light would extinguish any second. He shone the feeble beam into the darkness searching for the source of his anxiety. The faint track of light from the dying flashlight could barely illuminate objects beyond his own reach.

With the stealth of a jaguar and with the oar in hand, Banks slid into the first row of petroleum products. Nothing. The second row was even darker. He labored his eyes to focus down the second row. Another sense rushed forward, disturbing his belief that he was alone, the olfactory animal instinct everyone possesses but rarely use—the smell of another creature's glands expressing fright. It was possibly the same adrenaline scent that had been left at McMaster's house thirty minutes earlier. Banks raised the oar slightly. He inched toward the final coal-black row of shelves. He was overcome with a sense of uneasiness. He desperately wanted to walk away but felt more peril by turning away and leaving than facing the unknown.

In his youth, Banks had played football as a linebacker. His size had saved him in more than his share of run-ins. But he could see his adversaries in those cases. At this moment, he could see nothing. He peered down the last dark aisle. It was an obscure, oily cave. A final row of shelves lined the left side of the aisle. The shelves' contents were impossible to discern, just shadowy outlines of inanimate objects. The grimy south wall of the shack lined the right side.

Banks slowly extended his neck, straining his eyes to absorb any remaining shafts of light. As his eyes traveled from the floor to the ceiling, they stopped on a microcosm of light sparkling from the reflection of the dam's floodlights. The bush pilot recognized the outline of a pair of very distinct Inuit mukluks. There were no mukluks stored in the float base. Above the leather hide outline, he could scarcely make out the silhouette of a man, a silhouette that suddenly came to life. Banks barely had enough time to raise the paddle. The first blow from the intruder crashed into the wooden handle of the oar. Travis was able to grasp the assailant by the sleeve and pull him out of the aisle toward the light of the small rear window. With all the strength his adrenaline could muster, he spun the attacker around. At the end of the pirouette, he let go. The stranger flew against the north wall of the shack. Banks raced at the intruder raising his oar. The roar of the blood pounding in his ears was deafening enough to drown out the hydro station's generators. Banks' ferocity was now fueled by fear, not by confidence in his large frame. He reached his enemy in mid stride. His foe was lying on his back and, at the last instant, he kicked up his left foot.

Travis' groin was met with a thunderous blow. The searing pain engulfed his entire being and he instantly fell to the floor, too overcome to even cry out in pain. His instinct of self-preservation became his driving motivating force. He feared for his life. Using the paddle as a crutch, Travis pushed himself up onto one knee. Waves of nausea washed over him. His foe circled around the room before the wet leather of mukluks took a step back and came smashing against his head, soccer-style. Banks crashed onto the hard, oily floor. Blood and sweat trickled down his forehead and burned the open wounds on his face as the mixture encircled his eyes. Through the corner of his bloody left eye, he could see the uninvited guest slink down and stare at Banks' bruised temple.

The room fell silent except for the labored breathing of its two occupants. The attacker slid forward perching himself on one knee. He reached forward, taking a handful of Travis' hair, and pulled up the pilot's head. Travis feigned unconsciousness, picking his moment. The image of Ed Bellichek's frozen, half-submerged, and tattered body steamrolled through Banks' mind like a freight train. There was no time to think, just respond. The initial fear of death had passed and anger now ruled supreme. He wanted to kill the son of a bitch who lurked over him. The old football player dug into his linebacker memories and concentrated on the visceral rage the coaches had instilled into him before each game. The hate. The desire to rip someone's head off.

Travis' fingers, opposite to the attacker, surreptitiously crawled across the shadows until gripping the Cessna 185 oar. He clutched the handle with such zeal, the blood rushed from his fingers, turning his knuckles white. With all the force he could muster, in one swift motion, Banks arched his back and drove the wooden handle into the groin of his surprised attacker. The dark silhouette of his enemy screamed, groaned, and fell backward rocking on the floor, clutching between his legs. Banks took the opportunity to force his body up and quickly twist the oar around so the flat horizontal blade resembled a huge butter knife. The dark figure slowly began unfolding and rising from the floor. Travis wound up fully intending to kill his nemesis. With a decapitating swing, Banks grunted like a shot-putter, slicing the oar through space and slamming it into the neck of the intruder. The thud of flesh was an ovation to his aim. The side of the shack shuddered as the reeling dark silhouette crashed into the wall. Amazingly, the bastard started rising again, his hand clutching the side of his neck. Banks balanced on the oar's handle.

The two debilitated figures stared at one another, too exhausted to move. Travis was beginning to black out when his foe slowly began to back out toward the small office in the other room. Unable to intercede and give chase, Banks allowed the attacker to stagger out the office door and flee into the dark freezing night. When the last stumbling footsteps could no longer be heard in the foggy consciousness of the beleaguered pilot's mind, he let go, veering to the right. He collapsed painlessly onto the oily, encrusted floor and listened to the whining noise of the snowmobile's engine disappear into the roar of the hydro dam's rumbling turbines.

Powell disliked the Airport Chalet to begin with. The fact that Banks was a half-hour late only exacerbated his foul mood. Travis' snooping around in Yellowknife for information on Ed Bellichek, the principal in an ongoing police investigation, made Powell even more cantankerous. McMaster and Powell stared at one another waiting for the wayward pilot. It was not a very happy "Happy Hour."

Of all the drinking establishments in Whitehorse, Powell preferred meeting his two friends at the Klondike Inn, not the Chalet. The Klondike was a cavernous, dimly lit bar in which an individual could be inconspicuous for a lifetime. It was a hole-in-the-wall where he was anonymous. He could relax. But not at the Airport Chalet lounge where, according to him, it was one big happy "disgusting, interbred" airport family. No strangers to socialize with, just one large incestuous family. He constantly ribbed Banks that he recognized cast members from the movie *Deliverance*. From eavesdropping on conversations in the past, he was sure that everybody had slept with everybody else. Powell's wife was forever pestering him about an RCMP constable being seen in public at a bar, especially at the Chalet. As if police didn't drink. Dale was forever teasing Powell that cops drank more than everybody else combined. They just had to hide it.

Powell was here tonight only because Travis had located Bellichek's brother.

Staff Sergeant Powell was tired of waiting for Banks. Dale had informed Powell about the break-in at his apartment and the constable was convinced it was simply a random act of bored kids with nothing to do. Especially considering that nothing but some negatives were taken. Powell, knowing Dale, assumed the negatives were pornographic.

Powell also informed McMaster that they found absolutely nothing new at Primrose Lake. He did add that it was odd that Radcliff had spent the better part of an entire day looking under every snowflake for a moose dropping or something else that might explain the last moments of Ed Bellichek's disgusting life. They had come across a formed perch on a ridge near the cabin where someone may have sat looking down on the lake and Bellichek's cabin, but eventually came to the consensus that it was only a moose's lair. After that, they spent only twenty minutes looking over Bellichek's cabin and the surrounding area.

The snowmobile tracks Banks had seen were gone. It had snowed at the lake during the night covering any evidence of Travis' theory. Radcliff dismissed the pilot's postulation as the product of an overactive imagination. Whether or not the tracks were still there wouldn't matter to Banks. He knew what he had seen the day before. The pictures from Dale's camera would be all the proof he needed.

They had waited for nearly an hour when Banks slowly limped into the Chalet lounge through the door leading to the parking lot. He was applying a compress on his right temple. It was a grease rag wrapped around a snowball.

"Jesus, Travis . . ." Dale pushed the table out from the wall. "Are you all right?"

"Sorry I'm late, fellas." Travis gingerly slipped behind the wooden table, seeking the soft vinyl bench along the wall.

"What in God's name happened to you?" Powell took Banks' forearm and helped him land.

"Nothing really. Just can't stop chasing cars," he exhaled and paused before becoming serious. "I interrupted some Neanderthal at the float base who was looking for something."

Charlie Charlie came prancing over with a drink and a smile for his favorite pilot. When he saw the lump on the side of Banks' face, he wadded up the bill perched on the edge of the table and tossed it into the fire. Perfect. Charlie Charlie had someone who could party all night long with him for medicinal reasons. All tax deductible. Travis became a charity right before their eyes.

Banks slowly raised his head and looked up at the other two men. "Where are those prints, Dale?"

McMaster slid the pictures toward his injured friend. He glanced through the seemingly innocuous prints.

The bush pilot looked at the police constable. "Remember the film, Leon? Dale had the negatives stolen tonight from his apartment. The other film was taken from the float base. Are you still going to call what's going on around here a damn coincidence?"

"What was on the film that was so important?" Powell questioned Dale.

Banks answered with a snap, tossing the benign prints across the table at Powell. "Who knows? Just another winter in paradise."

Powell wanted to ignore Travis, but it was getting harder to dismiss what was happening. He was beginning to wonder himself what exactly had transpired at Primrose Lake and how and why McMaster and Banks were involved.

The off-duty cop faced Banks again. "Did you see . . .?"

"No idea who it was, Powell," Travis knew the question before it was asked. "Too dark. It was like ant shit on pepper in that back room at the float base. It's too much of a coincidence. It's got to be the same guy who ransacked Dale's apartment. Anyway, he won't enjoy a date anytime soon. He's got an Cessna 185 oar tattooed on his privates. I rocked the bastard's family jewels hard enough to make his grandkids dizzy." Banks found solace in the memory.

Dale grinned at his friend's recollection and licked a Zig Zag cigarette paper, sealing a hand-rolled smoke.

Travis sipped his beer and felt the welt swelling on the side of his head.

McMaster piped up, "You need to see Michelle. That's a nasty lump."

"You think that's swollen." Travis peered between his legs. "If only you could manage swelling like this, Dale, you'd sell a lot more brushes," he smiled painfully. "I'll be all right." A moment later, Banks dropped the smile and gave Powell a nasty glare. The Staff Sergeant had to wake up and smell the coffee soon. Hopefully before someone else got hurt.

Powell saw Banks boring in and wouldn't budge. "I told you to stay out of this Bellichek business, Travis." He straightened up and instinctively waved Dale's cigarette smoke out of his face. "Have you told me everything about Yellowknife?" Powell was agitated, confused, and trying too hard to defend the RCMP.

"You're not answering my question, Leon." Travis pressed. "Did you tell Radcliff about Dale's pictures?"

The big cop leaned forward and lowered his voice, "No. But what difference does it make? He saw Dale with the camera. Even if he hadn't seen them, I would have told him. Jesus, Travis, he's in charge of this police detachment. He's entitled to *any* and *all* information I receive. McMaster shouldn't have been out there at a crime scene with a camera in the first place."

"If you recall, Powell, we were there first. Before we even knew it was a crime scene. Like you said yourself, Radcliff saw the camera and didn't give a shit."

"He might have, if he knew you were starting your own investigation."

"I thought I was just delivering groceries, for Christ's sake. Had I known we were going to land in the middle of a homicide, I would have told Dale to leave the goddamn Nikon at home," the agitated pilot growled sarcastically.

Banks was growing tired of Powell's unwavering support of Nick Radcliff.

Powell's face reddened. "Travis, listen to me, and listen closely. I've known you a long time. We're friends. But this is my career," he warned. "I don't have a choice. The death of Ed Bellichek is an open case still under investigation. I told you yesterday to stay out of it! I can't believe you went snooping around Yellowknife." He took a deep breath and paused. "Jesus, Banks, I'm trying to do you a favor. I can't save your ass if you tangle with Radcliff. He already dislikes you. Yesterday didn't help."

"Leon, someone just tried to beat the crap out of me over some seemingly meaningless pictures that only five people knew existed. The first person is the student RCMP pilot who probably can't find his way home from the airport. Two of the others, you and Dale, were sitting here staring at one another while I bounced off the walls down at Schwatka Lake. That's four out of five. Grade one math tells you who's left."

Banks wanted to tell his racquetball foe more about Yellowknife, but not until Powell's love affair with protecting fellow cops was over.

"What are you saying, Travis?" Powell laughed. "Inspector Nick Radcliff, commander of the Whitehorse RCMP detachment, is actually a slasher who beats people up for pictures of snowmobile tracks?"

On the surface, it sounded ridiculous. But Powell didn't have the information the men across the table had dug up earlier at the Yellowknife library.

"I don't know what it means yet, but it might be too late to ask us not to get involved." Banks pointed at the swelling near his temple.

"I'll go with you to the Regina Hotel only because I know you're going anyway and I'm off duty. Which won't save my ass if Radcliff finds out. After that, you're finished as a private dick. Understand? Any information I get tonight, I'm going to use tomorrow. If you want to become a philanthropist and locate the families of dead people, move away from here or wait until we've finished our investigation."

Banks glared at the Staff Sergeant. Travis thought he'd taken his tongue-lashing rather well except for the one brief instant about "private dick." At that point, he'd have given his paltry kingdom to drive a racquetball into Leon Powell where the sun never shines.

Banks realized that for the time being, Powell needed to believe they had delivered all the goods from Yellowknife. Travis wasn't going to mention Kelly Margaret Radcliff, the dead little girl, or the fact that Bellichek and possibly Nick Radcliff, stood inches apart twenty years ago on the police station steps in Yellowknife. He trusted Powell, but not anyone he worked with. The information on the younger Bellichek was the only information Banks would divulge. At least for now. Maybe Brock Bellichek could fill Powell in on Nick Radcliff's family history and save Travis the trouble.

Charlie Charlie unwillingly took their money and nearly broke down in tears. He thought they were there for the duration.

They all got into Dale's truck and headed downtown to the Regina Hotel to find Brock Bellichek.

The manager of the Regina Hotel knew perfectly well who Brock Bellichek was but hadn't seen him since early the previous night. He said the three men could probably find Brock at the Fifty Below Zero Tavern. First, they went upstairs in the old hotel and knocked on the younger Bellichek's door. There was no answer. Travis suggested they peek into his room but Powell lifted the side of his jacket exposing his handcuffs. Banks saw the look in his friend's eye. Powell would probably arrest him if he stuck his nose into Bellichek's room.

They left the truck parked at the hotel and walked the west sidewalk the two blocks to the seedy tavern.

It was eight o'clock and the place was a quarter full. It didn't start attracting its vile patrons until after every other bar in Whitehorse was closed. The bartender was doing some preparations before another episode of "Wild Kingdom" began. He wiped down the bar and ignored the three men until Travis spoke up. Powell didn't want to be seen in the decrepit bar while he was off duty and slid into the shadows.

"What'll it be?" The bartender was busy but acted jovial. The three men were the best-dressed patrons the joint had ever seen and the barkeep had visions of a big tip.

Banks leaned across the still damp counter. "I'm looking for Brock Bellichek."

"So am I." He smiled.

"Is he here?"

"If he was, he'd be at the top of the stairs stuffed into a snow bank." The bartender's demeanor took a momentary sharp turn. "That son of a bitch walked out of here again last night without paying."

"Do you know where I might find him?"

"No idea." He eyed Banks as he pulled glasses from a putrid-smelling sink full of brownish suds. "Who's asking?"

Travis felt like he was in a grade B detective movie. This guy might have total disdain for the Bellichek boys, but they probably paid his salary single-handed. "I work up at the airport and have some news concerning his brother."

"Ed?" The bartender smiled at some distant recollection.

"You know him?"

"A little. He's an oddball. Doesn't say much. When he's in town, both he and Brock live here at nights. Haven't seen him since he went back to his trapline. Brock may not show up tonight."

"Why's that?"

"He's probably still sleeping. He always gets shit-faced, but last night was worse than usual. He got so drunk he could barely walk." He flipped a dishrag in the air that had been following him around on his shoulder and pointed. "Brock sat right over there in the corner and tied one on. Problem was, he left without paying. It ain't the first time. The upside is he never remembers. The next day, when he shows up and gets plastered, I just take what he owes for both nights and he don't know the difference. Have you tried the Regina?"

"They haven't seen him either."

"What about their cabin up the river?"

This was news to Banks. "Their cabin?"

"He and his brother have a cabin twenty miles up the Yukon River just off Wickstrom Road, on the east shore of the river, where Labarge starts. They tan pelts, raise sled dogs, get drunk; hell, I don't know what they do at that cabin and I don't want to know."

Travis thanked the guy with a $5 bill and decided never to see the inside of the Fifty Below Zero Tavern again.

The three men climbed the stairs out of the filthy bar and looked up and down the street. Travis filled in the other two on what little information the bartender had divulged about Ed Bellichek's little brother.

Powell spoke first. "Well, gentlemen, he left here early this morning and never made it back to his room. What's that tell us?"

"It doesn't tell us anything." Dale was cold and tired. The only thing on his mind was bed. "Bellichek could have found a ride, passed out somewhere else, or driven to his cabin without the Regina knowing. Let's call it a night and look tomorrow."

Banks didn't say anything. He was becoming more and more suspicious every time something happened that was out of the ordinary. The hotel manager stated it was unusual for Bellichek not to return in the winter.

They walked down the opposite sidewalk toward the truck parked at the Regina. Passing an alley off to his right, one block from the hotel, Banks spotted the oil and the familiar tracks. He slowed and, without saying anything, followed the tracks in a large circle. The traffic during the day had obliterated most of the tracks in the center of the street but not the impressions near the curb, or the ones leading over the bank of the Yukon River.

"Dale, look here." He pointed to the lug tracks approaching the curb and the banks of the river.

"What?"

"Look familiar? Those are the same tracks I saw at Primrose."

"I can't see anything." Dale bent over, eyeing the ground. He finally stood back and took in the whole image. "All right. Maybe. But look at the middle of the tracks."

Banks could see what McMaster was studying. "They're all wiped out. Like they were towing something."

Powell had joined them and could see the tracks by the riverbank. He saw what the other two were pointing at and could no longer deny the obvious.

"Maybe he was."

Banks looked up the Yukon River that wound like a white snake into the dark toward Lake Labarge. It slowly disappeared into the expansive Arctic night.

Travis glanced at his watch under his parka's sleeve. "It's too late to drive up to his cabin tonight."

The three of them quietly stared at the aurora borealis dancing colorfully across the Yukon skyline, their thoughts remaining within themselves. It was deathly quiet and serene. The peacefulness of the moment reminded the aging Banks why he had returned to the North. His senses relished the import of the image engulfing him, a sensual experience few ever encounter. His eyes smiled brightly at the aurora's beauty. He could smell the stark winter that encompassed the three of them, a winter that could ravage as well as seduce.

"You might find your next of kin at that cabin, Powell." Dale spoke slowly.

Leon turned away and headed for Dale's truck. "That's what I'm afraid of."

The events of the past two days had worn on all of them. Travis didn't want to think about the possibilities that lay up the river at Bellichek's cabin. Tomorrow he would head up there, but only after eight hours of sleep.

"Dale?" Travis' mind was twenty-four hours ahead.

"Yea?" McMaster didn't look up.

"Is your suit dry-cleaned?"

DAY 3

THE LIEUTENANT had the atrium doors wide open. The sweet aroma of Danish coffee and fresh-baked scones filled the air of both halves of the duplex. The delightful bouquet had even found its way up the stairs and into Banks' bedroom.

He had been sound asleep, dreaming about the boss. They were sitting up in bed about to eat warm scones. The two of them acted silly and casual with each other as if they had spent the night making wild passionate love. Their hair was disheveled and the sheets were tossed about. Like every dream it was too good to be true. Travis had no memory of the sex part—the dream hadn't begun until all the torrid sex was over. Typical. He finally sleeps with his beautiful boss, albeit in his dreams, and all he could remember was serving her breakfast in bed and doing the dishes. Regrettably, the pulsating swollen groin he was now experiencing was not caused from the pleasurable effect of his romantic dream, but rather the result of his family jewels being used for soccer practice the previous evening.

The sugary scent of Monty's breakfast had awakened the sleepy pilot five minutes earlier. He lay in bed smiling over his dream but kept his legs comfortably apart to accommodate his healing midsection. He eyed the plastic dry-cleaning bag hanging in his closet, wondering about the possibilities for later that evening.

On his night table were the prints Dale had managed to salvage from Primrose Lake. Banks fluffed his favorite pillow, sat up in bed, picked up the prints and studied each one closely.

Dale was an excellent photographer. He preferred high-speed film because of the time he spent in airplanes. One picture he snapped on their trip to Primrose was amazing. McMaster had shot over the Beaver's nose at a Dall sheep standing alertly on the jagged edge of a steep cliff. Not only was the sheep crystal clear in his majestic stance, the exposure showed two blades of the aircraft's propeller perfectly motionless and exact. The loader's photographic skill was remarkable.

On the third time through the stack of prints, Banks noticed an odd rock, or bush, in the corner of one frame. It had a clear or opaque center, and didn't look like anything he'd seen Mother Nature produce. It had been taken with a zoom lens. Maybe Dale could use his photographic expertise to clear up the image.

Travis looked at his watch. He had plenty to do before his date. Mindful of his injuries, he gingerly showered and dressed.

Banks' timing was always impeccable. He arrived at the exact instant Monty's Aga stove gave birth to a dozen steaming brown angels. It was the only recipe the Lieutenant had memorized from his beloved wife's English cookbook, and for good reason—Mindy's scones were a slice of breakfast heaven. They were so delectable that when one was inserted into your mouth, you lost all control of your eyelids. They automatically shut as if the brain wanted nothing more than to concentrate on the warm dough rolling around the inside of your mouth. Best of all, it kept Banks from Charlie Charlie's delicious but cholesterol-laden breakfast. Still, the scones were a treat his flight surgeon suggested he indulge in only several times a year if Travis intended to keep his first-class airman's physical.

Monty was up and about, lathered up in Brut aftershave and impeccably dressed. He had even trimmed the almost imperceptibly thin line of gray hair he referred to as a mustache that marked the midpoint between his upper lip and his nose. Picking his moment, Banks would inaccurately point out that Monty had missed a spot shaving. The perfectly groomed gentleman couldn't take the risk of not looking in the mirror, even if he knew his accuser was Banks, a teasing louse. The Lieutenant would excuse himself, rush to the mirror, and come back moments later grumbling about Banks' childish Yankee humor. It was the least Travis could do. It would be his last jab before the Lieutenant spent the rest of the morning criticizing Banks' flying.

Monty was anxious to finish breakfast, get to the airport, and act as Banks' copilot and pseudo-check airman. It was a routine the two had played out many times. The old RAF pilot would be polite for several minutes with the staff at Arctic Air and then wait until they were alone in the airplane. At some point, usually during the taxi, Monty would suddenly turn into Charles Lindbergh and gamely criticize Banks' "Yankee" airmanship while trying to overhaul all of Travis' aeronautical bad habits. This would persist all the way to their destination, which this morning was Finlayson Lake. Travis had forgotten about the invitation he had extended to Monty the day before. There were no passengers, just freight, and the Apex mining camp was a regular customer and never objected to him bringing the Lieutenant.

Banks was not sure what had bothered him more during the night. It was either what they might find at Brock Bellichek's cabin near Lake Labarge or having to face Michelle Baker about his promised date that evening with Kayla Jackson.

Travis had made a conscious effort over the years never to delve into that murky part of his brain that contained the twisted remnants of Psychology 100 and its perverted hillbilly cousin Psychology 200. They were mandatory courses, required mental gymnastics for every university student. Regrettably, no matter how hard he tried, he wasn't able to purge the psychobabble Freudian crap from his system. The end result was, when he least wanted it, Psycho 100 reared its ugly head to inform him just how dysfunctional and insecure he was concerning some insignificant fact about which he couldn't care less about. Right now, Banks' college memory was lecturing him about the true reason he felt trepidation about the approaching evening. It wasn't the fear of informing Doc Baker; it was that he was looking forward to his evening with Kayla Jackson. Whatever it was, he hadn't slept worth a damn.

Travis walked into Monty's breakfast nook and took a seat by the foggy picture window. The Lieutenant already had the fireplace stoked up and roaring in the living room. The heat radiated warmly on Travis' back. The peaceful gray winter morning could barely be seen through the half-dead ferns sprawled across the opaque frozen glass above the old white enamel sink. Banks had little desire to fly this morning. The thought of staying in front of the Lieutenant's fire drinking Guinness Stout all day and arguing about damn Yankees was far more appealing.

Travis tried to sound awake and cheery in the only European accent that came to mind. He sat and added sugar to his coffee. "Top of the morning to ya, Lieutenant."

"Jesus Christ, Travis," Monty stopped dead in his tracks and jerked his head up in Banks' direction. "The only thing more aggravating than a bleeding Yankee first thing in the morning is a goddamn Irishman. Pick another accent, will you?"

It was going to be a long day. Apparently, the Lieutenant hadn't slept well either.

Monty opened the oven door of the old copper- and ceramic-covered Aga stove. "How many of these damn things are you going to eat today?"

"Two will be fine, thanks."

"Right." He stared at Banks incredulously. "That's what you said last week and you ate a bleeding half-dozen." He dropped the hot pan on the counter and placed several steaming scones in a red-and-white checkered cloth-lined basket. Moments later, lathered in marmalade, the first one slid into Travis' mouth and danced harmoniously with his pallet. They sat in silence enjoying breakfast.

The ringing phone was barely audible in Banks' half of the duplex. He excused himself temporarily and trotted quickly back through their communal doors into his seldom-used kitchen. Pratt and Whitney had been eyeing Monty's half of the atrium but knew better than to enter. The Lieutenant had made it clear—Travis was invited but the "bleeding rodents" were not. They had invaded Monty's side once a long time ago, and although Travis had no idea what had happened, the cats now eyed Monty's home as if a dozen feline-eating pit bulls drooled and lurked around each corner of a house of horrors.

Banks wasn't able to beat the answering machine. It kicked on and began playing his unique version of "Hi, I'm not home now but if you leave your name and number . . ." Rick Meyers, the owner of Northern Tracks, cursed and began leaving his message. Travis managed to pick up before Rick hung up.

Rick's shop was the Yukon's best snowmobile repair business. He had worked hard to make it profitable. Meyers had had to give up coffee the year after he opened. The first year in business he consumed enough java to positively affect the gross national product of Colombia. Besides not sleeping for the better part of a calendar year, he invented an array of new gastrointestinal anomalies not yet to be discovered in any medical journals. He convinced himself, while teetering near bankruptcy, that the coffee bean, alone, contained enough nourishment to sustain human life. Several hundred gallons of cherry-flavored Maalox later and two lengthy hospital stays, he recovered enough to acknowledge the errors of his lifestyle and give up the coffee bean. Instead, he found a new life-sustaining substance. Cigarettes. He now smoked three packs of unfiltered butts a day. Banks barely got out a hello before Rick started talking. Travis could hear the smoke billowing out of Meyer's mouth and into his ear via the phone lines.

"Travis? Rick here. Remember that Polaris 440 you called about?"

"Yeah."

"If you want to meet the guy who ordered the oil sump for it you better hurry up and get down here. He just phoned and said he'll pick it up 'this week.' For your benefit, I lied and told him that wasn't good enough. If he didn't get here today before noon," he paused and told a customer he would be right with them before continuing, "I was sending it back to Edmonton. I told him I couldn't keep inventory lying around for unpopular machines . . . some line of bullshit. Anyway, that seemed to get his attention. He was a bit pissed off but finally agreed to come over and get it. He said he'd be here any minute."

"Do me a favor? If I'm late, get a name, address, phone number, anything so I can find out who this guy is."

"I'm a little swamped right now. I'll see what I can do. Get your butt down here and you can talk to him yourself. Gotta go." He hung up the phone.

Banks knew it was a long shot but it was all he had. He was sure Ed Bellichek had been murdered. Bellichek's brother, Brock, was missing. The head of the local RCMP detachment, Inspector Nick Radcliff, had a brother, Simon Radcliff, who was also a cop. Nick and Simon's sister,

Solange, had died at an early age from God knows what, and the remains of Simon's daughter, Kelly Margaret Radcliff, had recently been discovered in Yellowknife, which was about the same time Inspector Nick Radcliff transferred to Whitehorse. Banks had a grainy newspaper photo that might possibly be the Bellichek and Radcliff brothers side by side twenty years ago. The problem was Nick Radcliff denied any surviving family. Banks had been beaten up over some pictures of snowmobile tracks. The only link between the death of Ed Bellichek and the disappearance of his brother Brock was the snowmobile that leaked oil and rode on metal lugs. All this might be inextricably connected by whoever owned the snowmobile. Granted, it might simply be a coincidence. But what were the odds that the owner of the snowmobile was at both scenes on the days in question, and didn't know anything about it? Unlikely. Whoever owned the Polaris 440 should at least be able to answer a few questions.

Banks hurried back into Monty's kitchen, grabbing his parka along the way. Pratt and Whitney were unusually bold and were peeking around the corner of Monty's living room. Banks asked the Lieutenant to call Dale—the Lieutenant referred to him as "Travis' horny little friend"—and have him meet Banks five minutes ago at Northern Tracks. Dale would know what it was about. Banks then needed Monty to call Kayla and explain that he was running a few minutes behind and would be at the airport shortly. With no passengers going to Finlayson Lake, Travis knew it wouldn't be a problem. He apologized for rushing off during his wonderful breakfast but Travis assured Monty he would pick him up on the way back to the airport. The Lieutenant nodded silently and handed Banks one scone "to go" while helping him out the door. Monty had another scone clenched in his left fist.

As soon as the door closed Travis heard its purpose: feline target practice. Banks knew the old man wouldn't hurt the cats but he would certainly get their attention. There was the sound of a piping hot scone hitting a wall followed by a squeal as either Pratt or Whitney retreated quickly back into their half of the duplex. If Doc Baker knew that Banks let Monty use the cats as scone target practice, he was sure that getting her approval to escort Ms. Jackson to dinner that night would be no problem because she would never talk to Banks again. Travis smiled at the thought of the Lieutenant running around the duplex trying, in vain, to catch his stealthy and agile cats. Banks jumped into his cold truck and fired up the engine. He would be downtown at Northern Tracks in less than ten minutes.

Rick Meyers's shop was on Second Avenue near the river. It sat across the street from the modern, square, three-story glass and darkly stained cedar creature known as the Yukon Government Building. Northern Tracks was a single-story, white stucco building with a small room protruding from the side, probably the original pick-up point of an old drive-through. It was next to the town's oldest fast-food joint, a KFC. A&W had actually arrived first with one of their historic drive-ins but it had closed years earlier. Someone in A&W's marketing department had found that people in the far reaches of the Northern Hemisphere did, in fact, enjoy a big greasy burger, but failed to take into account that a hamburger freezes rather quickly sitting on an open tray in fifty below-zero weather. The cost alone to provide the waitresses with snow tire-clad roller skates and asbestos-lined underwear probably turned the venture into a losing proposition. It was a terrible miscalculation on A&W's part. The same inept sales expert was now either attempting to market Jewish ice cream in Lebanon or had joined the competition, making buckets of McMoney.

Banks pulled into the back of Rick's shop where the parking lot was hidden from the street. If there was any possibility that Radcliff was involved he didn't want to be seen. He wasn't planning on being there very long and didn't plug in the heaters.

Banks knocked twice on the back door, pulled the latch, and was met by a wall of warm air mixed with cigarette smoke. Rick was cursing and swearing with a cigarette hanging from his lips and two more smoldering in ashtrays around his blackened workbench. He used his forearm to wipe the sweat from his brow and barely glanced in Travis' direction to see who had caused the intrusion. He had a small chain saw engine tightly clenched in the jaws of a bench vise and was attempting to loosen a corroded nut. Based on the language spewing from his lips, he was not having much luck.

Rick looked up at the receding bruise on the side of Banks' head. "I assume the other guy's dead?"

"I hope he's here," Travis responded.

"You're late." He barked from the side of his mouth without removing the cigarette bouncing around the middle of his black goatee.

"I got here as quick as I could."

"Wasn't quick enough. The guy's gone."

"Damn." His arms fell to his side in anger and frustration. "Did you talk to him? Did you recognize him?" Travis looked over Rick's shoulder toward the front, past the saloon-style swinging doors. He was hoping the stranger might have come back for some unknown reason, but he didn't know what he was looking for. His imagination was in overdrive, conjuring up some big, hairy, dirty creature with a beard and bloody leghold traps hanging all over his shoulders.

"I thought you were going to hang onto him until I got here." Travis' disappointment was palpable and his frustration boiled over.

"First of all, Travis, I'm not in the habit of forcibly detaining my customers. Secondly, I went outside to run this sorry piece of shit." He indicated the engine locked in his vice by whacking it with a three-eighths-inch open-ended wrench. "Anyway, Sammy up front sold him the part. Hell, if you'd stop bitching at me you might still catch him. He only left a minute ago."

Banks marveled at Rick's casual attitude until it occurred to him that Rick had no idea why he was after this particular customer or what the customer may have done two days earlier at Primrose Lake.

Banks took off through the swinging doors and out the main entrance. Sammy had overheard his boss talking about his innocent mistake and felt guilty enough to stick his head out the main glass doors of Northern Tracks and give Banks a blow-by-blow portrait of the elusive customer. Travis didn't look at Sammy but he paid attention to the description that filtered in from behind. The bush pilot scanned the streets in both directions. A tall man in a brown fur-lined parka was not unusual this time of year in Whitehorse. But one with Inuit mukluks that kept his hood up and his sunglasses on while indoors was unique.

Banks spotted someone seemingly matching Sam's description. It was hard to tell. The man was two blocks away, moving in the opposite direction, turning east toward the White Pass railway station. Banks nearly knocked Sam over running back through the store to get his truck when the unmistakable sound of Dale's two-cylinder-functioning V-8 Ford banged and sputtered, limping to a crawl in front of the shop. Travis ran out into the middle of Second Avenue, rolling one arm around in a sweeping motion telling Dale not to stop. McMaster slowed down enough for Banks to jump in the passenger side door. Travis pulled himself up through the passenger window and looked back over the cab's hood at Sammy standing on the white sidewalk.

"Sammy! Did the guy limp?" Banks shouted.

Sammy shuffled forward cupping his hands over his mouth and yelled back. "How did *you* know?"

Travis gave him a thumbs-up and slid back into the warm cab.

"What's up, Sherlock?" Dale smiled and instinctively hit the gas.

"There," Banks pointed down the street toward the old rail station, "on the right-hand side of the street. Walking away from us."

Dale leaned forward toward the dash trying to follow the imaginary line beginning at the end of Banks' glove. Two blocks away there were a dozen people crossing the street and slowly navigating the treacherous wintry sidewalks. Before Dale could see what Travis was looking at, the figure turned the corner and disappeared.

"Make a right on Hemlock," Banks ordered.

Dale glanced at his passenger. "Your head looks better. How's your pecker?"

"Sore. Do you want to see it?" Banks quipped.

Dale politely declined the invitation to view Banks' injury up close, certainly not while in the confines of his dilapidated truck. With their recent luck, Leon Powell would walk up to investigate the parked vehicle and peer into the truck while the grandiose purplish viewing was in progress, an incident that would, no doubt, compel both Dale and Travis to move to different hemispheres.

"Is that the guy from Primrose?" Dale was excitedly pointing at their target now only a block away.

"Who knows? It's a guy who bought an oil tank for a Polaris 440 snowmobile. It only proves he's guilty of needing a new oil tank, not murder."

Dale had the accelerator pushed into the slushy black rubber floor mats. The view in the rearview mirror would have been disconcerting if they were in an airplane. Black and blue smoke rolled out from underneath the twenty-year-old chassis as if they had been shot down in aerial combat.

The two excited men were half a block from Hemlock when Dale's truck made a grinding mechanical noise followed by a loud bang. Banks grabbed the armrest, which was bolted loosely to the door, and felt his body stiffen with concern. If they were in an airplane, Travis would have already transmitted a Mayday and been preparing to bail out.

"Jesus, Dale, when was the last time you had a tune-up?"

Dale ignored the insult and spun the wheel quickly to the right, causing the truck to slide around Second Avenue and onto Hemlock, almost hitting another pickup traveling in the opposite direction. He punched the gas one more time, creating an ear- shattering, explosive backfire. A several-block radius had been rudely advised that there was a new hole in McMaster's muffler. The blast from the exhaust pipe was actually a blessing. Everybody on both sides of the street stopped dead in their tracks and spun around terrified, facing them, wanting to get a momentary glimpse of Armageddon's arrival. The parka-clad figure with the Inuit mukluks also came to a stop. He turned and faced the two men in the truck. Dale took his foot off the gas and coasted toward the man standing in front of an alley less than a half-block away. He was obviously startled by their interest in him, and the parka-clad image peered back at the pilot and loader, expressing more interest in them than the other pedestrians. Dale and Travis stared back, squinting, and their eyes boring into the dark shadowy face that was engulfed by the parka's wolf-trim hood and aviator-style sunglasses. As hard as they tried to recognize the stranger, it was impossible. Dale slowly steered the truck down Hemlock. They passed the man, who held the box emblazoned with the red and black logo of Northern Tracks and which contained the newly purchased oil tank. The unrecognizable figure stared back, seeming startled by their persistence. They crawled by, without stopping or turning toward the stranger.

"Do you recognize him? Is it Radcliff?" Dale asked.

"I can't tell from here, not with the sunglasses and hood up." They slowly turned ninety degrees in front of the stranger. "But he was limping."

"Fascinating, Travis," Dale uttered sarcastically. "So what?"

"I rocked someone's family jewels last night at Schwatka Lake," Banks reminded him.

"Take it easy, Banks." McMaster interrupted. "This guy might have just stepped on a nail."

Banks kept his eyes on the stranger. "Let's find out. Pull into the Edgewater Hotel."

They both craned their heads around, keeping a vigilant watch on their quarry. Dale pulled into the "For Patrons Only" parking lot at the Edgewater Hotel. The stranger hugged his package even tighter and suddenly seemed to recognize something or somebody. He quickly darted to his right and disappeared down the alley.

Without a word, McMaster and Banks jumped out of the warm truck and ran across the icy street toward the alley. Even with his delicate "injury," Banks arrived first. They saw nothing. The garbage-infested back alley was only fifty feet long and then hit a wall with a T-intersection that branched off in both directions. For a few moments, all they could hear was each other's breathing. The silence was broken by something that sounded like a couple of planks dropping on one another. It originated from the tributary of the alley that veered off to the left toward the White Pass railway station and Yukon River. They broke into a full gallop toward the noise.

As they turned the corner, sunlight became darkness as something struck Banks and McMaster from the rear. An old stained two-by-four quickly joined them on the alley floor, both men stunned and in shock. Banks slowly rolled around on the cold, icy, soaked asphalt trying to get his bearings and stand up. Neither he nor Dale had blacked out but it took a few seconds before Travis was able to help Dale to his feet. They both rubbed the backs of their heads and turned to look for the stranger.

A block away, at the end of the alley, the stranger stood, poised in a shooting stance. The two men saw the glint of blue steel twinkle in the morning sun. They both took a headlong dive into the surrounding boxes of garbage. Several gunshots rang out, the alley cracking with thunder and echoing loudly in their ears. Banks saw one bullet strike the building twenty feet above his head; brick and mortar chips cascaded onto his head and shoulders. Travis was unarmed and desperate to know if the shooter was coming back in their direction. Dale was among the garbage on the other side of the alley, facing in the opposite direction and breathing heavily. Banks slowly peeked around the corner of a trash container and exulted in the sight of the man running near the river, slowing down his sprint. The large parka-covered figure gingerly mounted a snowmobile that, being illegal in the downtown area, had to be kept at the edge of the river. McMaster and Banks slowly got up and inched in the direction of the man who had just shot at them, keeping an eye on anything that would provide cover in the event Jesse James started firing again.

Half a block away, they heard the snowmobile's screaming engine come to life. The two friends couldn't reach the stranger in time nor did they really want to. They watched as his powerful machine spun 180 degrees, spewing snow, then tore rapidly down the street before launching over the edge of the Yukon River and disappearing behind the bank. By the time McMaster and Banks made it to the White Pass station, the silhouette of the man and his machine were gone. He had either quickly exited the river toward town to the west or raced into the bushes along Wickstrom Road to the east. His tracks paralleled those from the night before until they mingled with an indistinguishable web of old snowmobile markings.

Banks looked around at the ground. The marks left behind in the ice and snow were unmistakably familiar. They were surrounded by the same metal lug tracks and leaking oil found the night before, less than a block from where they now stood. They were also the same tracks found at Primrose Lake.

"This asshole is really starting to piss me off," Dale shouted.

"He wasn't trying to shoot us," Banks observed, keeping most of his body weight on his left leg. It seemed to alleviate stress on his private parts.

"Could have fooled me." Dale was incensed.

"He fired twenty feet over our heads. He was just trying to scare us."

"Well, he fucking succeeded." Dale bent over, putting his hands on his knees, trying to catch his breath. "Jesus Christ, I've never been shot at before. And I can honestly say I didn't enjoy it. I think I need to change my shorts."

"It was him, Dale."

"Are you sure?"

"No doubt about it. I saw those same mukluks last night up close at the float base. One of them kicked me in the head. It's not something you forget quickly. But it doesn't make sense. If this is the guy who fed Bellichek to the wolves, why shoot twenty feet over our heads?"

"Maybe he's a lousy shot."

"Or maybe he's as sane as you and me but he's after someone else."

Dale stared at his friend. "Who?"

"I don't know yet." Banks looked back over both shoulders at the surrounding buildings. "I need to phone Radcliff."

"You're joking, right? You gonna tell Radcliff someone tried to shoot us? Hell, he'll probably come down here and finish the job."

"I need to see if Radcliff's at work."

Banks slowly headed toward the lobby of the Edgewater Hotel to find a pay phone. He had one thing on his mind and left Dale chasing after him. Travis knew that he might be able to answer a very important question if he moved fast enough.

The Edgewater lobby was empty at that time of the morning, a lobby that wouldn't make "Lifestyles of the Rich and Famous." It drooled of crassness, with burgundy velour walls, matching broadloom, and gold-braided ropes hanging from every corner. The rotund, bald manager was barely visible through a gray billowing cloud of cheap cigar smoke.

"Hey, you guys hear a gunshot?"

"Car backfired." Banks put his hand up to his right ear miming a phone. He stared at the silhouette behind the smoky front desk. The desk clerk pointed at a hallway leading to the men's restroom.

Travis flipped open the thin white Whitehorse phone book to the "Rs" and found the number. He placed a dime in the slot, heard the dial tone, and dialed. It was answered almost before it rang.

"Whitehorse Detachment RCMP, Constable Mike McRaney, may I help you?" McRaney's lack of enthusiasm was proof he'd been answering the phone for too many years.

Banks had phoned in the past regarding Arctic Air airplanes the RCMP had chartered. They seemed to relish the opportunity to make him wait an insufferably long period of time before someone picked up the phone. The day had just taken a turn for the worse and Banks didn't feel like waiting. He couldn't. He needed an answer quickly. The pilot cleared his throat and coaxed his voice up a couple of octaves before proceeding in his most effeminate tones.

"Hi! Is Officer Radcliff in on this beautiful day? Isn't it just a glorious day?"

The shock registering on the other end of the phone was unmistakable. Constable McRaney may have been answering the RCMP phone a long time but he had never experienced this.

"May I ask who's calling?" the officer responded.

Banks could tell a smile was creeping across McRaney's face. Travis took another deep breath. "Why, of course you can. This is Jacques!"

"Jacques?"

"Yes. Jacques!"

"Jacques who?"

"They just call me Jacques."

"I see." McRaney couldn't believe his ears. "Well, Jacques, may I ask what this is pertaining to? Inspector Radcliff is a very busy man."

"Oohhh! You're telling me! You see, I'm the manager at the Unisex Hair Salon on Third Avenue and he's supposed to have his hair done and mustache waxed this afternoon. Well," Banks paused as if he was Ed McMahon about to divulge a sweepstakes winner. "He asked me to phone him, *right away*, if I had an appointment open up any earlier. And guess what? I've got one!"

McRaney barely got out, "Hang on," and partially covered the phone before he broke out in uncontrollable laughter. Banks was sure the entire detachment knew of the call by now.

McRaney temporarily regained his composure. "I'm sorry, Jacques, but Officer Radcliff is not in yet." McRaney struggled with his amusement. "I'll have to take a message. But you can be assured I'll let him know you called the second he gets in."

"Aren't you sweet!" Banks lost a bit of his edge, wondering if Radcliff was touring around somewhere on a snowmobile while the two men were talking. "If you ever need your hair styled we offer a big discount for our men in blue and gold. There's nothing more handsome than a man in uniform! Don't you think so?"

"Yeah, sure, Jacques. Hang on a second, will you?" McRaney paused and Banks could hear him cover the receiver.

A moment later he piped up, "Jacques, you're in luck. Inspector Radcliff just stepped in. Hold on, I'll get him."

Banks wanted to hang up but not until he heard Radcliff's voice. Travis looked at his watch. It had been almost fifteen minutes since the stranger had disappeared over the banks of the Yukon River. Could Radcliff have ditched the snowmobile and made it back to the station in such a short period of time?

Banks didn't have to wait but a few seconds before the unmistakably gruff voice of Nick Radcliff started barking, short of breath, into the phone.

"Inspector Radcliff. Who is this?"

Banks kept the phone on his right ear and slowly pressed down on the chrome cradle. The Whitehorse RCMP squad room must have been in hysterics. Banks was glad they were finding this amusing. He wasn't. He looked over at Dale who was staring wantonly at the dark and seductive bar.

"Radcliff just showed up while I was on the phone. He sounded short of breath." Banks thought a moment before continuing. "It seems everybody around here is heading toward Lake Labarge." Banks pointed out the door in the general direction of the large lake north of town. "I think it's time we found Brock Bellichek."

"What about Leon?" Dale was somewhat concerned about what the law might think of their little jaunt. "He said last night he wanted to come with us."

"Don't forget, last night he was nervous about going to the Regina Hotel looking for Brock Bellichek. I'm not interested in getting him in anymore hot water with Radcliff. The less he knows about this trip to Labarge the better. I'll fill him in when we get back. Besides, I'm like you. This jerk on the snowmobile is getting under my skin. There's no law preventing us from going for a drive. Is there?"

Banks placed another dime in the phone and dialed Arctic Air. He successfully requested Kayla commandeer somebody else to fly the Finlayson Lake trip. Monty would be disappointed but there would be ample opportunities for him to denounce Banks' flying skills at a later date.

Kayla easily found a substitute pilot to fly the Finlayson Lake charter. Hal Reynolds was hanging around the hanger, as usual, looking to pick up any garbage trips that fell into his lap.

Hal Reynolds was an enigma. He was a middle-aged pilot who seemed to have been conceived in some strange genetic experiment using Captain Kangaroo and Mr. McGoo as parents. There were stunning physical and personal similarities: he was endowed with a monstrous bulbous nose and without his glasses; he was as blind as a bat. He loved kids and his wardrobe was mostly army and navy surplus. He hadn't started flying until his early forties. He took his entire retirement account, built over twenty years of teaching in the slums of east Los Angeles, and cashed it all in for a commercial pilot's license. Everyone at Arctic Air considered it the strangest midlife crisis anyone had ever heard of.

It occurred to him one day that teaching grade three science to high school kids wasn't fulfilling. He managed the last five years as a teacher by being continually plastered and owning a dog willing to be kicked every day at four in the afternoon when he staggered home. It nearly ruined his marriage of twenty-five years. His wife, Mary, a veritable angel, was about to leave him when the metamorphosis took place. She actually encouraged him to switch careers in midlife. He was much too old for consideration by the airlines but that had never been his ambition. He was happier now than he had ever been and constantly gushed about his newfound career to anybody willing to listen. Every experienced pilot was aware that Hal's enthusiasm would eventually wane. Meantime, it was mildly refreshing and often entertaining.

Kayla had hired him the previous year out of sympathy, more than anything else. His experience level was marginal at best. But he was sober, stable, had a loving supporting family, and would probably stay with Arctic Air for years—a pleasing thought for Ms. Jackson who, like all small operators, was tired of paying for the training of every young airline pilot. He was affable, likable and respected the younger and more experienced pilots. He listened well and was a quick study. Those two qualities alone might keep him alive long enough to enjoy a normal retirement as a bush pilot in the North. Hal Reynolds was one of the most agreeable local pilots, probably because he hadn't been a bush pilot long and this job was, more than likely, the pinnacle of his career. Banks often wondered how long it would be before he could convince Kayla and the insurance company to make Hal Reynolds the chief pilot.

He had taken off within minutes of Banks' phone call and was now somewhere between Whitehorse and Finlayson Lake, whistling and smiling over the dash of the Beaver's round cowling.

Kayla didn't bother to dig into the reasons why Banks had willingly let a lucrative trip slip through his fingers. Luckily, she also released Dale for the day. Travis liked the idea of company, considering the isolation of Bellichek's cabin on Lake Labarge.

Kayla must have assumed Banks was on a clandestine shopping spree to buy a new suit and some Hi Karate cologne for their date, now only hours away. Which reminded him that he still had the unpleasant task of informing Doc Baker.

Travis knew the RCMP would be paying the cabin a visit sometime during the day, and he wanted to get there first. Once Radcliff got hold of Ed Bellichek's younger brother, Brock, he would be off limits. What Banks and McMaster had learned in Yellowknife would remain a mystery. They needed a head start, so Banks would talk to Michelle on his return. If he caught her just as she was waking up after eight hours of sleep, she might be reasonable and understand the evening for what it was. The problem was, Travis wasn't sure himself what the evening was about.

Banks had found the only suit remaining from his urban airline days only hours earlier, just prior to indulging in the Lieutenant's scones.

Hanging in the closet, the plastic dry-cleaning bag had been smothering it for what must have been a decade. He'd seen the bag so often over the years he'd actually forgotten what was in it. Not having to rely on Dale's suit or renting a tux was a good omen. He was looking forward to the evening.

Dale and Travis pondered the quickest route to the cabin. It lay somewhere on the south end of Lake Labarge. Having flown nearly every square foot of the lake over the years, Banks knew of only two cabins in the area described by the manager at the Regina Hotel, both on the southeastern shore of Labarge. One was accessible by heading north on the Alcan Highway via Tahkini Hot Springs Road, the other by Wickstrom Road. It couldn't be the first one, which had been abandoned by an old dying miner years earlier and bequeathed to his tenderfoot son living in Oregon. The other cabin had to be accessed by following Wickstrom Road along the east shore of the Yukon River.

The ride would take at least an hour in Banks' truck, several years in Dale's heap. The two men headed back to Northern Tracks and switched to Travis' truck.

Twenty minutes later they engaged the four-wheel drive and headed north past the hospital. They turned headlong into the snow-covered, tree-lined, dark winter trail known as Wickstrom Road. The first ten miles had been plowed several times over the winter months but it wasn't long before they hit virgin snow and the drive became treacherous. Dale tried several times, unsuccessfully, to roll a cigarette. He was experiencing nicotine withdrawal and was becoming edgy. Banks tried to assure him it wouldn't be much longer. It wasn't exactly true, but he was concerned about stopping and getting stuck with only a handheld come-a-long winch in his toolbox.

They slid back and forth between the ominous tall spruce and pine trees and soon realized they were the first vehicles on wheels to have come this far in months, maybe since the previous summer. There were no other tire tracks, just the odd snowmobile indentation zigzagging back and forth in front of them. From what the manager at the Regina told them, Banks assumed Brock ventured to his cabin at least several times a month. There certainly were no signs of him driving up here recently.

After an hour of grappling the steering wheel as if Banks were a bull rider about to be thrown, they broke into a clearing, which extended for several miles. The picture ahead was familiar. Travis could see the peak constituting the southern tip of the Miners mountain range and Pilot Mountain off to his left on the western skyline. To the east, over their right shoulder, snow-covered Joe Mountain reflected the morning sunlight. The view straight ahead, over the truck's hood, was full of low brush, an indication they were close to their destination. Lake Labarge was not in view but was approaching fast.

Pilots gain a unique sense of direction over many years of flying. Banks didn't have it when he started nor did he read about it in any aviation textbook, being acquired as it is through osmosis. It may have something to do with spending endless hours staring at a magnetic compass while keeping subconscious logs of the body's relationship to the sun. He had no idea why, but a pilot's directional orientation becomes uncanny over a lifetime in the air. He could envision exactly where Dale and he were. It was as if Banks was in the sky overhead, looking down, following the truck by air.

He knew they were getting very close to the lake and the cabin. Travis kept glancing to his right, out Dale's window, looking for a tree stand, recalling that the cabin was nestled into the cover of several acres of trees. After another ten minutes of bouncing up and down and listening to Dale's bitching about his sore kidneys, the road slowly wound itself to the right. One mile ahead, they could see a stand of trees and the frozen southern shore of Lake Labarge. Banks knew exactly where he was.

The ground was hard, so traction wouldn't be a problem. Banks came to a stop and shut off the engine. He told Dale to go ahead and roll himself a smoke. Travis opened the door, put one foot on the running board, the other on the top door hinge, and pulled himself onto the truck's roof. He stood and soaked in the 360-degree panoramic view.

The cold, dry, fresh air filled his lungs and woke his senses, which had been dulled by the truck's warm cabin.

Banks could see the first ten miles of Lake Labarge sprawling to the north. Spring would arrive soon, transforming the barren black and white view in front of him into a vast array of wildflowers, rich and lush in a multitude of colors. There wasn't a sound until he heard Dale roll down his window, blow out a lungful of smoke, and curse. He couldn't see McMaster, but he could hear the exasperation in Dale's voice.

"Shit, Travis." He paused, totally frustrated. "What *are* you doing?"

"Paying homage." Banks zeroed in on his target.

"Homage?"

"That's right. Homage." Travis could see the cabin several hundred yards away in the trees up ahead.

"What the hell's 'homage'? Sounds like some type of Hungarian sausage."

"It's publicly paying respect, you nitwit. In this case, to Mother Nature." From his vantage point, Banks could see no vehicles parked at the cabin.

Travis leaned over and peered into McMaster's window, upside down. "Would you mind passing me the binoculars, they're in the glove box." The pilot paused, waiting for Dale to retrieve them. "I'm relishing the closest thing to heaven we have on this planet."

"Oh. I see." Dale shook his head sarcastically and passed the binoculars over his right shoulder out the window. "And who, may I ask, are you paying 'homage' to?"

Banks marveled at the staggering beauty surrounding him while focusing the Nikon lenses on Bellichek's cabin.

"Whoever your higher power is," Travis replied, adjusting the binoculars.

Banks needed a respite before approaching the cabin. He'd seen something on the drive for the past ten minutes that was very familiar but unsettling. A set of snowmobile tracks ran from beneath the truck's frame toward the cabin. He had noticed them several miles earlier, when they had joined the road from the Yukon River side about two miles back. They were similar to those he had seen in the street near the Fifty

Below Zero Tavern the night before, tracks with something being towed from behind a snowmobile. He had an ominous feeling that the cabin 300 yards ahead, the one Dale couldn't see yet, might contain more questions than answers.

"Well, Banks, is it necessary for you to pay 'homage,' to . . . the Dalai Lama, Buddha, Allah, or whoever you're supposed to pay homage to, while I'm freezing my ass off?" Dale snorted rhetorically.

There was no discernible movement at the cabin. The chimney showed no signs of fire. Thirty or so yards away from the cabin, in a tree line of lodgepole and balsam fir, Banks focused on about a dozen husky dogs, each tied to its own tree. The two men's voices obviously carried quickly through the dense arctic air. First one of the dogs, then the others, started stirring. They had been curled up in a tight ball, half covered in snow. The first one to stand shook the snow off his back, stretched, then stared straight back into Banks' binoculars. Probably Bellichek's lead sled dog. His piercing blue eyes locked on Banks. Travis could see the hair slowly stand up on the dog's back and his throat swell with a growl. Seconds later the ruckus began as he howled, stirring the others into a barking crescendo.

Dale stuck his head out the window. "What the hell's that?"

"I assume Mr. Bellichek owns some sled dogs. The cabins up ahead on the right."

Dale jumped out, keeping his hand on the truck door. He stood futilely on his toes trying to see the cabin, finally joining Banks on the roof.

The dogs kept barking. Travis turned the binoculars and aimed at the cabin's main door, hoping and waiting for someone to appear and investigate the dogs' agitation. The door never opened and the ragged window shades never moved.

"I don't think anybody's home. Let's go take a look."

Banks hopped off the roof and climbed into the truck. In one fluid motion he started the engine and engaged the transmission. Dale flopped in as the wheels slipped and spun to life. The snow-covered ground had been windswept and provided solid traction, and they covered the last quarter-mile quickly and easily.

They approached slowly and finally came to a stop, parking the truck in front of the cabin.

Brock Bellichek's cabin was much more of a home than his brother's "trapper" cabin on Primrose Lake. Travis felt silly calling it a cabin. From the outside, it was actually an attractive home. It needed a lot of work, but if Banks had been house-hunting for the perfect fix-it-upper in the wilderness, he'd certainly be interested in seeing the inside.

The cabin was constructed of medium-grade cedar siding that had been stained and treated with care over the years. The roof was covered by what appeared to be relatively new, hand-cut cedar shakes. A set of two by ten Douglas fir steps, connected to cedar saplings, led to the long front porch and main door of the cabin. The attractive cedar porch, extending across the entire front of the house, supported a huge empty wooden cable spool, presumably used as a table, and several old schoolhouse-style chairs. Bellichek had even hammered several flower boxes on the outside of the porch's railing. The boxes were obviously barren of any vegetation this time of the year, but his attempt at a green thumb surprised Banks nonetheless. He had planted many small trees around the house; some had perished due to the harsh winters but most had survived. There were two unusually large but attractive picture windows on either side of the main door. The cabin was an odd juxtaposition of character, compared to its owner.

The two men stayed inside the truck's cab and rolled down the windows. They sat quietly for several minutes, assuming that if someone were around they would come at the urging of the animals. Other than the crying dogs, there was no other life.

McMaster tried his luck calling out Bellichek's name. There was no response. Banks zipped his parka and climbed out slowly, making sure all the dogs were securely fastened to their respective trees. They were jumping wildly, pulling hard on their tethers, and barking hysterically. They seemed confused, but maybe Banks and McMaster were the ones confused. It was hard to tell if the dogs wanted to attack the pilot and his friend or play with them. The northern dogs wagged their tails madly while serenading Banks with throaty howls.

Dale eyed them warily from the safety of the truck.

"I sure wish you'd brought that handheld cannon you call a pistol."

"Maybe they're hungry." Travis moved twenty yards toward the tree line to get a closer look.

He turned and shouted back to Dale, "I don't think they're hungry, there's still caribou bones with some meat left on them."

"Well, I have no desire to be their first 'live' meal this winter," Dale retorted over their incessant howling.

"You stay here a minute," Banks instructed Dale. "I'll see if anybody's out back."

"Sounds good to me." He pulled his cigarette pouch from his breast pocket and slid back in the warm passenger seat.

There was a short trail leading from the main steps of the cabin to the back of the small property.

Off to his right, toward the tree line and the barking dogs, Banks could see Bellichek's work shed. It was a large rickety structure and in a state of absolute disrepair. The shed may have been the original residence on the property as it appeared to have been built years before the new cabin. Its lumber was weathered and warped and several gray slats of vertical cedar were missing from its sides, allowing sunlight to filter inside. The twisted main door was hanging by the bottom hinge, forcing the door to tilt outward at the top. There was a large section of birch, presumably used as a chopping block, perched against the door, keeping it open. The block of wood was covered with ax marks and dried blood. It looked like a monstrous biscuit. There was also a set of familiar and disturbing snowmobile tracks leading to the door of the shed. They were new, within the last twenty-four hours.

The dogs had slowly begun to calm down but as soon as Travis neared the rickety main door they came to life and once again began their howling concerto. Maybe the shed housed their food supply.

Banks held the door for support and wiggled the one remaining hinge. It was frozen with rust. Obviously, the door had not been swung either open or closed in years. The many shafts of sunlight pouring in from the missing wall timbers filled the interior with bright but uneven strips of sunlight.

He stood at the doorway sensing something. Something amiss. It was more than just the familiar tracks in the snow under his feet. There was a smell here more associated with summer than winter. He could smell the borax trappers used to decrease the drying time for pelts, but it was the accompanying smell that was odd. During moose hunting season half the local population had moose meat hanging and aging from the rafters of their garages and sheds. Aging moose smelled sweet, a trait of wild meat. This was not the smell of wild meat. Normally, winter's cold breath would cover the odor, unless it was a recent kill yet to freeze. It filled Banks' senses with an increased level of trepidation. He slowly stepped inside the shack, ducking his head to avoid striking the small door frame. He looked around the room, adjusting his eyes to the shafts of uneven light.

The walls were lined with workbenches covered in an array of junk: traps, rusty tools, yellow nylon ropes, canvas tarpaulins, engine parts, and every imaginable gadget to skin and tan hides. A two-handled, boomerang-shaped fleshing tool was embedded into the workbench. Its shiny edge glistened in the pale light. He assumed this was where Ed Bellichek brought his furs for treatment before sale. The middle of the room was oddly clean and tidy. Everything had been piled and placed on the encircling workbenches. There was a huge oval dark stain in the middle of the dirty dusty floor. It sparkled and glinted in the shafts of light. Banks walked over and knelt next to the moisture. He touched a drop and rubbed it between his index finger and thumb before bringing it up to his nose. It was from no wild animal he had ever smelled before. The memory of the kill site they found at Primrose Lake came flooding back. He suddenly felt uneasy, as if he was being watched. A large drop of cold blood fell from above and splashed thickly into the stain at his feet. He slowly twisted his head, looking upward. He stared, confused, at the old wooden ceiling. Something dangled from the rafters.

Banks stood up and circled the room keeping his head craned toward the beams, not letting go of the horrifying image before him.

A sprawling figure, resembling a crucifix, was swinging from the rafters. A wooden stretcher used for tanning hides was elevated ten feet off the ground by a pulley attached to the ceiling. It resembled a giant flying squirrel, wings spread, as if about to land. The sun drew ribbons of bright light across the dangling macabre image.

It was a human hide. It had been skinned, stretched, and hung. The flesh was still weeping plasma. It was a recent kill. The meat on the skin was still full of moisture and had just begun to dry and recess inward toward the hide. There was no sign of a head, or hands, or feet, just the unmistakable missing section of flesh where the appendages should have been.

Banks' stomach rolled and he could feel the tiny hairs on the back of his neck creep to attention.

Just forty-eight hours earlier at Primrose Lake, he had discovered something as ghastly as what now hung before him: Ed Bellichek. Now, he gawked at what he assumed was the remains of Ed's brother. Banks quickly looked around the room one more time and headed toward the door and some much needed fresh air.

He made his way back to the truck. "C'mon, get out. I think I've found our missing brother. I won't know until I find all the parts."

Dale's face contorted, "Parts?"

Banks took Dale back to the shed, but not before warning him about what he was going to witness. It didn't help. When Dale looked into the rafters, he placed his hand over his mouth and nearly vomited. He quickly exited the shed for some fresh air.

Banks followed Dale and reminded him that they didn't have much time. Having not heard from them, Leon Powell was sure to head this way with Radcliff before sundown.

If they were going to gather any information inside the home, they would have to move quickly. Dale's lack of objection surprised Banks. Running away and drinking was his normal approach to stress.

They both headed quickly toward the cabin and scaled the ten steps to the porch.

A leghold trap hung over the front door, dangling by a chain one-third the way down. In front of the trap, bolted to the door, was a heavy metal plate. Banks could only guess that it was used for knocking. He was dumbfounded by the concept. Who would ever drive this far from Whitehorse to knock on this strange little man's door? Just as the thought crossed his mind, Dale picked up the leghold trap and gave the cabin's main door several hard whacks.

"McMaster, do you know something I don't? I doubt the owner can come to the door right now. He's hanging out back in the shed." Banks tried to break the tension they were both feeling with humor but it didn't elicit a smile from his very nervous partner.

Not surprisingly, no one answered their knocking.

Dale felt around the door frame for a key but didn't find anything except a splinter for his finger. He began wandering along the sturdy deck, peering past the window shades into the cabin's interior. He stopped and cupped his hands around both temples in order to see past the reflection caused by the bright morning sun.

"Well?" Travis urged.

Dale fogged up the windows, working hard to see inside.

"I can't see shit in here. The shades are drawn too close. The only gap is in the curtains and, well, it's blacker than molasses. It's a safe bet nobody else is home."

"Let's try the door." Banks peered into the glass but had the same bad luck.

"I think Leon would describe that as breaking and entering. I'm not fond of prison."

"Dale, it's only a B and E if you break and enter. I'm not suggesting we break anything. Just try the doorknob."

McMaster shrugged and approached the main door with a distinct air of uncertainty.

He stopped and looked at Banks again. "Why am I doing this? What if the guy who's running around pretending to be Hannibal Lecter is in there with a 12-gauge shotgun on his lap pointed at the door waiting for us, with a bib on?"

"You've been watching too many movies. Go on. I'll try one of these windows."

With a newfound resolve, the loader approached the door quickly and turned the knob. The door was locked.

"Well that's that. Let's go." Dale turned toward the stairs, exuding the same uneasiness he had manifested at Primrose Lake.

"Hang on." Banks stopped him and pointed to the window on his right, "try that window next to the door. This one's locked or painted shut from the inside."

Dale eyed his ex-roommate suspiciously before walking back and, with fingers spread, pushing up on the large window closest to the door. It moved slightly, only two or three inches, but it was a start. He grasped the window by the bottom frame and grunted with all the force he could muster. Finally, it creaked and squealed upward, opening halfway.

He looked at Banks. "Now what?"

Travis walked over to the opening and stuck his head through the window. The cabin was still. He climbed inside.

Banks pulled back the curtains, flooding the musty room with bright sunlight. Millions of dust particles wafted through the air, reflecting the morning light. He found himself standing in the middle of Brock Bellichek's living room.

The cabin interior was much more of a cabin than it appeared on the outside. There was an old red brick inset fireplace but it had been modified. A tin potbelly stove had been permanently inserted and plumbed into the chimney vent. Around the exhaust duct, a makeshift mantel held a half-dozen Coleman and kerosene lamps. Two of the walls, along with the entire floor of the room, were still raw plywood. The interior of the cabin had never been completed nor did there appear to be any intention of doing so. Several large, cheap oil paintings of wildlife were securely fastened to the plywood walls, suggesting that no fancy wallpaper was on order. In the center of the room, two dilapidated, rumpled couches were covered with stained brown blankets and separated by a soiled multicolored throw rug. Several banged-up bent recliners were evenly spaced around the couches facing toward the wood burning stove. The kitchen plumbing was exposed at the far end of the room. A tiny chrome and acrylic breakfast table, encircled by mismatched wooden chairs, sat near the propane gas stove next to the last window. Banks wandered toward the kitchen and was surprised to find the stove's gas pilot light out but the propane refrigerator still running.

A string of profanity spewed at him from the open window. Banks hadn't been able to unlock the main door without the key for the dead bolt lock, so the window was the only access they had. Dale had decided to join Banks inside but his large frame was finding it hard to negotiate the small gap in the window. Finally, he squeezed through, cracking the back of his head on the bottom of the window frame. Once in, he looked around nervously, decided it was time to have a smoke, and gently lowered himself into one of the bent recliners next to a small end table sporting a metal ashtray.

"Hey, McMaster, don't sit or touch anything!"

Dale looked around the room perplexed. "Why not? I doubt the owner gives a shit anymore."

"The RCMP took fingerprints from Primrose Lake. When they find what's left of Brock Bellichek they'll dust the whole south end of Lake Labarge."

That got his attention. He leaped up and wiped off his seat while putting away his pouch of cigarette tobacco.

Off the living area was a doorway to the back of the house. Banks left the kitchen and headed there. As he reached the dark hallway, he felt Dale's footsteps on his heels. The first room off to the right was the bathroom. Brock Bellichek must have had a dam supplying water to the cabin or an electric generator supplying power to a pump that sucked water from Labarge. The house was fully plumbed with a kitchen, shower stall, and toilet. Travis turned the small handles above the porcelain sink and got nothing. Not surprising, as most people turn off their water in the winter when they leave for extended periods of time. The small bathroom smelled of urine. The toilet's lid was up exposing the empty brown-stained bowl. The cabin had been shut down and there were no signs of anybody having come back. Assuming the thing hanging from the rafters was indeed Brock Bellichek, he never got the cabin turned on before he became airborne in the shed. The water was still off and the stove was cold. The cabin had been empty for some time. Banks was still miffed at why Bellichek would keep his refrigerator running while he was away.

"Travis!" McMaster called from somewhere down the hallway. "In here."

Banks followed Dale's voice down the hall into Brock Bellichek's bedroom. The room was too dark to see anything clearly. The window had black roofing tar paper stapled to the frame—a common makeshift shade people used in the North during the long, bright, twenty-four hours of summer daylight. Next to the bed, a small lamp sat on a wooden crate. Dale took out his Bic lighter, keeping his gloves on for fear of leaving prints. He removed the glass chimney, lit the kerosene lamp, adjusted the flame, and seconds later the room came alive with a warm glow.

The bedroom made the living room look like the lobby of the Waldorf Astoria. It was disgusting. The mattress on the metal-framed double bed was soiled and tattered and several stained sheets were tossed in a ball at the foot of the bed. Dirty clothes, along with an array of shoes and boots, lay strewn about the floor. The closet door was open, exposing several dozen pairs of long johns and winter coats. In the back of the closet stood a stack of cardboard boxes. Whatever the top ones contained, it provided sufficient force to crush the lower boxes. Banks took stock of the disheveled room, then stepped over the littered clothes and retrieved the first box. Dale took the second one and the two men placed them on the bed, curious as to their contents. Travis suggested they both keep their gloves on.

In silence, they spent the better part of an hour rummaging through the boxes. What they were doing was highly illegal but it didn't faze either one of them. They would simply tell the police they found the body in the shed and not mention their foray into the house and they never stopped to discuss the issue. Travis had a stinging reminder on both his head and groin that they were involved in something up to their necks whether they liked it or not, and although they had far more questions than answers they had obvious misgivings about approaching the police. This might be their best chance to gather information that would lead to an explanation of the events of the past two days. A sense of urgency burgeoned in both of them.

The first several cardboard containers were filled with insignificant records, covering the spectrum of tax receipts to rabies vaccination forms. They moved as quickly as possible, reminding each other it was more than likely that Inspector Nick Radcliff would make an appearance today at Brock Bellichek's cabin. Banks felt confident that Leon's sense of duty would compel him to inform his superior about the directions to the cabin they had all received the evening before at the Regina Hotel. McMaster and Banks were acutely aware of the consequences of Radcliff finding them climbing out the living room window of a man who, presumably, had been skinned alive and whose brother had been ritually murdered two days earlier; forget the fact that they had whiled away the morning rummaging through his personal effects. Several times, the two stopped like deer staring blindly at headlights, convinced they heard approaching police vehicles.

The last box was the most interesting and most perplexing. It contained personal letters, family photos, and several packets of small manila envelopes wrapped in rubber bands. Travis and Dale divided up the booty and began the final search.

A pile of old black-and-white pictures of both brothers at the cabin showed them posing outside while hunting, trapping, fishing or drinking. Banks' guess was the Bellichek brothers were drinking in all the pictures. The image was often at an angle or blurred. Travis kept wondering who was operating the camera. The pictures were almost exclusively of the two men together. Finally, Banks found two pictures that included other men, none of whom he recognized. It also struck him there wasn't even *one* picture of a woman.

One of the photos jumped out at him. It was taken many years earlier with both Ed and Brock wearing suits. There was no date or place written on the back, but Travis was sure he had seen the picture before, possibly at Ed Bellichek's cabin at Primrose Lake. He slipped several of the photos into his pocket.

The rest of the contents of the last box contained an array of handwritten notes. Most of them were not addressed and were signed only with a first name or initials. Dale picked out the first one that struck a chord.

"Jesus, Travis, look at this." He passed it to his friend.

It looked relatively new. The envelope was postmarked from the Beaver Creek Post Office north of Burwash. Banks read the scrawled, handwritten note.

Four and whore rhyme aright
So do three and me,
I'll set the town alight
Ere there are two.
Two little whores, shivering with fright,
Seek a cozy doorway in the middle of the night.
Jack's knife flashes, then there's but one,
And the last one's the ripest for Jack's idea of fun.

Travis rubbed his temples with his left hand before wiping off the edges of the note and placing it in the envelope and back in Dale's box. This was a very odd family.

Dale kept staring at his partner. "What the hell's *that*?"

Banks raised his eyebrows in Dale's direction. "If my memory serves me correctly, it's Jack."

"Who?"

"Jack the Ripper. That was part of a note he left for Scotland Yard during his killing spree in the late 1800s."

"How in the hell do you know that?"

"Believe it or not, I retained one or two things from my college days."

"What's it doing here?"

"Dale," Travis didn't hide his sarcasm very well, "it's not the original note."

"Banks, don't treat me like an idiot just because I don't have some useless degree in English! I know it's not the original fucking note! Jesus Christ." He threw his arms in the air. "I'm asking why would someone keep this in their personal effects?"

Banks didn't answer. He didn't have an answer. He went back to the last pile of wrapped notes and kept reading. He soon found another perplexing letter, also postmarked from Beaver Creek. He mumbled the last paragraph out loud:

Brothers Ed and Brock,

It's not too late. It's never too late! Fill your lives with Christ. The Almighty is at hand. Redemption and salvation are yours. Reach out

and be saved! Either Heaven awaits you or eternal damnation!
MJ

Banks slid the letter into his pocket.

"What were the names of the other two miners in the pictures we found in the Yellowknife Library? The ones with both Bellichek brothers?"

McMaster rummaged through a half a dozen pockets of his parka before pulling out a packet of folded photocopied pages. He opened them, flipped them upright, and pointed at the article with his finger.

"Let's see . . . here it is, William Watt and Mike Jansen. Why?"

"I don't know. It's hard to believe a religious fanatic would be friends with these guys."

"Maybe he wasn't always a religious fanatic," Dale observed astutely, then added matter-of-factly, "there's been a few times, usually after a bad date and several weeks of penicillin, I thought of joining the priesthood. But one stiff drink and I'm over it."

"I'm sure priests all around the world will take comfort in that knowledge." Banks tossed the remnants of their search back into the box as a switch clicked on in his head.

"Let me see those papers you brought back from Yellowknife."

Dale handed Travis the stack. He flipped through them until he found it. He knew he had seen it before. Banks took the photo out of his pocket showing the Bellichek brothers in suits. It was the same one taken in front of the courthouse or police station. Somehow, the brothers had managed to get an original black-and-white photo that appeared in the Yellowknife newspaper more than twenty years earlier. Travis held up the other picture he had slipped into his pocket earlier, showing the two strange men with Ed and Brock at the Labarge cabin. The pilot compared it to the photocopy brought from Yellowknife. It was a match. It was the same foursome.

"I think Mike Jansen and William Watt are in trouble."

Dale was trying to stay with his partner. "How so?"

Banks looked at his watch. It was late afternoon and time to go. The RCMP would be arriving soon and he remembered his evening plans included being in Whitehorse escorting his boss to a formal dinner.

"I'll tell you on the way back."

They put everything back the way they had found it and headed for the window, but there was one thing that had been bothering Banks from the moment they first crawled through the window: the refrigerator. Travis wandered over to the kitchen and opened the fridge door as Dale put one leg out the window.

"What the hell are you doing, Travis? You gonna make yourself a quick sandwich?"

Banks opened the door and fought the desire to gag. The creature hanging from the shed's rafters was definitely the remains of Brock Bellichek. The object on the top shelf of the fridge stared back at him, eyes opened, terror plastered all over the sliced face. Travis slammed the door and ordered Dale out of the house as quick as possible.

Banks silently marched through the snow toward the dogs. He wanted a better look at the bones they had been gnawing. The refrigerator's contents led him to believe the bones scattered among the dogs were probably the remnants of a human skinning.

Dale saw Travis was not going to the truck, and found security in numbers. Just as McMaster arrived and looked over Banks' shoulders, Travis picked up a small human finger bone just outside the reach of one dog's tethers. He handed it to Dale and turned toward the truck.

"What the . . ." McMaster paused, staring at the small thumb bone he held in his hand. He still didn't realize what he was holding. Dale suddenly flung it in the air as if it were a poisonous snake oozing the Ebola virus. "What the hell was that?"

"You really want to know?" Banks jumped into the truck and spun his wrist on the keys, bringing the engine to life.

"Yes. I really want to know." Dale opened the passenger door and jumped in.

"Those are fresh human bones scattered all over the tree line amongst the dogs. I'm assuming they belonged to Brock Bellichek."

"Holy shit!" Dale rolled up his window as if a sword-wielding samurai was loose on the property. "Are you sure?"

Travis looked at him confidently, "I'm sure."

The wop-wop of rotor blades approaching was aural proof they hadn't left soon enough.

Banks hit the dash. "Damn!"

"What?" Dale looked at him, confused, at the same instant he heard the helicopter.

"Remember, Dale, we never set foot inside the house. Our footprints are all over the shed. So that's the only thing we found, that hide hanging in the shed."

The Bell 206 of the RCMP was approaching quickly from the south. Banks turned off the ignition and slid back in his seat. He resigned himself to the fact that, once again, he was going to be answering questions from Inspector Nick Radcliff about a dead man he just happened to discover before anybody else. The problem was, this time he didn't have a valid reason for being here. The RCMP had chosen to fly instead of driving to the cabin, which proved they had too much taxpayer money at their disposal.

The Jet Ranger went into a hover fifty yards from the truck, creating a whirlwind of snow and ice. The ice particles blasted the side of Banks' new red paint job, the whirling snow hitting the windscreen, sticking and then melting. The truck rocked slightly as the chopper pilot pulled up on the collective and touched down. Moments later, after a short idle, Banks heard the turbine engine pitch down as the fuel cock was shut off.

It didn't take long before one very irate inspector opened the side door and jumped out. Radcliff marched toward the two men in the truck; head down under the decelerating rotor blades. The Chief Inspector of the RCMP started shouting long before Banks could hear anything he was saying.

Travis took a deep breath, regained his composure and stepped out of the truck with Dale.

Banks had never seen Nick Radcliff so nearly on the edge of losing his composure. Snow kicked off his boots as he stormed toward the two men like a rabid linebacker. McMaster didn't like what he saw coming and took a step in behind Banks. Radcliff was slipping slightly in the icy snow and it was impossible to discern if he was favoring a leg.

"Banks!" Little bits of foam shot from his mouth. He stopped inches from the taller man's face and, with teeth clenched, tried to lower his voice. "What in the hell are you doing here?"

"Good afternoon, Inspector." Travis paused, his imagination picking up speed as he invented his implausible lie. "Ah . . . well . . . Dale and I were rabbit hunting on Wickstrom Road and it occurred to us that we hadn't paid our respects to Brock Bellichek. Thought we'd shoot up here and tell him how sorry we were about his brother. I assume you've informed him of his brother's tragic death?"

"Rabbit hunting? Don't give me that shit. How long have you been here?"

"Not long."

He removed his glove and placed his bare hand on the hood of Bank's truck. It was cold. He glared back at Travis.

Banks was drowning fast. "Would you believe just long enough to cool off the engine?"

The Arctic Air bush pilot could actually see the heat of Radcliff's anger radiating from the inspector's face.

"I told you to stay out of this at Primrose Lake. This is an on going police investigation."

Dale opened wide and inserted his size fourteen foot.

"Well, Inspector, your investigation is about to get a whole lot more interesting."

"Shut up, Dale." Banks said without looking at him.

"What's that mean?" Radcliff snorted.

Banks watched every nuance of Radcliff's demeanor. He certainly didn't seem disingenuous in his query of Dale's comment. If Nick Radcliff was involved in the death of Brock and Ed Bellichek, he was either an accomplished liar, or he didn't have a clue as to what he was about to find.

There was no point in trying to convince Radcliff that McMaster and Banks hadn't found anything. If they acted as if they were coming clean with the skinned body of Brock Bellichek, Radcliff might believe them when they denied being in the house.

"Inspector, you'll find part of Brock Bellichek in the shed."

"Part of him?" Radcliff's head turned toward the shed then back toward Banks. "Which part?"

Radcliff's eyes darted between Dale and Travis.

"The outermost part." Dale grunted before continuing, "Bagging evidence is not for the fainthearted today, sir. See those bones scattered all over the hillside, the ones the dogs have half eaten? Well, they belong to a two-legged critter. Probably belong to the hide in the shop. Parts of this guy are everywhere!"

Radcliff marched off to the shed and tree line where the dogs were howling ecstatically. The furry animals had probably never had this much company or excitement. Radcliff waved his arms in the direction of the two other constables, one of which was Leon Powell. They quickly marched toward their boss.

When Leon passed by Banks, he mumbled without looking up, "Travis, I warned you."

Several minutes later, Radcliff, a little more somber but still livid, came out of the shed. He looked and pointed straight at McMaster and Banks.

Dale sealed their fate, "What did we tell you, eh? Even all the king's horses and all the king's men couldn't put Humpty back together again."

"Constable Powell, arrest them!" He pointed at Banks' truck. "Escort these two men back to Whitehorse in their vehicle. When you get to the station, I want you to explain their rights to them and then charge them obstruction of justice."

"You can't arrest us!" Dale was beside himself. He hadn't missed happy hour on a Saturday at the Klondike Lounge in years.

"You don't think so? Powell! Cuff them as well! You drive."

They drove in silence the first several miles. Once out of sight of the cabin, Constable Powell drove with one hand and unlocked the handcuffs with the other. After coming across a flat spot on the road with good traction, he stopped the vehicle and switched places with Travis.

Leon hated driving Banks' truck. He claimed it didn't handle well and Wickstrom Road in the winter was only exacerbating his negative opinion.

Dale broke the ice. "You're not really going to arrest us, are you?"

Powell smirked, "Too late. You're already under arrest." Powell could see no humor in Dale's face. "Don't worry, McMaster, Nick just wanted you out of his hair. He needed to get your attention."

"He's got it." Dale nodded.

"Before I get halfway through processing you guys, he'll be back and cut you loose. A first-year law student working for legal aid could get this thrown out of court." Leon shook his head. "He should have charged you with stupidity. That might have stuck. I still can't believe you came out here by yourselves. I thought you said last night you were going to let me know. I could have given you an unofficial heads up."

Banks fought with the steering wheel over a snow-covered rut as they all bounced off the roof in unison. "We didn't want to risk getting you in any hot water."

Dale was squashed inbetween the pilot and police officer and added sarcastically, "So we decided to take a trip up shit creek and get ourselves arrested instead. You know, being the good friends that we are."

Leon was deft at ignoring Dale. "So, you think that thing hanging in the shop was Brock Bellichek?"

"I know so." Banks didn't take his eyes off the road.

"How do you know for sure?" Powell was afraid of his flying friend's answer.

"Because I found his head in the refrigerator."

Dale choked on his unlit cigarette and started coughing wildly.

Powell leaned forward, stunned. "You found his what, where?"

"His head. It's in the refrigerator."

"Oh Christ, Travis. I didn't hear that." Leon rubbed his face in his hands, knocking off his blue and gold uniform hat. "Shit! You broke into the house! Didn't you?"

"Technically, I suppose we did. But figuratively speaking we didn't. Nothing's broken."

"Your prints will be all over the place."

"We kept our gloves on the whole time. Even wiped our feet on the front porch."

"Well, that's it." Leon threw his hands forward in defeat. "I can't help you this time. If they find out you were inside that cabin, as my last act of friendship, I'll notify your next of kin."

"It was his idea." McMaster looked at Powell and pointed at Banks.

"We didn't have a choice, Leon. I'm involved. Whether I like it or not. I think there's a better than fifty-fifty chance Dale and I are in trouble."

Powell chimed in, "I can guarantee you you're in trouble."

"Whoever committed those atrocities to Ed and Brock Bellichek certainly won't hesitate to shut us up if they think we know something."

"You did that to yourselves," Powell observed dispassionately.

"Fine. Maybe you're right. For some unknown reason I felt compassion for Ed Bellichek. All he had was his brother. Knowing what I know now, I would have probably helped butcher both of them."

"What's that supposed to mean?" Leon said, trying to interrupt Banks.

Travis ignored his question for the time being and continued. "The facts remain: I was mugged, Dale's apartment was ransacked, this morning someone nearly killed us by whacking us over the head with a two-by-four, and when that didn't work they shot at us." Banks had Leon's undivided attention and continued.

"These two hillbilly brothers are involved. I think I know how. And now Brock Bellichek's cabin is going to be tied up in a big yellow police bow for years. It'll probably end up being a goddamn tourist attraction once the public finds out. I had to get in there before you guys put every gnat's ass in a plastic bag. It's a good thing I did. But you're not going to like what we found." Banks paused and glanced at the sergeant. "Leon, I have proof that Radcliff knows an awful lot more about Ed and Brock Bellichek than he's letting on."

"If you know something about these deaths that we don't, you tell me right now if you want my help."

"I promise I will, Leon. Just let me make one more stop in Whitehorse first. I can assure you, I've gathered enough information and facts to go to your internal affairs department and lodge a complaint if Radcliff comes after me. They don't have to know where or how we got our information."

"Don't kid yourself. They'll want to know everything." He stared out the window, realizing he had already crossed the line regarding his job and their friendship. "What other stop do you have to make?"

"I'd rather not say. You wouldn't let me do it."

Banks' friend Leon Powell paused momentarily before bluntly summarizing his feelings.

"When you get this information, whatever it is, I want to see it. If you have tangible convincing evidence, I won't say anything else to Radcliff and I'll assist you in any way I can. But mark my words, if you accuse Nick Radcliff of some complicity or legal impropriety in this Bellichek matter, and it turns out to be untrue, you'll not only ruin his illustrious career but more than likely our friendship as well."

They drove in silence the rest of the way. En route to the RCMP police headquarters they passed the Whitehorse Baptist Church on Second Avenue. The lights were off. It was late Saturday afternoon.

William Watt's girlfriend had found the disturbing letter addressed to Watt two days earlier. In a sealed envelope, with a stamp but no postmark, it somehow found its way onto their kitchen table. She had checked the door of the small apartment on Jeckell Avenue. It showed no signs of forced entry. The windows boasting a view of the SS *Klondike* had also been untouched.

The SS *Klondike* was an old paddle steamer used early in the century to haul misguided miners to their imaginary pot of gold on the Klondike River near Dawson City. It was now a tourist attraction and sat grounded next to the Yukon River just below the Schwatka Lake dam. With the traffic passing in front of his apartment, it would be unlikely anyone could break in without being seen. It was as if the clandestine postman had a key to his dirty little dwelling. Watt couldn't figure out how or when it had been dropped off. The apartment manager had said he didn't let anyone in. Watt and his girlfriend were scraping by on welfare and were almost always home except for trips to the liquor store and the welfare office.

When Watt had refused to let his abusive girlfriend in on the letter's contents, she assumed it was from another woman and cut loose in a drunken rage.

But Watt thought he knew where it was from. It was signed "M." He assumed it was from his sordid past—a forgotten memory. He had tried unsuccessfully to contact the Bellichek brothers for the first time in nearly twenty years. He thought maybe someone was becoming untrustworthy, and he was growing more anxious. The other letters had arrived in his mailbox. This was the first one that found its way into his apartment. The religious ranting and raving in the last letter was particularly strange, worse than the others.

He started getting the notes six months ago. This time, the author claimed he needed to see Watt, that it was urgent. The writer had actually set a time and place along with more stuff about salvation being at hand. Watt decided to go and meet whoever this loose cannon might be. There should only be five of them, unless someone told someone else. He needed to confirm that their dirty little secret would remain concealed.

Watt had no car. The walk would take twenty minutes. He told his girlfriend to drink up and shut up, he would be back in an hour.

It was late Saturday afternoon and the Baptist Church on Second Avenue was deserted. He used the side door as instructed.

The church was as dark inside as Whitehorse had become outside. An array of candles had been lit throughout the church, filling the air with an incensed red glow, the smell arousing memories of his childhood. Sundays were church days. He hated Sundays. After praying about love, family, and forgiveness, his dad would go home, get drunk, and then beat the shit out of him.

The wooden sign near the side door claimed there was no service until Sunday morning at 11:00. He strolled in like he owned the place, entering from the side pews. He called out several times, but there was no response. He slowed down, looking at the sacred surroundings. The walls closed in on rancid memories. He walked to the back of the church and opened the inside doors leading to the small atrium that separated the church from the street. He attempted to open the church's main door but it was bolted shut.

He turned and looked around at the small atrium. Two small tables against the walls were littered with religious paraphernalia. Pictures of Jesus were everywhere. He pushed open the doors leading back into the church and walked cautiously up the center aisle, peering into every pew. He became uncomfortable. Apprehension began to envelop him. There didn't appear to be anyone in the church. He made his way to the front and sat in the first pew on the left, the end seat next to the aisle, exactly as instructed. He waited.

He sat there for twenty minutes, checking his cheap watch every minute. He had the unsettling feeling that he was being watched. Watt had arrived early and was angry nobody had showed up.

He grew increasingly apprehensive about the whole visit, but as he rose to leave, a voice boomed from every corner of the church.

"Genesis, 49:18. *'I have waited for thy salvation, O Lord!'*"

Watt spun around, trying to locate the source of the voice.

"Who is that?" he shouted.

"*'Work out your own salvation with fear and trembling.'* Philippians 2:12."

Watt didn't recognize the voice.

The blood was quickly draining from William Watt's face. He looked at the main door then spun around, chasing the echo. The side door he entered was now decorated with a large brass lock on the inside. There was no exit. He looked up at the altar. It was empty except for burning candles. A crucifix hung on the front wall and was tilted toward the white satin-covered altar. There was something on the crucifix, something covering Jesus' face. He inched closer, squinting to see what it was.

"*Living well is the best revenge!*" The voice continued to reverberate throughout the church.

Watt continued to look around as he climbed the three shallow steps to the altar. He got close enough to see what was obscuring the face of Jesus. It was a photo, a picture he hadn't seen in years. A newspaper photo of an eleven year-old girl. His knees became weak. He reached out to catch himself and grabbed the edge of the cloth on the altar, but the satin cloth slipped off the waxed marble. He lost his balance and crashed to the floor.

"*He only is my rock and my salvation: He is my defense; I shall not be moved!*"

Lying on the floor, Watt finally isolated the source of the voice: it was coming from above. He could see the organ loft, elevated, at the back of the church.

"Who the hell are you?" Watt slowly rose from the carpeted burgundy floor and stared blindly at the silhouette looking down on him from the rear of the church. "What do you want?" he shouted fearfully.

Watt squinted up at the figure and saw an outline of something he never imagined he would see in a church. The lines were unmistakable. It's just that he had never seen it from this angle. He was staring at a loaded, high-powered, hunting bow. Unwavering, it bore in on its target. He cringed and wiped the tears from his eyes.

The voice from above slowed in pace, lowered its volume, and became frighteningly ominous. It took on an air of familiarity.

"Repeat after me, sinner. '*We bless thee for our creation, and all the blessings of this life . . .*'"

Tears of fright began gushing forward, "I don't know . . . "

"Say it!"

"Ah . . . ah . . . bless creation and . . . "

"No! '*We bless thee for our creation, and all the blessings of this life.*'"

Watt urinated in his pants. "We bless thee for our creation, and all the blessings of this life . . . "

"'*But above all, for thee inestimable love in the redemption of the world by our Lord Jesus Christ.*'"

"But above all," Watt's voice was beginning to crack, "for love. . . . Oh shit. I can't do it . . . What do you want from me? Look. I'm sorry! O.K.? It wasn't my idea." He began to sob uncontrollably.

"Stand up." The voice from the organ loft changed pace.

Watt slowly pulled himself up, never taking his eyes off the steady image in the loft.

"Please. I'll do whatever . . ."

"It's time." The voice trailed off.

"It's time for what?" Watt trembled.

"The Gospel according to Saint Matthew, 26:18. Rejoice. You are about to be saved."

"Saved?" Watt answered trying to smile.

"'*My soul is exceeding sorrowful, even unto death!*'"

The whip sound sliced into his ears. The razor sharp spinning tip of the arrow zipped through the dark church. A pulsating glint of light flickered off the tip and it slammed into his chest with the force of a sledgehammer. He went reeling backward into the wall behind the altar, the taste of blood quickly filling his throat and trickling from the corner of his mouth. He struggled trying to walk forward. The arrow's tip had passed through him and impaled him to the wall.

He glanced down and saw the feathered back end of the arrow protruding from his chest. Around the entry point, his clothes began to swell with a dark crimson red stain. He was becoming dizzy and felt a warm fire rush through his body. His head slumped backward and he stared up directly into the crucifix of Jesus Christ and the haunting photo of a forgotten memory. The church's fragrant incense exhaled one last time from his lungs.

Moments later, the figure from the organ loft approached William Watt and stared into his terrified face. The hunter smiled and gently laid his hammer and nails down on the altar.

Dale and Travis were still being detained at police headquarters. It was getting late. It had been dark for two hours. Travis couldn't imagine what was taking Radcliff so long at Lake Labarge.

While the two waited to be processed, Constable Powell easily managed to find an empty interrogation room. It wasn't anything like Banks had seen in the movies or on TV. It was similar to a modern conference room you would find at any Holiday Inn or Marriott. Every RCMP interrogation room across Canada probably looked like this one. A government bidding war had allowed the RCMP to buy several warehouses of identical chairs, tables, carpet, and coffeemakers. It was new with bright contemporary furnishings. There was no rusted cage in the corner for animalistic prisoners or a large two-way mirror for peeping prosecutors. The table wasn't an old carved-up wooden relic, covered with last year's issues of *Popular Mechanics.* It was chrome with a black acrylic top. The navy blue carpet showed the paralleled lines where it had been vacuumed repeatedly. The room even smelled new.

It was early Saturday night and the evening's festivities of bar fights, break-ins, and alcohol-related domestic violence were not scheduled to commence for several more hours.

Dale was bored and jokingly asked Leon for the umpteenth time if it was O.K. to run over to the Taku Hotel and get a couple of cocktails to go.

Almost every call Banks made resulted in a busy signal. He paced like a nervous cat. He had two hours to make an illegal house call, shower, put on a suit, remember how to dance, and pick up his boss who was, by now, probably wondering where the hell he was. He hadn't spoken to Kayla since earlier in the day and couldn't remember what time he was supposed to pick her up.

Leon was pestering Banks about using the phone. Powell laughed and said Travis had already used up his one call phoning Monty. The Constable suggested Banks call Clarence Darrow if there was a hope of staying out of the electric chair. Powell was loving the bogus arrest Radcliff was putting them through.

When Banks finally got through to Lieutenant Winston Montgomery he graciously offered to check Travis' answering machine. There were three calls: one from Ms. Jackson, another from Doc Baker, and the third from Travis' sister, Karen, in Anchorage.

Banks quickly got hold of Kayla. She informed him she had left the office early. Ms. Jackson had not left the office before eight o'clock since he'd met her.

Kayla was at home and about to take a shower, a fact she shouldn't have mentioned as Banks missed what she said next. His overactive imagination boiled over and commandeered all his cerebral functions. He could see her about to climb into a shower; the wire- rimmed glasses on the sink, the hair twisting and flowing over her shoulders, the towel sliding down her smooth silky body as it came to a rest on the floor next to her perfectly manicured and polished toes; all the curves and lines of her exquisitely proportioned body seductively moving as she stepped over the bath's sill. Banks needed to pick it up a notch that night and become slightly more aggressive.

His daydream popped like a bubble when he heard his name being hollered into the phone. It was tragic timing. He was just about to undress and get in the shower with his imaginary Kayla.

Travis apologized to Ms. Jackson, explaining his apparent lack of attention was due to being arrested, not the fact she was currently prancing around naked in his mind, rubbing whipping cream all over his body. She responded to his arrest by not seeming too surprised. Travis briefly explained what had happened at Labarge and promised to fill her in with the details later in the evening. He gave her his word; he would not be later than eight o'clock. In reality, unless Radcliff got back soon, he had no idea what time he would pick her up.

As he hung up the phone, it suddenly occurred to him that the RCMP phone would probably call anywhere in the world. Dale was smoking by the vending machines and Leon was busying himself with a mountain of paperwork. Banks quietly closed the door to the interrogation room and dialed 9, getting an outside line. He pushed 1 and then the area code. He didn't get any weird noise informing him long distance wouldn't work, so he dialed the rest of the number and moments later the phone rang in Anchorage, Alaska.

Karen hurriedly answered the phone before it even rang.

"Hello."

As an infant, Banks couldn't pronounce her name and always used his two-year-old adaptation.

"Hey, Kram. It's me!"

"Oh, it's only you," she deadpanned with the scream of a hairdryer in the background. A second later it was turned off.

"It's good to hear your voice, too." Travis feigned hurt.

She laughed. "Just kidding, Travis. I thought you were my date phoning to cancel."

"There's the voice of experience. Who is it this time? Some big FBI stud who's only been married three times?"

"How'd you guess?"

Her love life was more complicated than the tax code, but he didn't want to venture down that road right at the moment.

"Kram, I need your help; more to the point, your professional opinion regarding a pretty odd individual."

"That's what I get paid to do," she hesitated, listening to the tone of his voice.

She had joined the FBI for academic reasons. It was either the FBI or law school, and at the university she'd concluded that most law students were latent criminals seeking ways to steal from the rich in order to give to themselves. Not an honorable profession, the way she saw it. She'd decided that a master's in criminology might offer an explanation as to what drove criminals and lawyers alike. Her master's ended up a doctorate.

"It'll have to be quick," she pressed, "why are you talking so quietly? Where are you?"

Banks kept an eye in the direction of the squad room. "In jail."

"In jail! What have you done now?"

"Nothing. Just pissed off the local boys. It's a bogus bust to keep me out of their hair while they scour over a murder scene. I stumbled across a butchered old trapper near Whitehorse today."

"Stumbled across?" She said it sarcastically, knowing him too well.

"Well, let's just say I had a hunch. The problem is, it's the second murder I've hunched across in three days."

"If you're leaving a trail of dead bodies behind you, I'm not surprised you've ended up in jail."

"The thing is, Kram, they're not soliciting any outside help. These local guys are way over their heads. If I know that, they must. The irony is they're probably starting to wonder if I'm involved. I know for a fact that the chief investigator in the case is withholding information." Travis was keeping his voice just above a whisper.

"You're sitting in his police station right now, telling me all this? You need a lawyer, not a criminal psychologist," she sighed. "What can I possibly do?"

"I think whoever committed these killings suspects I'm on to them."

"How so?"

"Dale and I followed someone this morning, I'll call him a suspect for lack of a better word, who, we thought, might be involved in the killings. We followed him into an alley where the bastard hit us with a two-by-four and then took a shot at us. The weird thing is, he missed us by a mile. It was as if he wanted to miss."

"You need to tell all this to the police."

"Kram, you're not listening. I know the RCMP investigator is withholding information, I just have no idea why. I'm going to have to find this guy without their help. Preferably, before he gets nervous and comes after me. But I need to know what I'm looking for. What kind of guy can take a trapper and slice and dice him up like julienne fries?"

"Calm down, Travis. How do you know it's a guy?"

"Well, if you had seen the mess . . . "

"Lesson number one: don't assume anything. I've seen women do things that would make Attila the Hun toss his cookies. What exactly has this *person* done?"

Over the next several minutes, speaking softly, Travis relayed, in detail, all the events of the past several days: the brutal slayings, the history of the victims, and the tenuous but undeniable connection between Radcliff and the victims.

This information got him Karen's undivided attention. He could tell she was no longer concentrating surgically on her vanity mirror and was seriously digesting what he had told her.

None of the gore fazed her.

It was several moments before she chimed in with, "Travis, over the phone, based on your sketchy outline, I can't possibly give you an accurate profile of the specific individual you're looking for, but I can give you an academic psychological overview of someone who behaves in such a fashion."

"Fine. But keep it short and in layman's terms. Radcliff is due back any minute."

"These aren't *lustmord* killings—that's German for joy murders. Unquestionably, the heinousness of these acts indicates calculation and premeditation. This person gave this a great deal of thought beforehand. This was also pleasurable to the perpetrator. Not pleasurable in the sense you and I experience pleasure. Relief might be a better word. The killer took pleasure in the relief. It was required to aid in his attempted catharsis.

"There are usually only a couple of reasons why spree or serial killers start killing. Keep in mind, it's difficult for a rational mind to fully grasp a demented irrational mind. I've studied Theodore Bundy and his motives for years and I'm still not sure why he butchered dozens of women. Often, it commences in an effort to exorcise some ghost from their past; a twisted mission statement, if you will. It can be caused by an abusive parent, a traumatic sexual experience, something that rattled them as youngsters, perhaps. More and more scholars in psychiatry believe these traumatic events have to be linked to an individual who already suffers from actual physical brain damage or some other type of mental disorder, like schizophrenia. If all these elements are lined up in proper order, they have all the mental baggage required to step off the deep end and start killing."

Banks interjected, "If you had seen what this guy did, and believe me it's a guy, you'd know he was crazy."

"Crazy is not a term we use. It doesn't mean anything. Let me finish. Once they start killing, it becomes increasingly difficult to stop, for a variety of reasons. If the outbreak stems from a sexual dysfunction, killing may become the only way for them to relieve the stress. Then, as the media fuels their notoriety, it becomes their identity. They become celebrities. Sometimes a huge suicidal act is all that will stop them. That usually occurs only if they are cornered and know the gig's up."

"The media doesn't even know what's happened here, and if you had ever laid eyes on the Bellichek brothers, well, I can assure you someone sexually assaulting these guys would be the last theory to pop into your head."

Karen was on a roll and pushed on as if she was reading from a book.

"People have a tendency to paint a picture of some mentally incompetent homeless person living in the sewer and only coming out at night to mutilate people. Quite the contrary. Often, these killers come from middle- or upper-working-class backgrounds. They can have a wife and kids. They're intelligent, moderately well educated, and impossible to uncover by physical appearance. You could pass this guy on the street, and he'd smile and say hello."

Travis Banks was slightly startled when the squad room door opened up, sending a blast of cold air sweeping across the room. He momentarily covered the receiver with the palm of his hand and peeked around the door, which was open a crack. It wasn't Radcliff. He quickly put the phone back to his ear and heard Karen finish a sentence he had totally missed.

"Kram, this is all very fascinating, but where does the rubber meet the road here? I hate to hurry you, but can you cut to the chase?"

"Based on what you've told me, there are two possibilities. First, the individual in question is in the middle of some sort of a requital."

"A requital?"

"Revenge. Payback. I doubt this fellow is any more 'crazy,' as you call it, than you or I. Not in that sense. Maybe crazy with grief or remorse, but he's not a fruitcake on an undefined mission."

Karen's brother was puzzled. "Wait a minute. I thought you said a minute ago 'crazy' is an inappropriate term in your profession, but now you're telling me *fruitcake* isn't?"

"I used that term for the benefit of my audience."

"What's the other possibility?"

"The depravity and ritualistic style of the killings bodes well for the argument that this could be a religious fanatic, someone suffering from homicidal religiosity. They could be attempting to rid the world of all drunk, profane, sexually corrupt lowlife. He won't stop until the debt is paid. In other words, he keeps going either until he delivers all those individuals to hell or he gets caught."

"He's got a lot of customers around here." Travis pinched the phone between his shoulder and ear, sat back in the chair, put his feet on the table, and pulled out the note they found at Lake Labarge. He read it to his sister:

Brothers Ed and Brock,
It's not too late. It's never too late! Fill your lives with Christ. The Almighty is at hand. Redemption and salvation are yours. Reach out and be saved! Either Heaven awaits you or eternal damnation!
MJ

Kram couldn't help but think how striking the note was in terms of her analysis.

"There's a good starting point. I'd suggest the police pay a visit to whomever wrote that note. It's got 'zealot' written all over it. You might want to check and see if there are any religious fanatics within the police department. That is, if you truly suspect someone on the investigation team."

"What about the fact that Dale and myself have possibly seen him?"

"I would suspect as long as you stay clear of him you're safe. He's not interested in you. Unless, of course, you try and stop him, or get in his way."

"Great! What you're saying is, as long as I don't do anything and just let him keep killing in peace, I'll be all right?"

She ignored his question. "What happened to the little girl's father?"

"Simon Radcliff? I don't know. I think he's living in Norman Wells. He is, or was, an RCMP officer. His brother is running the detachment here in Whitehorse. I could only dig up some sketchy information in Yellowknife. If you've got any access to information I'd appreciate it."

"My home computer is wired to my office's mainframe. There are several common destinations our FBI computers have with both local law enforcement in Alaska and the RCMP in Canada. I know personnel files aren't accessible, but I'll run his name and see what I come up with. I'll call you later tonight or tomorrow."

The voice of Nick Radcliff echoed in the squad room. Banks sat bolt upright and covered his lips with his free hand, whispering quickly,

"Kram, I've got to go. Thanks for everything. You're a doll. I'll call you later tonight."

"Little brother, you take care. Don't do anything stupid. I can't accurately predict what this guy might do and I'm wrong sometimes."

"I know. I grew up with you. Gotta go." He hung up quickly.

Dale, Leon, then Inspector Radcliff rolled into the room. Radcliff was still unwrapping himself and disrobing from all the winter attire he had saddled himself with for the Labarge helicopter trip. The temperature had dropped back into the minus thirties since McMaster and Banks had arrived at the RCMP day care center. The cold helicopter ride must have been brisk for Radcliff and his crew, his cheeks being red and stiff, and his speech slightly numbed. He threw his navy blue parka and keys down on the tabletop, sending an empty glass ashtray flying off the table and onto the floor. His demeanor hadn't mellowed since their encounter at Labarge. He sat in the chair facing Dale and Travis from across the table, his silhouette engraved into the sparkling downtown city lights. Not even a glow remained across the northern sky. The chief inspector of the Whitehorse RCMP began his admonition without ceremony.

"Who was that?" Radcliff lifted his chin in the direction of the phone sitting on the table in front of Banks. "Your lawyer?"

Travis had no intention of answering his silly question. Radcliff knew Banks had been there for hours with ample opportunity to contact a lawyer. More importantly, Travis didn't need a lawyer and Nick Radcliff knew it.

"What were you two doing at Lake Labarge?" Radcliff was in no mood for games.

Banks spoke up before Dale had a chance to make things worse. "I told you, Inspector, we wanted to give our condolences to Brock Bellichek. I'm pretty sure Ed was the only family he had."

"Other than the shed, did you see anything else?" The Inspector was actually calm in his question. He certainly knew by now that Brock Bellichek's head was in the refrigerator but Banks wasn't about to mention he'd broken into the house and seen it as well.

"Nothing." Banks lied.

Radcliff stared at the two of them across the table for a long time.

"I'll say this one more time," he waved his index finger between Dale and Travis, "you two gumshoes stick your nose in this investigation again, and you'll go to Kingston prison. Is there something in what I just said that's unclear?"

"Nope," McMaster and Banks said in unison. Radcliff was behaving more arrogantly than usual.

"Powell," Radcliff said, standing up and leaning over the table, "go ahead and release them." He collected his coat and keys before heading to the door.

"Excuse me, Radcliff." Banks caught him from behind. Travis was beginning to dislike the man more and more and wasn't going to massage his ego further by using titles or unnecessary platitudes. "Are you going to be here for a while?"

"Why?"

"In case I think of something else."

He gave Banks a blank stare.

"Something about the investigation." Travis raised his eyebrows as if extending an olive branch. It was a lousy attempt to cover his true feelings about Radcliff. You could hear a pin drop in the squad room.

"Just stay out of it, Banks."

"Sure. Great. Only trying to help." Travis headed for the door.

Radcliff mumbled something barely audible to Leon. Banks heard enough to confirm that Inspector Nick Radcliff would be at the station for a while longer but, unfortunately, Travis also overheard something that quickly ruined his appetite: Radcliff would be leaving by eight due to "a Chamber of Commerce Dinner" the mayor wanted him to attend.

Now, the possibility existed that within two hours, Nick Radcliff and Travis Banks would be sitting next to each other chatting about their Cornish game hens and wild rice. The day was going from bad to worse.

Banks and McMaster made their way out to the dark parking lot and climbed into the pilot's frozen truck. The plastic bench seat was as hard as concrete. The engine starter engaged without objection but the pistons labored begrudgingly in the cold thick oil surrounding the cylinders. The motor groaned several times before rumbling to life. Travis didn't wait for the oil pressure light to extinguish before putting it in gear and heading quickly in the direction of Porter Creek.

Dale was shocked by his partner's uncharacteristically rough treatment on the truck.

"You in a hurry?" He looked around puzzled and soon realized Banks wasn't heading toward Northern Tracks where they had left Dale's truck earlier in the day. "I thought you had to get ready for a 'date' with the boss."

"I do."

"Why are you headed to Doc Baker's?"

"I'm not. Were going to Radcliff's house."

"Why? He's not there. We just left him. I thought you said he was going to be at headquarters for a while." Dale was confused.

"Exactly."

The realization of what Travis was about to do slowly gripped Dale's imagination and ire.

"You're joking, right? You're going to break into a second house today? A murder victim's home wasn't good enough? So, now you have to break into the house belonging to the guy in charge of the Whitehorse RCMP? Brilliant! Why?" Dale didn't wait for a response before continuing. "Can I remind you that a few minutes ago Radcliff said if he catches us snooping around anymore, he's going to send us to prison. I don't think he's bullshitting."

"It'll only take a minute. I'm looking for something. Anyway, we know he's not home."

"That's not the point. What about snoopy neighbors? How do you even know where he lives? It's got to be unlisted."

"It is. When I slipped behind the duty officer to ask if I could borrow the phone book, I saw Radcliff's address written on the guy's desk. I know exactly where he lives. It's a new extension of Porter Creek. I haven't seen it but the name of the street is familiar."

There was no moonlight. It was either overcast or another lunar cycle had begun and there was an invisible new moon in the arctic sky. Banks' crooked high beams cut through the darkness.

The wind started to pick up on the ten-minute drive to Porter Creek and blew ice and snow across the road in front of their truck, obscuring their view of the Alaska Highway. They headed north and soon passed the Kopper King Tavern on their left. The excited patrons were lined up and beginning to file in. They were laughing, giggling, arms around each other, already behaving intoxicated at the mere thought of the beer, smoke, and fiddle music that would soon engulf their senses. A mile later, Banks turned left onto Centennial, the first exit northbound for Porter Creek. Nick Radcliff lived in the rear of Porter Creek, in a new subdivision.

The two men passed all the new houses, which were painted with soft pale blues, whites, and grays. They were not identical, but it was apparent that there were only a handful of architects and building contractors behind the designs, who had decided that everyone would have the same amount of lawn and common trees planted in the front yards.

Radcliff's house would be only blocks from the honorable Dr. Baker, which reminded Banks, once again, he had failed to notify Michelle about his dinner engagement with Kayla Jackson, an engagement now less than two hours away.

The inspector's forbidding two-story brick home stood alone on a dead-end street, strategically embedded in the trees. There was one light on, burning from the tiny one-car garage attached to the house. A new fluorescent streetlight shone barely enough of an orange glow down the street to locate the mailbox at the end of the short driveway. Radcliff had obviously been seeking seclusion and had been astoundingly successfully. There was no attempt to make the outside of the house inviting. It was new but painfully bare and mediocre. With the dark street at their backs, it reminded Banks of one of those houses, as a kid, you steered clear of on Halloween.

Being in charge of the local RCMP detachment had its obvious advantages. Radcliff's home was complete. The building contractor had never finished the other homes on the street before winter's cold hand gripped the neighborhood, and they stood empty, half-completed frozen wooden skeletons.

The odds of being seen or caught were going to be practically nonexistent. An entire two-block radius seemed bereft of life. Banks pulled around the block and parked on the street in front of another partially erect structure. The two men climbed out of the truck and saw a path leading through the trees to Radcliff's backyard. The wind had picked up considerably, crackling and howling through the evergreen trees. The route Banks and McMaster needed to follow had branches whipping and thrashing just above the ground. They pulled the fur-trimmed hoods of their parkas up and around their faces in an effort to keep out the biting cold. Besides the wind, the only other sounds they heard were the crunching of frozen ground beneath their feet and the buzz of the fluorescent streetlight less than a block away.

It didn't surprise either one of them that when they broke from the tree line they found themselves standing in front of a privacy fence covering the back of Radcliff's home. Everyone knew Nick Radcliff was a loner, but the wall of privacy rising before them was shocking. It was at least ten feet tall and wound around the entire perimeter of the back of the house. Scaling the monstrous cedar wall was out of the question. Travis and Dale walked around both sides until they stumbled onto an unlocked gate blocking a small gravel walkway, which snaked its way to a wooden step leading to a glass door at the back of the house. They made their way down the path and up to the door.

Banks pulled on the wooden handle and the glass door slid open. It was almost too easy. The two men kicked and wiped their boots across the edge of the wooden step. The dry and powdery snow and ice easily fell off the frozen exterior of their soles. They quietly stepped inside the home of the chief law enforcement officer of the Whitehorse RCMP detachment.

Banks dug through his parka's inside chest pocket and retrieved the small black metal flashlight Monty had given him as a stocking stuffer the previous Christmas. He spun the tip, hoping the batteries still had some juice left. They did, but the small shaft of yellow light pricked the darkness and did little to illuminate anything more than his next step.

The kitchen was apparently off to their right. Banks could see the outline of the sink and oven created by the dim greenish glow emanating from the counter. The refrigerator's compressor jumped to life, startling both men and freezing them in their tracks.

Travis motioned to Dale with his arm to take a look around the rest of the house while he checked out the den. McMaster responded into the tiny beam of light with a porcelain smile and an erect middle finger. He wasn't about to leave the only light in the house.

The two of them briskly walked around the single-story structure, mentally absorbing the floor plan. The den seemed to be the only room Radcliff used regularly. The formal living room contained no furnishings except a vacuum cleaner, which was still plugged into the wall.

The master bedroom was modern and meticulously clean. It looked like a bedroom in a model home. The king-size bed was made with crease lines so sharp they might cut the skin. A year's supply of bright navy blue and gold starched police uniforms hung in the closet. An array of black polished RCMP-issued boots and shoes lined the floor. Radcliff's bathroom was painstakingly organized. Surgery could have been performed on the commode with no risk of infection. It wouldn't have surprised Banks if he collected his whiskers while shaving and disposed of them in the order they were harvested. The man was pathologically neat, prompting Travis to remind Dale to watch his step—if they happened to move some dust spores, Radcliff would surely notice.

The two spare bedrooms were empty except for several pictures waiting to be hung. One large chrome-framed photo looked like an RCMP graduating class from the '60s. There were several medallions dangling from the corners of wooden-framed citations of merit, which sat on the floor and leaned up against the walls.

The den was very small. An attractive navy blue and gray braided throw rug lay on the varnished hardwood floor. There were two burgundy leather chairs side by side with matching ottomans. All four walls were lined with modern teak bookshelves containing everything from police manuals to Alexander Solzhenitsyn's *The Gulag Archipelago*. The guy was no literary slouch. Banks had always considered himself well-read but he couldn't pronounce half the titles that now stared back at him. This made any notion of Radcliff's involvement in the killings all the more implausible.

The inspector's desk had several papers lying across it on an old-fashioned ink blotter. They had not been stacked precisely, the corners were not lined up meticulously, edge on edge. McMaster and Banks whispered sarcastically that Radcliff must have been in a hurry to leave such a mess. Everything else on the desktop had its place. Travis moved the stapler, expecting to see its chalked outline as if it were the victim of a homicide.

Travis attempted to open the desk drawers. The top pen drawer was open, the side file drawers were locked. He wanted to discover a clue to Radcliff's veiled past or some indication of his clandestine involvement in the present, but there was absolutely no information in the top drawer. There was nothing on the surrounding bookshelves. It was unnatural, almost calculated. The bush pilot looked around, wondering why a person would have so little in their home relating to their past. It didn't make sense.

Dale finally found the courage to wander off by himself. He shuffled down the hallway, which led to the small laundry room. The one lightbulb shining through the small window in the doorway leading to the garage gave him sufficient light and prevented him from having to use the walls to navigate. He turned the corner and disappeared.

Banks went back to the bookshelves to see if he had missed something. He held the little flashlight above his shoulder and next to his right ear, aiming it in concert as he turned his head back and forth. In order to see the upper portion of the bookshelf he took a small step back and high above him, barely visible, was the corner of a small cardboard box. It was on top of the shelf and nearly touched the ceiling. He stood on his toes and gripped it loosely. As he pulled it toward him, several books, hidden from view, tumbled down with the shoe box. One of them was a large Bible that hit Banks square in the forehead. He chuckled. Maybe it was divine intervention urging him to finish up and get out. He bent over and picked up the box, mumbling and cursing all the priests from his childhood. How had they managed to so artfully fill him up with so much religious rhetoric that he was now standing here in the dark conjuring up guilty religious thoughts? No wonder people gave away their life savings to some ex used-car salesman screaming

"Hallelujah" on the boob tube on Sunday mornings. He had to remember to have his cable disconnected before he turned fifty.

Travis placed the butt end of the small flashlight into his mouth, holding the box and removing the lid with his mitt-covered hands. He raised his jaw until the light shone directly into the small pile of letters and photos. He quickly flipped through the box's contents and found nothing of any significance. It was more benign material—gas receipts, dry-cleaning bills, and interoffice memos. Disappointed, Banks carefully placed it back on the same shelf, making sure to leave the corner exposed as he had found it. He picked up the books that had cascaded down on his head. The bible that hit him was the Old Testament. The education he'd developed during his religiously manipulated childhood now leapt to attention and pondered whether there was any religious significance to the fact that he had been holy crowned by the Old Testament as opposed to the New Testament. Usually able to castigate and make him feel guilty about anything, his religious memory drew a blank.

He did have one recollection that rang a bell. Granted, the memories were sketchy, but the Bible in his hand was much heavier than any Bible he had ever attempted to study in Sunday school. He sat on the arm of one of the leather chairs, steadying the flashlight clenched between his teeth. He opened the hardcover version to see if he recognized anything other than the first line of *Genesis.*

It was a unique Bible. The center of all the pages had been precisely cut with a razor from Genesis to Malachi, leaving a clean cavity an inch in from the edge of the pages. Where the cutout pages used to be, there sat a small metal lockbox. Banks plucked it out and tried to open it. The box was locked but it was a cheap lock. A letter opener on Radcliff's desk provided enough leverage to pry it open, revealing its contents of several dozen color photos and personal letters.

One set of pictures triggered some memories. Banks couldn't place them at first. They were pictures of a hunting trip, in a specific geographical area. They were pictures of a man in a parka, kneeling down, rifle in one hand, pulling up the horns and head of a sheep in his other hand. The man had a smirky grin and was proud of his kill. There was another picture of the same man hanging a sheep's hindquarter from a chain tied between two trees. There were several other pictures of campfires, tented campsites, and snowy mountain peaks. They were pictures of a hunting trip.

All the pictures showed only Nick Radcliff, except the last one. It was of two hunters, bundled up in parkas, their respective rifles slung outward and their arms draped over each other's shoulders. The second hunter wore a smile but was holding up his arm as if to block his face from the picture. He had failed and his face was exposed. The foreground of the photo was blurred. Banks' guess was that Nick Radcliff had set the timer on the camera to get a shot of them together, and he was the hunter on the right. Recalling the newspaper pictures in Yellowknife, the face on the left, trying to hide, belonged to his brother, Simon Radcliff. On the bottom right-hand corner of the photo was the orange printed date: 11/15/81. Banks unfolded one of the letters. It was signed MJ, just like the one he and Dale had found at Bellichek's cabin. Its contents were even stranger.

> *He will swallow up death in victory, and the Lord God*
> *will wipe away tears from all faces.*
>
> *'A good name is better than precious ointment, and the day of death than the day of one's birth.' Did you see the paper? They uncovered a dirty little secret. It's time. Twenty years is a long time. It's time to tell the people. It's time to reach out for the Father and cleanse the soul. I will free them. Hypocrisy can be evil. 'There is death in the pot.' I AM SALVATION!*
>
> *We have made a covenant with death,*
> *and with Hell are we at agreement.*
> *Prophet Isaiah*
> *MJ*
> *9/28/81*

Dale called out Banks' name in a harsh whisper. "Travis. Travis! Get over here."

Banks put the letter and pictures down on Radcliff's desk.

Before he made it down the hall to join Dale in the laundry room, the high-pitched sound of an approaching snowmobile filled his ears. It wouldn't have concerned Travis if not for the fact that he was standing inside a policeman's home without an invitation. Oddly, the noise was approaching from the rear of the house through the woods, the same surreptitious approach Banks and McMaster had taken.

Dale urged Travis toward the laundry room. He pointed through the small window on the locked side door, which lead to the garage. Surrounded by a large red Craftsman toolbox and enough cut firewood to heat the small home for several winters sat an aqua and black Polaris 440 snowmobile. They didn't have time to study it any further.

The approaching whine was so shrill it sounded as if it were about to come through the side of the house. Someone was about to crash their clandestine party.

Travis grabbed Dale by his parka's sleeve and headed for the rear glass-sliding door in the den. The lights of the howling machine had illuminated the entire back of the house, and the den was aglow and soaked with light. The two men stopped running forward and spun, looking for an alternate exit, crouching and scurrying away from the light. The custom-made front door of the house was an inviting possibility. The two of them furiously fumbled in the dark with a plethora of locks. The door must have accidentally been dropped off in Whitehorse instead of Manhattan, New York. Banks thought New Yorkers had set the gold standard on home security; although in spite of years of airline layovers in the Big Apple, he couldn't recall such an elaborate array of locks there. It was designed with dead bolts, knob locks, chains, and even sliding floor locks. If Harry Houdini had been trapped underwater with this door he would have drowned. Why in the hell did Radcliff have all these locks on the front door but left the rear sliding door unlocked?

The name of the dead bolt sent a jolt up Travis' spine. Vario. He reached into his parka and rooted around for the small ring of keys he had found at Primrose Lake two days earlier but which, until now, he had totally forgotten.

Dale was beside himself. "What are you doing?"

"I found a key in the snow at Primrose two days ago."

"So what?" He looked toward the noise approaching from the rear.

Banks cursed under his breath as he tried to locate the small ring hidden among pens, lint, candy wrappers, and God knows what else. He hadn't cleaned out the inside vest pocket of his parka in years.

"Dale, maybe our mystery man who used my balls for batting practice wasn't after the photos. He might have been looking for these." Travis pulled the keys out of his pocket and flipped them around until the odd-named one, Vario, stared back at him. He slid the key into its female counterpart in the front door of Radcliff's house and turned. The dead bolt slid open.

Dale kept looking back and forth between the door and the noisy snowmobile.

"That doesn't mean anything. Radcliff could have dropped them when he was out there investigating Bellichek's death."

Banks stared at the lock for a moment before looking up at his partner. "Dale, I found them *before* Radcliff arrived!"

"Those can't be his." McMaster stumbled for an explanation. "I saw his keys on the table tonight, downtown, at headquarters. You remember? He threw them down on the table when he got back from Labarge."

The sounds of silence gripped their attention. The snowmobile's engine had been shut off.

Banks pulled the key out of the dead bolt and looked around for an exit. They didn't have the time to try every key in every lock. Instead, they scampered through the empty living room toward the kitchen, opposite the den. There had to be a pantry, a storage room, someplace to hide, but they recognized that an essentially empty house is not the ideal place to conceal more than 400 pounds of parka-clad intruders. Running in the dark, Dale tripped over the vacuum cleaner cord, sending himself and the machine flying through the air. He quickly got up and stood the Panasonic vacuum back up, though not precisely where it had been—he didn't have time.

Panic-stricken, the two men looked around the dark kitchen. They were marginally aided by the green glow generated from the digital clock in the microwave. Next to a small breakfast nook, surrounded by a bay window, there were two accordion wooden-slatted folding doors. It didn't look big enough to accommodate the two of them but it was worth a try. They had run out of time. Out of the corner of Travis' eye, he could see an indistinguishable dark silhouette turn the corner of the privacy fence and march toward the back sliding door of the den. The figure marched with an authority suggesting ownership oft this home, yet he still looked over his shoulders in both directions. If he had heard Dale's encounter with the vacuum cleaner, McMaster and Banks' attempts to hide would be futile. The two exhaled in sync and slid into the dark storage room, quickly sliding the doors shut behind them.

The instant the wooden slatted doors were shut, the glass-sliding door to the den slid open. The stranger stepped in and closed the door behind him. Cold air crept through the back of the house, eventually swirling around Banks' feet in the pantry. Several large cans of soup along with boxes of cereal and other assorted nonperishable supplies poked into various parts of their anatomy. Dale stood next to a mop holder glued to the wall. The hook on the mop holder was embedded into his cheek. Neither man dared move an inch.

The silhouette in the den leaned over and clicked on the switch of Radcliff's desk lamp. The colorfully beveled glass on the tiffany lamp hood illuminated both the den and kitchen with warm colorful light. They could see that the stranger was a tall man wearing a black ski mask. He might be able to see the two men hiding in the pantry, but McMaster and Banks were unable to identify the intruder. Suddenly, the wooden-slatted doors seemed to offer no protection from being discovered. The light poured through the slats, making the pilot and loader feel as if they were standing naked in Times Square. They were both too petrified to budge. Banks felt like a live human being in a store window pretending to be a mannequin. His breathing had crawled to a hibernating pace.

Travis could see thin slices of the figure hunch over Radcliff's desk, pull a key from his pocket, unlock a drawer, rifle through some papers, and then stand up, placing a wad of $20 bills into one of his pockets. Between the slatted interruptions in Banks' line of sight and the stranger's ski mask, he was unable to identify who it was. Travis moved his head slightly and was able to get a better look at the prowler's movements.

The intruder pulled back the door leading down the hall. On a hook, behind the door, was a pair of orange overalls with a white stripe running down the pant leg. The initials "WDC" ran across the back of the jump suit. Banks had seen that type of overall before. "WDC" stood for Whitehorse Department of Corrections. Minimum-risk prisoners wore them during community service, cleaning downtown Whitehorse or the gravelly shoulder along the Alaska Highway before the tourists arrived each spring. The masked man threw the overalls across his shoulders and hurriedly returned to the desk. He opened another drawer, rifling through its contents as well and pulling out a set of handcuffs. He paused. Something had caught the prowler's eye. Banks clenched his teeth in disgust—he had left the hidden letters and hunting pictures on Radcliff's desk. The intruder studied the pictures and carefully unfolded the odd religious letter signed *MJ* that Banks had read. The masked man raised it closer to his eyes.

Moments later, the letter slid from his hands onto the desk. He grasped the edge of the desk for support, then violently slammed his fist onto the blotter. The angry trespasser spun around, clenching his fist to his forehead. His entire body trembled and shook. Banks couldn't see his face, but the pain or rage the person felt was obvious and palpable. His actions were terrifying. Dale and Travis stopped breathing. Whatever the intruder had just read had seriously rocked his demeanor. A few minutes later, the masked man regained his composure, and resolutely closed the drawer and then locked it. He started behaving as if he was consumed with a newfound resolve. Suddenly, he looked over his shoulder to the kitchen and then back down the hall as if he had heard something, acting as though he knew something was wrong. He clicked off the light. The room fell pitch-black again, except for the microwave's clock. He turned to leave.

In several moments, the prospect of not having been detected and escaping into the night might become a distinct possibility. The mop hook sticking into Dale's cheek had become more than he could bear and he couldn't wait to celebrate their apparent clandestine victory over the stranger. He moved slightly to the right to relieve the pressure on his impaled cheek. A box of something behind Dale's back fell forward, hitting his neck but not falling to the floor. It wasn't a loud noise but loud enough to be heard over the wind whistling around the house. Dale leaned backward to prevent the box from falling farther, but Banks glanced over and saw a box of cornflakes perilously close to tumbling. He mouthed the words, "Don't move." McMaster glared back petrified.

The silhouetted figure by the glass door stopped dead in his tracks. He turned with lightning speed and stared straight into the kitchen. He slowly approached the two trespassers in the pantry and drew back his parka, the greenish glow from the clock exposing the intruder's left hip. On his leather belt there was a large sheath connected to a gigantic bone-handled knife that could have easily substituted as a sword. He delicately grasped the handle with his right glove and slid it up and out of the sheath. It was even bigger than Dale had imagined. The grotesque image of Brock Bellichek flying spread-eagle in the rafters was dancing in McMaster's head and filling Banks with a sense of urgency. Travis slid his hands down around his waist, searching for something, anything to grasp and hold in case the figure approaching him pulled back the door to their hiding place. The only thing within reach felt like a dustpan. It wouldn't be a fair fight. The stranger with his sword, and Banks with his dustpan. Dale looked at Banks as if he would pitch in with his box of cornflakes.

The dark silhouette crept forward, turning his head from side to side, craning around each corner. He had covered the entire distance of the kitchen floor and was now standing in front of Banks and McMaster, hidden in the pantry. Travis stared through the wooden Venetian blinds of the door, amazed that the unknown stranger had not seen them. Only the dark holes through the mask where his eyes and mouth were located exposed any flesh. As he approached, he reached up and slid the ski mask off over his head. Banks cursed under his breath. It was still too dark to see who it was.

Travis had seen the shadowy outline of this face before, but he had no idea where. The dark face of the intruder leaned forward inches from Banks' face and twisted his head to glimpse through the wooden slats.

Travis was so close he could feel the man's warm breath creep through the slats of the door. Banks still couldn't get a good clear glimpse of the person's face.

The stranger's free hand reached down and grasped the pantry's little wooden knob. Banks' body tightened and his heart stopped. Travis felt Dale's body tense next to his, readying for the inevitable. Banks wasn't sure about Dale, but he didn't feel like waiting for the stranger to open the door. Travis had been taught, at a very young age, most fights are won by the instigator. Every muscle in his body was rigid and coiled like a leopard ready to pounce. The pilot leaned backed slightly and grabbed whatever the hell was in his hand. It was time to introduce himself to whoever was standing in front of him.

The silence was shattered. The ringer volume on Radcliff's home phone must have been set high enough to raise the dead, and the unmasked silhouette in front of the hidden men was as startled as they were. The intruder spun around wildly, letting go of the pantry's doorknob. The accordion doors opened slightly. Neither Dale nor Banks were seen through the crack in the door. The lone trespasser momentarily looked back at the pantry before racing into the den, opening the glass door, and stepping outside. Banks' stomach seized a second later. The masked man's head slowly poked back inside the house and gazed directly toward the men still hidden in the closet. He raised his right arm toward them. His hand was in the shape of a gun. Banks' eyes bulged locking on the black holes of the stranger's ski mask. The departing intruder pointed his index finger right at the wooden slats in front of Banks' face. The stranger clicked his thumb forward firing the imaginary gun.

The dark figure knew someone was behind the pantry doors.

The head covered in the ski mask disappeared outside and the sliding door slammed shut.

Banks opened the pantry door and peered around the corner. He got a last second glimpse of the intruder fleeing down the path and into the night. Seconds later, the whine of his snowmobile filled the night air. The back of the house lit up with his headlights before the light bent outward and around the property and disappeared into the arctic winter night.

"That son of a bitch knew we were here." Dale was so scared he was short of breath. "He couldn't have known who we were. Right?"

Banks doubted Dale's assessment. "If it was the same guy we chased downtown this morning, I seriously doubt that he's forgotten what our truck looks like. He came in the back, just like us. He probably saw our truck parked behind the house."

The answering machine could finally be heard as the snowmobile's metallic screaming engine subsided into the night.

Banks wished he had heard the entire message. He didn't know if it was good or bad. It was Leon's voice, half finishing a recording. " . . . able information . . . the photos are benign. I've seen them. I know these men, sir, they're not involved. Enjoy your dinner." The machine peeped.

Dale looked at Banks. "What was that?"

"Leon's just doing his job. Filling his boss in on the pictures we took from Primrose. "

Before leaving, Banks showed Dale the odd letter from *MJ* before placing it in the lockbox and putting it back on the bookshelf. Assuming this was another of Mike Jansen's letters, he was an extremely odd individual. But where did Radcliff get the letter? If he got it at Ed Bellichek's cabin at Primrose Lake why was it in his home and not downtown as part of an investigation? The intruder might know. Something in the letter had violently upset him.

Dale was not interested in staying one more second. He urged Travis out the door.

The intruder had left the phone book open at the residential white pages: last names starting with "J."

Banks and McMaster pulled left off the highway down Two Mile Hill and were back downtown before Travis' heater was hot enough to fill the cab with warm air.

Banks had a lot of questions about the stranger in Radcliff's house, assuming it was an uninvited intruder. And if it was, why would he turn on lights? It couldn't be Radcliff. He wouldn't park in the back of his own house and sneak around wearing a ski mask. If it were a burglar, why didn't he take something of value? The fact that one of Radcliff's house keys was at Ed Bellichek's murder site before he even got there was more disconcerting than any other development. Even Leon Powell couldn't ignore this new information.

Banks told Dale that the condition of Radcliff's Polaris 440 snowmobile was confusing. It didn't look as if it had been used in a while. It was hard to tell after just looking for a second through the window in the garage door. Travis had seen a layer of dust on the snowmobile's seat, but Dale disagreed. He hadn't seen any dust and was not interested in going back to investigate. Not now, not ever. There definitely were no oil stains in the tracks they saw behind the house on the way back to the truck. According to Dale, that didn't mean squat. The guy may have installed the new oil sump earlier in the day. What was impossible to see in the dark was if there were any broken or missing lug nuts.

Dale wasn't interested in anymore talk. It was "Miller Time" and he wanted out at the Klondike. He'd get a cab to his truck later. They stopped in front of the Klondike, but before Dale got out of the truck, Travis tossed three photos across the bench seat onto his lap. They were the pictures Banks had studied in bed that morning.

"Can you make these any clearer?"

McMaster angled the photos toward a streetlight and looked down at them. "Maybe. Why?"

"Look at the top left corner of the second one. There's something red or bluish near the tree line. It's too fuzzy to tell. Hell, it could be nothing."

"I'll have to use the prints to make new negatives and enlarge them. Sometimes you loose clarity, but I'll see what I can do."

They agreed to meet early in the morning and find the missing two Yellowknife miners: the religious one, Mike Jansen, and William Watt, the one they knew nothing about. Dale jumped out of the truck and disappeared into the Klondike Lounge.

Banks sat in the truck for a moment trying to organize his thoughts. There was something nagging him about his illicit visit to Inspector Radcliff's house, besides having just feared for his life, something that he had seen or heard.

He looked at his watch. The whole excursion to Porter Creek had taken just over an hour. He was supposed to be picking up Kayla Jackson in less than ten minutes. Banks was going be late.

Whatever the stranger had taken, found, or left behind at Nick Radcliff's house would remain a mystery for the time being.

Banks showered and jumped into his old suit in less than twenty minutes. He had only worn it at funerals for fallen aviation comrades. Eight funerals, to be exact.

Travis felt like a heel for never having informed Michelle Baker about his date with Kayla. The doctor had even left several messages on his answering machine. He hadn't had the time to contact Michelle earlier in the day and now didn't have the time to answer the messages on the machine.

Banks trotted downstairs through the atrium with his combed hair still wet. The frozen night air was inexpensive hair spray; it would soon freeze his "do" in place. He hadn't tried this hard to look good in a long time, and he galloped into Monty's living room waiting for the accolades.

Banks stood proudly. "Well, what do you think?"

The Lieutenant was stoking both his pipe and the fire. He placed the fire poker down and stood up supporting the small of his back with the palm of his right hand. He turned and looked at Banks as if the pilot were on fire.

"What?" Travis looked down to see if his shoes were on backward.

"I thought you said you were going upstairs to get ready for a date," Monty snorted.

"I did."

"Then what's this?" He glared at Banks motioning with his arm up and down.

"What's wrong?" Travis waited for a response but didn't get one. "C'mon, you obviously think something's wrong."

Monty exhaled. "The missus, God rest her soul, used to watch this bloody awful American TV show . . . what was it called . . . it featured one of those Gabor trollops . . . Cha Cha . . . or Ya Ya . . . or . . . "

"You mean *Green Acres*." Banks couldn't imagine where the Lieutenant was going.

"Yes, that's it. 'Green Acres.' That was it. 'Green Acres.'" He hesitated.

"And?"

"Well," his voice picked up tempo, "with that bulging vest you look like that fellow with the pig. Mr. Haney." The old soldier started getting worked up. "Good God, man, do you want to bed this beautiful creature or not? Where's your top hat and cane?"

Travis didn't know whether to get angry or laugh.

"First of all, Lieutenant, this is not the '30s. Top hats and canes are not the 'in' thing. Secondly, I am not out to *bed* Ms. Jackson."

"You ought to be, man! What's the matter with you? Wait until you're my age. You'll look back on squandered sexual encounters as if you had missed the last bloody lifeboat on the *Titanic*."

"What about all that B. S. 'don't dip your pen in company ink'?"

Monty's eyebrows scrunched toward his nose as he took little puffs off his pipe.

"Did I say that? Yes, well, you're half right. It *might* be bullshit. Depends on motives. If you feel special about the bird, the company and your work come second. I see it in your eyes. She's different, eh?"

Banks hesitated. "I don't know."

"There, you just answered my question. Anyway, I probably said that was the *honorable* thing to do, not what a red-blooded male *should* do!" He sighed. "Now, go on! Get. Have a good time. As Continental men go, I guess you look fine. By the way, when you come home tonight, if you come home tonight," he winked, "make sure you lock up. You left your back window open this afternoon."

"I didn't come home this afternoon."

"Well, then, you left it open this morning. I had to close it when I got home from the market. My fireplace wasn't designed to heat up Whitehorse."

Banks must have had a puzzled look written across his face.

Monty snorted. "Maybe the cats knocked it opened." He shrugged his shoulders before changing gears and tossing a set of keys in Travis' direction. "Here, it hasn't seen a date in years. Drive carefully."

The Lieutenant was gracious enough to lend Travis his pristine 1969 Ford Galaxy 500 to take Kayla Jackson to the Chamber of Commerce Dinner. Monty looked after the vehicle as if it were starring in an auto show every weekend, and Banks' truck was in dire need of a cleanup. Kayla might hop in and sit on Brock Bellichek's half-eaten pinkie. After the past few days, his imagination had lost all conventional boundaries of gore. God knows what might be on his truck's floorboards.

Banks' suit fit reasonably well, as long as he didn't exhale. He'd gained a few pounds since his last encounter with it. He undid the bottom two buttons on the vest and top button on his pants. Instantly, the fly on his zipper slid south an inch relieving the intense pressure around his waist. He'd have to remember to zip up when he arrived at the honorable Ms. Jackson's house in Riverdale.

The pilot peered up into the rearview mirror. He stretched his neck left and then right, tightening up his tie knot while driving with his knees. Mr. Haney? Hell, he didn't look that bad. The old limey had hit Travis with a zinger. Banks figured that commenting on Monty's poor shaving techniques every chance he got would be fair payback.

Banks didn't want to be any later than he already was for his first date with the boss and he hit the gas pedal too hard. The big Ford's tires spun for an instant, twisting the car sideways.

He had forgotten what it was like to drive a real car built before the Japanese took over the automotive industry. It was a good thing he hit the brakes on Monty's wombat a few blocks before Kayla's home. The 3000-pound ballistic missile on wheels took a half-mile to stop. The snow-covered Alsek Street, where Kayla lived, might as well have been an ice rink. The Lieutenant's car took off as out of control as a bull moose in rut. Travis Banks hung on the steering wheel and watched the neighborhood spin by, hoping nobody was out for an evening stroll. He came to a stop close enough to the curb and Kayla's house to shut off the engine and pretend he had actually planned to park where he now sat, got out, and walked across her neighbor's crunchy white lawn. Banks made a mental note to drive a little slower on the way back into town.

The tight-fitting black patent-leather shoes strapped to his feet were not ideal winter footwear. He had worn them only a few times and the soles were slick-buffed leather. He nearly killed himself edging along the driveway and stumbled up the walk as if he was having some type of seizure. Steadying himself, and trying to look casual, he rang the doorbell. It was a quarter to eight.

Travis could not have prepared himself for what greeted him when the door opened.

Kayla Jackson was unequivocally ravishing.

She was wearing a gorgeous long black evening dress and was covered at the shoulders with a matching shawl. Her streaked blonde hair was exquisitely and tightly bound on top of her head, exposing her long, soft neck and perfectly sculpted shoulders. She certainly didn't need makeup, but the little she had applied enhanced her already delicate facial features. A dazzling pearl and gold necklace hung around her neck, and matching elegant earrings dangled from each lobe. The strong smell of fragrance spilling from the house suggested she had recently doused herself with her favorite lilac perfume. It was quickly becoming Banks' favorite as well. Unfortunately, it nearly incapacitated his sense of honor. Neanderthal instincts are a scary thing. He was glad that society passed laws preventing people from acting on impulse. He desperately wanted to scoop her up and sprint to the bedroom.

"Hi." She gave the handsome pilot a quick smile. "You're late." She picked her navy blue winter coat off the coat rack by the door and swung it over her shoulders for the walk to Monty's Ford missile, switched off the hall light, and stepped outside.

Carefully, she placed her house keys into her dainty black dinner purse and snapped it shut. In her free hand, she held her high heels by the straps. She was wearing running shoes. Smart woman. Banks wished he'd thought of that. She tossed the purse over her shoulder and looked up at him.

"Well. Shall we?"

He was still drooling.

"Is there a problem, Travis?"

"Not at all, Ms. Jackson." He hesitated. He didn't want to sound too forward but he had to acknowledge the obvious. "You look . . . well . . . stunning!"

She smiled. "Thank you. You look very handsome yourself. You're to be congratulated as well."

"Why is that?" He stepped into the trap.

"You obviously bathed." She smiled.

He returned the smile and raised his elbow, extending a silent invitation to assist her over the icy ground. She took his offer and gently wrapped her arm through his.

"I saw your acrobatic performance coming up the driveway. Are you sure you don't need *my* help?"

She had won the first battle but Travis wasn't about to play dead.

"Tell you what. You promise not to wear those running shoes when we dance, I'll let you help me to the car."

"It's a deal. Only if you promise *me* one thing."

"Anything."

"Before we get on the dance floor, you'll remember to do up your fly."

Banks looked down below his belt. She had won the war.

The ballroom at the Klondike Inn was already full when Travis and Kayla arrived. There was a large foyer with several small bars dispensing four standard cheap liquors, California wine and Moosehead beer. Banks peeked into the Teslin Ballroom and observed the waiters and busboys scurrying around filling water glasses and preparing for the onslaught of the finest in Whitehorse's business community. Large cheap chandeliers covered the ceiling, brightly illuminating the room in sparkly white light. There were at least fifty identically set tables, each with eight pyramid napkins and a centered small silver sign advertising which company was to sit where. The long head table was elevated and split with a wooden lectern. A flexible microphone bent back from the lectern toward a flushed, red-cheeked fat man in a bulging, rolling suit who was slurring, "Test, testing one . . . two . . . three."

Travis tried to imagine how the hotel's special events manager ever obtained any satisfaction from orchestrating such artificial evenings. It was a high-class drunk. Nothing more, nothing less. Is an individual more valuable if he gets drunk in the gutter wearing jeans as opposed to a ballroom wearing a rented tux? Travis thought about his social contributions. He transported drunken miners and trappers who might moonlight as child molesters. Who was he to pass judgment on anyone or anything?

The cocktail hour in the foyer had come and gone without them. The crowd had started migrating to the Sterno-heated buffet line. Banks hated buffets. Florida was full of them. Airline employees referred to them as "hobble and gobbles," an unkind description of retired folks feeding from a trough.

Somehow, Arctic Air's only flight attendant and receptionist, Peggy Rand, had procured an invitation to the festivities and was surrounded by a speechless, gagging audience. He casually inched close enough to ascertain the subject of her latest story in aviation terror. She was explaining how the recent DC-3 crash in Rwanda was caused by a love affair gone awry between a Hutu flight attendant and a Tutsi captain. She continued to expound, in detail, how the Ministry of Transport and Federal Aviation Administration define death caused by BID: "blunt impact damage." In a nutshell, BID refers to the action of an airplane striking the ground and having the nose impact to a halt while the tail continues through the cabin, shredding its occupants in the process. Several members of the group surrounding her coughed into their drinks and politely excused themselves, scurrying to the bathroom with napkins pressed firmly to their lips. None of these members of the Chamber of Commerce would be chartering Arctic Air's DC-3s anytime soon.

Peggy caught a glimpse of Banks and motioned him toward her, imploring that her "favorite captain" join her stunned audience. He smiled politely, shaking his head and pointing toward Kayla as if he were tied to a leash and had no permission to leave.

Travis stood alongside his date eyeing the crowd. He knew several people but had no intention of mingling unless forced to do so, or he became fully anesthetized on cheap scotch.

From his hidden vantage point, he watched Nick Radcliff wander in and out of the ballroom several times, looking around quickly like a deer, eyeing the crowd, as if he were trying to find someone. He certainly didn't seem to be enjoying the proceedings. Moments later, desperate for a sedative, Banks left Kayla chatting with a half-drunk louse who thought his money would "bed" the boss, as Monty would put it.

Travis headed back outside into the reception area to fetch Kayla a wine spritzer and buy himself a beer before the "free" happy hour bar closed for dinner.

He thanked the bartender and turned to leave. In front of Banks stood a surprised doctor.

"Hello, Travis."

"Michelle!" He managed to act excited, confused, and stupid all at the same time. "What are you doing here?"

"Same as you, I assume. Having dinner. Celebrating commerce in Whitehorse." She turned and looked in the direction of the ballroom and Kayla Jackson. "Unless of course you're celebrating something else?"

He stared at his drink somberly. "Michelle, I'm sorry. I tried to call several times but I . . . "

"Please, Travis. Remember our deal? No explanations." She was hurt and acted like she wasn't.

"Ms. Jackson asked me at the last minute. She needed an escort. She felt she could trust me."

"She's not as smart as she looks." The doctor stabbed the swizzle stick into her drink, impaling a slice of orange. "Just kidding, Travis. That was uncalled for. I'm sorry. You have the right to see whomever you want."

"I'm not *seeing* her, Michelle. Look, I explained what it was . . . " He gave up. "Never mind."

She was doing "it." He wasn't sure what "it" is, but only women can do it. It's the subtle manipulation of describing a man's actions until the man feels like a heel. Suddenly, he feels awful and ends up with a wallet full of receipts for flowers and Chateaubriand for two. He thought there ought to be a law against women screwing with a man's psyche.

"It's as much my fault." She smiled slightly. "I tried calling you. I had that information you wanted and I was going to see if you would've liked to join me this evening. I should've gotten in touch with you sooner. I didn't realize how popular you were."

"Travis." Kayla Jackson approached from the dining room.

"Oh, Kayla, I'd like you to meet . . . ah . . . my good friend and Whitehorse's own female version of *Quincy*, Dr. Michele Baker."

Kayla Jackson didn't skip a beat. She was truly a class act.

"How do you do, Dr. Baker?" She extended her hand. "I've heard many wonderful things about you. Especially, how you saved Travis' life after his mishap several years ago."

Michelle gritted her teeth. "Yes, well, to be honest, I didn't save his life." The grit broke into a slight smile. "I've felt like taking his life a few times since the accident, but all I did was sew up a few holes." Dr. Baker put her index finger over Banks' lips. "I missed one big festering one, didn't I?"

They all laughed uncomfortably.

Travis handed his boss her drink and they all stood around staring at one another, wondering who was going to jump in and make some silly remark about how cold it had been recently. Never had Banks felt so awkward, but the moment didn't seem to bother Kayla. He felt Michelle was squirming but she smiled straight ahead. Travis looked around, hoping to spot a raging fire somewhere in the ballroom, anything to facilitate the building's immediate evacuation and his removal from present company. He was about to get his wish.

Peggy Rand was his unexpected salvation. She staggered up to Banks trying to be sexy and slurred into his ear. It was a blessing she didn't unwind often. She then either blew into his ear or licked it after imparting her message. A cab ride home was in her near future.

Peggy didn't make much sense. She said someone in the lobby paged her but really wanted Travis. It sounded odd but before he could get her to explain herself, she gave him a kiss on the cheek and ran off, ready to terrify another future air traveler. The strange story she told him was a welcome request. He excused himself and trotted off, curious as to who might be looking for him. Only a few people knew his whereabouts.

A gaunt elderly woman was on duty behind the registration desk.

The smell of gin on her breath could have peeled wallpaper. Her gray hair was gathered into a disheveled bun half hanging off the right side of her head. Years of cigarette smoking had given her a set of dark sunken eye sockets, and these glum eyes, along with her pointed facial features, made her resemble a raccoon. She must have been behind this desk since the cremation of Sam McGee.

Travis identified himself and she motioned for him to pick up a house phone across the hall directly around the corner from the pay phones. He quickly covered the distance and picked up the phone on the first ring.

"Hello." He was curious to know who tracked him down.

"Betty?" The Lieutenant's voice was unmistakable.

"Betty?" Travis chuckled.

"Hi, Pumpkin." Monty cooed

"Monty, is this you? Who the hell's Betty?"

"How's my little crumpet?"

"Lieutenant, this is Travis. I suggest you climb out of your brandy glass and get some sleep."

"I'm sorry, dear, but I can't see you tonight." Monty continued on as if he weren't hearing a word Banks said.

"Monty, what the hell's going on? You're sounding senile." In the background Travis could hear several male voices.

"You won't believe it, Betty." Monty dropped his voice an octave. "You know the young pilot who lives next door?"

"Monty, who's there with you?" Banks was quickly becoming concerned.

"He killed a man this afternoon." Monty half covered the receiver and explained to someone in the background he was breaking a date with his "little crumpet." He promised to be off the phone in a second.

Monty continued. "That's right. Killed a man. I overheard the police say it was a trapper. William Watt. This Banks fellow shot him with his personal, monogrammed, high-powered bow in a downtown church and then nailed him to the crucifix above the altar. They found the dead man's wallet in Banks' kitchen drawer. Isn't that awful? Never did trust the lad."

Travis pressed the phone to his ear, "Monty, what are . . . "

"Don't worry, pet," he wasn't explaining as much as instructing, "the police are looking for him right now. Anyway, sweetie, you wouldn't want to come here tonight, the place is crawling with bobbies. I have to go now. I'll see you tomorrow."

"Wait! Monty!"

"Love you too." The phone clicked dead.

Banks' skin crawled. A sense of panic rushed through his veins like hot lava.

He tucked himself around the corner of the lobby and out of sight. He leaned against the wall by the house phone and felt his chest tighten. He needed to sit down.

The men's washroom was across the hall. It didn't say MEN. It had a small picture of a placer miner on one knee panning gold. The women's door, several yards down the red-carpeted hall, was adorned with a scantily clad follies girl holding her dress high, one leg pointed skyward, doing the cancan. This location was going to get busy once the crowd in the ballroom got its fill of liquor and their kidneys needed bailing.

He had to find someplace to think, to comprehend what Monty had just told him. *The young lad next door, the pilot, killed a man, William Watt.* Someone must have stolen Banks' monogrammed hunting bow, killed William Watt with it, and then planted the victim's wallet in his house.

"Travis." Michelle startled him from behind. She smiled from across the lobby. The good doctor quickly walked over to his enclave near the house phone. She pushed her body lightly up against his and took his hand.

"I'm sorry if I acted like a bitch in there," she cooed.

He'd been seeing this woman, on and off, for years. She'd never been this aggressive or physical with him in public.

"I hate to admit this with all the silly promises we've made to each other in the past but when I saw you arrive this evening with Kayla, well, I guess I was a little jealous. I'm going to Vancouver tomorrow. Another medical convention. I'm leaving on Pacific Western in the afternoon and I don't want to leave with any hard feelings." She stood on her toes and kissed his cheek lightly, followed by raising a tissue to wipe off the lipstick.

"Anyway, I had to find you and let you know that I'm sorry."

Obviously the shock of Monty's call was affecting Banks' deportment. Her smile slowly faded and the expression on her face became deadly serious.

"Travis, what's the matter? You look like you've seen a ghost."

"Michelle. I've got to leave. You told me back in there by the bar that you had some information for me?"

"You mean about Nick Radcliff's brother and sister?"

"Yes."

"What's the matter, Travis?"

"Please, Michelle, just tell me what you've got. I'll explain everything to you once I understand it myself."

"If you're in some kind of trouble, you need to tell the police. Nick Radcliff is wandering around inside the ballroom. I can go get him and …"

"Michelle!" He interrupted her. He tried to keep his voice down and still get her attention. "Listen to me, do *not* tell Nick Radcliff you've seen me. Understood? Just give me the information you have and go back to the party."

He had never been so stern or unpleasant to her in all the years they had known one another. She was shocked and hurt. She answered defiantly in spite of being on the verge of tears.

"Well . . . Solange Radcliff died as a teenager."

"I know. But how did she die?"

"She was abducted and sexually assaulted."

"Christ, Nick's sister *and* niece were murdered." His voice tailed off. He wasn't prepared for that answer.

"What do you mean?"

"Never mind. Go on."

"I didn't say she was murdered." Baker wiped the corner of one eye.

Travis was confused, "You just said . . . "

"She survived the attack," Michelle continued, "but she died several days later in the hospital of exposure. Whoever attacked her left her alongside a road in the dead of winter."

"Where's Simon Radcliff?"

"I don't know, other than that he's probably dead. His medical records were purged from the system three months ago. That usually means a person has left Canada permanently or they're deceased. He's definitely not with the RCMP anymore and hasn't been for a while. That's all I could find out."

"Michelle, listen to me. I found a very strange letter today written by a man named Mike Jansen. See what his medical records have to say. Please. And don't tell anyone, I mean anyone, what you just told me. O.K.?"

"All right."

He'd never seen her look so frightened. He gave her a quick kiss on the lips.

"Go back in there," Banks pointed to the festivities, "and have a hoot. But don't mention to anyone you've seen me. The fact you're talking to me right now puts you in danger." He took her hand. "Michelle, you're going to hear some news in the next twenty-four hours that's all bullshit. Don't pay any attention to it. Try and get that information to me on Jansen before you leave tomorrow."

Radcliff's voice bellowed somewhere near the lobby.

"Now, go. I'll call you when you get back from Vancouver." He blew her a kiss.

Michelle quickly trotted off, totally confused. She looked back over her shoulder at Travis once or twice before entering the ballroom.

Banks considered exiting through the front door, but Radcliff was walking toward him, head down, playing with his cummerbund. It seemed the RCMP constable was pushing every button on his beeper trying to silence the chirping plastic black box. Had Radcliff seen Banks? Travis couldn't get out of the hotel yet. He had to get word to Kayla. The only escape was to the bathroom, but Radcliff might be on his way to the toilet. There was nowhere to go. Banks retreated around the corner and quickly picked up the house phone, hunching over into the small enclave.

One ear buzzed with the sound of a dial tone. Radcliff stopped a couple of feet short, around the corner, flinging a dime into the pay phone.

Banks had a lot of information to process, but what was happening was slowly starting to come into focus. His most pressing concern was the Royal Canadian Mounted Police. Monty had just informed Banks that he was suspected of killing one of the gang from Yellowknife. That's three dead trappers. There was only one to go: Mike Jansen, the religious fanatic. Apparently William Watt's wallet had been found in Banks' kitchen, and Watt had been killed with his hunting bow. He owned two bows, one which was in his survival kit and one, the monogrammed one Dale had given him as a gift several years ago, was at home. Banks hadn't fired it in years.

Monty had told him he'd found a window open earlier that day in Banks' half of the duplex. Travis never locked the windows but he hadn't opened one that day either. Pratt and Whitney would have to be on steroids to raise those old metal things. Could it be that while Banks was breaking into Radcliff's house, someone was breaking into Banks' house? That alibi wasn't going to sound very convincing in court. It would have to accompany an insanity plea.

Radcliff hadn't noticed the bush pilot hunched over around the corner. Banks tried to eavesdrop on Radcliff's conversation.

Travis overheard the RCMP officer bark, "Send two cars over right away."

Radcliff hung up the phone and walked to the registration desk.

Now was the time to leave. Banks pulled an old receipt from his suit pocket and scribbled a quick note for Kayla. He was obviously rattled. He should have given the note to Michelle when he had the opportunity. When he was done, he tossed it into the house phone cubicle. If Kayla looked for him before Radcliff sealed off the Northern Hemisphere she might find it. If Radcliff found it, he wouldn't know what it meant or whom it was from. Unfortunately, Kayla might not either. It simply said:

Kitch Olson wants you to call him at his summer residence as soon as possible.

Banks saw Radcliff raising his hand above his head, giving a description of someone's height to the woman behind the counter.

Banks slipped across the hall and into the men's room. After several seconds, he carefully pushed the door open a crack. The clerk behind the registration desk pointed in Banks' direction, toward the bank of phones across the hall, then shrugged her shoulders. Radcliff looked around and darted back through the open doors that lead to the ballroom. Banks had a better idea. He pushed open the washroom door and swept up the note he'd left by the house phone. Walking carefully across the hall, toward the lobby check-in desk, he pulled out the pen in his breast pocket and scribbled Kayla's name on top of the note.

Miss Raccoon looked surprised. "Where did you go? Someone was just here looking for you."

"Do me a favor? Page Peggy Rand and give her this note."

She raised her reading glasses, placing them on the tip of her nose. "It says Kayla."

Banks didn't need this relic's help. He took her liver blotched hand and gave it a kiss. "Please. Just give it to Peggy Rand." He turned to leave. "One other thing," he gave her a warm smile, "that fellow that was looking for me. He's an old friend and he doesn't know for sure if I'm here yet. We've got a surprise for him tonight. Don't mention that you saw me. O.K.?"

The old lady took a hard drag on her long Q-tip thin cigarette and smiled.

"Let me guess. Bachelor party. A stripper's going to jump out of a cake?"

"Something like that. He's a cop. We went to school together. Anyway, the other cops should be arriving soon for the party. Remember? Mum's the word."

Banks turned and headed toward the main lobby door.

It was too late. The frigid arctic night air was alive with the flashing blue and red lightning strikes of two RCMP cruisers pulling up under the overhang of the hotel's main entrance. The white and light blue Chevrolets slid to a stop, nearly hitting nose to nose. Four officers jumped out, leaving the strobes cracking away on top of their vehicles, lighting the inside of the lobby with red and blue flashes.

Banks tried to look casual as he turned back toward the four double doors leading back into the ballroom. He heard Peggy Rand being paged and looked toward the registration desk. The old lady on duty was winking at him as she spoke into a cheap microphone. She must have believed she was involved in some big secret. She was, but it had nothing to do with cakes, strippers, or Nick Radcliff getting lucky. Banks saw Radcliff heading to the lobby, searching the inside of his breast pocket. Without exposing it to anyone behind him, Radcliff pulled out a small revolver and checked the chamber before quickly stowing it back in its holster. Banks had cops in front of him and behind him. The receptionist was to the left and the washrooms were to the right. He smiled at the clerk and pointed at the arriving cops, and he told her the rest of the guys were here and the party was about to begin. Travis placed his index finger over his lips. She gave him a thumbs-up and he darted into the men's room.

There were six stalls and four urinals. On the floor in one of the stalls was a pair of suit trousers piled up on a shiny set of black wing tips. Someone had arrived since he had last departed. As soon as Banks entered the washroom, the unknown occupant started whistling. Travis assumed it was a polite attempt to advise him of the occupied stall. It wasn't necessary. The room reeked.

Under the two sinks was a ventilation grate. Banks quickly turned on both the hot- and cold-water faucets in one sink. He didn't want the whistler to hear what he was doing. Bending down on both knees, Banks slid under the counter-top. He snaked his fingers between the grate's metal baffles and gave a hearty pull. The ventilation cover popped off on the second tug and fell to the floor. The noise of the running water partially covered the noise of the metal hitting the ceramic floor tiles. The ventilation shaft was small and he was claustrophobic. Unfortunately, he didn't have a choice.

He used the counter to pull himself up. Reaching forward, his face barely making it over the countertop, he spun both faucets off. He stopped momentarily and stared straight ahead. The steamy hot water had left moisture on the left side of the vanity mirror while the cold-water side of the mirror was clear. His face looked cut into two, one side clear and precise, the other opaque and confused. It was the reflection of someone he didn't recognize. There was a unique fear written on the divided face and Banks knew he'd entered uncharted territory. He'd done nothing wrong but the wheels were turning and jerking out of control. For some reason, some unknown reason, he was now deeply involved in something out of his control. He needed time to think and sort it out. He had been framed. Why? By whom? He was determined to find out.

He ducked under the counter and squeezed into the small ventilation hole. There was a T-intersection several feet in front of him in the bowels of the dark shaft. He managed to turn himself around, slide back to the bathroom opening and quietly pull the grate off the floor back into its mounts. The moment the grate was in place, the washroom door swung open loudly, hitting the opposite wall. Through the cracks in the grate, he could see the shiny black boots that were standard issue to Northern officers of the Royal Canadian Mounted Police. Miss Raccoon must have caved in at Radcliff's first deadly stare.

Banks wanted to start crawling away but he was afraid if he let go of the grate it would fall back to the floor, putting an early end to his great escape. He could see the gold, striped trousers of the RCMP officers moving along the row of toilets, pushing open door after door. As each stall door slammed open, the guy in stall number two whistled a little louder. Soon he was whistling the *William Tell Overture* so loud that Banks thought the intestinally challenged occupant behind door number two might blow a rectal gasket. The poor fellow needn't worry. The odor would have kept Hannibal Lecter at bay. One of the officers bent over and looked under the door of the surprised whistler. The guy finally stopped chirping and barked, "Do ya' mind?"

The officers identified themselves and asked the perturbed whistler if anyone had come in or out in the past few minutes. Considering the cops had just rudely invaded his smelly space, he wasn't too keen to help. It became apparent he was slightly drunk. He curtly slurred that people had been coming and going since he arrived and he "hadn't kept a log, pardon the pun." He laughed. The RCMP officers didn't.

One of the officers bent down again and turned his stare in Banks' direction under the sink. Travis quietly pulled the grate as hard as he could and untangled his fingers from its baffles. He took his chances by letting go, but it didn't fall. He began pushing himself backward into the dark ventilation shaft that snaked throughout the old hotel, and managed to slip into the shadows before one of the officers bent down and looked into the dark shaft. He turned around and asked his partner for a flashlight. Banks twisted and contorted himself as quickly as possible and managed to turn a corner and slip out of sight. He struggled to control his breathing—the metal walls were pushing hard on his ribs like a vise. The instant he tucked his arms to his sides, the aluminum interior of the ventilation shaft filled with light. He held his breath. The side of his right nostril reflected the beam of light roving up and down from the trooper's hand. Could they see him? If they had spotted him, he'd know about it shortly. Banks lay perfectly motionless, breathing thimblefuls of air. Finally, the light went out and shortly thereafter the washroom door opened and shut. The man behind door number two finally stopped whistling. He belched and flushed simultaneously, cursing the police.

Travis slowly crawled around looking for another exit. He could hear chatter emanating from the women's washroom. Dropping in on them would land him in jail as a murderous Peeping Tom. Not the legacy he had in mind. He looked ahead in the darkness for another exit, and shimmied along for what seemed an eternity, but was probably no more than twenty minutes. At one juncture, he crawled up a steep angle as the shaft headed to another floor. There was no opportunity to turn around. He started to consider just hiding in the shaft for the next twenty years in his own arctic version of *Phantom of the Klondike*. He reminded himself that he hadn't done anything wrong. He was wanted for a crime he didn't commit and he was going to prove it.

The first elevated exit he came across was ten feet above a sizzling, smoking deep fryer. The kitchen was a hive of activity. Men and women wearing monstrous puffy chef hats and white double-breasted uniforms jockeyed for position. They were screaming and hollering at one another while flinging a flock of baked Cornish game hens onto stacks of white plates adorned with wild rice and parsley. Kayla was about to eat without him, though by now she must have begun to wonder what had happened to him. If she got his note, it wouldn't be long before she would start calling.

He had to get out of the hotel. Quickly. And preferably without running into the arms of Nick Radcliff and his men. If he wound up in jail, he had a hunch he'd never be able to prove he hadn't killed William Watt.

Electing not to end his predicament by leaping headfirst into a vat of boiling beef tallow, he wiggled forward and continued along the ventilation shaft another fifty feet.

The next vent opening was not only bright but also hot and humid. The grate was slightly detached at the bottom. Light crept into the shaft from the bottom seal. The vent cover would be easy to open. The shiny walls of the sheet metal aluminum shaft were dotted with moisture and corrosion near the opening, seemingly the long-term effects of humidity. The baffles of the grate were at such an angle that he was unable to see clearly into the room below. Other than the rhythmical cadence of machinery, there was no other activity. He must have found the hotel's laundry room.

He was hot and panic-stricken. Sweat dribbled into his eyes and claustrophobia was beginning to make decisions for him. He didn't care if someone was in the room; he wasn't about to back up and search for another exit. He gripped the loose grate and flung it into the room. Slippery and wet, he slid out of the wall. From below, it must have looked as if the hotel had given birth to a fool in a suit. Travis didn't hear the grate hit the floor but he felt himself land with a painful and resounding thud.

Banks rolled over and grasped the back of his neck. He had sprained or pulled something in his upper back on impact. A voice startled him.

"Jeez, that's gotta hurt, eh?"

Travis spun around with his legs straight out and pushed his back up against the wall. Sitting less than five feet away on a rickety old wooden school bench was a round-faced native Yukon Indian dressed in uniform white slacks and shirt. A black belt matched his black work boots.

Banks assumed he was face to face with the Klondike Inn's night shift maintenance man.

Telling the age of a Native Indian within a quarter of a century was almost impossible. This man's brown skin was severely wrinkled and his hair was shot through with silvery gray streaks. Banks guessed the Indian was in his '60s. With his round cheeks and hook nose he reminded Banks of the old Indian actor, Chief Dan George. The old fellow was scrubbing the lint off a filter that must have come from one of the large commercial dryers that lined a wall of the room. The rest of the room contained several other huge dryers and washing machines, only two of which were spinning. They kept the room humming and vibrating at a low pitch. There were several large tables covered in green plastic and a dozen laundry bins on wheels parked throughout the room, and the door on the opposite wall was slightly ajar, letting in cooler air.

The native Indian looked up only for a second, acting as if this type of intrusion was a common occurrence at the hotel. He sat with his back to one of the dryers, around the corner from the door. It was as though he were hiding from someone as well. A phone sat on the table next to him.

"Police, eh?" He asked as he went back to work on the filter.

"Excuse me?" Banks was stunned at the man's lack of interest in his presence.

"Must be cops." The Indian didn't look up. "I figure there's only two reasons why a white man would nearly kill himself jumping through a hole in the wall, eh? One, if his wife caught him cheatin', or, two if the RCMP was after him. Since you're in that fancy suit and not your underwear, my guess is it's the cops." He paused, waiting for a response.

By not answering, Travis answered his question.

"What they chasin' ya for?" he inquired.

"Believe it or not, I'm not sure." Banks was in denial. He still found it hard to believe what Monty had said over the phone. "Whatever it is, I didn't do it."

The Native chuckled. "My ancestors' been saying same thing for centuries, eh? Don't worry," he pointed at his chest with his thumb, "I spent a couple of days in the slammer once. It's not all that bad. Three squares a day. Mind you, you gotta be careful when you take a shower . . . "

"I'm innocent." Banks insisted.

The Indian smiled. "I was innocent, too. Could've used a white man in a fancy suit when I went to court. But you folks never fall out of the wall when ya need one, eh?" He paused. "What's your name?"

Travis massaged the top of his spine. It hurt like hell. He knew he had to get out of the hotel but he needed to catch his breath and he was hoping Radcliff was looking for him somewhere else. Hiding in this laundry room for a few minutes was as good a place as any to stay out of sight.

"Travis." Banks sat up and extended his hand. "Travis Banks."

The Indian shook Banks' outstretched hand politely and nodded at the same time. "Nice to meet you, Travis Banks."

"Likewise." They were both acting as if they were part of the festivities in the hotel ballroom rather than the hotel laundry room.

The two sat quietly and said nothing for several seconds.

"Marvin." The Indian spoke softly.

Travis looked up. "I beg your pardon?"

"Marvin. That's my name. I figured you were about to ask." The Indians eyebrow's hopped up. "A true Indian can see into the future."

Marvin was indeed a prophet. Banks was indeed about to ask.

"Marvin." Travis said nodding his head slowly, as if the name suited the fellow sitting in front of him. Banks had lived in the North for a long time but never heard of a Native Indian called Marvin.

Travis tried to be polite without smiling or sounding disrespectful. "That's not Cherokee or Kootenay, is it?"

"Nope." Marvin deadpanned. "I think it's whiskey. My dad was plastered when he named me. In fact, from what I can remember, he was always sloshed. Who knows what he was thinking."

"Marvin what?" The pilot had to ask.

The old Native continued to fiddle with the filter in his hand. His silence seemed to indicate Banks' question was intrusive.

Travis jumped in, "I'm sorry, I suppose it's none of my . . ."

"It's Yoblanski." The Indian mumbled, picking up a different tool.

"I see." Banks wasn't sure how to respond. He hesitated. "It's a pleasure to meet you, Marvin . . . Yoblanski."

Marvin continued. "It was hard enough growing up around here an Indian. Try it as an Indian named Marvin Yoblanski."

Travis sat silently, trying to avoid any possibility of discovering Marvin's middle name.

Marvin went on. "His grandfather was Polish. Came up here from California in the '98 gold rush. Him and hundred thousand other fools. Only 400 got rich. He managed to stake a claim on Bonanza Creek."

"Did he get lucky?"

"Sure did. Nailed my grandmother in a Dawson City whorehouse. She was 100 percent Native Indian. I was never able to figure out how a good woman like that could create the drunken louse who called me Marvin."

"Why didn't you change it to something . . . I don't know, native?"

Yoblanski stopped working for an instant and rested his elbows on his thighs. He looked up, trying to conjure up a distant recollection. "My dad did give me an ancestral Native name as a child."

"What was that?" Banks expected the great historical name of an Indian warrior.

Marvin leaned forward and stared seriously into Banks' eyes. His speech started slowly and then sped up to a crescendo.

"'Little Brown Running Pain in the Ass!'" Marvin clapped his hands and gave a hearty laugh, rocking back on his bench.

Banks realized Marvin was no threat to his being discovered.

"Marvin *is* my name." He continued, "Over the past seventy-five years I've gotten used to it. Besides, it drives you white folks crazy. Everybody nods politely, just like you did. They don't usually say anything but I know it's driving them nuts. They want to know how an Indian got the name Marvin Yoblanski. You're one of the few who have ever asked. Great conversation piece—when all you have in common is a name." He chuckled, knowing that was exactly what they were doing at that moment. "Don't you think?"

"I see." Travis wasn't sure why Marvin was working in the laundry room. He should've hosted his own psychology talk show. He understood human behavior better than most shrinks.

"I live by myself in that new reservation housing north of town near

Fox Creek. No living family." He became somber for an instant. "Yeah, Fox Creek. It's the reservation you white men built because you felt guilty about something you did against us Indians. They say you took all our land up here in the Yukon, eh? Well, you can have it. Hell, I got cable hooked to a twenty-one inch color Hitachi. Friday nights I get a large Pizza Hut deep-dish supreme delivered right to my door. God, I love the white man." He laughed some more before continuing. "If it wasn't for you people, I'd be living outside in a fifty-below-zero tepee. I'd be huddled up in some stinky caribou hide trying to stay warm by burning moose skin dipped in seal fat. I think *you* people are that 'second coming' you always talk about, eh?" He gave a wide smile.

As Banks sat there, it occurred to him that in all the years he had lived in the North he had never had a protracted conversation with a Native Indian. Marvin made Travis realize the population of Yukon Indians wasn't all drunks staggering around the White Pass railway station. Many had jobs and were hard workers. He'd simply never paid attention.

Marvin went on, "I know some white people dislike the Indian. They just don't know us. Never taken the time."

Banks stared down at his feet wondering if Marvin was referring to him.

"What ya do when you're not in that fancy suit crawling around hotel walls?"

"Fly airplanes."

"Oh, yea." He thought about what Banks said for a moment. "Big ones or little ones?"

Sitting here in his current predicament, Travis thought it best not to alarm Marvin by confiding with him he was once an airline pilot.

"Little ones."

Marvin eyed Banks for a second before responding. "That suit makes you look a lot smarter than you are, eh?"

"How's that?"

"If you were a smart pilot you'd fly the big ones." He went back to work before mumbling, "I always wanted to go for an airplane ride."

Even the guy working in the hotel laundry room was chastising him for leaving the airlines. Travis decided to let him believe he wasn't smart.

If he couldn't explain to his peers why he had left the airlines, he didn't have a prayer with Marvin.

Marvin Yoblanski quickly stood up and looked at the door.

"Get in basket," Marvin ordered pointing to a large cloth tub next to Banks.

"What?" Travis slowly got up.

"Just get in!" His voice whispered loudly as his old body struggled to pick up the ventilation grate. With a Herculean effort, he climbed onto one of the tables, and thrust the grate back into the wall. Banks clumsily fell into the tub, which subsequently rolled into a 360-degree circle. A second later a heavy pile of bedsheets was dumped on top of the startled pilot. The door to the laundry room swung open and Marvin did his best impression of a slow old Indian.

"Howdy, Officers. Is there a problem, eh?"

Banks couldn't see a thing but white cotton.

The voice was stern. "Have you seen anyone down here tonight that's not supposed to be here? We're looking for a male Caucasian in his late thirties, a little over six feet, probably wearing a suit."

It was Leon Powell. His voice was distinct. Travis resisted the urge to jump out of his laundry tub like a stripper out of a cake and hug his racquetball foe. Marvin had said "officers." There must be more of them. If Powell had a partner with him, Banks would be putting Leon in a bind if he stood up. Powell was probably as confused as Banks was regarding the bogus murder charge. Banks had to speak to him later, alone, but for now he continued to lie still.

A second young voice piped up. "The suspect is wanted for murder."

Leon came to Travis' defense and put his young zealous partner in place, "We simply want to question the subject regarding an ongoing investigation."

Banks had a sixth sense that Marvin was staring at him in the tub, debating whether or not to hand Travis over to the police. Banks assumed Marvin had no idea he had just spent the last five minutes with a murder suspect. Banks sat motionless, hearing nothing.

The pilot's instincts were sound. Marvin was unflappable.

"The only suits I get down here, Officers, are dirty and empty. Sorry, but nobody's been down here." He chuckled for their benefit.

Banks heard Leon thank Marvin for his time and then the door creaked closed.

Moments later the sheets were lifted from Banks' head and replaced with a small caliber handgun that shook nervously in Marvin's hand.

"Murder? You've been a bad white boy, Travis."

Banks started to pull himself out of the tub but Marvin pointed him back into the hamper with the gun.

"For Christ's sake, Marvin, I didn't kill anybody! Do I look like a murderer?"

"Don't know. Never met one before. Least not a white one wearing a fancy suit."

"Well, you still haven't met one. Are you going to put down that gun and let me out of here?"

"Who'd you kill?"

"Nobody!" Banks implored.

Marvin stared at Banks, wanting more information. Travis acquiesced.

"According to the police, I killed a trapper. A trapper, I might add, I've never met."

"Was he Indian trapper?" Marvin snapped.

"No, Marvin. It wasn't an Indian trapper." The old man had Banks confused. He thought for a moment of the grainy pictures in the Yellowknife newspaper. "Well, Marvin, hell, I don't know. I don't think it was an Indian. I've only seen a picture of him. He was white, I'm sure." Banks looked up at the old man incredulously. "Why, would you turn me in if he had been an Indian? What's that got to do with anything?"

Marvin looked into Banks' eyes for a few moments.

"Nothing." A mischievous smile spread across his face. "But I'll bet you're more aware of the plight of the Yukon Indian now than you were before you dropped by my laundry room tonight." He put the gun in his pocket, turned away and disappeared.

Travis emerged slowly from the tub and peered over its sill. Marvin had his head out the door and was looking up and down the hall.

"Marvin, do you have a permit for that thing?" Banks eyed the gun in Marvin's hand. "It's illegal in Canada if you don't."

The elder Yoblanski pointed down with his index finger for Travis to get back into the tub.

"It's also illegal to help a murderer escape. We go now. You stay in hamper."

"Look, I'm not a murderer. Once I get out of here, I'll get the answers and I'll clear myself."

"Good. 'Cause you may not be a murderer but I *am* an Indian. If they find out I help you get away, they'll bring back hanging just for me." He smirked before throwing the same pile of sheets back on Banks' head.

"I'm taking you to the loading dock. If it's safe, I kick the side of the tub. Wait a minute or two so I can get back inside. Then you're on your own."

"Thanks, Marvin. I won't forget your help." A moment later they smashed through the swinging door of the laundry room and turned down the hall.

"If you clear yourself, you can take me for an airplane ride and we go hunting."

"You got it. How about a sheep in Kluane Park?"

"How 'bout a pizza in Fairbanks? Never had Domino's deep-dish. Looks pretty good on TV."

Radcliff had yet to figure out how Banks had gotten Kayla Jackson to the Klondike Inn. Apparently, she hadn't divulged it either. The astute RCMP officer must have known Banks' truck was at his home in Hillcrest. Banks' guess was Monty told the RCMP he had taken a cab to the Chamber of Commerce Dinner. A lot of people were sticking their necks out for Travis. He was now feeding off their faith. And he was going to get answers—he just had to sort out the questions: Who was the intruder in Radcliff's home and where was Mike Jansen? Maybe both questions could be answered by the same person: the person who killed William Watt.

Monty's car sat in the parking lot unattended. Fortunately, Travis had tucked it away from any streetlights toward the back of the Klondike parking lot. He remembered not wanting to be too close to any other vehicles when it was time to leave. Monty's missile had the turning radius of an eighteen-wheeler.

Banks crept up from behind the huge Ford and slithered in the driver's door. He hated carrying keys in his pockets. Out of habit, he hid them under the front seat. After a quick grope in the dark, he found the keys and slipped the long one into the ignition. The old V-8 was cold and cranky but eventually fired to life. The rearview mirror filled with billowing plumes of smoke. A few pumps of the accelerator and the coughing gave way to a smooth idle.

Travis turned left out of the parking lot onto Second Avenue. Three minutes later, he passed the Northwest Territorial Government Building and turned right. The South Access Road would take him to the fictitious summer residence of Kayla's late mentor, Kitch Olson. He kept his eye in the rearview mirror. He was rightfully becoming paranoid. Travis assumed any headlights tailing him belonged to an overzealous rookie RCMP trooper ready to bag his first "bad guy," but his fears were unfounded. The road behind him was clear. The only lights appearing in the rearview mirror were opaque streetlights becoming obscured by patches of drifting ice fog.

He turned left at the large turbines of the Schwatka Lake hydro station. Bright white halogen lights lit up the entire south end of the manmade lake. The heat from the facility kept the lake water at the south end from freezing, but the rest of Schwatka Lake was covered in a thick sheet of white, windswept ice.

The bumpy ride down the snow-covered, unplowed road rattled his kidneys. It was worse than the jarring laundry tub tour he had taken moments before through the Klondike Inn.

Banks arrived at the desolate Schwatka Lake office of Arctic Air within ten minutes of leaving Marvin's tub.

He parked Monty's car in the bushes near the summer boat launch, fifty yards down the shoreline. If a police cruiser circled the lake, they'd never see the car.

The lake was deathly still. Except for the drone of the hydro turbines behind him, there were no sounds. It was a perfectly quiet Yukon winter evening.

Banks assumed that the lake office would not have had any visitors since his three-round no decision the previous night. He was wrong. There were tracks all over the place. A new lock hung from the latch. Ralph Michaels, Arctic Air's diligent chief mechanic, had obviously been down earlier in the day to repair the door.

Cupping his hands around his face, he tried to look inside the office. The floodlights of the dam shone enough light inside to confirm that the office had been cleaned as well.

Unfortunately, he didn't have a key for the new lock.

When the office phone started ringing, he scampered the ten feet to the aboveground aviation fuel tanks on the frozen shoreline. The strong pilot picked up a rusty fire ax, ran back to the door, and in one motion, swung the ax onto the new lock. Luckily, it was a typical Arctic Air purchase: cheap. It exploded into a dozen pieces. Ralph would have to come back tomorrow to fix the door again.

Banks managed to get to the phone on the fifth ring.

He held the receiver to his ear and said nothing while catching his breath.

"Travis?" Kayla sounded shaky and unsure.

It was good to hear her voice. "Hello, Ms. Jackson," he said, taking a deep breath and exhaling. "You got my message. Welcome to Kitch Olson's summer residence."

"You're the only one I've told about Kitch's death. I knew what the note meant. Where have you been? I've tried calling for almost half an hour."

"I was busy helping an Indian do laundry."

"You were what?"

"It's a long story. Are the police still looking for me?"

"Yes. They wouldn't say who they were after but it was obvious when I got your message. They've been wandering all over the hotel. One of them even looked under the tables in the ballroom. Your friend, Powell, was here for a few minutes. He crept over to me and whispered some crap about your hunting bow being found at a murder in a downtown

Baptist church. I told him I doubted that you've seen the inside of a church since you were out of diapers." There was a slight cutting edge to her remark.

"Be fair. I go now and then, usually when I think crazy thoughts, like marriage. Anyway, I know for a fact I'm not a pagan; I think I'm spiritually agnostic."

"You might want to take up religion again. According to Powell, you're in trouble. He assumes you're innocent but he said his boss wants your scalp. He wants me to let him know if we make contact."

"Will you?"

"No, of course not!"

"Good. Where are you now?"

"I'm still at the Klondike. I'm about to catch a cab. I'll come and get you."

"No, you won't! Whatever you do, don't come down here."

Banks doubted Radcliff would tail her but it wasn't worth taking the chance.

"Kayla, where do you keep all your old charter tickets?"

She stumbled trying to gather her thoughts. "Well . . . ah . . . the ones from the current fiscal year are in my filing cabinet at the office."

"And previous years?"

"They're at home."

"I need a favor . . . "

She interrupted, "Travis, what is going on?"

"I'll tell you later. Just go home. Make sure no one follows you. Look up any old receipts you have for a fellow named Jansen. Mike Jansen. See if he's chartered us. I need to know where he lives, or at least what lake or airstrip we might have dropped him off at. It's probably somewhere near Burwash. I'll call you in twenty minutes."

Banks kept the receiver to his ear and pushed the right button on the phone's cradle, then he dialed Monty's number. He hoped the police would have left by now.

The Lieutenant picked up instantly.

"Obviously, they've left, Monty?"

"Yes, Travis, they're gone," he snorted in a disgusted English accent.

"There's one parked down the street watching the house. He's smoking so damn much, the inside of the car looks as if it's on fire. He's convinced I can't see him. Silly twit. I've a mind to go out there and tell him he'll die of lung cancer before they catch you."

"Leave him be. He might be of use. If Radcliff thinks the duplex is being watched, they'll keep their distance."

"How are you, lad?"

"Fine."

"Where are you?"

"Monty," Banks hesitated. "I trust you like my own father. But if I tell you my whereabouts . . . someone might conclude you're harboring a fugitive. I don't want you to lie if someone asks. Let's just say I'm safe."

"Who set you up?" Monty asked with the zeal of an old gumshoe. He didn't even consider the possibility that Travis was involved in William Watt's demise.

"I assume it's the same person who stole my bow."

"Who?"

"I'm not sure yet but I have an idea."

Banks mentally tried to place the time the intruder had arrived at Radcliff's residence and the time his bow was stolen.

Travis asked Monty, "How long were you gone this afternoon before noticing the window was open in my place?"

"It was only a few minutes. Maybe twenty, thirty at the most. Just after tea this afternoon. It wasn't long before you came home and washed up for dinner."

"And when did the police say Watt was killed?"

"They didn't say anything to me but I overheard one bobby say the body was discovered around four this afternoon. A janitor found him."

If Monty's timeline was accurate, Banks' bow had to have been stolen, taken downtown, and used to kill Watt. Then the killer had to come back and plant the victim's wallet in his kitchen, all in less than thirty minutes. It was impossible, unless the wallet wasn't planted until the police arrived to arrest him.

"Monty, who was the first RCMP officer to arrive at our house?"

"It was Inspector Nick Radcliff. He was all dressed up for the Chamber of Commerce Dinner."

Banks pulled the lapels of his suit collar up around his neck. The float base office was freezing but he didn't dare light the oil stove. If an RCMP patrol car was dispatched to visit the Schwatka Lake office, the white billowing exhaust from the heater would be seen for miles.

"What can I do?" The Lieutenant was desperate to help.

"Find Dale and tell him to prepare for a sheep hunt. He'll know what I mean. Have him wait at the airport until I contact him." If Jansen lived anywhere near his postmarked letters they'd need survival gear.

"Done." Monty unnecessarily scribbled the message down.

Banks' mind was racing. He didn't have much time. There was one piece of the puzzle still missing.

Monty continued with a touch of glee in his voice.

"How was the date, lad?"

"Well, I didn't *bed* her if that's what you want to know. It sort of died before it started. Nobody's fault."

"What happened?"

"Well, Lieutenant, if you must know, I spent most of the evening doing the two-step inside a hot ventilation duct instead of on the dance floor."

"Say what?"

"I also had a pleasant tête-à-tête with an eighty-year-old Indian named Marvin Yoblanski."

He was utterly confused, "What about the lovely Ms. Jackson?"

"It's a long story. Just get Dale." Banks slowed the pace of his voice. "One other thing, Monty, before I forget: thanks."

"Not to worry, son. We'll get to the bottom of this. I'm off. I'll find what bar McMaster is in and send him to the airport." He hung up. He hadn't experienced this much excitement in years. Travis wished it had been at someone else's expense.

There was silence. He sat in the cold dark office waiting to call Kayla Jackson back. He looked at his watch. Not even ten minutes had passed, and he was antsy about sitting in one place too long.

Travis felt the same trepidation that encompasses a pilot when an airplane breaks in flight but doesn't crash. Usually, nothing goes wrong. Hours of reliable boredom. But when something pops, snaps, or explodes, the rush of adrenaline-induced fear can be temporarily crippling. In order to think clearly, he needed to relax.

He looked out the window into the northern sky. The extraordinary night landscape helped take his mind off his current predicament and the bitter cold.

It was a magnificent arctic evening. The aurora borealis lit up the ink-black night sky as if it were his own vast planetarium. The colorful northern lights waved and danced among the stars in graceful rhythmic cadence. The stars themselves were as sharp as needles, and there were billions of them. He had never seen such pristine stars until he moved north.

The crunching sound of turning car tires and the accompanying reflections of headlights filled the surrounding night air. Banks ducked into the rear storage area and peeked out the back window. It was a car he didn't recognize and he watched it drive slowly along the frozen lake shore until the vehicle's taillights disappeared into the night. Probably young kids looking for a spot to examine each other's tonsils in peace.

Banks blew warm air into his hands and curled up on the diesel-stained couch. He crossed his arms tightly into his suit's armpits, trying to find some untapped source of warmth. His mind struggled to absorb the many details of the previous three days.

It was times like this he thought about the big bear of a man he called Dad. What he would give to pick up the phone and confide in him right now. The thought struck a chord—he did have family to call. He stood up and took the two short steps required to reach the old rotary phone on the warped oak desk. Travis dialed his sister's home phone number in Anchorage. While he waited for the call to connect, he pushed the light button on his watch. He was hoping Karen's hot date was over by now. And, in case it wasn't, as her little brother, it was his duty to end it.

She picked up on the first ring.

"Hi, Sis." Travis must have sounded melancholy. The stray thoughts of his father had permeated his disposition.

She chuckled. "You sound like your evening was worse than mine."

"You don't know the half of it."

"How can it be worse than this afternoon?" she asked rhetorically.

"Well, let's see. This afternoon I was only being questioned for *interfering* in a murder investigation. As of right now, I'm *wanted* for murder."

Karen Banks' voice had never been more subdued. "I beg your pardon?"

"That's right, Kram. Murder. You know, 'Book 'im, Dano.' That sort of thing. Anyway, don't worry. It's all just a big misunderstanding. I'm sure they'll clear it up before I'm electrocuted." His attempt at humor was not being well received.

The phone was silent. Karen tried to sort out whether or not he was joking.

"I was framed, Kram. Someone stole one of my hunting bows, a bow I haven't used in years, and whoever stole it didn't waste much time before using it. They killed an old miner with it in a downtown Baptist church," he paused. "Now I know why Mom wanted us raised Catholic."

"Travis, this isn't funny."

"You're telling me." His sarcasm was mixed with anger as he began to realize how grave his predicament was. He didn't even like thinking about it. "So, enough about me, how was your evening?"

"Short, like my date." She caught herself answering his trivial question. "Who cares about my night? What have you gotten yourself into?"

Travis sighed. "It's part of the same mess I was in this afternoon."

"Where are you?"

"I'd rather not say." Banks took a quick look out the office window. He thought he'd heard something outside. "You didn't happen to punch up Simon Radcliff's name on your fancy FBI computer yet, did you?" He half stood up and looked outside the office's back window. There was nothing out there.

"As a matter of fact, I did. Unfortunately, I didn't come up with much other than the fact that he's dead."

"What happened?" He didn't know if he had expected that answer or not.

"The only way I found anything out was because he died in the United States. Or at least it was close enough to involve authorities in both countries. It was a hunting accident near the border. He slipped off a mountain ledge south of Northway, Alaska. Somewhere between Beaver Creek and Burwash. It was last fall. October."

"October?" The pilot jolted upright on the office's hard wooden swivel chair. "It couldn't be October, Kram."

"It was. I've got it right here."

"Where was he buried?"

"He wasn't. According to the official police report, which was filed with the sheriff in Northway, a winter storm hit before they could get to the body. They've never recovered him."

"Who reported the accident?"

The phone's speaker broadcast a distant shuffle into Banks' ear as she searched her notes in the background. "Let's see, umm, no wonder it wasn't investigated further." She mumbled into the phone.

"What?" Her brother urged.

"An individual didn't file the report." She paused. "That's odd."

"What's odd?"

"The accident was reported directly to Fairbanks police officials by the Northway Sheriff's Department." She was paraphrasing directly from printed notes. "The RCMP filed a similar report in Canada. It was reported by... here it is... a Canadian police officer. It doesn't say who."

"I have an idea." The pieces began tumbling into place.

"It's unusual for the police to directly file the report. Unless, of course, the officer was with the person at the time of the accident. It appears he was the only witness. That might also explain why there was no further investigation. A cop reported it."

"Thanks, Kram. I'm going to be fine. If the RCMP contact you, tell them the truth. You don't know where I am."

"Wait, Travis, I've got some vacation coming . . . "

"Stay there. I might need your help. I'll call you in a day or two."

No sooner had he hung up the phone when the person creating the noise outside violently swung open the front door and stepped into the float base office. Banks' heart froze and missed a beat. It had been several days since the intruder had shaved. A brownish-blond stubble of whiskers encircled the lit cigarette hanging from his lips. His breath filled the cold office with the unmistakable smell of alcohol. Dale McMaster held a flashlight up to his face and did an atrocious Boris Karloff impersonation.

"Goood eeevening."

"Jesus Christ, Dale." His abrupt arrival had rattled Travis' nerves and locked his diaphragm. He leaned over the desk and caught his breath. "Would you mind knocking next time?"

Dale emptied his lungs of cigarette smoke into the dark office. He flipped the smoldering butt into the frigid night air before closing the door.

He shone the flashlight on Banks and studied his face for an instant.

"You look like shit." Dale plopped onto the arm of the small couch and checked his watch. "I got your message from Monty. He paged me at the Chalet. I was about to get lucky."

"Based on what you consider lucky, I've probably done you a big favor." It was hard to tell how much he had drunk. He was good at hiding it.

"Made it here in less than thirty minutes. Not bad, eh? I parked at the boat launch. Next to you." He crossed his arms before continuing. "You've had a busy night. The Lieutenant tells me you're up to your asshole in alligators."

"How did you know where I was?"

"*That* was a no-brainer, Sherlock." He slid off the arm and onto the couch. "There's no other place you'd go. And if little ol' me can figure that out, so can the Keystone Kops."

McMaster was right. Banks quickly picked up the phone and dialed Kayla's number. He'd given her enough time. She must have been inches from the phone. She picked it up before it rang on his end.

"Travis?"

"It's me. Any luck?"

"I'm trying. I haven't even taken my coat off yet." She must have been holding the phone to her ear with her shoulder. She was barely audible. "I've gone all the way back to 1975 . . . wait . . . here's something."

"Please tell me you've got a charter ticket with Mike Jansen's name on it?"

"Hang on."

Banks could hear papers being tossed around on her desk.

"Here we are. It's the only one I've found so far . . . "

"One's enough. What's it say?"

"I don't know if he lives here, but seven years ago we dropped off a Mike Jansen at, get a load of this, 'Duke Lake.' The charter ticket says it's northwest of Burwash. Where in the hell is 'Duke Lake'?"

The name rang a bell. It was common for bush pilots when flying floats or skis in the far reaches of the North to name unnamed charted and uncharted lakes. There were thousands of tiny remote lakes on aeronautical maps that were nameless. Christening the obscure body of water with whatever designation that came to mind was a safety net for the passengers as well as the pilots. The name had to be somewhat absurd for memory's sake: Trout Lake, Long Lake, Big Salmon Lake were all names that had been used a multitude of times. Often, hunters and fishermen didn't know where they wanted to be dropped off until they saw it from the air. As you were the only person on the planet who knew their whereabouts, if anything tragic happened on the flight home or prior to their scheduled pickup, they might never be heard from again. Some of these lakes were several hundred miles from a trail, let alone a road. No one was usually dropped off in the winter, but during the summer months, pilots had crashed on the leg home and it took weeks of search and rescue to locate the terrified and starving passengers. Normal procedure dictated that, prior to departing an unnamed lake, the pilot call on the HF radio and give their company rough magnetic coordinates to the drop point as well as a new elaborate name for the lake, one people wouldn't soon forget.

A friend of Banks and fellow aviator had come up with the name "Duke Lake." He had died several weeks later landing short of a runway, ten miles short to be exact. He hit a mountain near Whitehorse in a blinding snowstorm attempting to shoot an instrument approach in an airplane with no instruments. It was Banks' first winter in the North. The friend was a skillful old-timer who was supposedly too seasoned to ever make such a mistake. Like all pilots, Travis convinced himself his friend's death was not in vain. Naïve, along with the other pilots attending the man's funeral, Banks agreed they should all learn from the pilot's death and not repeat his mistake. Since then, Banks had buried several of those pilots who'd attended that old-timer's funeral. They eventually made the same ill-advised mistake. It's one of the reasons pilots don't like to criticize a fallen airman's final decision—they may well make the same stupid miscalculation one day, resulting in their own demise. Over time, pilots realize that incorrect aeronautical decisions that result in death are best left uncriticized lest it become their legacy to the next generation of bush pilots.

The more Banks thought about it, the more he remembered. He knew exactly where Duke Lake was located, and if the cabin over the northwest ridge from Duke Lake belonged to Mike Jansen he knew exactly where to find him as well.

"Kayla, Duke Lake is southeast of Northway, on the park side, just behind Burwash. I've got to get there before daybreak. Please don't ask any questions. I'll explain when I get back. I'll take the Beaver. Don't report it stolen. I'm in enough trouble."

Kayla was in the dark but trusted her best pilot's judgment. "I'll file a flight plan and get them to gas up Kilo India Delta for you."

"Don't. I'll bet the RCMP are watching the airport."

Kayla hesitated. "Don't forget, Travis, KID is a Beaver. It isn't equipped to fly night instruments."

"I don't have a choice, Ms. Jackson."

"Travis," Kayla exhaled, "don't call me Ms. Jackson anymore." She was frustrated but resigned herself to the fact he was going to go. "O.K. What can I do?"

"Wish me luck."

She ended their call in a tone defying the traditional boss/ employee relationship.

"Travis, please be careful."

Banks hung up and looked at Dale. An uncomfortable quirky smile on the loader's face reflected his growing concern.

"What was that? What were you saying to her about flying?" Dale moved closer to the pilot. "We're driving to Burwash, Banks."

His ex-roommate didn't answer.

"C'mon, Travis. Say it. Say it! We're driving to Burwash. Right?"

Dale stood up. The smile was gone. The implication was obvious.

"Travis, it's pitch-black outside. It's the middle of the fucking night. The fog's thick as peanut butter up at the airport. The only Arctic Air aircraft capable of night instrument flight is the DC-3 and you don't have a copilot."

Banks smiled at him.

"Jesus Christ. I don't even have a pilot's license." He paused. "And I think I'm *drunk*."

"Calm down. Didn't you hear me? We're not taking the DC-3. I need the Beaver to land on Duke Lake. I have to get to Jansen first. His three buddies from twenty years ago have already been butchered. He's the key. He's either been doing the killing or about to be killed. Hell, he might already be dead, for all I know, but until I find out, he's the only hope I have to prove I'm innocent. Whoever framed me should be going after him next. If it's Radcliff, I've got to get there first and stop it. Radcliff might beat me to Burwash, but with the Beaver, I can beat him to Jansen's cabin."

"Then what's the big hurry? We'll take off at first light."

"Radcliff will be at Jansen's by first light. I can't *leave* at daybreak."

Dale wasn't convinced.

Banks prompted McMaster to use the phone. "Go ahead, call. My guess is they're gassing up that fancy-instrument Twin Otter as we speak."

Dale pounced on the phone like a starving jaguar and dialed the flight service station at the airport. He kept his eyes peeled on Travis, confident their trip could wait until morning. Dale reached Phil Meyers in the tower. A moment later, he slowly hung up the phone. The color had drained from his face.

"The RCMP filed an instrument flight plan for Burwash ten minutes ago. Phil said they're moving a prisoner. They're at the RCMP hangar fueling as we speak."

Banks looked at his friend. "Dale, Radcliff's counting on me driving to Burwash. It gives him an eight-hour head start. Flying the Beaver is my only ace. Unlike his Twin Otter, I'll be able to land the Beaver on Jansen's doorstep."

They were in Dale's truck and bouncing down the Schwatka Lake Road in less than a minute. The drive to the airport would take ten minutes.

Dale slammed his foot onto the loose clutch and into the rusty, icy floorboards. He ground the gear lever around in circles until he found a gear that worked on the slippery side road.

"Do you mind filling me in?" Dale's tone was plaintive. "Monty says you and I are going hunting. From what I can gather, you've already been hunting. Bagged yourself a full curl trapper tonight in church! How did you do it? Tree stand in the organ loft? Nail 'im on his knees praying?"

"Not funny."

"Lighten up. I know you were set up." Dale turned left onto the South Access Road. His truck strained trying to climb the steep strip of pavement up to the Alaska Highway. "You'd never kill a human out of season." He waited for a reaction before finally slapping his knee and laughing.

Dale had been drinking and relished his buzz. Banks turned sideways and cranked the window handle a few times. The cab instantly filled with freezing air. McMaster needed to sober up.

Dale quickly realized Travis was in no mood for lame drunken humor.

He asked, "How did the police know it was your bow?"

The pilot cocked his head sideways, raising one eyebrow. "Take a guess."

Dale gawked at him momentarily before rolling his head back.

"Oh, shit. It was the PSE bow I gave you for Christmas a few years ago?"

Travis nodded.

"Shit, I had your name monogrammed on it, didn't I?"

"Yes, you did, thank you very much. I can't ever remember even using the damn thing, but I'm sure my prints are all over it."

"Even Radcliff knows you're not stupid enough to kill someone and then leave the murder weapon behind with your name on it."

Dale kept one hand on the wheel and with the other reached into his parka, pulling out two large color photos.

"You might want to take a look at these."

He handed Banks his flashlight and two of the pictures from Primrose Lake. It was the two shots Travis had asked him to enlarge.

"Let me guess." Banks laid the pictures out on his lap. "You took a picture of something or someone who wasn't supposed to be at Primrose the day we found Bellichek?"

Dale was impressed and raised his brow, "Very good. Both of the above. You can see the something, but I don't know who the someone is."

"I think I might," Banks said, and paused. "I suspect whoever you've caught on film dropped their keys after butchering Ed Bellichek. Once they realized their keys were missing, they came back to retrieve them."

The first picture revealed the red nose cowling and two black ski tips of a snowmobile's front end. It was partially hidden along the tree line a hundred yards from the frozen shoreline of Primrose Lake, directly opposite Bellichek's cabin.

Dale had used a black marker on the second photo. He circled an image in the bottom right corner. Banks leaned closer, peering at the glossy photographic paper. He had to squint in the weak yellow beam of the dying flashlight.

There was a face, sitting on a stump, covered in furs. It was staring up at McMaster and the de Havilland aircraft rumbling overhead. It wasn't a bad picture considering they had been flying at more than 100 miles per hour.

"We weren't alone the morning we found Bellichek's body." Travis was speaking to himself as much as to Dale.

"It appears not," Dale deadpanned as he slowed before cranking the steering wheel hard to the right. They turned west onto the Alcan Highway.

Banks altered the flashlight's angle trying to maximize its energy against the picture, but the truck's lousy suspension kept him bouncing around, making his examination of the photos nearly impossible.

The enlarged telephoto picture was slightly grainy, and the circled face was partially covered with bundled furs, but not enough to deny the obvious. The eyes shook the pilot's senses: they were the same eyes he had focused on through the baffles of Radcliff's kitchen pantry door; the eyes of the sheep hunter he had seen in the photo in Radcliff's study; the hunter with Nick Radcliff on the hunting trip who tried unsuccessfully to hide his face; the same person in the photo locked up in the Old Testament. The eyes and protruding portion of face definitely belonged to that of Nick Radcliff's brother, Simon Radcliff.

The ex-RCMP officer was alive. He hadn't died in a hunting accident. Simon Radcliff had been at Primrose Lake the morning Banks and McMaster had discovered Ed Bellichek's body.

Travis chuckled and looked out the window toward the airport and mumbled, "Prisoner my ass."

"What?" Dale licked the edge of the Zig Zag cigarette paper while keeping his elbows pinned onto the steering wheel. Now Banks knew why the company called them Zig Zag papers. Dale's truck was zigzagging all over the damn road as he deftly rolled the paper between both index fingers and thumbs before sealing the thin cigarette.

"Remember the 'intruder' in Nick Radcliff's den? The one who picked up the orange prisoner jump suit and handcuffs? It's Simon. Simon Radcliff is the prisoner about to be transported to Burwash. I guarantee you that prepubescent RCMP pilot doesn't have a clue as to what Nick Radcliff's up to."

"You're saying that's Simon Radcliff in the picture?"

"I think so." Banks pulled one the pictures they had from the Yellowknife newspaper out of the inside breast pocket of his dinner suit jacket. He handed it to Dale and shone the flashlight on both photos. McMaster's eyes darted back and forth from the road to the two images and compared the pictures. He nodded his head.

"It's possible."

"Would you still believe it's possible if I told you Simon Radcliff was dead?"

Dale took his eyes off the road for only a second and gawked at his passenger with a blank stare.

Banks continued. "That's right. Simon Radcliff supposedly died in October."

Dale lit his smoke, focusing back on the road. He pointed quickly at the pictures with the hand holding his burning lighter.

"He's not dead if he's in that picture."

Banks turned and looked out the window. The frozen countryside slid past in the night, the occasional streetlight filling the truck's cabin with an orange halogen glow. The warm heater was finally thawing out his tingling extremities, but his face was close enough to the passenger window to feel the cold glass; his breath painted the window an opaque white. He thought about Simon Radcliff, thought of the tragedy the man had suffered and the insatiable anger he must have lived with, or still lived with, every day.

Dale continued gearing up. "What did you mean *supposedly dead*?"

Banks didn't answer. His mind was still following a different path. Another angle came to mind.

"The notes we found signed 'MJ' at Brock Bellichek's cabin on Lake Labarge, they were all postmarked from Beaver Creek near Northway, Alaska. Right?"

"So?" Dale fired several spits between his legs, cleaning his tongue of stray tobacco leaves.

"According to my sister, Simon Radcliff died in a hunting accident not a stone's throw from Beaver Creek."

"How'd he die?" McMaster queried a second time.

"Supposedly, he fell off a cliff. But his body was never recovered."

Dale watched the road closely as a gust of wind blew a wall of blinding ice crystals across the highway. He continued to lean closer to the dashboard, squinting into the white blustery glow of his headlights.

He geared down. The turnoff to the Arctic Air hanger was approaching to the right.

Dale bounced the truck off the highway onto the company's access road.

"Dale, stop!" The facts slipped together. Radcliff's hunting trip to Kluane in the fall was how it all started.

"What?" He took his foot off the gas.

"Pull over." Travis needed to verbalize the bits and pieces rattling around in his head.

McMaster pulled off the rough road and onto the snow-covered shoulder.

Banks started. "Tell me if this makes sense."

Dale turned off the headlights but kept the engine running and the heater on.

The bush pilot faced McMaster and collected his thoughts.

"In *September*, the Yellowknife coroner released a preliminary autopsy report. It was for law enforcement eyes only until it was confirmed. It indicated they may have finally discovered the remains of 'Kelly Margaret Radcliff' at Tetcho Lake. Remember Tetcho Lake? It was the past residence of four placer miners who were all suspects in the killing: Ed and Brock Bellichek, William Watt, and Mike Jansen. The next month, *October*, the bereaved girl's father fakes his own death. How do I know that? In *November*, the 'dead' father goes hunting with his brother, Nick Radcliff, and inadvertently, I assume, has his picture taken. The surviving brother, Nick, a tenured RCMP veteran, transfers to Whitehorse in the fall. Two months later, the four onetime suspects start being brutally executed. At one murder site, we find a set of keys that fit the front door of the chief investigating RCMP officer's home. The keys were at the murder scene before he arrived."

Dale leaned against his door.

"This is all pretty far-fetched. Why would Nick and Simon Radcliff, an ex-cop and a current inspector of the RCMP, conspire to commit murder?"

"It *is* far-fetched, but Michelle informed me that Solange Radcliff, their sister, also died from injuries caused by a sexual assault."

"Jesus." Dale shook his head in disbelief.

"I guess it's hard to imagine until your own daughter and sister are murdered by some pervert. Then, as you try to cope with the loss, your despondent mother and wife slowly commit suicide by drowning in a sea of booze and pills."

"For Christ's sake, why frame you?"

"My sister theorized that we would only become targets if we got in the way. Obviously, we have. I found a set of keys I wasn't supposed to find, and you took some ill-advised pictures. Why do you think Radcliff spent the entire day after we found Bellichek's body back at Primrose Lake? There wasn't anything to investigate. Even Leon was miffed at Radcliff's persistence. Nick Radcliff was trying to find those damn keys before anyone else did. There was a good possibility U.S. authorities might get involved. That's exactly what happened when they faked his brother's death. Why do you think he kept asking us over and over if we found anything? Remember? He continued to threaten us about how he was going to 'lock us up' if we didn't disclose everything we knew. He wanted his damn keys back."

"So, Radcliff is a killer?" Dale asked. He took a deep drag on his cigarette.

"*Simon* Radcliff. Not Nick. It's safe to assume Nick is riding shotgun for his brother. It's not a bad way to cover up your brother's tracks. Transfer in as a chief of the local police detachment. As an added bonus, if Nick keeps the case quiet, nobody's going to miss these four creeps."

"These are cops, Travis. There's no statute of limitations on murder. Why not arrest the men and charge them all over again?"

"You'll have to ask them. It's a good question. I guess they felt jail wasn't good enough for the bastards. Can't say I blame them. Can you?"

"Nobody should play God, Travis."

Banks couldn't believe his ears. The humanitarian had spoken. He responded incredulously. "What these creeps did to Kelly Radcliff was hideous. If it's true, these guys are diseased. I wouldn't waste much time trying to psychoanalyze them. If they brutalized the Radcliff girl they deserve exactly what they're getting."

"That's a big 'if.'" Dale laughed sarcastically. "Better watch out. It appears your buddies are setting *you* up to take the fall."

Dale's bullshit started to infuriate Travis. The pilot captured his anger, calmed down, and spoke quietly.

"I didn't say they were my 'buddies.' I said I understood."

McMaster and Banks hadn't argued in ages. They avoided arguing, especially when Dale was drinking. McMaster held dear to the political left and was convinced that life should be painless, there should be no tough choices. And when there are, an elaborate social system should be in place to protect them. Anything to soften the realization that, occasionally, life is not a "just" paradigm and often can be an inequitable royal pain in the ass. Plus, Banks didn't have the time nor the patience to lock horns with Dale. His situation was perilous and he desperately needed his friend's help. The stress was mounting and creeping under Banks' skin.

They sat in silence for a few minutes. Normally, it was Travis' responsibility to extend the olive branch. This time, Dale acquiesced and gently backhanded his passenger's left shoulder.

"Let's forget about it." His tepid apology slowly rolled off his lips.

Banks cupped the palm of his hand on the back of Dale's neck and shook him gently. "Good idea." Travis paused, adding, "I'm not the one playing God, Dale. I'm trying to exonerate myself and I need your help."

Dale took a deep breath and looked into the night. "You got it." He fashioned the remark in a way that made it clear to Banks that Travis was the closest thing to a brother or family Dale had.

McMaster quickly lightened the mood by changing the subject. "Why the hunting sheep message?"

Banks pulled the map of the Yukon and Alaska out of the truck's glove box and unfolded it.

"We need to get to Mike Jansen's cabin." Travis' finger wandered over the colorful topographical map until it found the small lake near Burwash known as Duke Lake. "Radcliff's hunting pictures indicated a pretty hostile environment. I'm sure I've been there before. I just can't place it yet. I suspect they already know where he lives."

"How?" Dale asked.

"I'm willing to bet the November hunting picture I found of Nick and Simon together was taken near Jansen's home; in the mountains somewhere, west of Beaver Creek. Jansen was probably their first target, which makes sense. He'd be the hard one. They had three of the men close to Whitehorse. Jansen was relatively far away, near Kluane National Park. They didn't want to end up in a situation where they punish the first three quickly, and then risk exposure by searching high and low to ferret out the last one, especially, near Kluane Park. That's some of the most treacherous terrain in North America. My guess is they just came up empty the first time. God only knows where Jansen was at the time. I'll bet after twenty years Simon was impatient. Once Nick told him about the Yellowknife coroner's report, he wanted to start dishing out a little 'eye for an eye' justice."

Dale confessed, "It makes sense, but it is ironic. A Catch-22. You need to find Jansen before they do. He's your bait. If you catch Simon your theory and alibi will fly. On the other hand, you wouldn't give a shit if Radcliff popped Jansen for killing the little girl. But, if they do, you'll end up being the patsy. Radcliff can't blame all this shit on Bigfoot. He'll have to nail someone and it looks like you're it. I don't need to remind you your defense sucks. I can just hear you in court: 'Your honor, it wasn't me. The real murderer is actually a retired ex-cop who died falling off a cliff . . . I think. And if he didn't really die, he was aided in these brutal murders by his brother, who happens to be in charge of the Whitehorse RCMP detachment.'"

Dale crossed his arms and exhaled before continuing. "I hope you like taking showers with large tattooed convicts." A beleaguered look crept across his face. "You're right. You better get to Jansen. You're miles up the proverbial creek. You could have saved yourself a lot of grief if you kept the hunting trip picture of Simon and Nick you found in Nick Radcliff's den."

"When I found them, I didn't realize Simon was supposed to be dead."

Dale put the truck in gear. "We better get going."

The truck fishtailed a little, spewing ice and gravel into the dark ditch as it gripped the slippery side road leading to the Arctic Air hangar. The road snaked back and forth for a half-mile before the hangar lights began to flicker through the unusually tall northern spruce that jutted up into the black night.

The rhythmical pulse of the unsynchronized propellers was unmistakable. Above the half-dozen hangars lining the south end of the

Whitehorse Airport, a red rotating fuzzy glow illuminated the ice fog overhead. It was the slow-turning beacon light of the RCMP turbine-powered Twin Otter climbing into the night. Radcliff had a head start on Banks and was on his way to Burwash.

"Are we packed?" Travis questioned Dale as he listened to the hum of the de Havilland DHC-6 Twin Otter disappear into the night.

"Yep. That was easy," Dale grunted, putting the old truck in gear. "I figured two aircraft survival kits would do the trick, yours and the Beech-18s. Yours is already in the Beaver. I've got the other one in the back of the truck. I swung by on the way to Schwatka Lake and picked it up. I had no idea you were crazy enough to fly tonight." He thumbed over his shoulder to the truck's bed.

Dale then backed off the accelerator and slammed his palm into the truck's headlight switch. The road disappeared, swallowed up into the black night. He braked lightly, slowing the truck to a crawl.

Banks leaned forward, squinting. "What is it?"

Dale used the moon's reflection off the snow-covered side road to navigate.

"Over there," he pointed to the tree line south of the Arctic Air hangar.

An RCMP cruiser sat, parked, on the edge of a logging road. Almost instantly, the blue and red strobe lights began stabbing the trees with blinking daggers. The car lurched from its perch and moved forward onto the main road spinning its tires toward the two men.

Dale cursed, eyeing the approaching cruiser.

"Shit, Travis, get out! I'll meet you at the airplane." He leaned over across his passenger's lap and pushed open the door.

The frigid night air slammed into Banks' face. His lungs hesitated and gasped as they filled with subzero air. McMaster slowed the truck for only a second attempting to assuage any suspicion on the part of the approaching RCMP cruiser. He barked again for Travis to get out. Banks looked for an accommodating landing zone alongside the snow-covered gravel road sliding by in the night. None existed. A small white knoll approached. It had to be old plowed snow. He leapt.

It wasn't "old plowed snow." The knoll turned out to be old plowed gravel. Banks hit with a resounding thud. His sternum made contact first, squashing inward and spilling the warm air from his lungs. The momentum carried him into the ditch along the road. Dazed and winded with collapsed lungs, he somehow managed to scramble into the woods and hide behind some fallen snow-covered birch tree twenty feet from the road. The cold was rapidly penetrating his thin suit and chilling him to the bone. He crouched behind the winter backdrop gasping for breath, but the white steam-engine-like breath, chugging from mouth and nostrils, told him he was going to live. The breathless pilot aimed the steam toward the ground; it could easily be seen from the road.

Obviously, the police hadn't spotted his leap of faith into the night. Dale hadn't gone thirty more yards from their impromptu drop-off point before the RCMP cruiser stopped him.

McMaster's cab light didn't work when he opened his door but the police car's overhead light lit up the entire white surrounding area. Banks saw the trooper exit his vehicle and place the officially issued winter headdress onto his balding head. The officer kept his high beams pointed at Dale's truck and left his flashing colorful strobes on to dance sharply among the surrounding woods. Travis watched from behind a snow-covered stump as Dale handed his driver's license to the officer. McMaster kept pointing back and forth between himself and the Arctic Air hangar. Other than trying to talk an unwilling date into intercourse, Dale wasn't much of a liar, and the truth would work here. All he had to do was explain how Arctic Air was his employer and he was simply checking some electric heaters on aircraft scheduled to depart early in the morning, a task all too common to Dale during the winter months. The trooper shone his flashlight around the inside of Dale's truck before walking back to his vehicle and pulling the handheld microphone out of the cruiser's door. He spoke into the mouthpiece several times. Eventually, he threw it into the cab and walked back to Dale's truck. He handed McMaster his license. The officer pointed through the woods to the white and blue RCMP airport 200 yards from Arctic Air's hangar. The water bombing tanker base, open only during the summer months, was all that separated Kayla's hangar and the police hangar.

Within a minute the police cruiser had managed a 180-degree turn on the icy road and was driving away to the RCMP hangar. Dale was in tow, close behind. It looked as though Banks' trip to Burwash would be flown alone.

The cold was becoming debilitating. The quickest route would be the road, but he had to assume Radcliff knew that. He felt certain that Radcliff had ordered the surveillance that caught Dale and almost caught him, knowing that the hangar was an obvious place for them to hide. There might be more police milling about, but Banks was confident Radcliff never considered him crazy enough to fly anywhere tonight, not in the dense ice fog that was beginning to blanket the airport. Radcliff would be watching the hangar, not the aircraft.

Banks set off, stumbling through the dark woods, driven by the knowledge that warmth awaited him. His slick dress shoes were no help. He spent as much time pulling himself back out of the snow as he did walking forward. It *was* crazy to even think of flying, but he'd run out of options.

An occasional glimpse of moonlight peeking through the crystalline fog helped light his way. Suddenly, he came to an abrupt halt, his progress impeded by the airport's Department of Transport perimeter fence. It was designed to keep people from doing exactly what he was about to do—sneak onto federal airport property. There were four strands of barbed wire jutting out at a forty-five degree angle on top of the fence. He looked around for a tree limb or anything that might help him scale the sharp wire, and found nothing. The cold was unbearable. He was beginning to lose the feeling in his fingertips. The warmth of Marvin's hot ventilation ducts at the Klondike Inn were bouncing around in his head like some fond childhood memory. He needed to get in the hangar, quickly.

He pulled off his last bastion of warmth, his suit coat. The perspiration on his dinner shirt collided with the cold air, instantly sucking any remaining heat from his abdomen. He held the jacket by the collar, making it as thick as possible in the midsection. With one very calculating toss, he launched it skyward at the barbed wire. It landed perfectly across the top, giving him about a foot of covered space to scale over the barbs.

He grasped the chain-link fence with his numb fingers and scaled it in three steps, pulling himself over the top and across the barbs. The reckless maneuver resulted in several minor cuts and tears. He landed clumsily on the other side and stumbled toward the hangar that slowly began to take shape through the cut images of the last stand of trees. As he approached the tree line, Banks slowed and cautiously surveyed the outlying area. To his surprise, the RCMP cruiser that had nailed Dale only ten minutes earlier was back in its clandestine parking spot.

The side door of the hangar was facing him fifty yards away. The police officer was parked 100 feet to the left, facing in the opposite direction. As long as Banks kept his eyes forward, toward the road approaching from the Alcan Highway, he would not be seen.

Arctic Air's ramp was cluttered with an array of old equipment. The Beech-18, or Widow-maker, as it was known in the North, was parked near the door. It provided plenty of cover once he crossed the ramp. The agile, freezing pilot darted between old airplane parts and other aeronautical junk until he was alongside the outer hangar wall under the old Beechcraft's wing, visualizing the heat inside the hangar. He couldn't remember the last time he had felt so cold. Trembling almost uncontrollably, he slid along the metal siding until he was able to grasp the hangar's south exit doorknob. It was locked. He reached into his pockets for his keys before realizing they were under the front seat of Monty's car at Schwatka Lake. In frustration, he grasped the doorknob and shook it wildly, trying to overcome the lock. His numb fingers, void of strength, slid from the metal knob. With his back against the corrugated metal wall, he slid down until his butt hit the ground. He realized there was no other entrance to the hangar except the front office door, which was normally locked at night as well. Not only that, he was sure it was being studied by a police officer who had been instructed that Travis Banks was a cold-blooded murderer.

He sat in the hangar's shadows for a few minutes, trembling with cold and fatigue. But slowly the shaking subsided and his body grew eerily warm. His wits were still intact. He realized exactly what was happening—he was experiencing the onset of hypothermia. He stared numbly into the fog twirling around the halogen lights that surrounded the hangar. He didn't want to move. He was becoming very comfortable, knowing such a feeling was typical of someone succumbing to exposure.

Banks heard footsteps from behind. Boots on concrete, inside the hangar. Someone had heard his feeble attempts to overpower the hangar door. It opened slowly. Travis stared straight ahead, too cold to look up. Someone reached down and took his arm, helping him to his feet.

Kayla Jackson affectionately put her arms around Banks' shoulder and led him through the hangar into the pilots' lounge. He was too cold to speak. Taking several blankets, Kayla wrapped Banks up tight as a burrito. A minute later, she eased a cup of coffee laced with some of Frank Flemming's "hidden" brandy into his hand. Twenty minutes later the warmth of the office and the Colombian concoction had Banks thawing out. As he unfroze, the tiny painful needles of thawing nerves tingled throughout his body. Kayla continued to dart around the room adjusting the electric thermostat on the wall and looking for more blankets.

Travis finally stopped chattering long enough to speak. The words staggered off Banks' warming lips.

"Kayla, how did you get here without being seen?"

"They're not after me. But I took the service road as a precaution." She put one more blanket over his shoulders.

"Please understand that I'm grateful, but I told you to stay home."

"It's a good thing I didn't, or you'd be sitting outside near a hypothermic death singing 'Tiny Bubbles.'"

Kayla had the office heaters spitting fire in an attempt to warm him. She pulled up a chair next to Banks and took his freezing hand, rubbing it gently. "Now. What can I do, Travis?"

"You can get back in your car and leave before *you* end up wanted by the police." Travis' lips were slowly getting warm and the words passing through them were beginning to lose their slur.

Jackson stared angrily at the one pilot she truly respected. She was not going anywhere, and Banks saw her resolve.

"All right. You can do me two quick favors." His eyebrows stood up. "Then you promise to go home until this is over?"

"We'll see. What are they?"

"I'm going to get changed. First, could you make sure the Beaver is fully gassed up?"

"Already done."

"O.K. Then go down to the RCMP hangar and get the survival kit from the back of Dale's truck. It should be parked out in front. Put it in the Beaver for me. If anybody stops and asks, just tell them you have a trip going out early in the morning and you're here to check on the heaters."

Kayla gently put his hand down and headed out the hangar door. She spun around when the idea hit her. "Do you need a co-pilot?"

Banks thought about the invitation. Now that McMaster was detained he didn't like the idea of going to Jansen's cabin alone, but he had an overwhelming and inexplicable desire to protect this woman.

Travis looked her in the eyes. "I need you here when I get back."

Kayla Jackson blushed, smiled, and left the hangar.

The bush pilot stared at the door where Kayla had just departed. He was alone in the office. Something was happening, something unique. Thoughts were tumbling around in his head, thoughts unimaginable a week before. He had certainly never felt this way before about a woman. A woman he had known for years. It was as if they understood each other without speaking. The events of the past several days had made a marked impression on the pilot who was entering midlife. Travis had seen and read about an array of grief and misery in his life but now these thoughts brought a tear to his mind's eye as if his compassion had switched to a higher gear. He had been giving an inordinate amount of thought to the young girl who had been missing for twenty years, lost or abducted to die in the wilderness. What was the horrible end to her innocent life? Were these dying trappers involved? What was the last memory of the young girl's life under the expansive arctic sky near Tetcho Lake? What happened to her?

Banks had momentary painful flashes where he simply could not understand how the parents must have felt regarding the agony of losing a child. In the past several days the concept of parenthood had lost its veneer of difficulty, and he began to understand his journey might have a purpose. For the first time in his life, he felt the risks might be worth it, to embrace the responsibility and also the frightening gamble associated with parenthood. But what had the butchering of three trappers done to steer him in this direction? Or was it Kayla Jackson? He looked down at his pink frozen hands. It was probably hypothermia of the brain.

Within twenty minutes, Banks had changed into dry warm clothes. The several lockers of mechanics were a veritable Sears and Roebucks—longjohns, wool sweaters, socks, and boots. They possessed a rather interesting aroma but under the circumstances he was more than satisfied. After covering himself with his own blue aviation overalls, he donned someone else's parka that had been left behind on the office's coat rack. He was thawed out and ready to fly to Burwash.

Before heading out to the ramp, Banks picked up the phone in Flemming's office and dialed Leon Powell's home number. Apparently Radcliff had relieved him earlier in the evening and sent him home. It made sense. He didn't want Leon around asking questions.

Powell was asleep. It took a minute of ringing to wake him up.

A very groggy voice finally answered. "Hello."

"Leon?"

The frogs leaped from his voice box and he came to life. Banks could hear him sit up in bed.

"Travis! Where in the hell are you?"

"I'm at the airport. But don't bother jumping on your steed and charging up here. I'm leaving as soon as I wish you sweet dreams."

"Travis, I know you didn't kill anybody, but you have to turn yourself in until I can prove it."

"The only proof I have is about to disappear if I don't get moving. Did you know Radcliff took off twenty minutes ago for Burwash? He's supposedly transporting a prisoner. Isn't it a little odd for the head of your detachment to move a prisoner in the middle of the night? To Burwash, no less."

Powell hesitated. He knew it didn't make sense.

"Leon, you told me to give you proof before you would believe me about Radcliff. Did you know he had a brother?"

"Yes."

"Did he tell you he was dead?"

"Yeah."

"Then he lied to you and everyone else," Banks said. "Your boss just left. Go over to his house. The back door's unlocked. On the top of his bookshelf in the den, to the left, you'll find an Old Testament. In it are pictures of him and his brother, Simon, taken one month after Simon reportedly fell off a cliff and died. The date is on the picture. The death was reported by Nick himself. Simon's daughter, Nick's niece, was raped and murdered twenty years ago by four miners. Her body was recovered this fall. Three of the four miners have been murdered in the past week. I need to find number four before your illustrious commandant nails him and concocts some asinine story implicating me as his killer. You wanted proof? Well, you've got it. Go get the pictures. Meet me at the Whitehorse Airport tomorrow. I'll let you know when I'm landing." Banks didn't wait for an answer. Leon would ask too many questions. He hung up.

If Leon Powell didn't believe him now, he never would.

Luckily, Kayla had even hooked up the Herman Nelson heater to the Beaver. It was only a ten-minute shot of hot air into the frozen motor but it might make the difference between starting and not starting. Banks had not stepped outside the office yet. He didn't want to risk being seen by the RCMP cruiser, and he wouldn't until it was time to leave. His boss said the trooper parked in the woods wasn't there when she drove the several hundred yards to Dale's truck, but the constable was back in position again when she returned. The officer had stopped and questioned her but she had given their rehearsed answer. It worked.

Banks could've used Dale's help, but time was running out. He watched from a crack in the hangar door. Kayla Jackson disconnected the old Herman Nelson heater, pulled it across the icy ramp, and shoved it into a snowdrift behind the aircraft. She ran back to the ski plane and jumped into the left seat using the front strut for leverage. She tried unsuccessfully to start the Pratt and Whitney 985. In seconds, Banks could tell she had flooded the radial motor. It banged violently and exploded, spinning the Hartzell blade from a start to a stop. If the experienced pilot didn't relieve his boss quickly he might have to walk to Burwash.

Travis opened the hangar door and ran across the ramp, waving for Kayla to get out of the airplane. She hopped out smiling, shrugging her shoulders. Banks looked back to the side of the hangar and the parking lot. The RCMP cruiser sat in the shadows, the halogen-lit silhouette sitting in the front seat suddenly bolted upright. The red and blue strobes came to life.

Banks stumbled across the ramp, stopping in front of his boss. He gently took her by the shoulders and gave her a quick kiss on the cheek.

"What's that for?"

Travis noted that she looked surprised, but she hadn't objected.

"A good-bye kiss."

She smiled, and spoke over the roar of the gas heater twenty feet away. "Good-bye?"

Travis glanced quickly at the police cruiser headed toward the hangar. "Yes. Good-bye."

Jackson was stern. "We're not saying good-bye. I'm going with you."

"Oh, no, you're not!" Travis turned to leave.

"You need my help."

"Not bloody likely!" Travis hopped into the left seat and closed the door. He gave the Junior Wasp engine two shots of prime and pulled the mixture to cut off. "Now, get out of the way or I'll run you over." With both magnetos on, he engaged the starter, spinning the blade quickly to the right. After six revolutions, he pushed up the mixture handle.

Travis watched as Kayla wrapped her arms tightly around the left wing strut.

She shouted over the engine coming to life. "I'm going with you one way or the other, Travis. Either hanging on out here or in there with you!"

Banks was incensed. What had he been thinking a few minutes ago in the hangar? He would never settle down, never marry. Women were a lunatic species put on the planet to ensure that utopia would remain only a theory.

"Kayla! Let go of that strut!"

"No!" She was resolute.

Banks glared in disbelief. He pushed the throttle forward and the radial engine exploded to life. The tires had sat too many hours in the cold and had squared up. He quickly pumped down the skis and pushed up the throttle. The ramp's snow and ice were whipped into a cyclone, forcing Kayla Jackson to turn her face and twist in the wind. She hung onto the strut, dragging her feet. Arctic Air's ramp was engulfed in a man-made ice storm. The skis slid underneath the tail dragger as Banks fishtailed out of the ramp. The stubborn woman outside his left window would not let go. He pushed his door open slightly and screamed again for her to give up, but the owner of Arctic Air was stoic. The ice and prop wash slamming into her face prevented her from speaking, so she vehemently shook her head. Banks was amazed. His boss was a piece of work. Maybe taking this woman along wasn't such a bad idea. Jansen was a man; if Jansen took them hostage she might be able to frustrate the old trapper into committing suicide. Banks pulled the throttle back and the aircraft slid to a halt.

"Get in!" he shouted over the idling engine.

Kayla Jackson unwound her arms, ducked under the belly, and jumped in the right door, her cheeks bright and red from the prop wash.

"Thank you." Kayla said politely as if nothing unusual had happened. She tossed the hood of her parka backward exposing a disheveled mess of hair full of ice crystals. "You finally remembered who signs your paycheck."

Banks shook his head in disbelief. "Strap in."

There would be no official warm-up time, just enough to ensure the oil cooler didn't blow.

Banks taxied quickly to runway 36, keeping the engine turning at a 2,000 rpm. The cylinder head temperature was quickly rising into the low end of the green band. The oil pressure was pegged off the scale. He jerked the prop pitch handle back and forth several times, trying to circulate as much mildly warm oil as possible. The red cockpit lighting of the old aircraft was as ineffective as the aircraft's navigational instrument panel, and squinting at the gauges, he could only make out approximate temperatures, pressures, and headings.

It was a right turn out of Arctic Air's ramp onto the southbound "Romeo" taxiway. The fog was thick as molasses. His memory was doing the driving instead of his eyes. He had taxied this way a thousand times. With the skis deployed, it didn't really matter if he taxied off the snowy concrete; snow was snow. It didn't matter whether concrete was underneath it or grass.

He went down the slight incline toward runway 36. It was his best bet to get airborne before the beleaguered RCMP constable found an entrance onto the airport property. The only access by vehicle, at this hour, would be in the opposite direction, near the main terminal.

Banks turned on the aircraft's radio. The tower was closed but the flight service frequency was broadcasting that the airport was officially closed until further notice. Travis turned off the radio. Radcliff would have to do better than that.

Travis applied full thrust. The Beaver slid down the runway until the fog-shrouded, white center line lights alternated between red and white. He had less than 3,000 feet of runway remaining.

Squinting in the dark cockpit Travis could only guess his airspeed. That specific instrument was only partially illuminated. He looked outside to his left and saw the white runway lights, each one separated by exactly 200 feet. They appeared to be flashing by at a sufficient rate to lift a de Havilland Beaver into the air, at least a Beaver without any appreciable ice on its wings. He looked over at Kayla whose eyes were staring wildly into the white wall of fog rolling into the windscreen.

Banks yelled over the roar of the radial engine, "Don't worry, it'll fly."

Kayla Jackson's mouth was open and she was about to say something when Banks saw her gasp in terror. Her eyes suddenly shut and she threw her arms around her head.

The flashing strobes of an RCMP cruiser darted into their path from the left. The trooper didn't realize he was crossing the runway and locked his brakes directly in front of the Beaver, skidding and sliding sideways directly toward the aircraft. Banks slammed the right rudder all the way to the stops. The tail dragger yawed and slid violently to the right. If they had been on a dry runway with tires, they would have all awakened in the hospital or, more than likely, the morgue. The owner of Arctic Air, like any good backseat driver, pushed both feet forward to the floor-boards as if she were in charge of the brakes. There were rudders under her feet but no breaks were connected to the skis. Travis overpowered Kayla's instinctual assistance and managed to miss the RCMP sedan by inches. Passing the police car, he rammed the opposite rudder to the floor, attempting to regain control. As soon as the nose was straight the runway end lights appeared 100 feet in front of them. Banks had no idea if the airplane still had sufficient speed to fly, but he was acutely aware that beyond the end of the runway was a canyon that dropped 500 feet. He could never get the airplane stopped before he and Kayla would cartwheel into the gorge off the end of runway 36.

Using every single inch of remaining runway, he resisted the urge to force the aircraft off the ground and instead, slowly pulled back on the yoke, letting it fly off the runway. If he became airborne only due to ground effect, they were certain to settle back down into the approach lights of runway 18.

The aircraft lifted into the fog momentarily before a large thunder-ous bang echoed somewhere in the rear, lurching the round nose cowl-ing violently forward and compelling Banks to pull back hard on the stick. The stall warning began screaming in their ears and the aircraft shook violently. Travis had no choice. He was no more than a hundred feet above the ground but if he didn't relax back pressure on the yoke and trade some altitude for airspeed, they were about to be the first to arrive at a new accident.

The controls had become stiff and unresponsive. It was all he could do to keep the aircraft upright. They had stopped climbing just inches from the ground. Air was whirling around loudly somewhere in the rear. Kayla could see the fear in Banks' eyes and she leaped out and over her seat toward the rear bulkhead. She removed the access panel at the back of the small cabin with a thunderous kick of her right boot, stuck her head into the dark interior of the Beaver's tail section, and crawled into the rear up to her waist. A moment later she reappeared, petrified.

Kayla yelled over all the racket, "You might be able to land this thing O.K., but you can't take off worth a damn. Good God, Banks, do you fly like this every time I send you on a trip?"

"What did you find?"

"The belly's been punctured. We've got two approach lights stuck in our rear. They're wrapped up in the control cables."

Banks fought the controls like he was riding a runaway downhill bike with no steering.

He yelled over his shoulder toward the back, "Do something, Kayla, and do it quick." The experienced pilot was slowly losing the airplane. His control inputs appeared to work for several seconds and then the Beaver would begin to roll wherever it so desired. "Can you get the lights away from the control cables? I can't stop it from rolling right. Hurry up, for Christ's sake."

Kayla crawled completely into the tail section and disappeared. Banks struggled wildly with the shaking and lurching Beaver for what seemed an eternity.

Finally, the yoke nearly jerked out of his hands. For a pilot, total electrical failures and absolute loss of flight controls are the biggest nightmares. He felt as if the latter was happening. Suddenly, he could hold the control yoke firm and straight. It didn't fight back. He hesitantly rolled the airplane slightly left and then back right, trying to ascertain if the yoke was still connected to anything. He experienced no resistance. The airplane banked as requested. He didn't know what his boss had done but it worked.

He started to climb slowly. A minute later, Kayla reappeared over his shoulder, holding the two shattered runway approach lights.

"How is it?" she smiled, snapping on her seat belt.

Banks gave her a thumbs-up.

The white foggy image in front of them was a reminder that they were not out of the woods yet. The only reference Banks had to keep the aircraft right side up was the needle, ball, and airspeed indicators. The old and, hopefully, unreliable artificial horizon averred that he was in a twenty-degree bank turn to the right. Banks ignored it. The ball and needle were centered and the magnetic compass floated within ten degrees of magnetic north. He was heading in a relatively straight track.

Travis began climbing a little quicker, hoping that this inversion layer was thin and they would soon break out on top of the ice fog. He slowly banked right and picked up a heading to the south end of Lake Labarge. The valley that the lake sat in was an expansive geographical opening, giving them ten miles of terrain clearance off either wing tip. He'd flown this estimated track many times under visual flight rules and had subconsciously memorized the magnetic heading. It was about thirty degrees. He looked at his watch. Time and heading. They would have a good 15 minutes free of any obstruction ascending through the fog. That should be plenty of time to get on top of the cloud deck. Banks shook his head in disbelief. Here he was, seventy years after the Wright Brothers, still navigating by the seat of his pants.

Banks admonished Kayla for the dangerous stunt she had pulled back at the ramp, but remained focused on the milky outside surroundings. They were both anticipating quickly breaking through the overcast.

They were passing 5,000 feet, and it was taking much longer than Banks had anticipated. He had never seen a layer of ice fog extend this high above the terrain. If they didn't break out soon, he'd be in deep trouble. He had no idea were he was other than an educated guess. He couldn't turn around and descend to an airport with zero visibility in fog. He looked warily at his vertical speed indicator. They were climbing at a speed of less than 200 feet a minute.

Both pilots became quiet and jittery. Banks' makeshift "instrument" departure was running out of obstruction clearance time. They were getting dangerously close to the peaks of the Big Salmon Mountain Range. Banks cheated slightly west and turned five degrees back to the left toward Lake Labarge. Their rate of climb had become negligible. Kayla had flown enough to realize their departure was risky. She kept quiet relying on Travis' experience, but she knew a bad sign when she saw one.

"Travis." Kayla's tone was ominous. "Look here."

Banks shone his flashlight out the right window. His worst fears materialized. The leading edge of the right wing was covered with a heavy layer of rough, milky rime ice. Clear icing was the most dangerous. Both rime and clear icing could bring an aircraft down, but clear ice could do it with little or no warning. The pilot had to find a quick way out of the ice.

It appeared that they had left the fog some time ago and climbed straight into a cloud deck. He checked his watch again and cheated some more to the left. The fear in both of them was palpable.

Thirty-five minutes into their "blind" climb, they had finally stopped climbing. The ice started to pull the clumsy ice-infested airframe back to earth. The airspeed was bleeding away as Banks tried to maintain his present altitude. The controls became sluggish and unresponsive.

Kayla screamed and pointed. "Travis!"

Ahead and to their right, they saw a cloud with a large rock in it. At twelve o'clock, less than a mile, a snow-covered mountain ridge approached rapidly.

They were in a cloud, iced up, somewhere over the Big Salmon Mountain Range. The de Havilland Beaver was at 5,800 feet above sea level but only 100 feet above the ground. Banks knew if he turned around quickly with the aircraft covered in ice he'd stall, or at best, lose at least 1,000 feet of altitude and hit the mountain. Every little angle of bank depleted lift; he couldn't afford to lose one foot. He searched the recesses of his mind, trying to rediscover some obscure aeronautical technique that might save his bacon. Suddenly, the aircraft started to buffet and they began experiencing moderate chop. Surely they couldn't be stalling, could they? Banks squinted at the faded airspeed indicator. He was still several knots above the stall speed, but that was with clean wings. He craned his neck forward and peered up into the layer of cloud on top of them. A good friend winked back. Banks caught a glimpse of the moon. He had one more rabbit in his hat.

He grasped the flap selection lever and pushed it to the floor for flaps down. Next to it, he gently gave the flap pump handle a few short shots. The flaps crept down several degrees. A couple more degrees. The nose pitched over slightly. Airspeed decreased closer to stall. The airplane almost instantly gained eighty feet of altitude. A little more flap. A little less airspeed. A little more altitude. He pumped the flaps down until he was at the aircraft's stall speed. The stall horn honked intermittently. The moon flashed by several times before they were swallowed up by the weather again. They were skirting the top of the last layer of cloud. Banks pumped one more little shot of hydraulic fluid into the hydraulic actuator, forcing the flaps out one more inch. The stall horn became insistent that they cease and desist the extension of flaps. They were one knot of airspeed away from becoming a rock. The wings were above the flat smooth cloud deck but the cabin was still jumping in and out of the moisture. Between little breaks in the clouds, the two occupants saw the rime ice start to dry and break away in the clear air above. Moments later, the aircraft began accelerating. Banks started reeling the flaps back in a degree at a time. They began a shallow climb. A minute later they popped out on top of the clouds, free and clear from the deadly clutches of the icy grip below. The two occupants of the Beaver finally took a breath.

Ahead of them lay a flat white blanket of clouds. A million stars and the full moon lit up the cottony tops as bright as day, making the visibility seem endless.

Separated from the clouds, the ride smoothed out. The clean, ice-free wings were once again efficient and responsive to the pilot's touch. Banks looked at the treacherous, cold cloud deck rolling below and felt as if he were safely sailing across shark-infested waters.

Off to the west, Pilot Mountain reared its beautiful white and gray peaks up through the blanketed horizon.

Past Pilot Mountain was Haines Junction and beyond that Burwash Landing. In calm air, they would land at Duke Lake in two hours.

Banks filled Kayla in on all the events of the past several days, including the strange notes he and McMaster had found at Lake Labarge. The look on Kayla's face indicated she might now be regretting the decision to accompany Travis on his trip to find Jansen and Simon Radcliff. She fully realized they were looking for a dangerous, unstable individual.

Travis and Kayla sat in silence. They knew they had just been dealt four aces; they could only hope lady luck would favor them for a few more hours.

Kayla rolled her parka up and placed it on the door next to her head. She leaned into it and was asleep in minutes.

Banks watched as she fell asleep. Moonlight wound its way through the soft strands of individual hairs that fell to her shoulders. The pilot worried about what might happen when they found Jansen. He couldn't watch out for both himself and Kayla, but proving his innocence was becoming no more important than protecting the woman who lay sleeping next to him.

At 2:00 A.M., the antiquated Automatic Direction Finder receiver started picking up the weak signal from the Burwash Non-Directional Beacon. The needle on the fixed-card ADF started swinging around, honing in on Burwash. The Beaver was indicating 90 nautical miles per hour. They'd be circling Duke Lake sometime between 3:00 and 4:00 A.M., depending on the head winds that would soon start pouring out from Kluane Park and the Lowell Glacier.

Banks fiddled with the radio's knobs as Kayla slept peacefully in the right seat. He was envious. He desperately needed rest before the trek to Jansen's cabin. The terrain at the foot of Kluane Park was cold and inhospitable. It would take a well-rested and nourished body to make the hike over the ridge from Duke Lake to the isolated cabin.

The warm exhaust heater along with the rumbling drone of the Pratt and Whitney 985 radial engine was intoxicating. Banks flew along half asleep, skimming the silvery cloudy highway that lapped at the bottom of his aircraft's skis.

They were fifty miles from Burwash Landing. To keep busy and awake, Banks spun the VHF communication radio around to 126.7, locking into the Burwash Flight Service Station. He tuned in just in time to hear the RCMP Twin Otter announce its intention to commence an instrument approach into the tiny strip at the Burwash Airport. It was a high minimum NDB approach. Banks knew that if Radcliff managed to land in Burwash, he and his boss would be able to slip underneath the overcast and crawl toward the Kaskawulsh Glacier, head north, and around into Duke Lake.

He tuned the VHF radio quickly back to the Edmonton ATC frequency.

All instrument flight plans are required to be canceled by the pilot, either in flight during visual conditions, or once safely on the ground. Most pilots, having made visual contact with the airport, will advise air traffic control of the weather conditions and where they were on the approach when they visually acquired the runway. It gives the next pilot shooting an instrument approach a headsup as to when they can expect to break out of the overcast and see the field and/or runway.

Several minutes of silence was finally interrupted when the RCMP pilot canceled his IFR flight plan taxiing on the gravel strip in Burwash. More importantly, he gave Edmonton Center the information Banks was looking for. The Twin Otter had broken out visually on the approach 2,000 feet above Kluane Lake. The weather was not a factor, high ceilings and no precipitation. The Beaver pilot should have little problem getting up to Duke Lake.

The overcast layer started to break up. It was becoming a broken-to-scattered cloud deck. The only drawback was that the moon's bright light diminished appreciably under the broken overcast. The odd streetlight alongside the Alaska Highway started to blink up at Banks from the holes in the white carpet at his feet. He could see long stretches of the southeast shoreline of Kluane Lake. It was time to dive below the layer underneath and find the glacier.

The coordinated negative "G" dive through one of the breaks in the cloud deck gently lifted Kayla off her seat. The abrupt "level off" smartly put her back in her seat and woke Kayla with a start.

She looked around, dazed, gripping the inside of the airplane with both hands. "What . . . "

"Bad dream?"

"Jesus . . . " She took a deep breath.

"Rise and shine." Banks pointed to the small cluster of lights twenty miles off the right wing tip that represented the tiny community of Burwash Landing.

Jackson yawned, stretched, and then exposed her bloodshot eyes.

"I had this awful dream, Travis. You would've liked it. Some asshole pilot was trying to take off in the fog with me hanging onto his wing."

Travis looked at her and smiled.

"Actually," she added incredulously, "it was a nightmare. But if I pretend it was a dream, maybe I'll forget it quicker."

Banks brought the throttle back slowly and gently descended to the dark southern end of Kluane Lake.

They passed over the abandoned community of Silver Creek at 3,100 feet above sea level, 500 feet above the ground. The southern end of the Kaskawulsh River snaked back and forth beneath them, emptying itself into Kluane Lake. The northern end of the river turned into ice and jutted upward at a seemingly impossible forty-degree angle, becoming one of the most breathtaking glaciers in North America.

It was an elongated wall of glass-blue glacial ice, thousands of feet thick. The Kaskawulsh Glacier wound upwards for twenty miles, peaking at Mount Logan, the second-tallest point in North America. Mount Logan topped out at nearly 20,000 feet above sea level. At his aircraft's absolute operational ceiling, he wouldn't be halfway up the majestic peak.

Banks planned to get in behind the Kluane Mountain Range and approach Duke Lake and Jansen's cabin from the south. The route would surreptitiously get him directly behind Burwash and, if his memory was correct, it contained enough room to turn and crawl out of the valley should the weather sour. Banks soon found his memory was lousy.

They turned right ninety degrees into the narrow gorge. The view below them was a typical Alaskan rain forest, the walls of the little gorge lined with dense ferns, brambles, and small half-frozen waterfalls. Spruce and alder nipped their skis as they continued to climb and outpace the rising terrain.

Banks tried to see familiar signs from the last trek up this small valley. It was so dark. Small patches of fog gripped the low-lying rocky peaks. They started to bounce around in light to moderate turbulence, the result of dense icy air oozing down from the glaciers, creating gusty and unpredictable winds. The highest peak in the valley lay straight ahead, and he remembered the falls. In the summer months the cliff ahead was a waterfall. Now, in the dead of winter, it was a frozen sheet of ice. If he could get over that last hurdle, the valley would fall away into a small body of water known as Duke Lake. The increasingly nervous pilot pushed all the handles on the throttle quadrant forward to the windscreen. He banked back and forth slightly, giving the aircraft as much time as possible to scale the frozen geography.

Kayla began getting that look on her face Banks had seen several times during the evening.

"Travis, are you sure?"

"I think we'll be all right." The pilot spoke unconvincingly.

"Wait a minute," Kayla gawked at him, "what do you mean, 'You *think* we'll be all right'?"

"We'll be fine. Relax."

His heart began racing as they approached the frozen ledge. He had less than a mile to go and they were still several hundred feet below the top of the iced falls. The sick feeling swelling in his gut was years of experience telling him he had just screwed the pooch. They weren't going to make it over the crest.

He looked out his window to the left, eyeballing the dark, snow-speckled canyon walls caving in on them. He'd waited too long to act. He no longer had sufficient distance to turn around.

He stopped thinking and did what every seasoned pilot did facing death—he panicked and became a test pilot. He kept METO power—Maximum Engine Take Off—blowing out the exhaust and lowered the nose slightly.

Kayla watched in horror. "My God, Banks, what are you doing?"

"I'm not sure."

The airplane started a nosedive and lost altitude. The vertical speed indicator pointed south and the altimeter wound down while the airspeed indicator started climbing rapidly. He was trading altitude for airspeed, stored vertical energy for horizontal energy.

They had lost altitude and the ledge of the rocky cliff ahead was now 1,000 feet above them. It was also less than a half-a-mile away. Banks had a plan. Not a good one but something nonetheless. He was about to kill or save them both.

"When I tell you pump the flaps down, Kayla, pump them and pump them hard, all the way. Understood?"

Panic-stricken, Jackson nodded obediently.

Banks looked back and forth between the approaching ominous gray-white rock face in front of them and the airspeed indicator. It reached 160 knots. He waited and watched the jagged rock fill the windscreen. His hands trembled on the yoke. He descended farther. More airspeed. Not yet. They were less than a quarter-mile away. Just another second. Arctic Air's owner began to gag in unabashed terror 175 knots. It was time.

"NOW!" Banks yelled.

Travis heaved back on the stick with every ounce of energy in his biceps.

He couldn't remember the maximum positive G forces allowable on a de Havilland DHC-3 Beaver. At this moment, he didn't give a damn but he knew they were being severely exceeded.

The wings shuddered and his body sank like a sack of concrete into his seat. In the corner of his eye, he watched Kayla bent over near the floor fighting the heavy G forces and furiously pumping the flap handle.

The Beaver was like an elevator with wings. It seemed not to be going forward, just straight up. As the flaps came down, Banks began pushing forward on the yoke, keeping the airplane's nose from pointing too far up and stalling. The rock wall in front of them appeared to be passing the aircraft vertically as opposed to approaching them horizontally. For a moment, it looked as though Banks' asinine idea might actually work. The lip of the cliff was coming up at them as quickly as they flew toward it. The stall warning began to scream in their ears for the second time that night. They had cashed in all forward airspeed for lift. Less than twenty yards in front of them they leveled off at the same altitude as the precipice of the falls.

Banks nosed over slightly and released back pressure for a moment.

He screamed at his passenger. "More flaps, Kayla, more flaps. Give me everything!"

"I am! I am!" She wanted to look up but it slowed down her pumping.

"Don't look! Just pump!" Banks shouted. "Believe me, Kayla, you don't want to see this."

The wings rocked back and forth close to the stall. Travis Banks gently manipulated the 3,000 pounds of metal toward the crest of the rocks.

It was almost as if he had planned to land on the edge of the cliff.

Kayla had the flap handle pumped down so hard she'd bent it into the floorboards. She sat up to watch herself die.

Banks held on as the edge of the cliff slowly glided beneath the aircraft's belly. Kayla subconsciously gripped both sides of her seat as impact approached. Banks' chest tightened, but he kept the aircraft right at the stall. The horn continued to holler in their ears. The aircraft hit the ledge.

One ski bounced off the crest of the jutting snow-covered rock. The other ski brushed the ground. The engine continued to roar and its maximum thrust pulled them over the ground. Several sharp jutting rocks were approaching but the aircraft started gaining enough airspeed to start a shallow climb and allow them to begin retracting flaps.

They visually checked out the window to ascertain if the skis had sustained any threatening damage. They couldn't see any. It took several minutes for them to regain their composure. Maybe letting the Radcliff brothers go and spending the rest of their lives in prison was a more intelligent alternative.

Once out of the gorge and the darkening influence of the tall surrounding mountain peaks, the light offered by the full moon was a welcome sight.

The valley opened, giving way to an expansive plateau west of Burwash.

Banks touched Kayla on the back and pointed to a tiny lake looming in the darkness several miles ahead. His weary compatriot looked over the round cowling.

"Duke Lake. Jansen's cabin is just over the next ridge past the lake, less than a mile. Let's land and set up camp on the lake. We'll find Jansen in a few hours, before Radcliff has his first cup of coffee."

Duke Lake appeared larger in the winter. The frozen white body of water and its shoreline blended dangerously into the surrounding snow-covered meadows.

Banks gained altitude away from Jansen's cabin. He wanted to take a peek and see if Jansen was home, but he didn't want him to be alerted to the arrival of his unexpected guests. They climbed high enough over the lake to retard power on the small radial engine and glide to the northwestern ridge above his cabin. They soared silently in a high wide arc over the ridge and back to the lake.

They easily spotted the cabin from the air. The night was calm and clear. Hazy gray smoke waffled from Jansen's chimney into the night and settled in a wispy transparent ash blanket around the small valley. Jansen was home. Banks and Kayla would be the first ones by for breakfast. Radcliff would never attempt to reach the cabin before daybreak.

Without adding power, Banks silently dead-sticked the Beaver from 1,000 feet and slid it toward the ice near the east shore of Duke Lake. As they sank below the tree line, their height above the frozen lake was anybody's guess. He turned on the landing light and set up a slow descent of 200 to 300 feet a minute. Travis kept the wings level and took quick glances out the window over his left shoulder. Suddenly, the icy, windblown surface of Duke Lake hurled itself up to his belly. He pulled back on the yoke just in time to prevent permanent structural damage. The airplane hit hard and bounced several times, finally coming to a stop fifty feet from the frozen shore.

Banks took a deep breath and looked over at an ashen boss. Kayla was white as a ghost.

"Very nice. Do you do air shows? I don't know whether to kiss you or fire you." Kayla peeled her fingers from the dash. "I think I'll walk home."

Mixing gas into the oil was the only hope they had of getting the engine started in the morning. Banks held the dilution switch with the motor still running. After a forty-five second dilute, he pulled back on the mixture and let the blade spin to a stop. He slumped back in his seat, totally drained of energy. His mind was still racing. How long could he sit there?

The thermometer on the cabin air intake tube accused the ambient outside temperature of being thirty-three below zero. He looked at his watch. It was 3:45. They'd used up almost three hours of gas. He had a little more than two hours left, assuming the wing tip tanks had been totally filled. He should have enough gas to return to Whitehorse.

Banks' brain was numb from thinking and worrying. He checked his watch again. He had already forgotten what time it was. He would have to start the engine within three hours or the airplane might sit here until it sank in the spring thaw. The prop should be turning by 7:00 A.M. It would still be dark.

The pilot had only enough energy for one more chore.

He grabbed his toolbox from the back and hopped outside into the snow. At the rear of the fuselage, he used a Phillips screwdriver to open the access door leading to the aircraft's battery. Several minutes later, the warm battery was snuggling him in the cabin, wrapped in blankets. It would be his teddy bear that night. The intense cold could easily suck the cranking amps out of it. He had no intentions of not getting airborne the next morning. Once Simon Radcliff was in his care he would radio ahead and get Leon Powell to arrange a date with federal authorities from both sides of the border.

Travis and Kayla were so exhausted they decided to camp inside the airplane.

They broke open both survival kits and pondered what dehydrated delicacy to prepare for dinner. Kayla quipped about being too tired for steak and lobster and suggested freeze-dried lasagna and peaches. Considering both kits were only stocked with lasagna, they unanimously agreed lasagna was it. Banks leaned out the door and scooped up a small pot of snow. Kayla had wisely removed the back two bench seats when loading the survival kit in Whitehorse. There would be ample room to stretch out in their sleeping bags after supper.

Banks was too fatigued to give a shit about common sense. They were going to cook dinner inside the airplane. He propped the small Coleman stove on the wooden lid of his survival kit and lit a match next to the burner. The blue gas flame came to attention. Banks placed the pot of snow and ice over the flame on the burner. All he had to do was remember to shut the damn thing off before sleeping. He had no aspirations of being the title character in the contemporary sequel of "The Cremation of Sam McGee."

Within minutes, the little lid on the aluminum pot began to chatter. The act of boiling water aided in strangling the intense chill that oozed through every seal of the airplane's cabin. A few minutes later, Banks poured the steaming water into the slits atop the foil pouches. According to the directions on the back of the shiny packages, dinner would be served in five minutes.

Travis sucked the warm lasagna directly from the hot pouch. He leaned forward and spun the little gas valve on the Coleman stove. The air inside the plane instantly dropped ten degrees. Within minutes, the cabin would be freezing and their breath would, once again, be visible.

Something tickled Banks' chin. A dollop of hydrated tomato sauce dribbled down into his sleeping bag. He didn't have the energy to stop it.

The moon peaked in from the outside, illuminating the subtle lines of Kayla's sleeping bag. She was still awake. Light glinted from her eyes every time she blinked. Kayla Jackson, one of the North's most beautiful women, was just inches away from Travis. He longed to reach and touch her, comfort her.

She spoke gently. "Are you going to get some sleep or just stare at me all night?"

"I wasn't staring at you." Banks mumbled.

"Don't get any ideas."

He responded softly, slowly drifting asleep. "Why not? We're out of screaming range."

Kayla's smile sparkled in the moonlight. She reached over and took Travis' hand.

"Goodnight Travis."

"Uuuumm."

He didn't remember much else and wasn't able to stay awake long enough to savor his hydrated peaches.

Thoughts of Kayla Jackson in her evening dress permeated and intoxicated his soul. The dreamy image planted a smile on his face as he held her hand and collapsed into an intense deep sleep.

DAY 4

THE BEDROOM was tastefully decorated in soft pastels and floral patterns. The antique oak furniture had been dutifully cared for as evidenced by its shiny-waxed shimmer. The air was saturated with the aroma of lilac, cinnamon potpourri, and sex. Half-asleep, with his left leg over the side of the queen-size bed, he lay peacefully in a dream state.

He saw his reflection on the brass ball sitting atop the bedpost next to his right foot. The reflection of his smirk was odd, like what you see as a child in an eerie House of Mirrors when the carnival came to town. He looked away. It was surreal, as if he were dreaming. His body was powerless. He felt drugged. He wanted to sit up but his torso weighed a ton. He was exhausted.

It was like his childhood dreams. He would have frightening nightmares of being chased and unable to run because of crippling fatigue. The antagonist would gain on his sluggish image until he would awaken in a state of panic. He felt the exhaustion now but not the panic. He rather liked being there.

The lacquered hardwood floors reflected the morning sun streaming in through the windows, pink chiffon curtains waving gently in front of the open bay window. The dry cool summer breeze was welcome, as they were both saturated with perspiration.

She rolled on top of him, rubbing her firm and delicately sculptured breasts against the hair on his chest. Her nipples were aroused and hard. Kayla's golden-streaked locks were askew and they dangled in all different directions around his face onto the pillow. Her hands were softer than goose down. She reached down searching for something that was long gone. She leaned forward, licked the inside of his ear and provocatively whispered something about him being a wimp. She pleaded with him. "C'mon, Travis . . . get it up. Get it up!"

"Travis! Get up. Get up!"

Banks opened his eyes.

Kayla was staring down at him. Her breath shot toward him like the steam escaping the wheels of an old locomotive as she scrambled to set him free from her bedding.

Banks blinked several times staring up at the maroon vinyl-covered roof of the aircraft's cabin. He groggily took stock of his surroundings. It was pitch-black inside the cold airplane. The realization of his whereabouts was devastating. His hands momentarily searched the inside of his sleeping bag. He was grasping for Kayla. All he found was what she had desired before his rude awakening.

"Travis. Listen!" Kayla stopped pulling her parka on long enough for Banks to hear whatever it was that had awakened her.

Banks sat up. He used the gray sleeve of his wool long johns to wipe the condensation from the window above his right shoulder. He peeked out into the night. It was difficult to see through the milky plastic window. Leaning over Kayla, he popped open the passenger door. The air inside the cabin, kept relatively warm by their sleeping breath, clashed violently with the frigid blast that met them as the door swung opened. They both sat perfectly still, interrogating the silence. And it was getting louder by the second.

Then came the sound of several small engines. The cadence of the whining motors rose and fell, echoing through the valley. It sounded like someone struggling to cut down a large tree with a chain saw. The two Beaver occupants listened more intently. The high-pitched sound was moving from their right to left, east to west somewhere over the ridge in the direction of Jansen's cabin.

Unless several people were sprinting around Duke Lake at twenty miles an hour with chain saws whirling over their heads, the noise they were hearing were two snowmobiles, and both were heading in the direction of Jansen's cabin.

Saying nothing, Banks and his boss finished bundling up.

Travis looked at his watch. It was almost 7:00. They'd overslept. Three hours of sleep wasn't enough but it would have to suffice. Could Radcliff have traversed the rough and inhospitable forty miles between Burwash and Duke Lake in less than four hours? In the middle of the night? It was possible, if he hadn't slept or rested.

They threw their makeshift kitchen and bedding into a heap at the back of the airplane's small cabin.

Banks retrieved the Ruger .44 and its holster from the survival kit. Alongside the handgun was a box of home-loaded ammunition, which he slid into his parka's inside pocket. He handed Kayla the rifle and forced a box of shells into her coat pocket.

She looked at the pilot incredulously. "What are you doing?"

"Just in case." Banks propped up his boots on the back of the left front seat and laced them up.

"In case of what?" Kayla leaned around to catch Travis eye to eye. "Banks, for Christ's sake, these are RCMP constables. I don't think pointing a loaded gun at them is such a good idea."

"Kayla, you insisted on coming along with me. We're doing this by my rules. Actually, I'd prefer you stay here anyway. My philosophy is to always hope for the best but prepare for the worst. You'll live longer."

Banks swung open the door and jumped onto the snow-covered ice of Duke Lake. The full moon spread a bluish glow as far as the eye could see. Fifty miles away, the white peak of Mount Logan stood, rising majestically into the night sky, resembling a postcard from the Himalayas. Small clouds near Logan's peak obediently twisted and twirled in the 100-mile-an-hour winds that whipped through the atmosphere at 20,000 feet. Banks took a deep breath, rocking his sleepy senses to attention.

He looked back at his boss. "Well, are you staying or coming?"

Kayla scrambled to keep up, making no effort to hide her concern.

"Right. More macho bullshit. 'Prepare for the worst. You'll live longer.' Men. Is that one of your little jewels from the Banks' congressional library of brilliant ideas?"

She jumped out behind Banks, still sliding her parka onto one extended arm.

"Look, Travis," she raised both arms and spun around grinning sarcastically, "we're in the middle of nowhere. I'll 'live longer,' as you put it, if I *don't* resort to armed intervention with the police. We came out here to find someone, not shoot someone. Don't forget, you're still wanted for murder . . . "

"Not for long." Banks looked west at the dark ridge between them and the cabin. The aria of the snowmobiles grew louder. Based on the direction and the intensity of the engine noise, Banks figured he and Kayla could hustle up the ridge and possibly arrive at the cabin before the snowmobiles.

Kayla continued to rant. "Oh. I see. How stupid of me. So, to solve this little dilemma, we're going to pull a Rambo. Just march into the wilderness cabin of a religious fruitcake and perform a citizen's arrest of an RCMP officer." She threw her arms in the air. "Christ, why didn't I think of that?"

"I'm not sure. Maybe because you're not a guy."

He looked across the frozen lake trying to better gauge the distance to the ridge they would have to climb in order to reach the cabin.

Kayla Jackson shook her head in disgust. "Travis, have you lost your mind? You told me we were simply going to prove Simon Radcliff was alive."

"We are."

She wasn't listening. "If you ask me, I think you're preparing to get us both killed. You're acting like Christopher Columbus sailing us up shit creek. If we go knocking on Jansen's cabin door loaded up like the dirty dozen, I suspect we might meet the creek's caretaker."

"Relax, Kayla. I'm more concerned about protecting us from wildlife, not Jansen or Radcliff."

"Jansen *is* wildlife, Travis. You told me about those letters he sent to the Bellichek boys. He's a few logs short of a cord."

"Kayla, if I don't find Mike Jansen and/or Simon Radcliff, I may end up in jail for the rest of my life. Please. Either stay here and curse me all you want or come with me and be quiet."

The stubborn owner looked at Banks and saw his desperation. She begrudgingly agreed.

Banks surveyed the dark bluish horizon, seeing a color spectrum consisting only of blue, gray, and vast quantities of white. It was a stunning contrast to what would be seen in several months. The snow-covered fields surrounding Duke Lake would be transformed into warm green meadows covered in an array of reindeer moss, purple fireweed, brambles, and other colorful wildflowers. The barren deciduous spruce, alder, and birch on the ridges would burst alive in rich green foliage. Except for the dark green and prickly extremities on the odd northern pine, the valley was currently devoid of any vegetation.

The ridge separating them from Jansen's cabin would be a hearty climb. The windswept icy lake would be easy to traverse, but the powdery icy snow blowing against the shore would make the climb a chore.

Travis gently took her by the arm and began to lead her in the direction of the ridge.

"Ms. Jackson, be assured, I have no intention of getting too close to that cabin. But there's more than one way to skin a cat. Don't worry. I don't want Jansen to get butchered like the others, but I promise I won't get us killed trying to stop it. I'd like both of them, but if I can only get one I'd prefer to get my hands on the invisible Simon Radcliff. If we can't catch him, we'll follow him. I phoned Powell last night. As soon as I know where Simon is going, I'll get on the HF radio and have Leon pick him up. If that's him on one of those snowmobiles, and I'm sure it is, we've already got him, and I'm an innocent man. He's a bug in a jar. As long as that Beaver behind us starts later on, he can't run fast enough to escape. Unless, of course, we do something stupid, like get caught."

They marched quickly together across the dark frozen lake toward the metallic whine of the snowmobiles. There was a thin glow along the mountain ridges to the southeast, as morning was slowly breaking. Cirrus clouds, tainted orange and magenta, were thinly spread across the eastern skyline. It would be another beautiful day in the North.

Five minutes later, the light of the diminishing full moon had lit their way across the small lake. They hopped off the lake onto the shoreline. Up close, Banks realized scaling the rising terrain was going to be harder than he had imagined. They were up to their hips in light powdery snow, but the noisy snowmobiles echoing in the background prompted them to push on.

They began scaling the 200 yards up the tiny ridge. The loose frozen vegetation below the icy snow provided little footing, and they slipped and slid up the incline, pawing their way to the top of the small hill. Their only assistance came from leverage gained by using the frozen brittle branches from dormant winter bushes.

They arrived at the precipice exhausted. It was not a peak. The top of the ridge consisted of rocky and rough snow-covered terrain the size of a football field. The entire area extended several hundred yards in every direction. The two climbers were winded and breathing heavily, burning their lungs with the sub-zero air. Off to the left, in the air above the valley, they found the location of Jansen's cabin. Like an atmospheric soufflé, layers of chimney smoke sat motionless, one on top of the other, covering the lower part of the small gorge. Although they couldn't see it yet, the cabin was in the valley below the gray smoky layered blanket.

Travis and Kayla crouched down and shuffled toward the west slope of the ridge, catching their breath. They crept in behind the rocks and finally got an unobstructed view, peering down into the small gorge where Jansen's cabin nestled in a thin stand of trees.

The moon was still bright enough on the surrounding snow to cast a pale blue hue on the cabin. It was at least thirty years old. The wood on all sides was gray, warped, and twisted. Patchwork was evident around the entire structure, which appeared no larger than 300 square feet, probably one room.

The fire trickling out of the chimney was scarcely smoldering. No light emanated from the small windows. If Jansen was inside, he hadn't heard the approaching snowmobiles and must still be asleep.

Travis and Kayla had barely arrived before the snowmobiles.

Kayla used the zoom lens on one of McMaster's cameras that he had left in the plane and Travis used the zoom lens on his binoculars to stare into the valley below. The snowmobiles were plowing through the deep snow less than a mile away. It was still too dark to see who the riders were but the second machine had the same color skis as the snowmobile Dale had pictured at Primrose Lake.

As they traversed the undulating snowy terrain, the two heavily dressed snowmobile riders rhythmically rode up and down as if they were athletic riders in an Olympic equestrian competition. A mile from the cabin, as if on cue, the two machines decelerated in concert and slowed to a stop. The motors idled, disturbing the winter night.

Kayla tapped Travis' shoulder and pointed at the cabin. A dull orange glow appeared inside the front window. The light grew brighter as the operator must have rolled the wick of the kerosene lamp skyward. The small Japanese engines of the snowmobiles had finally awakened the little valley, and Mike Jansen. Banks leaned forward and whispered into Kayla's ear not to miss any of this with the camera. Things were about to get interesting.

Any inclination Banks had to warn Mike Jansen of his uninvited arriving visitors had now passed. It was too late and too dangerous. The climb up the slope had been more strenuous and time-consuming than Banks had envisioned. He couldn't help but think his miscalculation might cost Jansen his life. Travis snuggled up to a boulder, pressing it against his right shoulder. It didn't matter anyway. There was no way he could get to the cabin in time and stop what was about to happen. It had been in the works for years. His conscience was clear. If Jansen had played a part in the horrible demise of the little Radcliff girl at Tetcho Lake twenty years earlier, then he was about to meet his maker. So be it. All Banks concerned himself with was proving his innocence and getting himself and Kayla out of here alive. He would document the unfolding events on film and try to intercept Simon Radcliff on the way out. Banks hoped to be exonerated; the Radcliff boys would have to face the system without their chosen patsy.

The snowmobile riders appeared to communicate, pointing left and right of the cabin. Banks squinted into his binoculars but could not make out who they were. They both wore ski masks under their helmets and reflective visors. It didn't really matter; he was confident he knew who was driving. It simply would have been reassuring to see the faces to finally prove his theory.

The two machines suddenly lurched forward and took off toward a tree line a quarter-mile west of the cabin. They were headed in the opposite direction of Banks' vantage point.

Moments later, the snowmobiles disappeared behind a wall of spruce branches. Silence fell across the valley.

It was odd. It took ten minutes after the noise subsided before Mike Jansen opened the door of his cabin. Banks couldn't understand why Jansen had waited so long to investigate the racket the machines had made. Being in a sound sleep might partially explain his tardiness, but this area was totally desolate. A visitor in the middle of the night had to be a rarity, and one that would certainly be cause for alarm.

Banks focused the binoculars on Jansen as his head inched out the door, reacting miserably to the cold as it met him head on. He was wearing only long johns and boots. With only his head sticking out, he looked in both directions. Banks' body became rigid, he caught himself not breathing. After the previous week's experience, Travis expected a gunshot to ring out and see Jansen's lifeless body crumple in the doorway. No sounds. Jansen tiptoed to the edge of his tiny wooden stoop and peered around back of his cabin, first down the left side and then the right. It was almost as if he were expecting someone.

Banks focused in with his binoculars. The sun was slowly creeping into the eastern morning sky and it added a touch of light to Jansen's face. The trapper stood ramrod straight, and was surprisingly nimble for a man approaching sixty. The only photograph Banks had ever seen of him was a grainy newspaper shot taken twenty years earlier. Travis had no idea what Jansen would look like now.

There were no signs of Radcliff or his brother. It had been fifteen minutes since they disappeared into the woods behind the cabin.

Kayla focused the Nikon zoom lens hanging around her neck onto the front door. She deftly rotated the lens in quarter turns, her left eye squinting while her right eye did all the work.

She spoke in a loud whisper. "Jansen's aged well. Must put formaldehyde in his bourbon."

Where was Radcliff? Something wasn't right. Banks searched the tree line behind the cabin. He darted the binocular lenses back and forth. Where in the hell were they? He pushed the lenses closer to the bridge of his nose, scanning the tiny valley. Banks was filling with a sense of urgency. Intuition told him to get away.

He scanned the ridge left and right, seeking a more clandestine perch on which to hide. Kayla was engrossed with the images filling her viewfinder and continued to stare down the incline toward the cabin.

"Maybe we ought to find better cover," Banks insisted to his boss.

One of the big disadvantages of sub-zero powdered snow is its reputation for being the perfect footing to surreptitiously approach someone from behind.

"You should have thought of that earlier."

Banks started to spin around.

"Don't turn around!" The voice from behind Banks and Jackson was all too familiar. There was no anger in the tone, just an odd sense of professionalism mixed with frustration.

"Listen carefully. First you, Ms. Jackson—move slowly—I want you to toss that rifle over your shoulder. Hold it by the barrel, not the stock."

Nick Radcliff didn't need to worry about anything from Kayla but full compliance. The only person Arctic Air's owner might attack at that moment was the employee she had entrusted to keep them out of harm's way. She threw the rifle backward and gave Travis a disgusted look while whispering an impersonation of him fifteen minutes earlier, "*unless we do something stupid like get caught!*"

"Banks, you're next. Take out that handheld bazooka you call a pistol and toss it back here without turning around. Use your left hand, and only your thumb and index finger on the grip."

Banks did as instructed. He complied by tossing the gun over his right shoulder and coyly turning around at the same time. He wanted to see for himself. Both men still wore ski masks. Nick Radcliff shook his head and lowered his service revolver. The other man kept his rifle poised on his target.

"Banks, I told you not to turn around." Nick Radcliff pulled on the top of his black wool ski mask until it stretched a foot in the air and slid off his head. His handle bar mustache emerged bent at a forty-five-degree angle. "That's been your problem for a while. You can't follow directions!"

No matter what tragedy was driving Nick Radcliff to this extreme, Banks never felt his safety was in jeopardy.

"What are you going to do, Radcliff? Shoot me?"

"Possibly." He swaggered forward closing the gap between them and leaning over to pick up the pilot's .44. "But first, I have some unfinished business to take care of." He checked the chamber for six rounds. "You don't mind if I use this, do you?"

"Be my guest."

Radcliff clicked the side release, rolled the chamber back into place and then gave Banks a serious glare.

"You couldn't keep out of it, could you?"

Banks didn't answer him. He looked at Nick Radcliff's partner—the man he was sure was Nick's brother, Simon. The mystery man stood motionless, breathing short blasts of condensation into the morning air. The sun rose up his back. Standing close, he was an imposing figure, a much larger man than his brother. Even the pictures Banks had seen didn't do his size justice. Travis could only imagine the terror Simon must have inflicted on Ed and Brock Bellichek in the last few moments of their miserable lives. The guy was huge, and standing there breathing slowly, with the sun at his back, knowing what Banks knew, Simon gave Travis a healthy dose of the creeps.

Banks pointed at Nick's partner. "What about Lurch here? You going to introduce us?"

Kayla crouched even lower.

Radcliff's demeanor changed instantly. His jaw tightened and the muscles in front of his temples bulged and rippled. Obviously, his big brother was a touchy subject.

Banks had to convince the Whitehorse RCMP inspector that others in Whitehorse had been apprised of his theory.

The pilot extended his hand and approached the masked man disingenuously. "Good morning, Simon. I'm Travis Banks. Pleased to finally meet you."

Nick Radcliff swung the butt of Banks' .44 and caught the side of Travis' head and neck. Banks fell to the ground in searing pain, which immediately transformed itself into anger.

"You son of a bitch, Radcliff." Banks rolled on the ground for a moment, holding the side of his neck. Kayla crawled to his side. Travis got up on one knee. "You think I left Whitehorse without telling anyone where the hell I was going and *why*? You're dumber than I thought."

The truth was, he hadn't told anyone *exactly* where he was going. Kayla Jackson hadn't left word either because she had no idea where Duke Lake was located.

Banks continued, "I know your brother Simon is alive. Go ahead, Simon," Travis turned and pointed at the tall silhouette, "pull off the mask. I know it's you. I also know . . ." he lowered his voice slightly and spoke softer and with reverence, "I also know what happened to your daughter. Believe me, I'm sorry."

Banks probably shouldn't have mentioned the girl. He thought Radcliff's anger had peaked. It didn't even come close to the explosion that ensued. The head of the RCMP in Whitehorse took two steps and kicked Banks in the ribs, knocking him sideways away from Kayla and onto his back. Travis' lungs pleaded with his diaphragm to flex and provide air. Through the corner of his eye, he saw the masked man come forward and put a hand on Nick's back as if to calm him down.

Banks saw Kayla begin to come to his aid. Radcliff motioned for her to stay back.

Nick Radcliff had lost his composure. He straddled Banks and the rage spat from his lips like an erupting volcano.

"You don't know shit! Do you hear me!"

The venomous statement spewed from his trembling mouth as his face shook with anger. He raised Banks' gun and pointed it at the pilot's temple. The RCMP constable pulled the hammer back with a quick jerk. Banks was wrong. This guy would have no compunction about putting a hole in his skull, right here, right now. The pilot had tapped into the recesses of a deep and festering wound by simply mentioning Simon and his little girl. For the first time in Radcliff's presence, Banks felt that his life was in peril.

Kayla Jackson cried out, "For God's sake, Radcliff, what are you doing!"

Banks closed his eyes and looked down. "Look, Nick, killing me won't solve your problem. I've already told people about Simon, and the pictures. The ones taken after he supposedly died in the hunting accident."

Nick's curiosity was titillated. He didn't shoot.

Banks pleaded, "I've never had kids, but I can imagine how you feel..."

Radcliff interrupted. The words seethed from his lips. "You have no idea how we feel." He was still angry, but the violent passion was ebbing.

The masked man walked up to him and gently pushed down Nick's forearm, forcing the gun away from Banks' temple. Whoever was behind the mask was probably saving Banks' life for the second time.

Travis piped up again. "Look, if I'd lost a member of my family the way you did, I'd react the same way. I'd try to kill the bastards responsible."

Radcliff had regained his composure and turned away, motioning to the other man. The man in the ski mask, who Banks confidently assumed was Simon, pulled two sets of handcuffs out from behind his heavy parka and approached the two new prisoners.

Nick Radcliff grunted in disgust in Banks' direction, "Like I said, Banks, you don't know shit. Simon and I haven't killed anyone . . ." he turned and stared at the cabin before finishing his sentence. "Yet."

"What do you mean, you haven't killed anyone?" Banks snickered uncontrollably and then quickly caught himself. Pissing this man off further was not a good idea but he couldn't believe what he was hearing. Even Kayla finally looked up, shock plastered on her face.

"Banks, you don't know half as much as you think you do," the RCMP constable stated, and turned to leave.

Radcliff had said "we" and "Simon." It was the first time he alluded to the fact his brother was alive. But what did he mean, they hadn't killed anyone? His answer sounded genuine and sincere. It rang of the truth. If what Nick Radcliff was saying was true, Banks' whole theory was sunk.

Kayla and Travis were led to a large pine near the edge of the clearing. The masked man wound their arms around the tree and then handcuffed them to the trunk. Radcliff conferred with the other man for several moments, nodded, and then they began down the slope turning sideways for better traction.

Banks stopped him. "Hey, Radcliff." Both men turned. "Are you sure the guy in that shack is Mike Jansen?"

Radcliff actually forced a smile across his chiseled face.

"You're a genius, Banks." He turned around again and began walking toward the cabin.

Banks had no idea what in the hell was going on.

The two officers slid down the slope, plowing through the knee- high dry fine snow. The icy crystals being tossed in the air mixed with the odd gust of wind and whirled around their faces.

Kayla pulled her head around from her side of their mutual hugging tree and, from inches away, stared into her employee's eyes.

"What do you know that I don't?" she implored. "If that's not Mike Jansen in the cabin, then who is it?"

Radcliff called back. "If you're good and don't make any noise up here, I'll come back and arrest your ass and put you in a warm jail. If you misbehave, I'll leave you here until next winter. Understood?" They turned and continued on their way down the ridge.

Kayla and Travis glanced at each other. They were both confused.

Kayla tried again. "Who's in the cabin, Travis?"

"I don't know. I assumed it was Jansen. Mind you, the guy was agile for an old man. He behaved as if he was expecting someone. Didn't he?"

"And what did they mean, they haven't killed anyone? It's been them, hasn't it?"

"I thought so." Banks was at a total loss to explain what was going on.

Kayla Jackson and Travis Banks sat in the snow, hugging the tree that rubbed their cheeks. They could both see Nick Radcliff and his mysterious partner plowing down the slope. Banks lost sight of them for a few minutes until they reached the bottom of the ridge. They reappeared fifty yards from the cabin. Both men marched erect and tall to Jansen's residence. This would be no surreptitious approach in which they surprised the occupant by nailing him in a bear trap and skinning him alive. These guys were being direct and almost professional in their approach. This certainly didn't follow the "modus operandi" of the other killings.

A minute later Nick stood in front of the cabin calling out to its occupant. His partner stood a few yards behind him to his left. It appeared as though Nick was holding up something in his hand. It looked like a wallet. He appeared to be displaying his identification. Kayla and Travis sat hugging their tree, mystified as to how this scene would eventually end in Jansen's mutilated death.

The door to the cabin swung slowly open, but Jansen didn't appear. Banks could see Nick urging the occupant to exit the cabin like a policeman directing traffic, heard him ordering "Mike Junior" to come outside where Nick could see him.

Kayla muttered, "Mike Junior?"

"That explains why they look alike," Travis whispered.

Kayla continued. "But if that's Mike Junior, where's his father?"

Banks shrugged, watching the scene unfold.

A muffled voice spoke loudly from inside the cabin. Nick glanced over his shoulder to his partner and motioned for him to lower his rifle. The tall masked figure obliged. Nick inched closer to the cabin, getting within ten feet of the front door. He leaned forward, trying to peer around the half-opened door into the interior. Several minutes passed.

Radcliff appeared to become impatient. He continued to creep forward, casually sliding his badge, wallet, whatever it was, back into his pocket. The inspector dropped a mitten into the snow at his feet. He brought his arm back to his chest and appeared to slide his uncovered hand inside his breast pocket, where he had hidden Banks' .44. Nick Radcliff slowly pulled the Redhawk from his parka.

Travis looked at Kayla. It appeared Radcliff was going to use Banks' gun to shoot Jansen when the trapper stuck his head out the door. Kayla was breathing almost inaudibly. This couldn't be how the other men met their grisly demise.

The tree huggers strained to hear the conversation below. They faintly heard the masked man ask Nick several times to confirm that this was Jansen's cabin. Nick faced his partner momentarily and nodded yes, adding, "This is it, Simon."

The two handcuffed on the ridge looked at one another. They both heard it. The man with Nick Radcliff was his brother Simon. Banks' theory was right on that account. All he had to do was free himself from the tree and apprehend Simon; then he'd become a free man. Feeling pleased with himself, he looked back down the ridge at the two brothers.

Simon raised his rifle and pointed sights at the cabin door for an instant. Then slowly, taking careful aim, he turned the gun in the direction of his brother, Nick.

Kayla and Banks looked on in horror. Simon appeared to be aiming at his brother's head.

Kayla began to speak, "My God, Travis. What's he doing . . ."

The gunshot was so startling that the two prisoners bound to the pine tree jumped and cracked their heads against the frozen bark so close to their faces. The valley echoed strongly as if several shots followed in perfect cadence. The small, heavily dressed figure of Nick Radcliff crumpled and fell backward, almost peacefully, and landed softly in the red-speckled snow. Simon Radcliff had just shot his brother in the head.

Kayla almost stopped breathing. "Oh, my God!"

They both wanted to run, in any direction, quickly. They shook the tree in a vain attempt to free themselves. They were stuck. Banks peered down the ridge, unable to add to Kayla's assessment of the horrific scene unfolding in front of them.

Immediately, gunfire rang from Jansen's cabin. Simon spun back around and began returning fire toward the cabin. He took cover behind a white and brown snow-coated stump several yards away. Bullets ripped the snow around Nick's body, sending icy plumes in all directions. Simon Radcliff continued to fire indiscriminately into the side of the old weathered cabin.

The window in the cabin that had contained the lantern exploded, glass flying out in all directions. Behind it quickly followed the barrel of a rifle. Instantly, gunshots rang out everywhere. Although several hundred yards away, even Travis and Kayla instinctively ducked seeking cover. Another round of gunfire soon followed as Simon ducked below the stump and slapped a new clip into the belly of his semiautomatic rifle, then he popped up from behind the stump and clicked off several rounds directly into the cabin window, splintering the frame and shattering the remaining glass.

The two bound observers on the ridge watched, speechless, as the scene in front of them continued.

After several minutes, the gunfire from the cabin finally ceased. From

Banks' vantage point, he could see Mike Jansen, Jr., decide to leave. Fully dressed for the elements, the younger Jansen ran out the back door and slipped into the woodshed behind the cabin. Moments later, the starting whine of a snowmobile screamed from the shed and violently penetrated the morning air. Simon peered over the stump trying to locate the noise. As he watched, the hidden machine crashed through one of the dilapidated doors of the shack and sped around the corner of the cabin toward him. A hail of bullets saturated the airspace between the two foes. Mike Junior used a handgun while Simon took careful aim with his rifle, one shot from the rifle shattering the snowmobile's windshield. The younger Jansen crouched and ineffectively fired a handgun over the broken Plexiglas. Luckily for the driver, Simon had emptied the new clip before Mike Junior got close. They both fired with handguns.

The snowmobile charged directly at the stump. At the last instant, the machine veered ninety degrees right, spraying the stump in a wave of ice and snow. Simon Radcliff attempted to fire once or twice more but had to hunker down. Unbelievably, the two fighting parties nearly collided, but neither one appeared to have been shot. Jansen spun around as he drove away and fired several more times. Simon sat up aiming to fire, but it was too late—all he saw was a snowy rooster tail zigzagging away. He lowered his gun in frustration.

Nick Radcliff was motionless. He had been shot in the head at point blank range. He had to be dead. Simon Radcliff walked over to his dead brother, put the toe of his boot under Nick's limp shoulder, and flipped him over. He pulled the hammer back on the pistol in his right hand and fired one more round into the back of his brother's head. He seemed devoid of any emotion. He turned and jogged to the tree line behind the cabin.

Less than a minute later, Simon shot from the tree line on his snowmobile. He raced fifty yards in pursuit of Mike Jansen, Junior, before coming to a stop. He looked up the ridge where Banks and his boss sat helpless and stunned after having witnessed the most horrific scene of their lives. Simon turned the snowmobile in their direction and accelerated up the hill.

Kayla began to panic. She rattled the handcuffs binding her wrists and shook the tree. "My God. Quick, Travis, do something, for Christ's sake."

Banks feebly pulled his handcuffs one time. It was useless. Normally, he wasn't one to give up, but there was nothing he could do. Even if their hands were free, Simon was on a snowmobile. They were on foot.

The situation was hopeless. They had just witnessed an RCMP inspector's execution. The executioner was about to pay them a visit, whether they liked it or not.

They heard the screaming engine approach but saw nothing until Simon and his machine leapt, completely airborne, over the ridge. He landed in a cloud of snow and ice less than 10 feet from the tree-bound prisoners, left the snowmobile idling and dismounted. He kept his ski mask over his face and walked toward them. For a moment, he watched Kayla and Banks pathetically hugging the tree.

Simon said nothing. He reached into his breast pocket and pulled out Banks' .44.

Travis studied the masked man curiously as he tossed the Redhawk handheld cannon into the snow ten feet from the tree.

Simon reached into his pocket again and pulled out a handcuff key. He dropped it into the snow near their feet, and turned to leave.

Travis and Kayla were shocked and confused. It seemed as if everybody had gone mad.

Banks shouted at the masked man's back. "Simon! If those four miners killed your little girl, I understand why you'd want to kill them. But your brother, why . . . why kill your brother. . .?"

He spun around and pointed a finger at the pilot. Travis had struck a nerve. Kayla whispered at Banks to shut up. Simon pointed at Banks exactly the way he had pointed in Nick Radcliff's den. The intruder the night before had been the masked man who now stood before them.

Simon regained his composure and turned away without speaking. The large man climbed on the snowmobile and, in a cloud of exhaust and flying snow, roared away in pursuit of Mike Jansen's son. Banks and Jackson watched for several minutes until the white rooster tail of snow disappeared.

Kayla looked at Travis, stunned. "What in the hell is going on, Travis?"

Banks had no idea. But he was beginning to think the answer lay in the bizarre letter he had found in Nick Radcliff's den. He couldn't rid himself of the image of Simon's rage when the devastated father had read the letter. He also would never rid his memory of Simon executing his brother.

Less than fifteen minutes after all hell had broken out in the desolate little valley near Duke Lake, silence returned.

As soon as the sound of the snowmobiles had ceased, Banks began trying to find a way to get the handcuff key resting on top of the snow at his feet. Every time he reached out with his boots, he kicked the key farther away. He was becoming agitated. Time was of the essence. Without the ability to move and keep the circulation active, the two of them were soon in jeopardy of suffering from exposure.

Banks was at a loss.

He looked straight up. The tree was thirty feet tall, covered in bare branches, and was two feet in diameter. They couldn't get over the top. Banks tried to lighten the mood by suggesting Kayla chew through it. His humor was not received well.

Arctic Air's owner questioned Banks. "Who did you tell where we were going? How long before they look for us?"

Travis dropped his head. "Do you want the good news or the bad news?"

Kayla was silent.

Banks continued, "Well, the good news is I told Leon Powell we were flying to Duke Lake."

"And the bad news?" Kayla prompted.

"I'm the only one who knows where Duke Lake is."

Banks could hear the frustrated sigh from the other side of the tree.

They said nothing.

The rising sun was warming the lowlands and allowing the cold dense air from the Kluane Mountain Range to start pouring down from the surrounding glaciers. The sub-zero wind was beginning to kick up and whip across their exposed faces. Kayla's lips were cracking in the dry freezing air, her facial extremities were losing their redness and becoming a purplish gray. If frostbite was gripping his boss, Banks was sure he must be suffering from it as well. Cold exposure is insidious, slowly overcoming an individual with little or no warning. Travis tapped his fingertips together. He felt nothing. The exposed flesh on their wrists was also succumbing to the freezing air. The sub-zero metal of the handcuffs was sticking to the exposed skin on their arms. They both tried to hold their heads down, out of the wind.

Banks had to think of something plausible. Leon knew Banks had headed in the direction of Burwash, but he wouldn't find this place for several days. At least not before he and Kayla had become permanently frozen to the tree.

Something nibbled away at Banks' conscience. There was something about how Simon Radcliff had conducted himself. Why murder your brother in cold blood and then let the only witnesses live? The letter hidden in Nick Radcliff's secret lockbox Bible must have held the key. The way Simon had responded to it was scary. Travis had to get the letter and Simon together in the same room. The elder Radcliff could explain something. Banks had no idea what it was, but he was confident it would exonerate him.

At least an hour passed.

They sat hugging their tree in silence, making ineffectual attempts to secure the handcuff key.

There was a slight slur to Kayla's speech. The cold was binding the natural elasticity of her cheeks.

"Travis? Why haven't you ever married?" She was being particularly careful in her choice of words. "I'm sure you've had the opportunity. Especially when you were with the airlines."

Banks looked up, surprised. "Good Lord, that almost resembles a personal question. You're obviously succumbing to hypothermia, Ms. Jackson."

"Travis, I'm serious. And, please, we've been over this, don't call me Ms. Jackson! I'm your age. You make it sound like I'm your first grade schoolteacher."

Banks smiled and filed that little tidbit of information away. He knew just what to call her down the road when he wanted to needle her.

She caught her breath and continued. "I mean you're a, you know…

well...you're certainly not ugly."

"Why, thank you." Banks interrupted teasingly.

Kayla was exasperated. "You know what I mean."

"No, I don't." He egged her on. "Are you saying I'm handsome, or cute? Women like the cute thing."

"I'm saying that I'm sure in your youth you were probably quite attractive, quite rugged in a way, and you're still . . . rugged, but, well, I mean we all age."

"Oh. I see. You're saying I've been ridden hard and put up wet a few too many times." He chuckled.

"I'm saying I'm surprised someone hasn't tried to nurture you and look after you. I see a lot of good. A lot of potential. You just won't let anybody get close enough."

"I prefer spending my money on fast women and slow horses. Any suggestions on whom I might let get close enough?" He was trying to be lighthearted.

Kayla was fed up. "Someone with a great deal of patience and a need to raise an adult child!" She whipped her head around to the other side of the tree away from Banks' face. "Just promise me if you ever find a woman with those qualifications, please, do us *all* a favor and don't breed."

Banks realized Kayla was beginning to open up to him and he regretted his offhanded and silly remarks. He became serious, trying to placate his superior.

"Kayla, I'd thought about what it would be like to have children. But having found out in the past few days the agony that some parents suffer from missing or abducted children, well, I don't know if it's worth the risk."

Kayla's voice had an edge. "Banks, you drive a car, don't you?"

Travis was perplexed. "You know I do. And I won't call you Ms. Jackson if you'll stop calling me Banks."

"In North America every year, almost 50,000 people die in auto accidents. It doesn't stop you or me from driving. Life is a risk. You've got to look at the possibility of reward."

Banks rubbed his runny nose against the tree. "Remind me never to go to Las Vegas with you. You could lose a bundle of cash thinking along those lines."

"If you've never had children, how do you know?" Her voice was solemn.

"Who are you trying to convince here, Kayla? You or me?"

The wind whipped some more snow around their faces.

Her voice was becoming weaker. "Maybe both of us."

They each smiled out of view of one another.

Ten more minutes passed. Time was of the essence. Banks looked up chuckling at the futility.

He was handcuffed to a tree near the Arctic Circle with his boss, who appeared to be becoming more than just a friend. He could spit on the keys that could free them but he couldn't touch them. They were on a ridge overlooking some unknown body of frozen water someone named "Duke Lake." Their tree stood in one of the most remote parts of the planet. They would be frozen to death by nightfall if they couldn't think of some way out. Banks started to laugh about what their rescuers would think when they found them dead, handcuffed to a tree.

"What's so funny?" Kayla slowly slid her cheek to his side of the tree. "I don't see what's so funny, Travis."

Banks could see her disposition was beginning to be affected by encroaching hypothermia. He tried to cheer her up. "We must look ridiculous from a distance."

Kayla's retort was instantaneous. "We look ridiculous from four inches." She paused momentarily and awoke becoming animated. "Travis, I have a hairpin in my pocket."

Banks smirked. "I don't think your next of kin will fight over it at the reading of your will."

"No, silly, can you reach it?"

"I can't help." The pilot studied her freezing face. "Believe me, if I could reach into your pockets, that's exactly where my hands would have been an hour ago." He eyed Kayla's pink ear lobes protruding from beneath her fur-lined hood. "Nice earrings. Dale has a set just like those. They look much better on you, though. I can't figure out why Dale started wearing an earring."

Jackson only heard the one word. Her mind was racing. "An earring!" Kayla shouted.

"That's right. Dale's ugly earring. How many secure men wear an earring? Only people searching for an identity."

"Can you reach it?" Kayla Jackson pleaded.

"Why?"

Her eyes demanded an answer. "*Dammit! Can you reach one of my earrings?*"

Whatever she was thinking, her passion made a believer out of Banks. "Maybe, if you lean back real hard."

Kayla tilted her head to the left and leaned back into the V where Travis' hands came together. "Just do it. And don't drop it."

Banks' numb fingers fiddled around in the hood of Kayla's parka for several minutes before he finally pulled the earring free from her lobe.

Travis finally realized what his boss was trying to accomplish. "Kayla, I can't get it to you."

"Push the end with the thin metal needle into the bark of the tree. Then we'll spin around the tree and swap places."

Banks did as instructed.

"Kayla, I know what you are trying to do but that's just garbage you see in James Bond movies."

"Really?"

Travis was watching Kayla's face contort up and down as she played with the metal clasp in her hands.

"These are RCMP-issued handcuffs, Kayla. I'm sure they've got the design down pat to where some moron cuffed to a tree in the Arctic can't undo them with an earring."

A blustery wind kicked snow and ice into his numb face. He lowered his head, turning it sideways into the trunk of the tree. A moment later, when he raised his head, his esteemed superior was standing a few feet away rubbing her sore wrists.

"Oh, ye of little faith."

Banks was still learning some of Kayla's talents. "Well, I'll be a son of a bitch."

"What little I know of your mother, God rest her soul, I sincerely doubt it. Now, do you want to dance some more with that tree or do you want off?" She bent over and picked up the key Simon had left behind.

The pilot held his hands straight out. "You'll have to teach me that trick, Kayla."

"Can't be done, eh?" Kayla continued to mumble aloud as she inserted the key into the lock on Banks' cuffs. A little click could be heard in the wind before the cuffs on his wrist fell to the ground.

Banks immediately thought of the letter in Radcliff's den and the knowledge that Simon Radcliff was alive. He needed to get back to Whitehorse and explain himself to Leon Powell. He felt it was only a matter of time before he was exonerated.

It took nearly an hour to reach the Beaver, install the battery, and get the aircraft started.

Banks slipped on his headset and tuned the radio. On the third attempt, he raised Arctic Air on the HF band.

"4049 Whitehorse, 4049 Whitehorse, Kilo India Delta, come in. Over."

Thousands of squeaky Mickey Mouse voices faded in and out. He hated the HF radio. Everybody sounded as if they were stoned on helium.

The squeaky speaker finally garbled something he recognized. The office heard his call sign. He listened intently, trying to make sense of what they were saying. For a fleeting moment, Dale McMaster's voice broke in and out.

"Kilo India . . . Message . . . Doc Baker . . .psychological evaluation . . . Jansen . . . mental facility . . . Burwash RCMP . . . Jansen spotted . . ." The squeaky voice faded away.

"Shit!" Banks hit the dash.

Kayla stared at Travis in the left seat of the Beaver. "What? What did they say?"

"Hell, I don't know. Something about Jansen seen in Burwash, somebody's mental evaluations. Damn. I don't know. A bunch of broken-up garbage. We've got to get airborne. I'll have a better chance to raise them on the radio once we're flying."

Travis thought about the broken message he had received. It had triggered something in the back of his mind. He strained to reason out what it was, he kept drawing a blank.

They bounced around on Duke Lake trying to get the Pratt radial engine sufficiently warm for takeoff. After ten minutes, the cylinder head temperature and oil pressure started to head in the right direction. The experienced pilot had to take it easy. If he was impatient and blew an oil cooler on this puny lake, he might never see Simon again.

He looked at his watch. The two men on snowmobiles had a two-hour head start. They would have certainly made it to Burwash. If he understood what he'd just heard on the HF radio, Mike Jansen Senior had been spotted in Burwash. Once he discovered his little boy was running around shooting at police officers, their religious crusade would, undoubtedly, have to start touring permanently. The question was, where would they go from Burwash? The only way to evade the authorities quickly was by air. If Jansen could get an airplane, he could easily get to Whitehorse or beyond.

The icy lake was rough and unyielding, and the gusty morning wind had created a sea of snowdrifts. They bounced along for two-thirds of the lake unable to get airborne. Every time they attained flying speed, they'd smash into a drift and lose twenty knots. As the opposite end of the lake approached, Banks attempted a glassy water maneuver used by float pilots. He rolled the wings right, lifting the left ski off the ice. The drag was slightly reduced. No sooner was the left ski flying than they smashed through an icy drift with the right ski. The impact launched them into the air just above the stall speed. He gently rolled the wings level, raised the flaps, and accelerated, banking the Beaver east. Once clear of the terrain, he tuned in 341 on the ADF. The Burwash NDB signal was strong and they were soon heading directly for Burwash Landing.

Travis motioned for Kayla to keep her eyes peeled below. Their track by air would take them the same route the younger Jansen and Simon would have taken if they were headed for the nearest road, the Alcan Highway.

The weather was clear and Banks no longer felt a need to hide. The letter in Nick Radcliff's home, along with Simon's explanation, might explain the madness of the last few days. He had to find Simon. Only the elder Radcliff could explain why he had killed his brother.

The broken message Banks received on the HF radio was eating away at him. Dr. Baker. Jansen. Mental facility. Evaluation. It brought to mind something his sister had said when he had called her from the RCMP headquarters in Whitehorse the day before. He had personally seen Mike Jansen's religious ravings in the letters he had found at Brock Bellichek's cabin and Nick Radcliff's den, and Jansen certainly appeared to suffer from what his sister labeled "Religiosity." She had described Jansen and his twisted religious motivations for the killings without ever having met the zealot. If Nick Radcliff told him the truth back at Jansen's cabin, that he and his brother did not kill the Bellichek brothers and William Watt, then Mike Jansen was a textbook serial killer. If Kram was able to correctly pinpoint the type of individual capable of such killings, then her assessment about them getting cornered and wanting to go out with a bang might also be accurate. If Mike Jansen knew the authorities had discovered that he and the others had killed Kelly Margaret Radcliff twenty years earlier, what could he do to fulfill that need to go out with a roar? There weren't many places in a small northern community like Whitehorse where a fruitcake could do something horrific enough to make the national news. There were no tall buildings. There wasn't one bus, let alone an intricate subway system. A palpable chill crept up the pilot's spine. There was an international airport in Whitehorse. It served transport-sized aircraft.

Banks quickly seized the radio handset and tuned in 126.7 on the VHF radio for Burwash Flight Service. Several attempts paid off when the groggy voice responded from the Burwash Flight Service Station.

"Calling Burwash Flight Service, go ahead."

Travis tried to erase any panic in his voice.

"Yes, sir, this is Kilo India Delta. We're a de Havilland Beaver en route to Whitehorse. Have you had any flights depart for Whitehorse in the last hour?"

The scratchy reply filled Banks' David Clarke headset. "The scheduled service left twenty minutes ago for Whitehorse. Before that we had a NORDO heading that way."

"A NORDO? What type was it, sir?"

"A Cessna Centurion, believe it or not. Charlie Mike Alpha Sierra."

Banks didn't reply. There couldn't be a Cessna Centurion on earth flying around without at least 10,000 dollars' worth of radios on board. It was a luxurious aircraft for private pilots and expensively outfitted. A NORDO Centurion was as unlikely as a hot January in the Yukon. Whoever was on that airplane simply didn't want to talk to anybody.

"Any idea who was flying?"

"It belongs to an outfitter at Wellsley Lake. It was the pilot and two other guys. They didn't file any type of flight plan. I'm not exactly sure where they were going. My DF steer indicated they were headed toward Whitehorse, if that helps. Are you based in Whitehorse?"

"Yes, sir."

"I think someone from Arctic Air phoned looking for you."

"I'm going to try and raise them right now. If I can't get them and they phone back, tell them to meet me at the Whitehorse terminal in thirty minutes."

"Sure thing." The operator hesitated with his mic button still keyed. "You might want to think about a different destination though, someplace other than Whitehorse. I just got a message over the telex. Here it is . . . the Whitehorse Airport has just been closed."

"Closed?" Banks paused. "Burwash, does it mention why?"

"Negative, sir. Just says it's closed."

Banks had an idea why. "Thanks, Burwash. Kilo India Delta out."

He spun the radio select knob back to HF. It was time to try and raise someone back at the hangar.

"4049 Whitehorse, 4049 Whitehorse, Kilo India Delta. Do you copy? Over."

Dale McMaster spoke excitedly into his ears. "Travis! This is 4049 Whitehorse. Go ahead. Are you all right? Over."

"I'm fine."

"Did you get our earlier message?"

"Roger."

"Dr. Baker phoned about that Jansen fellow. Said you'd want to know he's been evaluated several times for mental instability."

"Thanks, Dale. Has Officer Powell contacted you today? Over."

"He's standing right here."

"Could you put him on?"

Leon's gruff voice was solemn. "Travis, I did some snooping around after we spoke last night. I need to see you. I've got the Old Testament from Radcliff's den."

"I'm on my way in. But before I agree to land, I want you to assure me you've read what's inside that Old Testament. Over."

Leon ignored his request. "Where's Radcliff?"

Banks took a deep breath and looked across at Kayla who was monitoring their conversation through her headset. Travis didn't want the entire Northern Hemisphere hearing what had happened to the highest-ranking officer in the Whitehorse RCMP detachment.

"Leon . . . ah . . . Inspector Radcliff will not be returning to Whitehorse. Over."

There was silence. Leon Powell knew Banks well. He understood something had happened to his immediate superior. There was no reason to ask anymore questions over the airwaves.

He continued. "Leon? Are you there?"

"Go ahead. Over."

"You didn't answer my question. Did you open up the Bible in Radcliff's den? Did you find what was in the lockbox? The box contains pictures and letters that will go a long way toward explaining what I've been trying to tell you. I'm not even sure what the letter means, but the pictures are self-evident. Trust me on this one, Leon. I'll see you in twenty minutes. Over."

"I've seen it." Powell kept the mic button pushed as he hesitated to continue. "Travis, there's something else. Over."

"Go ahead," Banks said, prompting him to expound.

"When you flew for the airlines, didn't you fly the Boeing 737? Over."

"The Dash 300 series, that's affirmative."

"Pacific Western has one here, right now, sitting on the ramp." He hesitated before continuing, "And, well, until Radcliff returns, I'm officially in charge of the detachment."

The Beaver pilot stared straight out the window afraid to ask. "What are you getting at, Leon?"

"They want fuel."

Banks watched the southern tip of Lake Labarge approach in the distance. He really didn't want to pursue the conversation. He didn't like the direction it was headed.

"So? Give it to them. Over."

Powell's tone was ominous.

"They're being hijacked, Travis."

Karen Banks' apocalyptic description of what a man like Jansen might do reverberated in Travis' head.

Travis spoke softly. "Leon, when did this start?"

"The tower advised us about fifteen minutes ago. Over."

"Leon, don't let them leave. I think it's Mike Jansen."

Banks' mind churned. Could it be Jansen's son? If it wasn't, where were Junior and Simon? Had they both flown in the NORDO aircraft to Whitehorse or had Junior simply met up with his father in Burwash and left Simon behind in pursuit? If it was either one of the Jansen men, Banks had to assume they were both unstable and dangerous. If they were involved in the hijacking, Banks seriously doubted the people on board that airplane would survive if they got airborne.

"Leon, I suspect Jansen is planning to join the Almighty for dinner tonight. My sister says he won't go alone. You can't let that plane take off. Over."

Powell's voice was audibly shaken. "I'm not sure what in the hell I can do. There's no S.W.A.T. units here. No one knows a damn thing around here about a 737 except how to fuel it and load it with peanuts. They're demanding fuel as we speak."

"Tell the hijacker the fuel is on the way. Stall them. I might be able to help. And tell the tower to open the airport, long enough for me to land."

"What's your E.T.A..?"

"Less than thirty minutes." The conversation with Michelle Baker the night before at the Klondike Inn dinner hit Banks quickly. "One other thing, Leon." Travis' voice was tempered.

"Go ahead."

"Check the passenger manifest on that hijacked airliner. I think Dr. Michelle Baker is a passenger."

"I've seen the manifest, Travis. I'm sorry. She is on board."

"Understood. Kilo India Delta is clear." Travis pushed the throttle up to the metal stops.

Travis looked over at Kayla. His boss reached across the cockpit and squeezed his shoulder.

On final approach to runway 18, it was obvious there were problems at the Whitehorse Airport. Emergency lights flashed from atop a dozen RCMP cruisers strategically placed around the airport perimeter. The hijacked Boeing airliner was parked in front of the main terminal. There were no vehicles or service equipment within 200 yards of the 737. From a short final approach, Banks could see all the doors were closed. The APU's exhaust pipe in the tail was billowing heat waves into the cold, dense atmosphere. The aircraft appeared buttoned up and ready for taxi. Even the red beacon light flashed intermittently. From over a mile away, faces appeared in all the windows. If Jansen was on board, he appeared ready to join the choir of angels with a full load of innocent people.

Powell had arranged permission for the Beaver to land with the control tower. As Travis and Kayla touched down on the southbound runway, a police vehicle quickly drove in front of them and signaled for them to follow. Banks hoped like hell that Powell believed what he had read in the letter from Radcliff's den. He didn't want to taxi into a firing squad.

Once parked around the side of the terminal, they were escorted through the old World War II vintage structure by three Mounties.

The airport administrator's office was situated on the ground floor next to the ramp. Leon Powell stood behind the only desk in the office.

The wooden walls were lined with pictures of aircraft, ranging from Norseman to modern Boeing aircraft. Over Powell's shoulder, the only window was filled with the sight of the hijacked airliner sitting in the middle of the ramp.

Powell had Nick Radcliff's letter in his hand and looked up as Banks was ushered in. Leon's look indicated Travis was a free man.

"Thanks for calling off the dogs, Leon. I owe you one."

Powell was solemn. He handed Travis the letter.

"Do you mind explaining this?" His tone was confused, not accusatory.

Banks opened the letter. It was the one he'd found in Radcliff's Bible.

He will swallow up death in victory, and the Lord God will wipe away tears from all faces.

'A good name is better than precious ointment, and the day of death than the day of one's birth.' Did you see the paper? They uncovered a dirty little secret. It's time. Twenty years is a long time. It's time to tell the people. It's time to reach out for the Father and cleanse the soul. I will free them. Hypocrisy can be evil. 'There is death in the pot.' I AM SALVATION!

We have made a covenant with death,
and with Hell are we at agreement.
Prophet Isaiah
MJ
9/28/81

"I doubt even Sigmund Freud could explain *this*." Banks looked at Leon. "I sure can't. Other than to say Jansen is certifiable. I can answer all your questions once I find Simon Radcliff."

"That's not going to be easy," Leon snorted, "considering he's dead."

Travis leaned over the desk and picked up the pictures from the lockbox. "Dead? Haven't you looked at these?"

"It could be anyone."

"It's Simon, Leon, believe me. I know. I just left him two hours ago. My guess is he's here in Whitehorse. And if that hijacker is Mike Jansen, Simon is stalking this airport waiting to get his claws into him."

Leon Powell was at a loss. He pleaded with Banks as opposed to ordering him. "I don't have much time. What happened out there? Where's Inspector Radcliff?" His face reddened quickly. He didn't like not being in the loop. "Tell me what in the hell is going on, and do it quickly."

Banks asked Staff Sergeant Powell to clear the room. Other than Kayla Jackson, everyone left. It took several minutes to tell his racquetball foe everything he had discovered the past four days. Banks concluded by assuring Leon that he was certain the four trappers were responsible for Kelly Margaret Radcliff's death, and that Nick and Simon had staged Simon's death to aid them in killing the trappers. What Banks couldn't answer was why Nick Radcliff had been murdered by his own brother and why Nick was adamant they hadn't killed the other trappers. Only Simon could answer those questions.

Powell was stunned. As the acting boss of the Whitehorse RCMP he was being hit by one crisis after another, all urgent and all without any obvious solution. For a moment he remained silent, deep in thought. His decision made, he fixed his eyes on Travis.

"So you think Mike Jansen has hijacked this plane?"

"That's correct."

"You also said you could help. I'm waiting."

There were charts of a 737 strewn around the administrator's desk and Banks spun them around while he spoke.

"Two things. First, we need to stall the hijacker. You need to get close to the plane; therefore, you've just been promoted to aircraft fueler. Second, we have to set up communication with the pilots. While you're playing fueler, we need to get them off the airplane. Once they're gone, there's no chance of the airplane flying."

"How?"

"There are several intercom jacks on the 737. One at the nose for push-back crews, and another one used only by maintenance, in the main wheel well. The forward one is visible from the cockpit. You'll have to find and use the one in the wheel well. The problem is you'll never find it, not without my help."

"What are you suggesting, Banks?"

Banks continued to stare at Powell. The implication was obvious.

Instantly Powell began shaking his head. "No way! Absolutely not! Travis, there is no possibility you are getting anywhere near that airplane. There will be no civilians involved in this."

"Leon, we're running out of time. Don't look at me as a civilian. Call me a highly skilled technical advisor if you like." He paused. "I owe Dr. Baker enough to at least try and help."

Powell closed his eyes and rubbed his face with both hands. "The hijacker said only one fueler."

"Don't worry, I can sneak up the tailpipe. He'll never know I'm there. You need my help, Leon. It's the only way you'll get on that airplane and have a chance to save Michelle and those other passengers."

Leon Powell finished wiggling his large torso into the borrowed tight-fitting aircraft fueling uniform. He spun the chamber on his .38 caliber service revolver and saw no daylight in the six chambers. He continued to brush up on his five-minute fueler-training program.

"Remember, when I holler," he patted his walkie-talkie, "get your butt to the airplane quickly. I've got to appear as if I'm actually gassing them up."

Banks, the ex-airline pilot, reminded the RCMP officer: "Leon, it's jet fuel, not gas. Jet A. It's like kerosene. Don't say gas to the flight crew. You'll scare the shit out of them."

"Fine. Jet A." Leon continued, "According to what the pilots said on the aircraft's airborne communication computer, what the hell is it called . . . ?" he looked at Banks for the answer.

Travis obliged. "An ACARS."

"Right, ACARS . . . there's only one hijacker. We tried to confirm it. We couldn't." Leon flipped through the airline's passenger manifest. "And you think his son might also be on board? Or even Simon, for that matter?"

"It's a possibility, even though I can't believe Jansen would use his son as a mole."

"A mole?" Powell was getting anxious.

"It's a name used in airline security for hidden accomplices. One guy hijacks the airplane and the mole sits quietly, waiting to surprise any would-be heroes on board."

"Can you describe Jansen, his son, or even Simon, for that matter, give me something to look for?"

"I'm sorry, Leon. I only saw Junior from 300 yards through binoculars. The latest picture I have of Mike Jansen was taken before you RCMP guys switched from horses to cars. And I have no idea what Simon looks like. He never took off his ski mask."

"The pilots said the hijacker was quoting the Bible."

"That sounds like Jansen. You've seen his letters."

"He's kept the first-class curtain drawn since the ordeal began. That could be to our advantage." Powell spread open a colorful seating schematic of the passenger cabin pointing with his thick finger. "The passenger manifest showed only two first-class seats issued, with lots of room in the back. I'm sure they've been moved to coach by now or the curtain wouldn't be drawn. He'll want to be able to see everyone. I should get a clear shot once the curtain is pulled back. If the aisle is clear, it shouldn't be more than a hundred feet."

"Eighty at the most." Banks corrected him. "That's still one hell of a shot."

"For a pilot, maybe." Powell permitted himself a quick smile before continuing. "Don't be a hero. Our men on the perimeter have assured me he has a handgun. They're not sure, but it looks like a 9mm. They got a few quick glimpses of him through the windows before he made the passengers draw their shades. If you can get out there and set up communications with the pilots, I'll get them to evacuate. I'll use the evacuation ropes to get into the cockpit. If I get into trouble, the perimeter guys will move in, but that's messy. Undesirable. I'd prefer to do this without a big ruckus." Powell exhaled and tucked his revolver behind his bulletproof vest under his stretched uniform. "O.K., Banks, it's show time." He turned and started for the door. "Do me a favor, Rookie." He smiled and pointed to his walkie-talkie. "Keep in touch and don't do anything without asking first. If I get a civilian in trouble my pension won't buy me a free lunch." Powell lowered his hearing protection down over his ears and practically knocked down the door as he blitzed out onto the ramp.

Travis shook his head in amazement as Powell jumped into the fuel truck and sped off toward the Boeing aircraft parked on the airport ramp. What a hell of a lot of faith he'd put in Banks' rusty knowledge of Boeing aircraft.

"Mr. Banks, sir?" An RCMP officer came into the room. "We're ready to get you into position." His words were laced with mock respect. "That is, if you're ready, of course." Obviously he was less than thrilled that Travis had gone from wanted criminal to police advisor in less than twenty-four hours.

"Of course." The bush pilot tried to sound confident as he zipped up a borrowed fueling uniform. He looked over at Kayla, rocking back and forth on her heels against the wall. She looked scared.

Travis teased. "Are you sure you don't want to join me?"

Kayla took his hand but didn't smile. "I hope you know what you're doing, Travis."

The beautiful snow-covered Douglas mountain range loomed over the main terminal ramp and the air traffic control tower.

Banks slid in next to the ILS instrument approach shack, below the lip of the airport service road that stretched around the southeast corner of the Whitehorse Airport. He was flanked by two RCMP troopers. Lying on his belly, he looked across the ramp up the wide tailpipes of the two General Electric CFM-56 high bypass fan jet engines that powered the 737-300 aircraft.

He calculated that it would take about twenty seconds of hard running to cover the 150 yards to reach the belly of the Boeing aircraft. He kept turning the squelch and volume knobs on his radio, hoping Powell was trying to tell him it was all over and to go meet him in the Airport Chalet for a beer.

He could see Powell desperately trying to appear as if he had been refueling Boeing aircraft his entire life, without much success. The little refueling ladder toppled over several times while he ascended it, holding the large and heavy fuel hose over his head. The stream of profanity that poured from his gritted teeth made it all the way over to the ditch where Banks was hiding.

Finally, after several attempts, Powell held the fuel hose cam lock in place and successfully locked it onto the underwing fuel valve. To actually get fuel into the aircraft would be the real trick. A series of electrical valves had to be selected, both at the truck and the fueling panel. At least now it would look as though refueling was in progress.

Next, Powell ran under the belly into the main landing gear wheel well and started to look for the cockpit inter-phone jack. Banks had given him exact directions. From Banks' vantage point, Powell disappeared from the waist up.

After an interminable minute Powell managed to find the light switch and illuminate the wheel well. He stood amazed. The two-dimensional Boeing diagrams didn't do justice to the mechanical splendor that stared back at him. He scratched his cap in awe of the aeronautical Einstein who put this mess together. Metal spaghetti made up of hydraulic hoses and colorful electrical lines were twisting and turning in all directions before disappearing into the wheel well bulkheads. Above his left shoulder, two round modules with their respective pressure gauges looked back at him like large insect eyes. The Boeing diagram had indicated those were the small orbs that housed the engine's fire retardant. The system A and B hydraulic tanks were on the forward wall of the wheel well. The aircraft's flight control interconnect sat behind the metal tire screens, which protected the wires and hoses in the event the nitrogen-rich tires exploded. He could see the control cables coming from the cockpit. They were hydraulically boosted by the interconnect. He thought about simply cutting the cables, but that might piss off the pilots if they actually had to take off.

Leon Powell had gained a little experience with pilots when he represented Canada in a dual training exercise with the DEA and FBI at Quantico, Virginia. Most of the pilots he had met were self-centered, arrogant prima donnas that thought the world revolved around them.

Banks was the only pilot he'd ever met who seemed to break that mold.

Banks had tried to describe to Powell where the inter-phone jack was in the wheel well. Powell followed his memorized directions by bending down and sliding under the belly into the other cavity of wires and tubes that housed the left main landing gear. There wasn't much room. Slowly standing up, he peered around, trying to locate the quarter-inch hole of the intercom jack. Nothing. He was going to need Banks' help.

The voice filtered through the roar of the air-conditioning exhaust. It came from above. Leon tucked underneath the gear doors and cautiously wandered out from under the belly toward the front of the aircraft's huge left fan engine. It was monstrous. He'd never stood alongside the intake of a large turbofan jet engine. He figured he could have stood up in the intakes compressor section. The thirty-eight blades inside the cowling were as big as propellers. No wonder there were warnings painted in red all over the engine cowlings—the motor could have sucked the chrome off a car bumper.

"God waits for no one, my son!"

Powell looked up. Mike Jansen had cracked open the left front main cabin door and was pointing a 9mm Glock pistol at the police officer. Jansen might have been crazy, but he wasn't stupid. He didn't expose himself enough for one of the perimeter constables to get a clear shot.

The trapper was truly a *mad* trapper. His gray greasy hair was tousled around his pockmarked face. His clothes were filthy. His bulging eyes were bloodshot and almost vibrating with excitement. Acting afraid, at this particular moment, wasn't going to be hard for Leon, but pretending to be a fueler was difficult.

"Jesus Christ!" Powell instinctively raised his hands into the air, partially covering his face. "Take it easy. I'm doing the best I can. I'll have you gassed up in ten minutes."

The trapper peered down at Powell and barked. "*And He gathered them together into a place called, in the Hebrew tongue, Armageddon!*"

"I beg your pardon?" Powell looked up at the man totally bewildered.

"Five! You have five minutes, my son, not ten." Jansen smiled, dragging the head of one of the flight attendants into view. "The first lamb will be sacrificed in less than five minutes."

"All right, take it easy! You'll get your fuel." Powell didn't know how else to respond.

"*The last enemy that shall be destroyed is death!*" Jansen's smile turned to anger as he swung the door shut with a raging determination.

"Jesus." Powell pondered under his breath, staring at the closed door. He had just seen, firsthand, how certifiable Mike Jansen was. There was no possibility that the airplane could be allowed to leave Whitehorse.

Powell looked at his watch. Five minutes. Knowing Jansen was in the front of the aircraft, he quickly slid back under the belly into the security of the wheel well and screamed into his walkie-talkie over the roar of the air-conditioning exhaust ducts.

"Travis, this is Leon. Go. Now. Run. Go! Go! Go!"

Banks had no idea what was happening at the airplane. All he could see was Leon's legs from the waist down. He hadn't seen what had just transpired on the other side of the aircraft. Instinct took over. He heard "go," and that's precisely what he did. Travis dropped the walkie-talkie, jumped up onto the ramp, and began running across the hard icy concrete toward Powell and the stationary airplane.

A hundred and fifty yards never looked so far. The midday winter sun was drifting lazily across the southwestern horizon, partially blinding his view of the Boeing. The noisy breeze that had been at his back now equaled his running speed, and except for his rapid footsteps and the rhythm of his heaving breath, there was silence. Banks could see Powell emerging from the wheel well as he approached the aircraft. At first, Leon stood waiting. A moment later, the heavyset RCMP officer started frantically waving his hands. Banks couldn't tell if Powell wanted him to stop, retreat, or continue. Travis began to slow down and squinted through the sweat forming in his eyes to decipher Leon's approaching hand signals. Slowing down only prompted Powell to jump and wave with increased zeal.

With twenty yards to go, he could finally see the impending problem. The starboard aft entry door on the aircraft was slowly being opened. Jansen was checking to see if the authorities were doing exactly what they were doing, approaching the aircraft from the rear.

Banks knew he had passed the point of no return. He could never make it back to the safety of the ditch behind him. He couldn't stop. It would be too easy to spot someone standing in the middle of a concrete football field. Travis had to make it to the airplane before he was spotted. His lungs burned and his legs were beginning to wobble and ache. The big heavy Boeing door slowly popped opened. The exhausted pilot could see the muzzle of Jansen's 9mm peek around the corner of the half-opened door.

With ten yards to go, Banks lunged forward, grasping air with cupped hands. Stumbling forward, he twisted his body sideways with the zeal of an agile baseball player stealing second base. The contortion forced his flying body to hit the taxiway, head first, just to the left of the opening aircraft door. The collision with the tarmac tore a strip of flesh from his left wrist. His shoulder popped and burned as if he had dislocated it. Banks flipped over, pulling out his .44 in the same motion.

Straight ahead, under the wing and out of sight of the door, he saw Leon, weapon drawn, waiting to fire if the hijacker should look down under the belly in Banks' direction. Travis quickly pushed his body under the airplane, using the rubber heels of his winter boots. He lay in the shadows of the Boeing's greasy underbelly, breathing rapidly. He tried to keep the grip on his Redhawk revolver firm and the gun's sights pointed up and slightly out toward the lip of the door. The roar of the APU was deafening but it had probably saved the bush pilot's life. Jansen hadn't heard him running or hitting the tarmac.

The outflow valve that controls aircraft pressure was several feet behind the prone Banks. Next to the valve and directly above his position was the APU's drain mast. It was currently doing its job, expelling hydraulic fluid and excess jet fuel. The breeze died down long enough for a stream of fluids to hit him square in the eyes and on his bleeding wrist. Travis gritted his teeth and swallowed the burning pain. He could see the toe of Jansen's boot extending over the door's bottom lip. Neither he nor Powell could get a clear shot. If Jansen bent down and looked under the belly, the gig was up.

Moments later, the large plug door swung shut. Banks pushed himself up using his good shoulder, and Powell motioned for his friend to join him under the main wing spar. By the time Travis slid into the right wheel well, Powell was back looking for the intercom jack.

"I didn't approve of you carrying a weapon!" Leon was not happy.

"I forgot I had it," Banks lied.

Leon shouted over the noise. "I just spoke to that looney-toon a moment ago. He's crazier than a rabid dog. He said Armageddon's here if he's not fueled within five minutes."

"Who cares ? You can't let him leave anyway."

Powell looked at the flashing police lights surrounding the airport property. "We'll have to stall him longer."

Banks looked his racquetball partner square in the eyes.

"Leon, if my sister is right, you don't have five minutes. He's not up there making a political statement. He's insane."

"I know."

"You have to decide right now what you want to do."

"Shit. Five minutes. I don't even have time to call in the perimeter guys. I've got to go in now." Leon spun around with unparalleled determination.

"Where in hell is this intercom jack?" He placed his hand on the edge of the wheel well doors, imploring Banks' help. "I looked right where you told me."

Travis tapped his arm. "Did you try under your hand?"

Powell raised his hand and looked under the gear door's edge. He saw the small hole tucked under a metal overhang. He gave Banks a dirty look and quickly plugged the David Clarke headset into the quarter-inch jack. He pressed the dark green headset into his ears, trying to listened over the roar of the air-conditioning pack exhaust, which howled several feet away. He tried to ascertain if the flight deck was broadcasting blind.

Silence.

Powell spoke softly and professionally into the boom mic, assuming the flight deck speakers might be turned on and being monitored by Jansen.

"Ground to cockpit . . . ground to cockpit. Fueler here." There was a justified sense of urgency in his voice. "I've got a question about the auxiliary gauge," he lied. Several seconds passed before Powell tried again. "Hey, look, guys, I know you ain't having a good day, but believe me, I didn't pick this duty either. I need to know if the auxiliary system is the PATS system."

Banks shook his head. It was a dumb question. The crew would know instantly he was not a fueler.

"Captain Harris here. Who in the hell am I talking to?" came the curt and brisk reply.

"Sir, this is the fueler. Are you guys on headsets or cockpit speakers?"

A slightly panic-stricken reply blurted from one of the pilots.

"Look, whoever you are, if you're wondering where the freak is that's hijacking us, he's in . . . hang on . . . I think he's looking out the overwing exits."

Powell jumped in. "Get off! Can you use the escape ropes and get out the cockpit windows right now?"

"That's a rather interesting request coming from a fueler." The more mature voice of the captain filled Leon's headset.

Leon Powell had a short fuse.

"I'm no more a fueler than I am the reincarnation of Jesus Christ. But unlike the Almighty, I'm here, now, to save your sorry ass, providing you do exactly what I say. Understood?"

More silence.

"Now are you in a position to get off the airplane unnoticed?"

"No," came the whispered and humbled reply, "the son of a bitch looks up here every few seconds, waves a pistol in our face and tells us, 'Salvation's at hand.'"

Powell spoke freely. He stood in the wheel well trying to speak over the whine of the APU. With every word his anxiety level crept up. When he got excited that Montana drawl crept back into his speech.

"Look, fellas, I ain't here to gas you up and change your friggin' oil. Do what I say and there is a possibility salvation won't be at hand too quick." Powell took a calming breath. "Try and obstruct his view of the flight deck! Use the galley cart, cockpit door, anything that blocks his view. As soon as you are out of his line of sight, bail out."

The distinctive and aggravating voice of the captain piped up. "I'm not so sure that this course of action . . ."

"Just listen and trust me," Powell barked. "I'll keep acting like I'm fueling for as long as possible. You need to get out. You don't have much time."

"Shit," the intercom jumped, "he's on his way up here... wait...no... he's running to the back!"

Leon hollered into his boom mic, drowning out the air-conditioning packs, "Bail out! Now. Move it! Move it!"

Almost instantly, the cockpit side windows slid open. The two lumpy nylon emergency ropes, stored in the overhead above each pilot's seat, flew outward, cascading around the silvery nose of the Boeing aircraft. Powell threw down the headset and stared at Banks' bloody wrist and shoulder.

"You gonna be all right?"

"Fine." Travis nodded.

"Damn," Powell said to himself as he spun around in a small circle, running his powerful hand through his thinning hair. This decision was agonizing.

He stopped suddenly and pointed at Banks' .44. "Can you still fire that cannon?"

"If necessary."

"O.K." He turned away. "As soon as those pilots hit the ground get them out of here the same way you came. Once they're clear, stay under the ray dome toward the nose." Powell started walking backward to the hanging pilots. "Don't get on board. Understand? But if you hear gunshots and Jansen tries to leave without me climbing up his ass, you have my blessing to shoot the bastard."

"Leon, we don't know what happened to Junior or Simon."

Powell didn't wait for a response. He ran toward the pilots twisting in the breeze as they came down the ropes.

The first officer was young and slimmer than his counterpart in the left seat. The copilot hit the ground first. This was to Powell's advantage. He had been running along the right side of the aircraft and was able to leap at the copilot's escape rope without missing a step. The unsuspecting first officer never saw the Powell express train. With the agility and strength of a circus gorilla, Powell scaled the fifteen-foot rope from the ramp to the cockpit window within seconds. He grasped the emergency window release handle a foot below the window and quickly pulled himself up and poked his head into the cockpit. He placed his boot on the right Pitot tube and slowly slid his head through the cockpit window. Nobody home.

Banks quickly led the panting, pear-shaped captain and his first officer to the rear of the Boeing 737.

The bush pilot raised his voice to be heard over the APU's deafening exhaust. "You see that airport security truck?" Banks pointed toward the ditch. "Go!" He gave the copilot a slight push and had him off and running instantly. The captain stood firm.

"Is there a problem?" Banks inquired.

The four-striper recaptured his breath. "I want to stay with my ship."

By the slight hesitation in the captain's voice, Travis could tell the airline pilot thought he had some authority; that Banks was a police officer. He also knew Leon didn't want the four-striper around in the event the situation headed south. This pompous captain reminded Banks of a few cantankerous curmudgeons he had jerked gear for when he was a new hire with the airlines. Travis had always wanted to knock one of these overbearing egomaniacs down a notch.

He produced his .44 Redhawk and stuck the barrel in the captain's face. He tried to sound like a veteran cop.

"Captain, this isn't a goddamn Hollywood movie. Get your ass off this ramp now or *I'll* shoot you!"

The terrified look in the old airline pilot's eyes warmed the cockles of Banks' heart. There was only a slight hesitation as the veteran pilot digested Travis' sober disposition. He had verbally kicked the fellow's bowling pin-shape form into high gear and watched as he waddled off with the fluidity of a wounded pig.

Banks hugged the shiny aluminum of the aircraft's fuselage with his back and turned to the nose of the aircraft. The sight that greeted Banks turned his stomach.

He watched Leon Powell in horror. The muscular police officer was trying to get his large frame through the copilot's window. Powell's torso squirmed and twisted before his boots gave way and he slipped off the angle of attack vane mounted under the first officer's window. He lost his balance and grasped wildly at the smooth tractionless aluminum hull outside the copilot's window. Banks started to lunge forward to help but it was futile. The large RCMP officer caught his uniform on the air-speed Pitot tube, flipped through the air, and came crashing down off the side of the airplane, hitting the frozen ramp with a resounding thud. Powell's leg, halfway between his knee and ankle, snapped. It sounded like a gunshot cracking loudly in the cold arctic air. The constable gritted his teeth in agony but kept silent. He would not give away his predicament to the hijacker. Banks ran to the fallen officer. Powell's right leg was broken, probably in several places. He laid his head back in excruciating pain, not wanting to look at the jagged right tibia bone protruding from the cloth of his fueling uniform.

The perimeter officers had seen the fall. The walkie-talkie in Powell's uniform came to life. "Powell! Officer Powell? Are you all right?"

Banks listened to the scratchy voice. An RCMP officer with binoculars in the control tower caught a brief glimpse of the gunman in the cockpit. Jansen had a hostage in a headlock. A woman wearing a maroon scarf. Travis' mind filled with the Christmas memory he had of giving Michelle a maroon scarf. Banks looked back and forth between the stricken police officer and the cockpit rope swinging in the light breeze. Banks was desperate—it appeared Mike Jansen had taken Dr. Michelle Baker as his hostage.

Banks looked at Powell.

Leon knew what Banks was thinking and pleaded with his pilot friend through clenched teeth. "Don't, Travis! I'll get another officer. We can storm the aircraft from the tail section. Approach it like you did."

"We don't have the time, Leon." Banks hardly convinced himself with what he was about to do.

"Yes, we do!" Powell writhed in pain and fell back.

Banks instinctively covered his friend with his parka and crouched closer to the tarmac. Two gunshots rang out from inside the airplane. He was instantly filled with resolve.

"We *do not* have the time! The son of a bitch will kill everybody before your troopers get on board." Banks checked the chamber of his .44. "Just give me a couple of minutes, Leon."

"Travis . . . Don't . . ." Powell watched as Banks tugged on the cockpit escape twice before quickly scaling the side of the plane toward the first officer's window. The constable reached into his pocket and gritted his teeth, pulling the walkie-talkie from his overalls. He cursed at himself and put the microphone to his lips.

"This is Sergeant Powell. I'm fine. Do not approach the aircraft. I repeat, stay away from the aircraft. I'll call you back in a few minutes."

Banks finally got both feet through the small side window of the cockpit. Crouching down on the copilot's seat, he managed to hide his large frame behind the starboard circuit breaker panel. He squinted, straining to hear any voices or sounds emanating from the rear of the cabin. The muffled shouts of an argument wafted into the cockpit. Banks could see that the pilots had left in a hurry—a spilled cup of coffee dripped into the radio panel and the fire extinguishing handles that made up the majority of the center console.

The first officer's control yoke rammed into Banks' hip as a gust of wind hit the 737's tail. The electrical hydraulic pumps were both off. He grimaced in pain and inched closer to the circuit breaker panel and away from the gyrating control yoke. He glanced around the cockpit, looking for the source of an acrid electrical burning smell that polluted his senses. He found the problem—little white wispy waves of electrical smoke undulated upward between the throttles. The center console had drunk too much coffee. There was an electrical short. The master caution light began to flash in concert with outer lights around the cockpit. It wouldn't be long before the smell found the hijacker's nostrils.

Banks had to get power away from the radios. There was no on-off switch. The pilot looked at the circuit breaker panel. There were hundreds of breakers. He couldn't find the one that said, "spilled coffee." He started pulling all the breakers near the group "avionics." He made a mistake and pulled one breaker that should have been left untouched. Instantly, the APU shut down and killed the air-conditioning packs as well as all AC electrical power. An eerie silence fell over the aircraft.

Jansen must have suspected something was up. Banks jerked up the right sleeve of his tight uniform to give his shooting arm more mobility. He raised his Redhawk to shoulder height and slowly peeked past the cockpit door into the aisle of the cabin.

The door was half ajar, but the first-class curtain was fully open, allowing Jansen a direct view onto the flight deck. That's not what the pilots had typed into their on-board communication computer. Mike Jansen was busy running to the rear of the aircraft, screaming for everybody to stay down.

Banks leaped off the seat leaning toward the door. The copilot's oxygen mask got hung up on one of the endless number of zippers on his fueling uniform and fell to the floor with a resounding clang. He didn't stop. There was no way he could ambush Jansen in the tiny cockpit. He needed more room. He darted into the galley and caught his breath around the corner, pushing up against the coffee-makers. He was out of sight from the aisle. He faced the front of the galley with the open cockpit door to his left.

His gut told him he was on borrowed time. He leveled his .44 by extending his right arm and firmly gripping his right wrist. He lowered his head until his right eye peered down the blue steel sight of his revolver. If he pulled the trigger now, he would blow a hole in a can of Bloody Mary mix sitting on the juice shelf across the galley.

While in the firing position, he crouched and spun, pivoting on the ball of his left foot. There was no need to yell "freeze." The cabin momentarily filled with screams. Mike Jansen had been expecting someone.

The trapper chuckled. "*Well done, thou good and faithful servant, enter thou into the joy of the Lord.*" He had a headlock on Michelle Baker.

"Oh, please, Travis, please help me." Michelle was petrified.

"It's O.K., Doc." Banks kept a roving eye on the entire cabin as he shouted for everyone to stay down.

Jansen and Dr. Baker jostled in the aisle, slowly backing up. Mike

Jansen's gun was eerily relaxed in his right hand. He kept it pointed at Michelle's right temple.

Travis inched down the single-aisle cabin, keeping up with Jansen. He didn't want to get too far away, yet he also wanted to keep the other passengers in his field of view. Unfortunately, an accurate shot involving a hostage could only be assured from feet, not yards.

The bush pilot spoke softly but deliberately. "Look, nobody's been hurt. Put the gun down and let her go."

Unmoved, Jansen continued spouting scripture, "*This is an evil generation: they seek a sign!*" He raised his gun quickly. "Well, guess what? I'll give you a fucking sign. Drop the gun!"

"Mr. Jansen, I can't do that." He focused his attention on the metal sights on the barrel of his gun. He aimed at the bridge of the trapper's nose and then moved one inch to the left, centering on the right iris of the hijacker. This took the line of fire one more inch away from Michelle Baker. He reminded himself his gun was loaded with illegal overloaded ammunition; just grazing Jansen would blow his head off. Banks hooked his leg around the edge of a seat and pulled himself rigid to fire.

"You'll have to!" Jansen shouted angrily. "*The wages of sin is death, but the gift of God is eternal life.*" The religious fanatic changed quickly from scripture to schizophrenia. "Now, where the fuck is my gas?"

No training could have prepared a police officer, let alone a bush pilot, for dealing with a fruitcake of this magnitude. Banks needed only one clear shot.

"We're not going anywhere, Mike." Travis' voice became calm. He knew what he had to do. Powell was outside on the tarmac, probably going into shock, and Whitehorse's version of a S.W.A.T. team would soon storm the aircraft creating chaos and too many dead bodies. Banks looked into the terrified doctor's eyes. She was beginning to hyperventilate with short sharp breaths.

Jansen screamed. "I want my fucking gas and I want it now or I'll kill the bitch!"

Travis spoke softly. "Do what you have to do, but I'm afraid the pilots couldn't take all the excitement and they left. There's nobody to fly the plane." Michelle Baker looked at Banks in terror.

The muffled whimpers of crying passengers continued to waft through the cabin.

Murphy's Law: If something can go wrong, it will. Both Inertial Reference Systems, the aircraft's navigational sense of balance, had been deprived of APU-generated AC electrical power for too long. The IRSs had reverted to their backup DC current and announced the switch-over by activating their intense piercing warning horn. The passengers broke out in hysterics. Michelle Baker fainted. Her legs buckled and she inadvertently slipped out of the crazed man's headlock and fell to the floor. The hijacker turned and looked down to find her lying at his feet.

Banks never lost his focus. His gun was still aimed at the same imaginary spot in space. Instead of the gunman's right iris, his .44 metal sight found itself pointed at Jansen's left temple.

Banks had never killed anyone. He tried again. "For the last time, put the gun down!"

Jansen had lost his trump card. He giggled and smiled at both Banks and his fainted hostage.

"*Father, forgive them, for they know not what they do.*"

Jansen quickly aimed the dark-handled Glock 9mm at the head of Michelle Baker and began to move his trigger finger.

Time had just expired for Mike Jansen. He had lost and decided to cash in all his chips. Unlike the trapper, Banks had no choice. With the demeanor of a brain surgeon, he squeezed the trigger of his handheld cannon. The hollow unpressurized cabin echoed for an instant. Jansen's head rocked back and forth to the natural stops of his chest and upper back. His body heaved backward, collapsing rag-doll fashion in a lifeless heap. Mike Jansen never got his wish. He wouldn't be leaving Whitehorse. He was going to stay. In a box. God only knew if he found salvation.

Three rows of aircraft seats would have to be cleaned or replaced. The head is the body's most blood-rich cavity.

Banks maintained his firing stance while the entire cabin erupted in screams. One cry was particularly painful.

The pilot crept forward, ordering everyone to stay down. He never took his sights off the man lying in the aisle. He carefully stepped over

Michelle, who was beginning to regain consciousness. Banks slowly picked up the semiautomatic handgun that lay next to the twitching boots of the victim. The body ended up resting on its left side with the left arm contorted backward underneath the torso, the right arm thrown back with both legs half retracted toward the fetal position.

Banks was still on one knee searching for a pulse when someone approached him from behind.

Several passengers had the nerve to finally look up and see the accomplice approaching the bush pilot. Their only pathetic warning to Banks was more weak cries and sobs.

Banks peered into the terrified eyes of Michelle Baker. She tried to speak. Her lips parted but there was no sound. The dark-tinted lenses of her sunglasses reflected the one contingency Travis had warned Leon about, a mole. Banks looked into the reflection and saw the other half of the surviving Jansen clan.

Mike Junior was an angry man in his thirties. A tear ran from the dark circles that housed his raging blue eyes. His body and clothes reeked of perspiration, a by-product of his ride from Duke Lake. How the airline gate agents didn't remember this man boarding would remain a mystery. Since the inception of $50 air fares there was no accounting for taste.

The midnight special Mike Junior held in his left hand was unwavering.

There was no doubt in Banks' mind. If he didn't react quickly he was going to die.

"Don't move, you fucking bastard!"

Banks stared straight ahead at Doc Baker.

"You killed my father!" Mike Junior spat out the words.

Apparently, quoting religion was not a priority for the younger Jansen.

"You bastard!" He hissed one more time as he raised the gun to Banks' head.

Banks moved nothing but his wrist. He kept his weapon hidden in front of him over the elder Jansen's body. He slowly pointed the barrel under his left armpit trying to calculate his aim based on the reflected image in Michelle Baker's glasses.

Mike Jansen, Junior, missed his momentary window of opportunity.

Banks rejoiced at the familiar noise. He had beaten the junior Jansen to the punch. In such a short distance, the sound of a gunshot arrives no later than the carnage it inflicts, especially the thundering blast of an overloaded .44 Ruger Redhawk. The shot tore a burning path of cloth under Travis' armpit but the large-caliber bullet struck its target as aimed. The hole that a magnum-caliber hollow point bullet makes is much smaller going in than going out.

The trapper's sole surviving heir, Mike Junior, was rocked violently. His rib cage exploded forward, carrying him backward several rows of seats.

The screams from the cabin stopped as quickly as they had erupted. Silence returned with only muffled sobbing coming from the terrified passengers, huddled between their seats.

Banks dropped his smoking cannon onto the floor and helped the trembling doctor to her feet.

The passengers were escorted off the airplane one by one, searched, questioned, and released after identifying their luggage; the RCMP wanted to ensure there wasn't a third Jansen who had decided discretion was the better part of valor. There was no sign of Simon Radcliff.

Within an hour, the ramp was clear. The curious crowd of airport employees who had gotten wind of the hijacking and gathered along the airport's perimeter fence was gone.

As the waning orange sun slid halfway below the horizon, Dr. Michelle Baker had recovered enough to take over her official duties as coroner. It didn't take her long to officially pronounce the two Jansen men dead. Their bodies were loaded into black plastic bags and then unceremoniously wheeled into the coroner's van.

She came over to Banks and greeted him with a business-like kiss on the cheek followed by a very warm, non-businesslike hug. But it was different from any other contact they had had in the past. She held him tightly for a moment, then suddenly let go as if a bond had snapped.

She forced herself away and became a doctor again. It was obvious she was glad Banks was safe and grateful for his role in saving her life.

"*Do whatever you have to do?*" She mimicked Banks from earlier on when Jansen threatened to kill her.

Banks slowly shook his head. "Michelle, I care for you a great deal. I just said what I had to say in order to get a clear shot."

Banks tried to continue but Dr. Baker put her fingers to his lips, silencing him.

"I saw the look in your eyes, Travis. Both last night with Kayla and with me on that airplane. It's all right. I saved your life once, now you've saved mine. We're even." She smiled warmly, briskly wiped her eyes, handed him a piece of paper, and turned away toward the coroner's van.

Banks wanted to say something. Something he thought she wanted to hear. The problem was his true feelings would, in fact, hurt her. Michelle was a wonderful woman, but he didn't love her. She knew it. Maybe she knew more about him than he knew about himself.

He watched the wheels of the coroner's diesel-powered van spin on the icy tarmac and pull away. It climbed up the airport service road, passed the terminal, and disappeared into the traffic on the Alaska Highway.

Banks looked at the paper in his hand, and used the neon lights of the old hangar to read the official document. It was the information about Mike Jansen that he'd requested from Doc Baker the night before at the Chamber of Commerce Dinner. Dale had read some of the facts to him over the radio in the Beaver. The rest of the information was just as enlightening.

Mike Jansen had an interesting medical history.

At first, his scrapes with the law involved several charges of gross indecency. The report indicated those acts are now referred to as sexual interference. He had only been cited once for sexual interference. Then he found religion. Ten years ago, he began disrupting local churches. He had become a frequent visitor to several government-run mental hospitals.

According to the document, Jansen suffered delusion due to "religiosity." Karen Banks was right. The trapper had indeed become a mad trapper. He had become a sociopath because of his involvement in the death of Kelly Margaret Radcliff, some type of "guilt induced paranoid schizophrenia." He attempted to exorcise his demons by doing God's work and purging society of evil. What better place to start than with your old friends.

Banks scrunched the report into a ball and threw it as hard as he could toward the icy runway. It made his hands feel dirty. The little ball of paper tumbled and rolled until it disappeared into the snowy night.

Powell was the last officer on the scene. He sat up in a gurney waiting to be loaded into one of the hospital's emergency medical units. He took a deep drag off a menthol cigarette.

Banks reached him with a puzzled look on his face.

"You quit smoking years ago."

"I know. I'll quit again in a minute." Leon paused. "I asked you not to go on the plane." He looked at Banks and exhaled the remaining smoke in his lungs. "Anyway, thanks for not listening, Travis. Your bird-brain decision probably saved a plane-load of lives."

"You're welcome, Sergeant."

Banks surveyed the mountainous beauty surrounding the Whitehorse Valley and took a deep, cleansing breath. He thought about what he had done. Having killed someone, albeit justified, would take some getting used to.

Powell looked up. " So what do you suggest I do about the murder of Nick Radcliff? If I put out an all-points bulletin on Simon Radcliff, who, I might add, is a *dead* man, I'll be emptying parking meters in Moose Jaw, Saskatchewan."

Travis leaned against the car. "Leon, it was strange. He was so calculating and deliberate, you would have thought Simon Radcliff had the law on his side. Yet, on two separate occasions at Jansen's cabin, I'm sure Simon stopped Nick from killing me. Does that sound like a murderer? Hell, he gave me my gun back and also the keys to the handcuffs on our wrists. If he was so evil, why would he care if we died?" Banks threw his arms in the air. "Leon, I have no idea what you should do. Other than the fact he shot his brother at point-blank range this morning, I'd say Simon Radcliff appeared as lucid and sane as anyone else I've been around lately. If that makes any sense." The memory of Nick Radcliff's death came flooding back. He shook his head and watched as the paramedics loaded his racquetball partner into the ambulance.

Leon was only half serious. "Travis, if you see Simon, you let me know, you hear?"

Banks patted Leon good-bye on his healthy leg.

"I have a feeling, with Jansen in the morgue, we've seen the last of Simon Radcliff. By the way, Leon, it's a good thing you're not a horse."

The new head of the Whitehorse RCMP laid his head on the gurney's pillow and barked, "Why's that?" as the paramedics closed the back doors of the ambulance.

"With that leg we'd have to shoot you!" Banks knew Leon was inside the van smiling. The van's red taillights began to move away.

Banks headed toward the terminal a free man.

Dale McMaster met him halfway across the ramp with a bear hug. The loader had the biggest hand-rolled cigarette Banks had ever seen in one hand and a frothing bottle of beer in the other. He was humming his favorite tune from *The Wizard of Oz*, improvising "*Dingdong, the trapper's dead, the big bad trapper's dead.*" McMaster was celebrating his own survival of a night in the slammer, and Travis surviving his first hijacking.

"Someone wants to see you," he winked. "After what we went through, tell her we deserve a raise." He pointed at the base of the control tower. "Over there, by the security fence." Dale wandered off.

Banks walked past the rear of the hangar. The front of the old hangar was the terminal, the back of the building was empty. The offices were used for storing boxes of airline stationery and supplies. The last office inside the hangar had a small window that looked out over the ramp. Through the dirty windowpane, he could see the unmistakable image of a ski mask. He looked back and forth over his shoulders. Dale had disappeared and Leon was driving away in the ambulance, going in the opposite direction. Night had overtaken the ramp and Travis was alone.

He peered into the hangar and focused on the open office door. He cautiously exited the snow-covered tarmac and approached the dark room. Shafts of light from the airport's fluorescent fixtures spilled into the dusky office. Several wooden beams stretched across the low ceiling, making the room seem even smaller. The room was empty except for Simon Radcliff leaning against the back wall, looking out the window onto the ramp. The tall ex-police constable stood at the doorway watching Banks closely. The pilot didn't feel threatened or in danger. If Simon had wanted to harm Travis, he could have done so earlier.

The man in the shadows reached over his head and pulled off his ski mask, revealing facial features that were strikingly similar to his brother.

Simon looked down at his hands holding the mask. "So, I hope Mike Jansen was in one of those body bags."

"He was," Banks replied.

"Good." Simon Radcliff sighed and looked back out the window.

"Why?" Banks couldn't wait to ask.

"Why what?" Radcliff continued to look into the approaching night.

"Why did you kill your brother?"

Simon chuckled, turned, and looked at Banks. "I'm not sure if you deserve an explanation; but I'll bet you think you do."

A little animosity crept into Banks' voice. "Well, first you beat the crap out of me. Then you hit me over the head with a two-by-four. You broke into my house. You shot at me. You framed me for murder. And I watched you execute your brother." Banks nodded his head sarcastically. "Yeah, I think I've earned it."

"Possibly," Radcliff murmured.

Without leaving his spot by the window, Simon stuck his hand out, offering Banks a piece of paper. "Go ahead, read it."

Travis took the paper and tilted it in the direction of a stray beam of light. It was from the Recorder's Office in Yellowknife. It was a fax of a twenty-year-old mining deed for Tetcho Lake. The names of the deed's owners were scrawled across the bottom: Ed and Brock Bellichek, William Watt, Mike Jansen, and Nicholas Radcliff.

Simon crossed his arms and began talking. "I hadn't spoken to my brother in twenty years. Not since Sergeant Nick Radcliff headed the Yellowknife investigation into the disappearance of my daughter, Kelly Margaret. I was the girl's father and an RCMP officer. For obvious reasons, police department policy wouldn't allow me to participate in the investigation. I trusted my brother. Who else would you rather have running the investigation than your own brother?

"Well, Nick dropped the investigation in less than two weeks, before it even got started. Claimed he had to. Pressure from above because he had no case, no evidence. I tried to help but he claimed he would lose his job if I stuck my nose into it. I was accused of being too emotionally involved every time I protested. Although I trusted him, his dropping the case so quickly created a rift between us. We were never close after that. I even quit the force when Kelly's mother passed away. At that point, I had lost my sister, my daughter, and my wife."

The painful memory of the losses began to surface and fill the small airport office. Banks could see him in the shadows wiping his fingers across his eyes.

"Anyway, last fall, out of the blue, Nick calls me up and says they found Kelly's body. He also claimed to know who killed her." Anger slowly crept into Simon's voice. "I vowed I would get the person or persons involved," he hesitated, "provided I had irrefutable proof. Well, Nick had the proof. Coroner's reports, autopsies, detailed movements of the four men the past two decades. He knew everything about these guys." Simon dropped his head and smiled. "I mean, everything. There was no doubt. He had the right men. It was just that there was one name he left out. I was obsessed with killing those bastards. Nick planned everything. He even planned my phony death. Hell, I didn't care. My entire family was gone. All I cared about was exacting revenge. Nick and I knew they couldn't accuse a dead man. So, I died on a hunting trip. My brother assured me, as the RCMP chief in Whitehorse, he would destroy any link between me and the trappers' deaths. When it was over, I'd disappear and live a peaceful life, content in the knowledge I'd sent those four bastards to Hell. I just went along with him. That was, until last week, when I found Ed Bellichek at Primrose Lake."

Simon waited for the noise of a small plane to pass before continuing.

"*I* was supposed to be the one to kill Ed Bellichek. When I arrived at the lake, he was already murdered and planted in the ice. Now, that struck me as one hell of a coincidence. How often do two bank robbers show up at the same time at the same bank? Who killed Bellichek? I starting investigating his background myself, something, I had assumed, my brother had done properly twenty years earlier. Within a day, I came up with the information in your hand. Things began to fall in place quickly after that.

"I didn't want to believe what I was finding at first, but then it happened again. Brock Bellichek was skinned alive at Lake Labarge before I could have the satisfaction of nailing him myself. Nick couldn't, or wouldn't, explain it and began acting strange. Suddenly, he wanted Jansen killed immediately. No explanation. He didn't care about the risk of getting caught. I asked myself, why would he do that? Why would he behave like that? People only behave that way when they're being threatened.

"I quickly went out to Jansen's cabin. He wasn't there. By the time I got back to Whitehorse later in the day, William Watt was nailed to a crucifix in a downtown church. Nick was beside himself. He couldn't kill Jansen fast enough. His behavior had become terribly erratic. I knew something was wrong. I knew he wasn't being straight with me. The problem was we couldn't *find* Jansen. We finally agreed we'd have to go to his cabin and wait for him. And all this time, *you* kept popping up everywhere.

"Framing you was Nick's idea. He wanted to keep you guys out of the way and, at the same time, create a viable suspect if things got out of hand. You should have stayed out of the way. You don't take hints easily, do you?"

Simon couldn't get Banks to smile.

He continued. "And then a lifetime of questions were answered in that letter I found in my brother's den. The one you forgot to put away."

Banks interrupted. "You knew we were in the house?"

"Either you were there or had been there. I figured out you were there right before I left. My brother never closed the pantry door. He liked looking at all the cans neatly stacked in formation."

Travis rubbed his numb face. He thought he and Dale had been so clever.

Simon continued. "After I read the letter, I didn't care whether you were there or not."

The bush pilot jumped as he remembered his reaction to the letter. "What was so incriminating about the letter? You were awfully upset." Banks pulled the letter from his pocket. He had never given it back to Leon Powell.

"Did you read it?" Simon snapped sarcastically, crossing the room and jerking the letter out of Banks' hand.

"Yes." He tried to recollect its contents.

Radcliff looked at the paper in his hand. "Remember, this letter was mailed to my brother. It wasn't at any crime scene. '*A good name is better than a precious ointment. Hypocrisy can be evil.*' If you knew my brother at all, you knew that his reputation meant everything to him. He was Inspector Nick Radcliff of the RCMP. '*Did you see the papers. They uncovered a dirty little secret.*' And '*Twenty years is a long time.*' The Whitehorse paper ran a one-inch story last fall about the discovery of the remains of a 'young Jane Doe' in Tetcho Lake by an exploration company. '*I will free them.*' Jansen had flipped out, he had discovered religion. He decided to rid the world of his depraved friends, my brother included. He wanted to kill them and purge the evil. That's why my brother panicked. He was on Jansen's hit list. Then the kicker, '*We have made a covenant with death, and with Hell are we at agreement.*' I knew Jansen was guilty. And the guilty man had a pact with my brother. A pact involving 'a dirty little secret' that occurred 'twenty years ago.'"

Banks was still confused. "I'm not sure I understand . . ."

"Jansen and my brother knew each other. Look at the date." Simon handed the letter back to Banks.

"September 28, 1981?" Travis answered, unsure.

Simon Radcliff leaned one shoulder against the wall.

"That's right. September 28, 1981. Nick phoned me with his elaborate plan the first week of October. But he got the letter from Jansen *a week* before he contacted me. It was Jansen who forced Nick to contact me. My brother knew who killed my daughter two decades ago. He would never have set out killing these bastards if one of them hadn't gone off the deep end. He was simply protecting his own ass when he contacted me! He drafted me to kill Jansen and the others before Jansen, in some religious fervor, killed him."

The tall shadow slapped the palm of his hand against the wall. Banks could see the tears from across the room as they rolled down his cheeks. Radcliff stopped for a minute, regaining his composure.

He began again slowly.

"I remembered something the other day, just when the pieces began to fall into place. I had blocked it out for nearly thirty years." He took a deep breath. He was having trouble continuing. "Kelly tried to tell me one night. She was only six. It was after her mother and I had come back from a party. We had left 'Uncle Nick' to baby-sit." The words were becoming labored. "She lay in her little bed and cried in my arms when I put her to sleep. She was trying to tell me Uncle Nick had touched her in a bad way. I ignored it. I thought she imagined it. I mean, he was my own flesh and blood for God's sake. How could he?" His head trembled and the words seethed from his jaw. "My God, why didn't I listen?"

Banks couldn't believe what he was hearing. He moved closer. "Simon, are you saying your brother . . ."

The bereaved father trembled with pain, "He was the one who abducted her!"

Banks stood in the shadows, stunned.

They both were silent for several minutes.

Finally, Simon began circling the tiny room. "My *brother* passed an RCMP cruiser near Tetcho Lake the day he abducted Kelly. His truck's license plate number was entered into the police computer by the passing officer. A routine procedure. It's done to check on stolen vehicles. The plate number was entered near Tetcho Lake, less than an hour after school was dismissed. All this information is still available. Kelly wouldn't have gone with anybody else. She vanished. I still have friends in the department. I put all this together in less than a week. I remember we couldn't find Nick the day Kelly disappeared. He showed up the next day. Said he was out of town on police business. I believed him. Why wouldn't I?" He paused, taking a deep breath. "Well, those police logs are kept. He lied. He was assigned to Yellowknife that day. Nick knew the Bellichek brothers as far back as high school. When I read the letter Jansen sent him, I finally knew for certain. That's when I decided to ship the incestuous bastard off early for his date with the devil."

"Why shoot him at Jansen's cabin? Why not earlier?" Banks dug deeper.

"Believe me, I wanted to kill him earlier." Simon inhaled deeply. A moment later he blew his warm steamy breath into the chilly room. "I thought Mike Jansen, Senior, was hiding in the cabin. So did Nick. I'd decided earlier that their isolated cabin would be a good place to end all their miserable fucking lives. But I was concerned that if my brother actually laid eyes on Mike Jansen, he would have killed all three of *us* and buried his '*dirty little secret*' right there."

Simon's account of Nick's involvement in his daughter's murder was gripping and tragic. Banks put his back against the wall near the door and slid to the floor. He looked up at the man who still stared out the window.

Travis asked the question to himself as much as to Simon.

"Why would a brother do that?"

The silhouette looked across the room at Banks, amazed.

"How is a rational, sane person supposed to explain the thought process of a demented sexual deviant? I have no idea why. He was sick. And in the end, he got what he deserved."

They sat in silence.

Banks finally spoke. "Now what?"

The elder Radcliff chuckled out loud. "Would it surprise you, Banks, if I told you I didn't give a shit? All those bastards are dead. My daughter's death has been avenged. Amen."

Banks was drained just from hearing Radcliff's story. He couldn't imagine how depleted Simon must have been, having lived the tragedy.

"No," Banks paused. "It wouldn't surprise me."

"Well, then, what do you want to do? Lug me off to the slammer?"

Travis stood up. He didn't know if Simon was joking or not. This man had been punished all his life.

Banks walked over to the small window and stood beside the taller ex-RCMP officer. They both looked out across the ramp and watched the colorful aurora borealis begin to dance among the stars.

A minute later, Travis headed for the door.

He turned back one last time. "Would these help?" Banks reached into his pocket and pulled out his truck keys.

"No, thanks. I've gotten pretty good at riding a snowmobile." Simon tried to smile.

"Leon Powell just told me you're officially dead. I suspect Mike Jansen, Junior, will get credit for killing your brother." Banks put the keys back in his pocket and looked at the man in the corner. "Where do you go now?"

Simon grinned. "Do you really care?"

It was a good question. "I don't know. I suppose not."

Simon kept staring out the window. Maybe Jansen's death would finally give him some inner peace.

Simon Radcliff spoke for the last time. "Thanks."

Travis pushed himself from the doorjamb and walked away into the black freezing night.

"Travis!" Kayla was on the other side of the hangar next to the perimeter fence. Banks looked over his shoulder one last time. The silhouette from the hangar office disappeared.

"Where have you been?" She sniffled lightly, quickly wiping away one or two tears.

"Are those tears of joy or do you have a nail in your foot?" Travis was glad to see his boss.

"A nail." She smiled.

"Sorry. I got tied up for a minute. Gave directions to a lost soul."

"I beg your pardon?"

"Never mind." He reached the fence and with several hearty tugs, the agile pilot scaled it and jumped over the top.

They gave each other a polite cursory hug. She admonished his behavior and scolded him. "Travis, what you did was stupid. I was getting worried. . . ." She caught herself being too explicit. They were mature, middle-aged adults, not children. Casual sex might be acceptable, but communicating honestly would have to wait until they made a commitment.

Kayla backed away for a moment and hesitated. Finally, she leaned forward and gently pulled his neck and head to her lips. The kiss only lasted a few seconds. She was very gentle. Banks was hoping for more when she took his hand and began to guide them away.

"Where are we going?" he asked hopefully.

"I'm supposed to take you home for dinner. Monty insisted."

"Oh." His disappointment showed.

She was Johnny-on-the-spot with a seductive wink.

"Don't fret, I'm in charge of dessert."

Banks opened the passenger door of Kayla's small imported car as a distinctive voice called out. He turned around looking at the terminal. Standing on the sidewalk, near the terminal's entrance, was Marvin, his Indian friend from the hotel. The short, old Native stood with his hands in his pockets, wearing a Donegal hat from Ireland. The Cherokee Nation had lost one of its own.

"Hey, Travis Banks, you really are a pilot." Marvin smiled. "Are you a free man?"

"Yes, I am."

"Must be nice, eh?"

Travis wasn't sure if Marvin's response was another jab at how his ancestors had been screwed.

Marvin continued before Banks could answer. "Thought I'd come up here and collect on that airplane ride and pizza you promised, eh?"

Banks laughed. "Marvin, would steak and kidney pie with a Guinness Stout suffice?"

Marvin looked confused. "That's not a Native Indian dish, is it?"

Banks opened the rear door of Kayla's car and motioned for the Yukon native to get in. "It's British. Almost as good as a pizza!"

Marvin looked in both directions.

"You don't mind, eh?" he shouted over the roof of a passing car.

Banks shook his head.

The Indian smiled, walked quickly across the parking lot, and jumped into Kayla's car.

With Marvin inside, Kayla got back out and whispered across the roof of her car, "Travis, who is this? What about our dinner?"

"Kayla, I owe this man a big favor. Please. I'll explain later."

They both ducked into Kayla's small car and closed the doors. Kayla and Travis looked in the rearview mirror at the wide eighty-year-old smile in the backseat.

"Kayla Jackson, I'd like you to meet Marvin Yoblanski."